Herons Landing

"The connection between a deeply conflicted man slowly coming to terms with loss and a woman who understands him adds strength and intensity to a perceptive story that is more than the average friends-into-lovers romance. Vivid, detailed descriptions, real-life issues that resonate... Verdict: An excellent start to a promising community series with a stunning Olympic Coast setting."

—*Library Journal*

"Perennial favorite Ross delivers the emotionally intense first book in her small town contemporary romance series, Honeymoon Harbor... Ross has always been known for her ability to create truly memorable characters whose stories resonate sharply. This amazing book is touched by pain and grief, but also love and hope. A wonderful novel!"

—*RT Book Reviews*

"[A] sweet first book in Ross's Honeymoon Harbor series... Fans of cozy small-town romances will be willing to read further in the series."

—*Publishers Weekly*

"This book promises that the new series will offer the same kind of heartwarming appeal that made Ross's Shelter Bay series beloved by fans of small-town romance... I'm signing up for a return visit."

—*The Romance Dish*

Snowfall on Lighthouse Lane

"*Snowfall on Lighthouse Lane* is another deftly crafted gem of a romance novel by an author who is an impressively consistent master of the genre."
—Midwest Book Review

"Readers won't want to leave the heartwarming stories of Honeymoon Harbor and its characters' second chances at life and love."
—Publishers Weekly

"This is Ross writing her romantic best...
[It's] sweet-natured and well-meaning."
—All About Romance

"I laughed and cried throughout the book... There is nice closure and an unexpected happily-ever-after. I for one can't wait to be back in Honeymoon Harbor!"
—Romance Junkies

JoAnn Ross

Summer on Mirror Lake

HQN™

HQN™

ISBN-13: 978-1-335-01413-9

Recycling programs
for this product may
not exist in your area.

Summer on Mirror Lake

Copyright © 2019 by JoAnn Ross

The publisher acknowledges the copyright holder
of the individual work as follows:

Once Upon a Wedding
Copyright © 2019 by JoAnn Ross

This edition published by arrangement with Harlequin Books S.A.

For questions and comments about the quality of this book,
please contact us at CustomerService@Harlequin.com.

® and TM are trademarks of Harlequin Enterprises Limited or its
corporate affiliates. Trademarks indicated with ® are registered in the
United States Patent and Trademark Office, the Canadian Intellectual
Property Office and in other countries.

www.HQNBooks.com

Printed in U.S.A.

CONTENTS

Also available from JoAnn Ross

Honeymoon Harbor

Summer on Mirror Lake

As always, to my husband, Jay,
a master builder of beautiful wooden boats, who
was not only my inspiration, but my go-to expert for
everything (and more!) that I needed to know for Gabe
to build his Viking faering.

And in loving memory of our rescued
senior golden-paws Australian shepherd, Angel,
who made her appearance in *Snowfall on Lighthouse Lane*,
never left my side while I was writing
and gifted us with a too-short, but very special,
year of much love, laughter and joy.

CHAPTER ONE

New York

THE HEART ATTACK hit like a sledgehammer. As Gabriel Michael Mannion carried the casket of his closest friend down the aisle of St. Matthew's Episcopal Cathedral, his heart pounded against his chest, sweat beaded up on his forehead and at the back of his neck, and nausea caused his gut to clench and his head to spin. It took all his steely determination not to pass out.

Which he would not do. Not with Carter Kensington's grieving wife number four—wearing a black dress that probably cost more than Gabe's first car, and a pair of five-inch stiletto heels, suggesting that she was feeling a great deal steadier on her feet than he was at the moment—following behind with her three-year-old son. Gabe suspected that the blue coat the boy wore, which brought to mind the iconic photo of John Kennedy Jr. saluting his father's casket, was not a coincidence.

And he couldn't forget wives two and three seated in the pews, each with one of Carter's four children. Wife number one, Carter's college sweetheart and the mother of his eldest daughter, had chosen to remain in Santa Barbara. The daughter, Gabe remembered, was taking a gap year in Paris. All on Carter's dime, which he'd bitched about to Gabe nonstop while tossing back manhattans at the Campbell Bar in Grand Central Station like they'd time traveled back to the 1950s *Mad Men* days. Finally, sufficiently fortified, he'd taken the Metro-North home to spend a suburban weekend with his former swimsuit model wife and toddler son in their pricey home nestled into one of the country's wealthiest communities.

Despite having come from "old money," as he'd always point out sometime before Gabe would put him onto the train, and despite a trust fund that would have allowed a normal guy to live a comfortable life, Carter had been an indefatigable force of nature. He'd worked hard, played hard and had, like a comet flaring out, died young. In the bed of one of a string of mistresses, a detail that hadn't made it into his *New York Times* obituary.

Although Carter Kensington had readily acknowledged his many flaws, he'd been a boss, mentor and friend to Gabe. With the ink from his Columbia Business School MBA diploma still wet, Gabe had followed the yellow brick road to Wall Street when, on his first day of interviews, Carter had taken him under his wing.

"You've got the Midas touch, son," Carter had told him as he'd handed out a bonus in the high six figures at the end of Gabe's first year. Which was more zeroes than Gabe had ever seen written out on a check. Despite his small-town Pacific Northwest roots, he'd proven a natural at trading, and reveled in the take-no-prisoners, roller coaster 24/7 lifestyle.

Though he had to wonder, what good had the one-point-eight billion dollars Carter had taken home last year from Harborstone Advisors Group done for him in the end?

Dealing with more pressing issues at the moment, Gabe avoided that question. As he'd been doing for months.

You can do this, he instructed himself. *You will not drop a twenty-thousand-dollar casket*. Although his vision was blurred by vertigo and the sweat dripping into his eyes, his mind created a slow-motion video of the casket bouncing on the stone floor, breaking open, allowing Carter, dressed in his favorite James Bond Brioni suit and handmade Brunello Cucinelli shoes, to fall out and roll down the aisle of the Gothic stone church while the choir belted out "Nearer, My God, to Thee."

The church had eight steps leading down to the sidewalk. Although they were wide and not all that steep, standing at the top of them was like looking down into the Grand Canyon. Unfortunately, he and Douglas Fairfield, the managing company's sixty-year-old managing partner, were the first to tackle them.

You can do this.

As little black dots swam in front of his eyes like a cloud of gnats, Gabe grasped the brass side rail even tighter and lifted his end to help keep the casket level and prevent the body sliding downward and upsetting the balance even more. The six pallbearers managed to get Carter onto the sidewalk and into the waiting white hearse. Then in a group, they moved to the side, allowing Carter's parents, wife and son to make their way to their limo. It was only while Gabe was walking toward the car designated by the funeral home for the pallbearers that he felt himself folding to the ground like a cheap suit.

Then everything went black.

He came to in the back of an ambulance, siren wailing, while an EMT stuck an aspirin beneath his tongue, took his vital signs and assured him that he'd be okay.

"Nobody's ever died in my ambulance," she said.

"That's good to hear. So, I don't need to go to the hospital." Trading didn't stop just because one billionaire died. It kept ticking along, and every minute Gabe wasn't working was another opportunity missed and money lost, not just for him, but for the firm.

"There's always a first time," the woman said, her musical Jamaican accent at odds with her stern tone. "You don't get to choose a plan B. Once you hit that pavement, you handed the reins over to me."

"You don't understand. I have things I have to do."

"Yeah, I get a lot of guys who tell me that." She strapped an oxygen mask over his face, effectively shutting him up. "But here's the thing. In this case, you'll be glad that I'm the decider."

That said, she went back to monitoring his vital signs while the guy sitting next to the driver was letting the hospital know their ETA.

AN HOUR LATER, on what was turning out to be one of the most screwed-up days of his life, Gabe was lying behind a curtain, listening to what sounded like chaos in the ER. He was thinking that the hum, buzz, chatter and fast-talking reminded him of his summer internship days on the trading floor, when a different doctor from the one who'd examined him on arrival pulled back the white curtain and entered the cubicle.

"Good afternoon, Mr. Mannion," he said. "I'm Doctor David Kaplan and I have good news for you." He came to the side of the gurney and took Gabe's pulse. "Unless you get hit by an ambulance leaving the hospital, you're not going to die anytime soon."

"That's encouraging." What he guessed was an attempt at medical humor from a kid who looked as if he'd just graduated medical school had Gabe feeling a million years old. Which, given that Wall Street years were a lot like dog years, maybe he was. "So, my heart's okay?"

"It's still pumping. It wasn't a heart attack."

"Then what was it?"

"An anxiety attack. Or another term might be a panic attack."

"No. Way." You didn't survive in his business by being the kind of wuss who panicked.

Doogie Howser gave him a long look that suggested he'd heard that denial before. "The EMT said you're a trader."

"At Harborstone Advisors Group. It's a hedge fund," Gabe tacked on, realizing the name probably didn't mean anything to anyone outside the investment world.

He was wrong. The doctor whistled under his breath as he made a note on the chart attached to the clipboard he was carrying. "Small pond, big fish."

Which was exactly how Carter had described it the morning Gabe had interviewed.

"My brother worked there for a time," the doctor said. "It didn't suit him. Elliott missed the floor, which surprised me, because whenever I see trading floors on the news, they look a lot like what I've always imagined Bedlam to be."

"Says the doctor who chose to work in an emergency department," Gabe said dryly.

"Believe it or not, I've always found a well-run ED to be poetry in motion," Kaplan responded. "But we all respond to different stressors. The same way patients view ERs differently than medical staff working in them, Harborstone didn't match up well with Elliott's risk DNA. Also, my brother had lost all sense of any life outside The Street. Which is how I recognize the same signs in you."

That pissed Gabe off. "You don't know me."

"I know that your blood pressure is higher than it should be."

"Like you said, we all have our stressors."

"True, and landing in an emergency room could cause

anyone's blood pressure to spike. White-coat hypertension is a well-documented condition. However, the other pallbearers told the ambulance crew that you were already having symptoms of an attack before landing here. They first noticed them midway down the aisle when you got out of step."

"I did not." Gabe was sure of that. He thought.

The doctor's only response was a shrug. "Your cholesterol is also in the high range. I'm guessing from living on takeout."

Gabe couldn't deny that. "Contrary to what people might believe, my business doesn't allow for three-hour, three-martini lunches."

"Mine neither. Which is too bad. Not that I'm in favor of the three-martini lunches, but despite this being a hospital, the cafeteria food here is largely made up of carbs, sugars and fats, and Americans all need to take more time to eat.

"The French and the Italians have the right idea. They're not grabbing a bagel and coffee from a food truck, then gulping it down while checking their email. They walk to a café, drink coffee from a cup that isn't cardboard, and spend time talking with a friend. They're careful about what they eat, they walk more and believe in a slower pace of life with more time off. Which is why they live longer."

"Maybe it just seems longer," Gabe shot back.

Kaplan's half smile was more a smirk, suggesting that this was not the first time he'd heard this argument. "Six months after returning to the trading floor, my brother moved his family to Grenoble. He teaches skiing at a small resort at Les Deux Alpes during the winter and spring. Although the glacier there allows year-round skiing, he takes his entire summer off, then gives fall tours of the area before returning to skiing. From what I saw while visiting this past Christmas, his family is happier than they've ever been. And it didn't take a doctor to see how much healthier he is."

"I'm happy for your brother. But I'm not into skiing." He hadn't taken the time to go to any mountains since college.

"Neither am I, but that wasn't my point. An anxiety attack won't kill you, Mr. Mannion. But it should be seen as a flashing yellow warning light. When you're anxious, your body reacts in ways that put extra strain on your heart that could lead to eventual heart disease."

"Thanks for the PSA." Gabe looked down at his wrist to where his Rolex Submariner should be and found it missing.

"It's in the bag with your other things," the doctor said before he could ask. "Along with your cell phone, which I suspect you could use a break from."

"I need to get back to work."

"And I need to do my job. Which is to prescribe regular exercise, a better diet and a proper amount of quality sleep."

"I get all I need," Gabe said. Okay, so maybe he worked a hundred-plus-hour week, and maybe he was so jazzed when he got back to his apartment he'd need a couple or three drinks to chill enough to sleep, but that was the life he'd chosen.

"Given that you work at Harborstone, I seriously doubt that," the doctor said, writing something else on Gabe's chart. "And when was the last time you connected with your family and friends?"

"My family's across the country in Washington State." All except for his quarterback brother, who also lived in Manhattan. Burke, being far more social than Gabe himself was, had insisted on monthly catch-up dinners during his football off-season.

"Last I heard, planes flew west across the Hudson. When was the last time you hung out with friends outside work?"

"Earlier today."

"But the guest of honor at that party wasn't there. Because he happened to be dead."

"You know what, Doc?"

"What?"

"You've got one helluva smart-ass bedside manner."

"Thank you. It took several years to hone it. Your friend, and I assume he was a close one for you to be a pallbearer, died, according to what one of the other pallbearers at the scene told the EMT, at the age of forty-six. Given that the life expectancy of a male with his birth year is sixty-seven-point-four years, it suggests that while working on Wall Street may make you a very wealthy man, the lifestyle can kill you before you have time to enjoy it."

"Carter Kensington's life was excessive," Gabe argued. "Mine isn't."

"Being a workaholic is excessive in its own way," Kaplan said.

The damn guy just wouldn't let up. "You do realize that arguing my lifestyle probably isn't good for my blood pressure."

"Yet you feel the need to defend it," the doctor said mildly.

"To a guy who probably works the same hours."

"My work's not nine-to-five. But I'm going out tonight with my wife to watch our daughter's ballet recital. She's excited because her tutu has sequins and she gets to wear a sparkly tiara. Which she's going to wear afterward, when we go out for pizza. Because that's her favorite thing. Even if she does insist on pineapple on it. I blame that slight flaw in judgment on her mother.

"You're obviously an intelligent man, Mr. Mannion. Perhaps you ought to consider using some of your brainpower to come up with a way to achieve a better work-life balance. Before I see one of your friends having worried about dropping your casket thirteen years from now."

"Ouch. Mic drop."

Kaplan's lips quirked, giving Gabe the impression that the sadistic son of a bitch was actually enjoying this. "You're free to leave," he said. "But, seriously, you don't have to turn into a ski instructor. Why don't you try figuring out something that gives you pleasure, and make time for it? While you still have that option. Because I'd rather not see you back in my emergency room anytime soon."

With that he was gone.

CHAPTER TWO

Honeymoon Harbor, Washington

"OKAY," CHELSEA PRESCOTT SAID. "We have the summer reading challenge, art lessons with Michael Mannion, the trip out to Blue House Farm so kids can actually see where their food comes from, a tour of Herons Landing B&B from Seth Harper and Brianna Mannion, who'll point out all the renovations and tell the story of the Whistler mural, which the reading adventurers will have already learned about beforehand during the trip to the historical museum.

"What else can we come up with for the summer?" she asked her staff, which consisted of one other librarian, Farrah Shalhoub, who'd recently moved there from Spokane; two paid assistants; five volunteers; and the sixty something former librarian, Lillian Henderson, who, despite having retired, still checked in at least once a week to make sure the place hadn't fallen apart without her.

"This is beginning to sound more like a summer camp than a library," grumbled Janet Mayburn, one of the volunteers.

"We're in the business of opening minds," Chelsea said patiently. She'd been hearing those objections from Janet since she'd first begun planning the library's summer event calendar in January. She'd continued to bite her tongue, because the truth was that funds were low and she couldn't afford to offend anyone willing to work for free. "Books take readers on adventures to different places and times, but we're still talking about our very short Pacific Northwest summers, and although it may be hard for us to believe, there are a lot of kids who don't want to spend those sunny days *inside* the library."

"Those are the ones we especially want to reach," said Dottie Anderson, half owner of The Dancing Deer dress shop and a volunteer.

"Because reading is fundamental," said Doris, her twin and business partner.

"Exactly!" Chelsea was tempted to kiss them both. "Those who don't think of a library as a place to find adventure are the ones who'll get the most out of the program. Because once we get them inside the doors, we can hook them on reading."

"What about the liability issues?" Janet pressed.

"That's covered. Although Quinn Mannion is no longer a practicing attorney, he's still licensed, so he wrote a permission form for parents to sign. I also talked to the mayor, and he assured me that we're covered under the county insurance."

"People can still sue."

"Any idiot can sue for any reason," Lillian Henderson jumped in with a sigh of the impatience Chelsea herself was trying to hide. "That's what insurance is for."

Although the retired librarian had made her library a safe place for Chelsea during some very difficult childhood years, she'd also run a tight ship. No one had ever argued with her when she was behind the checkout desk. Apparently, Janet wasn't prepared to start now. She merely crossed her arms and shook her head. But, Chelsea noted, she didn't get up and march out in a huff.

"So," she forged on, "any other ideas?"

"How about a tour of Mannion's microbrewery?" asked Lily Carpenter, Chelsea's friend and fourth volunteer, who was director of marketing and promotion at Clearwater Community College.

"Great. Let's teach the kids to drink," Janet muttered.

"It could be a special event for the older kids," said Susan Long, who taught chemistry at the high school. "The same way going out to Blue House Farm can teach kids where their food comes from, learning about brewing can show them that by knowing chemistry, you can turn grains, hops, water and yeast into one of the world's oldest beverages. It makes science more relevant to everyday life."

"Also, the first evidence of beer production dates back to Egypt and Mesopotamia in the fifth millennium BC," said Farrah, who had received a bachelor's degree in Middle East studies at Pomona College in California before earning her MLS degree at the University of Washington. "So, there's an opportunity to throw some ancient history into the mix."

"I like that idea." With the exception of Janet, Chelsea loved her team. "I'll ask Quinn if he'd be willing to do that."

"He's already giving tours to guests staying at his sister's bed-and-breakfast," Mrs. Henderson pointed out. "I'm sure he'll be happy to do the same for us."

"Okay. Any more ideas?"

While her library admittedly wasn't the largest on the peninsula, Mrs. Henderson had left her some very big shoes to fill, and not only did Chelsea not intend to let the former librarian—and the town—down, she also wanted to make it the best small-town library in the state.

"You're already talking about a lot of activities," Janet pointed out. "And there aren't that many of us."

"I've got that covered," Chelsea said. "Kids need to demonstrate a sense of responsibility and community service to college admission officers, so I gave a talk about summer volunteerism at the high school last month, which resulted in more applications for volunteer interns than we can possibly use. I'll be choosing three or four this week. They'll be great at helping us herd kids. Farrah and I are going to take turns leading the adventures and Mrs. Henderson has agreed to return on those days to help hold down the fort. The volunteers will continue to work on their rotating schedule."

Janet folded her arms across her chest, but didn't object to what Chelsea had personally thought was a brilliant idea.

"I'm already working on the marketing and promotion," Lily said. "Adding the brewery will be a big deal, especially since we already have a course on craft brewing at the college. Quinn's spoken to the classes and he's both informative and entertaining."

"There's also the fact that he's not hard to look at," Doris said.

"The man definitely inherited those Mannion Black Irish looks," her sister agreed.

"Terrific," Chelsea said, bringing the meeting back to order as all the women's eyes, even Janet's, went a bit dreamy. "We've just about got this all nailed down. So, why don't we all think about it a bit longer—"

"Put our thinking caps on," Mrs. Henderson broke in with a decisive nod.

"Exactly." How Chelsea loved this woman who, along with giving her a safe harbor when she'd so needed it, had provided a focus that had saved her from sinking in the turbulent tides her life had once had. "That's exactly what we should do. We're all intelligent women, and with the program lasting six weeks, we certainly have more opportunities for engagement." She closed her planner.

"Let's ponder the possibilities over the weekend, and meet back here at five on Tuesday."

Monday was one of two days the library was closed to give everyone on her small staff time off. Although when she'd been growing up the library had been closed Sundays and Mondays, Chelsea had found that Mondays and Thursdays were the slowest days. Also, Honeymoon Harbor was a working-class town, and many people couldn't get to the library during the weekdays. Opening at noon on Sundays brought in a lot of people after church and, now with more restaurants in town, brunch. In addition, the library hours on Wednesdays and Fridays extended to eight o'clock to allow patrons to visit after work hours.

Mrs. Henderson lingered behind. "You're doing a dandy job. I was proud of getting funding for the bookmobile to reach people who couldn't easily come into town on a regular basis. But your summer reading adventurers will go down in the annals of Salish County as the same type of library milestone. Along with the coffee shop."

It was more like a large coffee wagon, located in a room that had only ever been used for storage. After Chelsea had presented the idea to keep the library as an important gathering space in the community, the town council had provided the funds to hire restoration and remodeling contractor Seth Harper to open up the room enough to put in some couches and easy chairs for patrons to sit and read.

Fortunately, the guys at Cops and Coffee had signed a two-year contract to supply the self-service machine. While it didn't offer the same array of choices as the actual store—their magnificent espresso machine had been special ordered from Italy—there were enough choices, including tea and hot chocolate, which had proved enormously popular during the winter and brought people back to the library.

As a bonus, the bright blue-and-white wagon could be wheeled to special events in the building, such as author readings and lectures; and they'd even presented travel videos, featuring a different location every month. So far, she'd been able to find local residents who'd returned from vacations with videos to share. Restaurateur Luca Salvadori had shown his own home photos and videos, answered questions and told colorful anecdotes about life in Italy. Luca had been born and raised in Honeymoon Harbor, but had moved with his family to Rome when he was in high school so his mother could care for her aging mother-in-law. Last year he'd come home and reestablished the family restaurant the town had sorely missed.

"Thank you." Her mentor's words meant a great deal to Chelsea. "Of course, if I screw up the reading adventurers program, it could end up an entirely different milestone." And the city council might fire her.

"You won't." They walked down a sunshine-yellow hallway lined with library-themed posters. "You have mettle, Chelsea Prescott." The first poster visitors saw when they entered the double doors read *Welcome! This is YOUR library! A Place to Discover. Read. Learn. Explore. Have Fun. Connect. Succeed!*

Mrs. Henderson pointed to the poster. "That was always my mantra. In the early days, I had it written on an old-fashioned blackboard."

"I know. I remember it well." Chelsea smiled. "Then you upgraded to brightly colored markers on a whiteboard. I hope you don't mind that I had Michael Mannion design the poster to replace that."

"You have to keep up with the times. As I did when I replaced that messy chalkboard. Also, having a graphic from an artist of Michael's caliber and fame is a true coup for the library."

"We do get the visitors who've come to town specifically to shop at his gallery." She'd been considering asking him if he'd be willing to give the library licensing rights to sell prints of the poster online. She was certain other libraries would prove a lucrative market, thus raising additional, always-needed funds.

"I do appreciate you keeping my words."

"I certainly couldn't have improved them." Hadn't the library under this woman's tenure been all those things to her?

"I noticed you also used them on the website design."

"I loved the previous header with the photo of the library and harbor behind it, but I thought putting up a mission statement in its place might draw more people in. I did keep the photo in the right margin where visitors can see it."

"I wasn't criticizing, dear," Mrs. Henderson assured her. "Speaking of the website, have you thought about adding an introductory computer class to the evening learning curriculum sessions? I remember when we first were able to get an internet connection. No one, including me, had any idea how to use it to our best advantage. It was definitely a self-taught, learn-as-you-go experience."

"There are still people who aren't computer literate," Chelsea said. "I doubt a week goes by that either Farrah or I don't help someone fill out a résumé and search for a job online. And then there's the rush of college applications and instructions on essay writing. Many of Honeymoon Harbor's students are the first in their family to go to college and it can be overwhelming."

"As it was before the computer. Though that's exactly the type of thing I had in mind. Also, I've bought items from local craftspeople who could reach more potential customers with websites. But I suspect many don't have the skills or the money to pay to have one set up, the way Doris and Dottie did when they opened up The Dancing Deer."

"Lily updated ours," Chelsea said. "Not only is she a whiz at marketing, she has mad website design skills. I'll ask if she'd be willing to teach a couple sessions. One for older kids, and another for the adults."

Mrs. Henderson nodded her steel-gray head, her hair flowing down her back in wild waves. No short, "age appropriate" hair for her. "That's a very good idea."

"It was yours."

"I know." Her smile took years from her face. "At my age, I don't have time to bother with bad ones."

They said goodbye and Mrs. Henderson left the library, walking with purpose down the front steps. Although Lillian remained hale, hearty and active, Chelsea always held her breath, waiting for a fall. There was a ramp next to the steps, but the elderly librarian refused to use it.

Chelsea waited until she'd reached the sidewalk, gotten into her Prius and driven off, before making one last check of the building. In a reading alcove off the children's section, she found two girls sitting on the chintz-covered love seat—as they'd been most afternoons after school for the past week, reminding her of a time when this very library had been her home away from home. Back when that dark, suffocating cloud had lowered over the pretty Prescott family Cape Cod home.

Chelsea mentally shook off the pain that still hurt all these years later, and brought out her friendly librarian smile. "Hello, girls," she said.

The eyes of the older girl, who Chelsea guessed to be

twelve or so years old, were guarded. "Hi." Her tone was flat. Disinterested.

"Hi!" the younger one, who looked about five years old, said. Her grin was as wide as a slice of summer melon. "I'm Hailey and this is my big sister, Hannah. We're reading about dragons."

"What fun. I like dragons."

"Me, too." Wheat-blond curls bobbed as she enthusiastically nodded her head. "They have fire coming out of their snouts." Her brow wrinkled, much as Mrs. Henderson's had. "But they only scorch and eat bad people."

"Then the three of us are safe."

"We are! That's why I don't have nightmares about them."

"I'm glad to hear that."

"Hannah gave me my own guardian dragon." Hailey reached into a Disney princess book bag and pulled out a fluffy green stuffed animal. "This is Daisy. My other one is invisible to everyone but me."

"That's very special. And I like this one." It was well-worn and missing a leg.

"Me, too. My invisible dragon is always with me, like a guardian angel. It burns away any monsters that might try to sneak up on me in the dark."

Chelsea glanced at the older sister, whose return look, like her earlier one, managed to be expressionless and stony at the same time.

"You're lucky to have such a good big sister." Chelsea remembered all too well how it had felt to be a big sister. From the time her parents had brought Annabelle home from Honeymoon Harbor General Hospital, she'd felt as if her heart had grown three—no, make that *four*—sizes the instant those big blue eyes had looked up into hers. And when the tiny hand had grabbed on to her finger, she'd known they would be bonded for life. What she'd had no way of knowing was how short her younger sister's life would be.

"I know." Hailey looked up at her sister. "Hannah's always taken care of me. Everywhere we've moved."

That explained why Chelsea didn't recognize them. Apparently they were new to Honeymoon Harbor.

"Would you like to take that book with you?" she asked. "So you can finish it at home?"

"Yes!"

"We don't have a library card." Hannah's statement was edged with a challenge.

"That's not a problem," Chelsea said blithely. "All you need is a parent, or guardian, to sign the application form for you, and you can have your own cards. Meanwhile, I trust you. And when you return it, I'll have other dragon books waiting for you."

"That would be awesome." Little hands with sparkly nail polish crossed over Hailey's heart. "Wouldn't it, Hannah?"

"Yeah." The older sister seemed less than pleased. Or, perhaps, she was merely guarded with strangers. Which was a good thing these days. Even in this small peninsula town.

Getting the message that the library was about to close, Hannah put the book into her own bag and stood up. "Come on, Hailey. We've got to go."

"Okay." The little hand took hold of the larger one. "Thank you, library lady," she said.

"You're welcome," Chelsea responded. "Could I call your mother for you?"

"She's working," Hannah said, a bit too quickly, Chelsea thought. There was definitely something going on here.

"Is your dad at home?"

"I have a key." Hannah pulled it out of her pocket. "We'll be okay. Like my sister said, I can take care of her."

"I'm sure you can. But it's raining."

"It's *always* raining." A pointed chin thrust up. "We don't melt."

"That's good to know. Because it would definitely be a disadvantage to living here in the Pacific Northwest," Chelsea said mildly. "Though you can't beat our summers. Nevertheless, why don't I drive you home?"

"We're not supposed to get into cars with strangers," Hailey said. "Because of the traffic."

"Traffickers," Hannah corrected.

Chelsea was relieved someone had taught the girls—who appeared to be on their own in the afternoons—child safety. "You've been in my library all week. Have I acted as if I'm a child trafficker?"

"I guess not."

"Would it help if I had the police chief come by to vouch for me?"

"No!" Both sisters nearly shouted in unison.

Hannah placed a hand on Hailey's head. Whether the gesture was meant to calm or warn, Chelsea couldn't say. Perhaps both. "That's okay," the older girl said. "I guess they wouldn't let you be a librarian if you were a criminal."

"There's a very extensive background check," Chelsea assured her, making a note to check with Aiden Mannion about what he might know about these girls' parents. "I was even fingerprinted."

Hannah bit her lip, considering. Then glanced out the windows at the summer rain that had, in the short time they'd been talking, gone from a gentle mist, to a drizzle, to a driving rain blowing in over the mountains. "Okay," she said. "Thank you."

"No problem," Chelsea said easily, even as her instincts continued to tell her that something was off. Why would two young children be so reluctant to have anything to do with the police? Now she was even more determined to ask Aiden about the family. She wasn't certain how much information the law allowed him to share, but if it could help keep a child safe, she had to try.

Hannah was quiet on the way to the address she'd given Chelsea, while Hailey continued to chatter away, her rapid-fire conversation jumping from dragons to wizards to a book about a giraffe who couldn't dance. "He had crooked knees and skinny legs, and when he tried to join the jungle dance, the other animals teased him," she said, her small face furrowed in a sad frown.

"Bullied," Hannah murmured.

Hailey continued undeterred. "So, he felt so sad. Because he really was a very bad dancer. He felt sad and alone."

Chelsea picked up on one of her favorite children's stories. Dottie Anderson, who'd organized the Saturday children's reading group, had read it aloud just last week. "But then while he was walking home, the giraffe looked up at the moon and while he was thinking how beautiful it was, a cricket suddenly appeared and told him how everyone is special in their own way."

"Yes!" Hailey said. "And when you're different, you don't need to feel bad or lonely because all you need is your own special song. So when the giraffe heard the moon playing a tune just for him—"

"His hooves started shuffling," Chelsea supplied.

"They did! And he swung his long legs around everywhere! When all the other animals saw him, they declared him the best dancer ever!"

"Like bullies are ever going to do that," Hannah scoffed.

"But they did," her sister insisted.

"Maybe in the story. But the giraffe still never gave the cricket any credit for helping him out," Hannah pointed out.

Chelsea glanced up into the rearview mirror, watching Hailey bite her bottom lip as she considered that idea. "Maybe the cricket is like the giraffe's older sister, who always takes care of him. And always tells the giraffe that he doesn't need thanks because he's just doing what big sisters are supposed to do."

Glancing again in the rearview mirror, Chelsea watched Hannah's eyes—which had, during their short time together, been only expressionless or hard—soften. "Maybe so, sprout," she agreed softly, reaching over to take her sister's hand in hers.

Dammit. There was a story there. Chelsea felt it. And not just because she'd been an older sister herself. But because she'd been about Hannah's age when her once perfect family had cracked apart. She knew all too well the need to make things better. Even when it was proved fruitless.

They'd reached the house, a Craftsman bungalow in a neighborhood that had once been mill company housing. But gentrification had brought change and now any of the small houses that had been renovated and given a modern interior floor plan could bring in several times over the original cost. It wasn't easy growing grass near salt water, and whoever lived in this home had apparently thrown in the towel. Where there would have been a lawn, or wildflower garden as many homeowners created instead, fir cones and needles were scattered over dirt studded with weeds.

Paint that appeared to have once been sky blue was peeling and a white shutter was hanging crookedly on its hinges. While the bungalow could have been darling, with its front porch and low gabled roof, it was just sad. Chelsea was reluctant to drop the girls off here all alone. Or, she thought, worriedly, perhaps not alone at all. Perhaps the reason for spending so much time at the library was because it was a refuge from being here.

"When does your mother get home from work?" she asked, turning toward the back seat.

"Anytime now." Hannah's hand was squeezing Hailey's smaller one so tightly her knuckles had whitened. Was she reminding her sister to remain quiet? Growing more and more concerned, Chelsea hoped Aiden would give her more information.

"That's good to hear," she said in a voice that even to her own ears sounded falsely perky and wouldn't fool the older girl for a minute. "I'll just wait here until you get inside."

"Bye, library lady," Hailey said.

After returning the cheerful goodbye, which suggested there wasn't anyone inside she was afraid of, Chelsea watched the two of them cross the broken pavement of the front walk up to the columned porch and, after Hannah had unlocked the door, disappear inside.

Then she pulled away from the curb, dialed Aiden and headed to the police station.

CHAPTER THREE

HOME, AS SOMEONE had once said, was a shifting landscape. Although many things in Honeymoon Harbor had changed during the years since Gabe had left Washington—including, he'd noted as he'd driven off the ferry landing, an influx of new businesses and tourists crowding the sidewalks and slowing traffic down with their motor homes—it wasn't, and never would be, like New York. Hell, it wasn't even like Tacoma. Or Olympia.

Which was why, even two weeks into Gabe's self-enforced sabbatical, he was already bored out of his freaking mind. How many miles could he run every morning? Not anywhere near what he'd been able to as a distance runner on UW's track team. Proving, dammit, the smart-ass ER doctor's diagnosis. He'd let himself get out of shape.

Which, hell, was fixable. He'd already come up with a goal metric, which he'd programmed into the schedule on the new smart watch that had replaced the Rolex. He'd also programmed it to report his heart rate, which was currently pathetic. Maybe he'd never been the ultimate jock his quarterback brother, Burke, had been, but he sure as hell hadn't had the heart rate of a couch potato.

The first three nights home, he'd enjoyed having dinner with his parents, grandparents, sister and brothers. His mother had always equated food with love, and who was he to discourage her? But it soon became obvious that they all had their own lives and couldn't spend their days and evenings entertaining him. Which, he supposed, was some sort of karmic payback for all the years he'd stayed away and the events he'd missed, like his sister Brianna's engagement party.

When he'd first heard his brother Quinn had walked away from his Seattle law firm to brew beer, Gabe'd thought he was crazy. But he was impressed with the way his brother had reclaimed the old preprohibition business.

"You do realize that you're driving customers away," Quinn said as Gabe entered into his second week.

"Me?" Gabe looked up from tracing lines in the condensation on the side of his chilled pilsner glass of Good Vibrations, his brother's new summer release. A not too sweet, light pilsner brewed with local fresh raspberries that blended well with its wheat malt, it was a ruby-colored pour that was pretty enough to almost be considered a girlie drink. But Quinn had captured summer in a bottle as perfectly as he'd always done everything else.

He glanced around, noticing for the first time that Quinn's restaurant wasn't as crowded as it had been when he'd first arrived. "It probably emptied out because we're between lunch and dinner."

"It's five thirty. And while I realize that after all those years living in Manhattan you're undoubtedly accustomed to dining at a big-city fashionable hour, Honeymoon Harbor tends to roll up the sidewalks after ten o'clock. Which means we should be starting to fill up with people getting off work."

"So what does that have to do with me?"

"The edgy vibe radiating off you is scaring people away," Jarle Biornstad, who'd appeared from the kitchen with Gabe's order of BBQ ribs, said in a deep, rumbling foghorn voice. After years of cooking for fishermen out of Dutch Harbor, Alaska, the Norwegian who claimed to have gotten tired of freezing his ass off during winter crabbing season had ended up in Honeymoon Harbor cooking for Quinn.

Personally, Gabe thought the red-bearded giant with a full sleeve tattoo of a butcher's chart of a cow was a lot scarier than he'd ever be, but he was also smart enough not to suggest that to a guy who made Sasquatch look like a preschooler. According to Quinn, Seth Harper had had to take out four rows of bricks in the doorway leading to the kitchen to prevent the six-foot-seven cook from banging his head.

"I'm not edgy." Edgy was too close to anxiety. Which, as something he'd already been through, he wasn't in any hurry to revisit. Thus this trip back to the peninsula. "Just bored."

"Antsy," Quinn diagnosed.

Gabe couldn't disagree. Apparently adrenaline was as addictive as caffeine or booze and he was definitely suffering from withdrawal. "My plan is to take the entire summer off."

Technically, three months and two weeks, given that he'd left New York a week after Carter's May Day funeral. With Harborstone already reeling from the death of one of the establishing partners, his announcement that he was claiming all the vacation time he'd never taken hadn't been met with enthusiasm in the boardroom. Fortunately, he'd made enough profits for the company over the years that no one was willing to complain and risk him jumping to another firm.

He'd arranged to have Phil Gregg, a longtime friend who'd entered the firm the same week he had, keep an eye on his portfolios. They weren't as close as he and Carter had been, and Phil hadn't risen through the ranks as fast, only because he'd married shortly after he'd gotten his MBA, already had one son, and a daughter on the way. Unlike Carter, and definitely unlike all the younger guys at the firm, he'd sacrificed promotions and bonuses in order to achieve normalcy in his personal life. Fortunately, since the accounts were all long-term investments, he usually only adjusted them, if necessary, every quarter.

"Good for you. Did this plan come with any ideas on how to spend all those days of leisure?" his older brother asked.

"The idea was to wing it." Gabe shrugged. "Maybe I'll go fishing."

"You've always hated fishing."

True. "Okay, sailing. Seth has a boat. So does Aiden. I could borrow one of theirs."

"Or you could build one," Quinn suggested as he drew a pint of his award-winning Captain Jack Sparrow from one of the taps and took it to a man wearing black fishing boots who'd just arrived and taken a seat at the end of the bar. The fact that Quinn had known exactly what the fisherman wanted reminded Gabe of how no one had ever had to ask Carter Kensington what he'd wanted to drink. Even wild, reckless habits could apparently become routine. Like drinking. Smoking. Drugs. Or apparently, in his case, making money.

"You enjoyed building boats before you headed off to the big city to make your fortune," Quinn reminded him.

Again true. When he'd been a kid, Gabe had spent nearly every free minute hanging around the town's internationally known boat school. By the time he was in the seventh grade, he'd been allowed to sweep up after the builders after school and in the summer. Over the years, he'd gained more experience and responsibility, even, while in high school, making a kayak and a skiff he'd sold to help pay for college.

He'd occasionally thought of those days on the rare occasion Carter would convince him to travel down to Newport for one of the New York Yacht Club regattas. Where the gleaming world-class yachts were a far cry from the boats that sailed Honeymoon Harbor waters.

"Why would I make a boat?"

"Because you'd enjoy it, it'd get you out of my pub, and because our mother would quit worrying about you."

That got Gabe's attention. "She is not."

"Is, too," Quinn uncharacteristically snapped back. Terrific, Gabe thought. Now they'd reverted to grade-school behavior. "She worries about all of us. Just in case you might think you were special. Or that she loves you more."

Gabe put down a rib long enough to salute his brother with his middle finger.

"You could make a Viking boat," Jarle said.

"You're suggesting I make a longship large enough for a crew of a hundred oarsmen, then go raiding off the coast?"

"No." Jarle folded his arms over the front of a T-shirt reading *That's too much bacon... Said no person ever.* "I'm suggesting you make a replica. And not one of those cutesy miniature ones old guys make that fit in a bottle, but one you could actually sail."

"You built that sloop for Seth," Quinn reminded him.

"True. But that's nothing like what you're talking about. It's a totally different process. I made the sloop stitch-and-glue, starting with the frame, the way American boats are made. The way I learned all those years working at the school. The Viking faerings were clinker-built, with the planks overlapping to form a hull." Apparently it worked for them since Scandinavians continued to build their rowboats the same traditional way.

"How about we make a deal?" Quinn suggested. "I won't talk brewspeak to you when we're discussing beers, and you'll talk about boats in a way normal people can understand."

"Okay." Gabe took a long drink of the summer beer. Damn, his brother was good. "Long story short, because a faering doesn't need a frame, it's lighter, thereby riding higher in the water, which let the Vikings go faster and travel down more shallow rivers for their raiding."

"Would've also helped them escape other guys who went after them trying to get their stuff back," Jarle suggested.

"Probably so. Your people weren't exactly an Amish community."

"We were fierce, that's for damn sure," Jarle agreed, squaring broad shoulders with obvious pride.

"So, why don't you build one?" Quinn pressed.

"Even if I wanted to, which I haven't said I do, it'd be a push to get a decent-size one done in three months." Which was his deadline. By then he'd be rested, at his fighting weight and ready to get back into the fray.

"Because your summer schedule is so booked."

Gabe gave him a hard stare. "You're pushing me."

"Just saying," Quinn said mildly. That was a funny thing about the eldest Mannion. Gabe couldn't remember his older brother ever yelling, or even raising his voice. Yet, somehow, just like his dad, who was the quieter of his parents, he always got his way, always made things happen.

"You must've been one hell of a lawyer," he muttered. Then tore another strip off a rib.

"No point in doing something if you don't do it well." Quinn dunked a glass into the sudsy water of the bar sink, rinsed it and dried it with a towel before putting it back on a shelf beneath the bar.

"This is a challenge, isn't it?" Gabe shot him a hard look. "The same way you double-dog dared me to go down that zip line when I was seven."

"That was Aiden who dared you," Quinn corrected easily as he washed another glass.

"Yeah. But I still remember your silence speaking louder than our bad-boy brother's taunts." Who, after following his own winding road, was now Honeymoon Harbor's police chief. *Go figure.* There'd been a time Gabe guessed even those oddsmakers in Las Vegas wouldn't have taken that bet.

"You could name her *Freya.*" Jarle jumped back into the conversation.

"Why?"

"Because Freya's the Norse goddess of love. Also sex, beauty, gold, war and death."

"The death part isn't exactly encouraging if you're taking it out on the Sound," Gabe pointed out.

"Just ignore the war and death part and concentrate on the love part," the Norwegian cook advised. "That's what I'd name a boat, if I had one."

"Until hooking up with Ashley Winters, Jarle fell in love at least once a week," Quinn said dryly. "Fortunately, it was always from afar, so I never had to fire him."

"What can I say? Our Norse blood makes us a passionate people."

"I thought Scandinavians were cool and distant," Gabe said.

"That's the Swedes," Jarle scoffed. "We Norwegians are more extroverted, laid-back and a helluva lot better at outdoor sports than other Scandinavians. Plus, we're better looking...

"There's an old joke about an American and a Norwegian who meet while sitting next to each other at an Oslo bar," he continued. "'Are you Swedish?' the American asks. 'No,' says the Norwegian. 'I'm Norwegian. But I've been sick.'"

"I'd be careful telling that joke around here," Gabe suggested as Jarle roared with laughter at his own joke. Descendants of the Swedish loggers who'd helped settle Honeymoon Harbor still made up a good share of the population.

Jarle shrugged shoulders as wide as Paul Bunyan's ax handle. "Our countries have had a long and complex relationship. But, despite our differences, we've always thought of ourselves as brothers. And like brothers, we make fun of each other. The same way you Mannions do."

"Can't argue with that," Quinn said as the door opened and a family who apparently wasn't put off by Gabe's vibe sat down at a table overlooking the water. "Just think about the boat," he advised.

His brother hadn't been kidding about the dinner rush. As the place began to fill up, and Quinn got busy mixing drinks, drawing and pouring beers, and waiting on tables when orders started to stack up, Gabe threw some bills on the bar and left.

THE HONEYMOON HARBOR police station was located across from the ferry landing and next to Cops and Coffee, which had been established by three detectives who'd retired from the Seattle police force. Not quite ready to take up fishing, they'd settled into small-town life, and given that the entire state of Washington seemed to run on coffee, they fit right in, catering to the caffeinated population. Playing on a cop stereotype, they also made the best doughnuts on the peninsula.

"I have your book," Chelsea greeted Donna Ormsbee, the manager and daytime 911 operator. She reached into her bag and pulled out a paperback featuring a woman standing in the middle of burning rubble. In contrast to her unrelentingly cheerful attitude, Donna always was first in line to put a hold on the latest apocalyptic novel.

"You didn't have to deliver it," the older woman said as she clutched the book to her chest. For as long as Chelsea could remember, Donna had dressed for the seasons. Today's blue shirt featured a summery beach scene with sugary white sand nothing like the Pacific Northwest's kelp- and driftwood-strewn beaches.

"I was dropping by anyway." She glanced past Donna's desk toward the glass door leading to Aiden Mannion's office. He was talking on the phone, but when he spotted her, he held up a finger, letting her know he'd be only a moment.

When he stood up, Chelsea allowed herself a moment of enjoyment at the way the dark blue shirt hugged a torso that she could remember being ripped, back when most of the kids at Honeymoon High spent the summer hanging out at Mirror Lake. Although his fiancée, Jolene Wells, was the lucky woman who got to touch, Chelsea figured that there was no harm in looking.

"Right after you called me, I made a call to the state patrol," he told her as he came out of his office, which was barely larger than her own at the library. Honeymoon Harbor didn't have that much serious crime, and those who committed it usually ended up in the county jail. "The kids went into foster care four years ago after their parents' SUV went off a coastal cliff. According to the officer who was first on the scene, the parents, who weren't wearing seat belts, were thrown out as their vehicle hit the rocks on the way down."

"Meaning they probably died," Chelsea said.

"The car landed upside down, and somehow, the older girl, who was eight at the time, got her younger sister out of the car seat and carried her away from the scene just before the vehicle caught fire."

"That's horrendous." Chelsea's eyes teared up at the thought.

"According to the older girl—"

"Hannah," Chelsea murmured, remembering how protective she'd been of her younger sister. No way could she have imagined this scenario.

"Yeah." He glanced down at his notes. "Hannah. She told the first officer who showed up at the scene that her parents had been fighting, which distracted them from seeing a deer run into the road. We found the doe's body on the other side of the road. I'm guessing that the girls' father instinctively swerved to avoid it—"

"And the car went off over the cliff."

"That's what the detectives deduced from the skid marks. The car was pretty much burned down to the wheels, so there wasn't any way to tell if anything had been defective, but the older girl told the police on the scene that her parents had begun drinking heavily in the weeks leading up to the accident, which was corroborated by the coroner's report putting both parents' alcohol blood level above the legal limit. There were also reports of an altercation between the girls' father and another soccer dad during a kids' game at the coast the day of the accident. Which could well have led to an argument on the drive home."

"Poor things." Once again Chelsea felt a personal connection with the two young girls who'd made her library a sanctuary. Just as she once had. And, she considered, if she were to be perfectly honest with herself, she probably still did. Everyone had a place where they fit. Where they felt that internal sense of belonging. The library had always been hers.

"Long story short, with no family to claim them, they landed in the system. I was talking with their caseworker when you got here. She told me they've been hard to place."

"That surprises me. They seem very well behaved and it's more than apparent that Hannah would do anything to protect her little sister, Hailey."

"That's part of the problem," Aiden said. "Most of the families who take kids in are already on tight budgets. Even with the monthly payments from social services, two kids cost a lot more out of pocket than one. But the last time they tried to separate them, the younger one ran away."

"To be with her sister."

"Bingo. Making matters worse is that the older one—"

"Hannah," Chelsea reminded him.

"Yeah. Hannah warned the caseworker that if they don't keep them together, they'll just take off."

"She's not possibly old enough to manage on her own, let alone with Hailey to take care of."

"Mrs. Collins, head of Salish County Social Services, knows that. As does her caseworker. And they both know that Hannah knows it, too. But no one's willing to take the risk."

"Thus the traffickers," Chelsea murmured.

"Traffickers?"

"When I offered to drive them home, Hailey said they weren't allowed to take rides from strangers because of the traffickers. The house didn't look all that well kept. And no one was home."

"Mrs. Hayes, their foster mom, often has to work over-time to make ends meet. It's my guess that taking in the kids helps with her budget, but from the inspection reports, the kids aren't in any danger."

"Just ignored."

He shrugged. "Probably. But they aren't the only latch-key kids in town. And their situation still sounds better than some of the kids I see when I go out on domestic violence calls."

Honeymoon Harbor was a beautiful town that at first glance seemed as if it could be a setting for a Pacific Northwest reboot of *Mayberry R.F.D.* But beneath its appealing quaint Victorian appearance and public spirit, it couldn't escape the problems shared by any town or city.

Chelsea thanked Aiden for taking the time to check the girls' history and left the office, wondering what to do next. While she didn't want to interfere with anyone else's lives, neither did she want to risk those two girls being so alone. Because she knew all too well how it felt, coming home to an empty house. Then later, as things spiraled more and more downhill, coming home to find her mother passed out on the couch.

"You're a librarian." She gave herself a pep talk as she drove to her apartment housed in a former 1880s lumber baron's Victorian mansion. Although it involved climbing three flights of stairs, her room gave her a wonderful bird's-eye view of the boat basin, where the boats that weren't out enjoying the perfect Pacific Northwest summer day bobbed peacefully on the water. There was also a row of houseboats that had been docked there since long before she was born.

Smoke drifted in on the salt-tinged air, suggesting that someone was grilling meat and making her wish that she'd stopped for something at the market deli section. She'd been so busy planning the Summer Readers' Adventure, she was down to Rice Krispies and some berries from Blue House Farm she'd bought at the farmers' market. Deciding that she wasn't hungry enough to drive back downtown to the market or one of the restaurants, she opted for the cereal, which she ate while Googling, hoping to find some way to legally help the girls without getting on the wrong side of social services.

Something she'd spent much of her childhood and teenage years trying to avoid.

CHAPTER FOUR

GABE WAS BACK out on the deck overlooking Mirror Lake, nursing a beer while watching a sailboat skim across a skyline that had turned rose gold. Maybe Quinn and the Norwegian cook were right about him taking up sailing again while he was here. The last time he'd been on the water had been the summer of his senior year of high school when he'd built an eighteen-foot Northeaster Dory. After taking it out to make sure it was fair, he'd sold it to an orthopedic surgeon from Tacoma for tuition money.

The conversation he'd had two days earlier with Quinn kept replaying in his head. The garage of the cabin—who needed space for five cars?—could make a good shop. If he were staying here. Which he wasn't.

His first sight of the ten-thousand-square-foot house named Eagles Watch owned by Ajay Deshpande, a Seattle tech billionaire he'd gone to UW with, was a revelation. And definitely more space than he'd bargained for when he'd taken his old fraternity brother up on the offer to use the house for the summer.

The only thing it had in common with a cabin was that both were made of logs. Still, when he'd called to ask about leasing it, Ajay had told Gabe that he was thinking of putting it up for sale because business was so ridiculously busy he never made it over to the peninsula. Plus, having hit his midforties and with no wife yet on the horizon, let alone the four kids he'd once thought he'd someday have, he had no need for the six bedrooms (three of them masters), seven baths, a home theater, gym, indoor pool with a roof that opened for the summer, a two-story library, the five-car garage and a commercial kitchen Bobby Flay would be more than happy to cook in.

And if all that wasn't enough, eighteen-foot-tall floor-to-ceiling glass doors accordion folded open onto the three-tiered deck boasting an outdoor kitchen complete with another stove, fridge, farm sink, three gas grills and a brick pizza oven.

A smaller one-bedroom cabin had been built next door on the seven acres for the intended live-in housekeeper who would, Gabe assumed, also cook. For now, a trio of maids from The Clean Team, a local cleaning service, came in weekly.

"Hell," his old friend had said, "feel free to stay as long as you want. Someone ought to get some use out of the place."

The house was an embarrassment of excess, yet at the same time, the builder had somehow created the feeling of the family home it had been designed to become. It was what Gabe would have chosen, if he'd ever planned to leave New York City to return west and start a family.

Still, with private, wooded waterfront space like this being in high demand from wealthy buyers from California to Canada, it wasn't as crazy an investment as it might seem. And unlike stocks and hedge funds, land was finite because God wasn't making any more of it. If he bought it, then leased it out while high housing costs continued to rise, he could turn a tidy profit. And, on the occasion he did come home, he'd have a place to stay.

Although it was still over-the-top for Honeymoon Harbor, Ajay's dark British Racing Green Range Rover in the garage was a lot less conspicuous than the Porsche 911 GT2 RS Gabe had leased last year. It wasn't as if he'd needed the outrageously priced car. Especially since he had a driver to take him from his apartment to his office. And he'd never driven it anywhere he'd even approached the need for its seven hundred horsepower. But as Carter had taught him, in the golden city he'd entered, a closet filled with designer suits, soft-as-an-infant's-bottom Italian shoes, a flashier new car every season and a young eager-to-please supermodel mistress in your bed were all a way of keeping score. While he'd bought into the heady financial hierarchy, Gabe had passed on the supermodels.

He'd forgotten how quiet life could be without the cacophony of city noise. The only sounds were the sigh of a salt-tinged breeze in the tops of the Douglas fir and cedar trees, the lapping of the Sound tide onto the sand beach, and the hum of bumblebees buzzing around the showy clusters of red, white and purple rhododendron blooms in the gardens surrounding the house. Last night he'd heard the hoot of an owl and the lonely howl of what could possibly have been a rare gray wolf, or more likely a coyote.

The sound of a car engine broke that silence, and since his family were the only ones he'd given the wrought iron gate code to, he stood up, walked around to the front of the house and watched the SUV with the Honeymoon Harbor Police Department seal on the door come up the drive.

"I come bearing dinners," Aiden announced as he climbed out carrying a familiar red cooler.

"Doesn't Mom have something better to do than cooking?"

"Live with it," Aiden advised. "I had to when I first came back. And with school closed for the summer, even with the classes she's taking to finish up her design degree, she's got extra time on her hands."

"Maybe she ought to take up knitting."

"Don't suggest that unless you want to be lugging a suitcase of sweaters back to New York." On top of the cooler was a red-and-white pizza box from Luca's Kitchen. "Dad brought me pizza when I was playing hermit out at the coast house. I figured it was the least I could do for you."

"Thanks. But shouldn't you be home having dinner with your fiancée?"

"Jolene and her mom are hosting a bachelorette party for a client at their spa, so I decided to come eat pizza and watch baseball with you. The Mariners are playing the Yankees."

"I may have grown up here, but I'm team Judge," Gabe said.

"Sellout," his brother countered. "But it'll make things more interesting. What do you want to bet on? The score or home runs?"

"Why not both?"

"You're on," Aiden said, as he set the cooler on the deck and the pizza on the table. "And to make things more interesting, how about going for a trifecta and adding in RBIs?"

"Works for me. What time's the game?"

"Seven."

"We've got time for the pizza. I'll get some plates and beer."

"Luca threw in some paper plates and napkins. I didn't know if you had anything that plebeian here at Versailles."

"So it's a bit excessive for Honeymoon Harbor." And yeah, he had sounded defensive.

"You think?"

"Yeah. I think. Right now it's home sweet home. Though I'm considering buying it."

"Seriously? I thought you were going back to New York after Labor Day."

"I am. It'd be an investment property. I happen to know the owner's ready to get rid of it, so I could get a good deal."

Aiden looked out over the lake, where the reflection of the mountains was turning glassy again after being crossed by a boat's wake. "When I came back home, I was at loose ends," he said. "While I was spending those weeks hiding out at the coast house, trying to figure out what the hell I was going to do with the rest of my life, I never, not once, imagined I'd end up police chief."

"I doubt anyone else did, either." Aiden had once been the Mannion family's black sheep and Honeymoon Harbor's bad boy. A born charmer, he'd talked his way out of more trouble than a lot of guys would've gotten away with until he'd made the mistake of boosting a twelve-pack from the back of a delivery truck outside Marshall's Market. That had been the last straw that had caused the judge to throw up his hands and threaten to send Aiden to juvie.

But without attempting to use the power of his office, which John Mannion had far too much integrity to ever try, their dad deftly worked out a deal where, so long as Aiden stayed out of trouble for the last two months of high school, he could enlist in the Marines when he turned eighteen and have his juvenile crime-spree record expunged.

"Dad had it figured out. At first I thought he was crazy. But—" he shrugged "—it turned out to be exactly the right thing for me to be doing."

"Good for you. And why do I get the feeling that there's a message in there?"

"I was just saying. Sometimes life can take some strange twists, like me getting through deployments without a scratch, then getting shot after becoming a cop, which brought me back here, but going with the flow can also take you interesting places you might not have considered."

Gabe got the message. Loud and clear. "Maybe coming home worked out for you and Quinn. But small-town life isn't for me. I like the rush of my life in the city."

"That landed you in the hospital."

Damn. Gabe never should've told Aiden and Quinn about that. But Aiden must've been one helluva interrogator during his days working LAPD, because he'd gotten Gabe to spill the beans about what had happened to have him returning home. It had been the day after he'd landed in town, a Monday afternoon, when his two brothers had shown up at the house with thick rib-eye steaks and fishing poles.

While they'd fished off the dock, Aiden had shared a story from his time as an undercover cop in LA that had sounded a lot like a modern-day gunfight at the O.K. Corral. A shooting in which he'd been wounded, his longtime partner killed, that had brought him home, where he spent his first weeks at the family coast house, trying to drink the state dry. But now he'd sobered up, gotten himself engaged, and was pulling trout out of the water, like Sheriff Andy Taylor at the fishing pond in Mayberry.

Which was why Gabe somehow found himself telling his brothers about passing out at Carter's funeral. Wife number four, now the widow Kensington, had chosen an open-casket viewing, and when Gabe had stood looking down at that artificially waxen face, its manic energy gone, it occurred to him that his now dead friend and mentor could have been brought to the funeral home from the Times Square Madame Tussauds.

That was when his heart started pounding against his ribs and vertigo had hit like a lightning bolt. *That could have been you*, a voice had pointed out over the wail and yelp of the ambulance.

No way, he'd shot back. Since he'd had an oxygen mask stuck on his face at the time, the argument must have been in his head, but it sure as hell had felt real.

Everyone dies, the nagging voice had said. *There's no escaping it.*

I'm not ready to go yet. He was only in his thirties. He still had a lot of living to do. Not that his life entailed much beyond work right now, but one of these days he was going to travel for trips that weren't all spent inside conference rooms. Maybe he'd even have a family. Not the crazy dysfunctional one like Carter's had been. But a real family. Like his mom and dad's. Not that he'd been a fully functioning member of that one for the past few years.

Despite his argument with the ER Doogie Howser, Gabe hadn't gotten to where he was by being dumb. He knew that every body had its limits. Even iron man Burke found that out two years ago with a concussion that had benched him in the last game of the league playoffs, derailing what all the fans and oddsmakers had considered the New York Gotham Knights' guarantee to make the Super Bowl.

But it wasn't too late. He figured that ER doc was more like Scrooge's Ghost of Christmas Future. He hadn't revealed what *would* happen. Only what *could*. Gabe was perfectly capable of changing his fate. All he had to do was make a plan. It wasn't all that different from analyzing financial data.

Which was why, the day after he'd arrived here, he'd started running a wooded trail along the lakeshore in the morning when the air was as still as the water. It might have been more like staggering at first, and any skinny freshman on his old high school track team would've lapped him, but the crisp, clean air was helping, and he was getting his stride back day by day. The thirty minutes of push-ups and crunches he'd done every morning back in Manhattan while watching the Asian markets had kept him looking fighting fit—which was more important than people might think in his profession—but apparently they hadn't done much for his stamina.

"Maybe I will ask Seth if I can borrow his boat." Sailing a small craft involved pulling lines, maneuvering the rudder, moving from port to starboard to adjust the sails, all which provided a good workout, and he'd always enjoyed being out on the water. It also would check off that stress-reduction box Doogie had prescribed.

Seth was so tied up with getting the remodel on his and Brianna's carriage house completed before their August double wedding with Aiden and Jolene, he undoubtedly didn't have a lot of extra time to go sailing. And as Quinn had pointed out, he *had* built his soon-to-be brother-in-law's boat back in the day.

"He'd lend it to you in a heartbeat," Aiden said.

That was true. Gabe considered that idea as he took another slice of pie from the box. Okay. Maybe he was eating the same way he had in Manhattan, but baby steps, right?

Besides, along with three kinds of meat, the pizza had tomato sauce and mushrooms. Which counted as vegetables. And the organic mozzarella sourced from happy cows down in Oregon took care of the dairy part of the food triangle.

"You don't have to get crazy and start eating at Leaf," he assured himself, so used to having only himself to converse with since returning home, he hadn't realized he'd spoken out loud.

"Why the hell would you want to do that?" Aiden asked. "I mean, the mac and cheese is surprisingly good, for vegan, and I know that doc told you to watch your cholesterol, but didn't some Greek say something about moderation being the best in all things? Or maybe it was in the Bible."

"Or Shakespeare."

Aiden shrugged. "Well, someone sure as hell said it. And it makes sense."

"Not going to get any argument from me." Gabe took another bottle of the Good Vibrations from the six-pack he'd brought out.

One problem with this rest and relaxation plan was that he'd apparently burned out his internal governor by the end of his first month at Columbia. He'd grown up accustomed to being the smartest guy in the room. With the possible exception of Quinn, but only because, being older, his brother had had more time to absorb information. But Gabe's first semester in business school had knocked him on his ass. Suddenly he was competing with the best and the brightest the country—hell, the whole damn world—had to offer.

Not willing to settle for second best, he'd kicked into high gear and his engine hadn't stopped racing. Until he'd found himself on that wedding-cake-white ferry plowing through the waters of Puget Sound toward home.

So now what? Although he hated admitting that his older brother always seemed to be right, since he didn't have anywhere to go, or anything else to do, it wouldn't hurt to go online and check out some boat plans. One thing he'd never been able to resist was a challenge—like that damn zip line—and building a faering could be one that would fill up all those days stretching out in front of him.

Then, at the end of the summer, he could donate it to some local charity to auction off. Win-win.

And if there was one thing Gabriel Mannion had always been once he'd hit Wall Street, it was a winner.

CHAPTER FIVE

CHELSEA HAD JUST ordered a skinny mocha Frappuccino without whipped cream, which admittedly didn't make all that much difference calorie-wise with all the chocolate syrup blended into it, when Brianna came up behind her.

"Small world," she greeted Chelsea with a smile.

"Small town," Chelsea responded. "Aren't you usually playing Julia Child to all your B and B guests this time of day?"

"We had an unexpected cancellation." Brianna browsed the case containing a plethora of doughnuts. "It seems that we have an open weekend."

"Oh." Chelsea paid for her coffee, adding a generous tip, having worked as a barista in college. "I have some time if you want to sit down and catch up for ten or so minutes."

"That sounds great. Seth is in Boise. Someone bought an Italianate Victorian just to tear it down and build a modern box house on the lot. There's a mantle and some other things he's bidding on before the remains get carted off to be trashed."

"That's so sad."

"It is. Honeymoon Harbor and Port Townsend are two of the few places in the state where you can find Victorians on the market. Of course all the early wealthy Seattleites built ornate Victorian mansions, but after the Great Seattle Fire of 1889, as the city literally rebuilt from the ashes, Seth told me that the styles shifted toward Romanesque, Tudor and foursquare construction." A table opened up in the corner, near the gift shop. "Why don't you go grab that and I'll order."

When a quartet of women Chelsea recognized as working at the Mannions' family bank came in while Brianna was at the counter, she was glad she'd manage to claimed the last table. With both of them in their busy summer season, spare time was at a premium.

"I couldn't resist the lemon poppy seed, cream cheese muffin," Brianna said as she arrived with her coffee. "Want to share?"

"Devil get behind me," Chelsea said on a laugh as she took the extra paper plate and napkin Brianna had brought to the table.

"It's no fun to sin alone."

"That would be true."

Brianna bit into the muffin, closed her eyes and held up a hand. "Sorry," she said. "But I was having a moment. I wonder if the guys would give me the recipe."

"They undoubtedly would. You're not really breakfast competition. So, what gives you this free time during the wedding high season?

"Apparently the groom-to-be got drunk and banged the stripper at his bachelor party on the coast."

"Isn't that a little cliché?"

"I suppose. But making it a threesome with the cocktail waitress hired for the party may have pushed it over the top."

"Sounds as if the bride-to-be lucked out."

"I told her the same thing, but I'm not sure it helped. She was swinging between sobbing, cursing, screaming about how she was going to sue his ass for the cost of the wedding, including the hundred-dollar bottles of champagne, at least one of which she'd apparently opened before calling me, and finally deciding to fly to Maui for the honeymoon on her own. She sounded a bit tipsy by then."

"Still, it's a good plan. Maybe Mr. Right will turn out to be a hot, tanned cabana boy."

"Given that she also mentioned revenge sex, I suspect she'll be looking for Mr. Right Now," Brianna said dryly.

"I can't say I blame her. With Seth out of town, I take it work has stopped on the gatehouse?" Chelsea licked some cream cheese frosting topped with finely grated lemon zest off her fingers and took another sip of her coffee.

After the two of them had restored Herons Landing to its original glory, while modernizing it at the same time for her bed-and-breakfast, Brianna and Seth had moved into the gatehouse he'd been restoring for the past few months.

"It's getting closer to completion," Brianna said. "The finish carpenters are creating a coffered ceiling in the master bedroom as we speak. We're finally down to the kitchen, which I kept moving to the end of Seth's list. I knew it was going to be horribly inconvenient, but thanks to takeout from every place in town, we're surviving. We're going to have a no-gifts-allowed housewarming party to show it off when it's done. I hope you'll come."

"I wouldn't miss it. Though I'm surprised you're taking on throwing a party while running your B and B and planning a wedding."

"I took Herons Landing off the rental market the week before and the week of the wedding. Although it's our busy season, I didn't want to disrupt guests with preparations and quite honestly, I don't want any guests getting in my way. As for multitasking, the wedding's proving easy. It's going to be super casual out at the farm with a reception barbecue. Desiree is baking the cakes and singing with Bastien, the flowers from Blue House Farm are ordered and I've rented a dance floor from a place in Port Angeles. Believe me, it's a lot easier than planning a mid-six-figure, high-end formal wedding for two King Charles spaniels."

Chelsea almost spit out the drink she'd just taken. "That's just...crazy."

"You should have been there. Looking back, I'm surprised I'd come to accept crazy stuff like that as part of the job. Once I got on the hospitality track, after dreaming of it all my life, I just kept moving forward, never looking anywhere but forward and upward." She took a thoughtful sip of her coffee. "From what Quinn told me when I'd decided to buy Herons Landing, he'd been the same way with the law. I suspect that may be the place Gabe's in. Did I tell you that he's home from New York?"

"You didn't have to. It was up on the Facebook page minutes after he stepped off the ferry." Gabriel Mannion was seven years older than Chelsea, so they'd never actually personally interacted. But it had been impossible not to notice all the Mannion boys when they came swaggering into town from the family Christmas tree farm, and she'd definitely agreed with all her girlfriends who'd declared Gabriel swoon-worthy going back to middle school.

Although she hadn't seen him since his return, he had been spotted at Cops and Coffee, where according to reports, he'd become even more of a hottie since moving to New York. She'd also heard that he'd been making money hand over fist and was undoubtedly the only one-percenter ever to come out of Honeymoon Harbor.

He'd also become an angel investor for Jolene Wells, who, in the way of small-town degrees of separation, was currently engaged to Aiden Mannion. Which, she figured, was the reason he'd invested. If you couldn't help family, what was the point in being rich? Jolene's skin care line, which she'd begun while working as a Hollywood makeup artist, was wonderful, and certainly no investment risk on his part.

And not only that, Jolene and Brianna were having a double wedding in August. Chelsea had already agreed to be an attendant, which would make it the second summer in a row she'd been a bridesmaid. Not that she was envious, but all the other brides seemed so happy in their marriages that there were admittedly times when she was sitting at home watching yet another couple find their happily-ever-afters on the Hallmark Channel that she wished some fairy godmother would show up with the perfect man for her.

"Did you also hear that he's spending the summer building a Viking boat in the boat school shop?"

"An actual Viking ship? Like they raided with?"

"Well, not nearly that big," Brianna allowed. "But it's going to look much the same."

"I recently acquired a Caldecott Medal–winning children's book on northern myths. There were already collections in the library for older kids, but every age loves fairy tales. Thanks for letting me know. It'd tie in perfectly with our visit to the history museum."

She hadn't even known Gabriel knew how to build wooden boats. Not that there was any reason to. All she knew was that, like all the Mannion brothers, he'd always been sex on a hot stick. She was, however, curious—not just about his Viking replica, but why the wealthiest man in Honeymoon Harbor would return to his hometown to build boats.

"I wonder if he'd be willing to let the kids visit the boat shop and see it. I could weave in the history of the Vikings with stories of the Scandinavians settling here on the peninsula. And maybe throw in a myth or two."

"I thought you might be interested in that idea. But I have to warn you not to get your hopes up. And please don't get your feelings hurt if he seems rude. He's been a loner out at the lake, and extremely noncommunicative even with us. I have the feeling something significant happened in New York, but if anyone knows what it was, it'd be Quinn, and he's not talking."

Everyone knew that Quinn Mannion held secrets as tightly as a priest hearing a confession at St. Peter the Fisherman's church. Which was why he undoubtedly knew personal things about most people in Honeymoon Harbor.

"Well, it wouldn't hurt to ask," she decided. "All he can do is say no, right?"

"Right. And good luck. Quite honestly, I think it'd be as good for him as it would be fun for the kids."

The rest of her week was filled with meetings, including a budget report to the town council. Then this weekend she was driving down to Portland to attend an Oregon state library convention and talk about her reading adventurers. Then her first day back would obviously be busy. While Farrah was a wonderful librarian, the staff was so small, every loss of personnel mattered.

There wasn't an immediate hurry, she decided, taking out a pen to write a tentative date into her planner. She had enough to keep the kids busy for a few weeks once they got out of school, but she would make a point of dropping by the boat-building school to ask Gabriel to take part in the Summer Readers' Adventure. If nothing else, a group of enthusiastic kids could bring anyone out of the doldrums.

CHAPTER SIX

GABE HAD CAVED, as Quinn had undoubtedly known he would. Two weeks after sharing that pizza with Aiden, he was hidden away in a back corner of the Honeymoon Harbor wooden boat–building school, running a piece of sustainable, plantation-grown, British-milled Okoume marine-grade hardwood through the table saw when the door opened, the sun backlighting a woman wearing a tidy black pencil skirt that ended at her knees, a sleeveless, pleated-front tuxedo shirt with the top two buttons open, and black flats.

Burnished brunette hair had been pulled up into a messy bun and, as she came closer, he watched her pupils widen behind her black-framed glasses to adjust to the shadows in the depth of the shop.

"Hi," she said, with a quick, wide smile. "I'm Chelsea Prescott. You probably don't remember me."

He could lie to save her feelings. But knowing that he'd eventually be caught out on some miniscule, long-ago hometown detail, he opted for full-out honesty. "I don't think—"

"Don't worry about it," she said, with an airy wave of her hand. "There's no reason that you would. You'd already graduated high school when I started, and it wasn't as if I was a social butterfly... I'm Honeymoon Harbor's librarian."

"What happened to Mrs. Henderson?" A memory of having to spend a sunny summer Saturday dusting shelves to pay off his library fines flashed through his mind.

"She retired. But she's still on the library advisory board."

"I didn't realize libraries had advisory boards."

"Many do." Twin dimples appeared in her cheeks as she smiled. She was, as his grandfather Harper would say, cute as a button. Even as her naughty librarian glasses had him imagining unbuttoning a few more of those buttons, Gabe reminded himself that he didn't do cute. "Though in our case, it's admittedly more a group of volunteers I've dragged in to help. Mrs. Henderson checks in at least once a week to make sure I haven't ruined the place." She talked with her hands, which seemed to flutter around like meadow butterflies. "Not that I'd have it any other way. She always has helpful advice and has been a friend and mentor to me most of my life."

"That's nice. For both of you." From the day he'd applied to work at Harborstone, Carter Kensington had played the same role in Gabe's life, although he guessed the elderly librarian's mentoring had been a lot more staid and hadn't included the excess of alcohol Carter's had.

"It is." She flashed him another of those wide, Julia Roberts smiles. "At any rate, we've always had a summer reading program."

"I remember." During his younger years, when his high school principal mother had insisted all her children take part, Quinn always won the award for not only the most books read, but also for the best written reports. Gabe, who'd enjoyed reading, mostly about captains of industry and robber barons, had written some of Burke's reports, while the family jock spent the summer honing his QB skills. Honeymoon Harbor's bad boy Aiden hadn't even pretended to care about the competition for most books read, preferring to spend the school break at the lake and getting into trouble. By the time Quinn had gone off to college, Brianna was old enough to claim his reading program crown.

"This year we're downsizing it a bit to try something different."

"Okay." He folded his arms and waited for what the hell that had to do with him.

"Since the goal is to expand minds, I thought that at least once a week we'd break out of the walls of the library and explore other learning opportunities." She glanced down at the drawing of a plan he'd chalked onto the hundred-year-old wood plank floor. "Brianna mentioned that you're building a Viking ship."

"A faering." Which would undoubtedly mean nothing to her. "It's from an Old Norse word meaning 'to row.'"

"Now, see, that's exactly why I'm here. You already taught me something I know the kids would be interested in. Before we go to the museum, I was planning to prepare the readers with a few days at the library exploring Norse folktales. I just acquired this wonderful book about Vikings for the younger children." She paused and he could practically envision the ideas bouncing around like pinballs in her head. "Maybe we could even make costumes."

"Just don't make the mistake of putting those horns on the helmets or you're going to piss off a lot of locals who know better."

"Don't worry, I'd never do that... Do you know where that silly stereotype came from?"

"No." And he really didn't care, though he had the feeling he wouldn't be able to stop her from telling him.

"It's all Richard Wagner's fault. Well, not really his, but Carl Emil Doepler's."

"Remember when you didn't know what a faering was?"

"Of course. It was less than a minute ago."

"That's how I'm feeling about now." It also had him

thinking of Quinn telling him not to talk so much in boatspeak.

"Oh. Well, Wagner wrote operas."

"That, I know." Occasionally, when Carter had gotten super soused, he'd started singing the stuff, which was when Gabe first learned about his friend's six-year relationship with a soprano from the Met. A mistress who'd outlasted wives two and three. It had predictably turned into a tabloid headlines breakup with the soprano and subsequent divorce from wife number three, which had been every bit as overblown and dramatic as any opera.

"Okay." She blew out a breath. "So, when he staged his *Der Ring des Nibelungen*, consisting of four operas—"

"*The Rhinegold*, *The Valkyrie*, *Siegfried* and *Twilight of the Gods*."

"That's exactly right. Wow." This time her smile was like one of those gold stars elementary teachers used to put on all-perfect Quinn's papers. Gabe's grades had been good enough to get him into the honor society, but he'd be the first to admit if a subject didn't involve boats, or the math he'd learned that was necessary to build them, he tended to blow it off.

"I had a friend who was into opera," he told her. A familiar ache had him rubbing his heart whenever he thought of Carter. Sure, the guy had been majorly flawed. But he'd also been his best friend. "He particularly liked singing from *The Ring*." Usually after the third or fourth manhattan. Which had been even more grating than Carter's drunken rendition of "New York, New York," which probably had Sinatra spinning in his grave.

"Well, to be honest, it's always seemed a bit overdone for me, but there's no denying that it lies at the heart of nineteenth-century culture and had an incalculable effect on European, particularly German, culture."

"You know what?"

"What?"

"Having grown up with Mrs. Henderson heading up the library, I was having trouble making the shift in my head. But now I definitely buy you as a librarian."

She tilted her head. As she studied him, appearing to decide whether or not she'd just been insulted, her bluish-green eyes, which appeared to be a barometer of her mood, turned cooler. He hoped the woman never played poker, because she couldn't bluff worth a damn.

"If you're not interested—"

"No, I am. Keep going." Although he'd never given a damn about opera, there was something about her earnestness that had slipped past the emotional drawbridge he'd slammed down when he'd gotten the call about Carter's death.

"Well. When Wagner staged the operas in the 1870s, Doepler, who was his designer, came up with horned helmets for the Vikings. And thus an enduring and rather ridiculous stereotype was born.

"There had been discoveries of ancient horned helmets in the nineteenth century that later turned out to predate the Vikings. Greeks and Romans had also written about northern Europeans wearing helmets adorned with feathered wings, antlers and horns. But that was at least a century before the Vikings appeared and those were probably only worn for ceremonial purposes by Norse and Germanic priests. Because, while wearing horns into battle might help intimidate your enemies, and perhaps poke out an eye, they'd be more likely to get tangled up in tree branches."

"Or embedded in a shield."

"That's exactly what I've always imagined!" She rewarded him with another smile that lit up the shadowy corner of the shop and tugged at something inside him.

Not lust, but a feeling Gabe couldn't exactly name. "But getting back to my point, and I truly did have one, it would be so wonderful to bring the group here to see you building your wonderful boat.

"Sorry, *faering*," she corrected herself. "Just looking at all those boards and pieces of wood, and trying to imagine them turning into an actual boat from that plan on the floor is amazing to me."

"Confession time. I've never figured out the Dewey decimal system."

Oh, damn. Her laughter tugged that same chord again.

"You're not alone. Which is why we also have a digital catalogue and a user-friendly search engine for library visitors to use… Please don't feel any pressure because it's only a suggestion." She held up her hand again. Her short nails with their clear polish would have seemed suitable to the stereotypical librarian, had it not been for the perky daisies painted on both ring fingers. "I was hoping that we could team up."

"You want them to work on my boat?" Hell. No.

"Oh, no." Her expressive eyes widened even as her forehead creased with concern. "I'm sorry, I'm usually more succinct. After delving into Norse myths from the books—I considered asking Jarle at the pub to tell some stories, but his language can get a little colorful—I decided to teach the children the history of the Scandinavian immigrants who settled in Honeymoon Harbor. I'm hoping some will be able to interview family members about their ancestors so we can include those."

Since his own family tree didn't include a lot of Scandinavians, at least that he knew of, Gabe still didn't see what that had to do with him.

"Next, I'd like to tie that in with a visit to the museum. And hopefully wrap it all up in a pretty red ribbon with a visit here to see an actual Viking boat in progress. It would also be wonderful if you'd be willing to explain what they used the boat—the faering—for."

"They used it for raiding. Which, not being up on ancient Norse history, is all I'd be able to tell them, so I wouldn't want you to waste everyone's time coming all the way out here."

"It's a small town," she pointed out. "Even out here on the end of the peninsula, you're not that far away from the library. And the museum, which we'd be coming from, is even closer."

"Sorry, but the shop's liability insurance doesn't allow kids in here." That was a lie, but she didn't have to know that he'd begun hanging around the summer between third and fourth grades.

"Even if I promise that they won't touch a thing?"

"Even then. Which, given them being kids, undoubtedly isn't a promise you'd be able to keep." It was his turn to hold up a hand to forestall the argument he sensed coming. "I'm only trying to keep them safe."

Color bled into her cheeks as he belatedly realized his comment also implied that she wouldn't be able to corral them. But it was too late to call the words back. Nor did he apologize for them, which would open him up to more conversation.

"I also promised this would be finished in time for the buyer to sail it in the Labor Day wooden boat regatta."

While considering whether or not to build the faering, he'd decided to donate it to Welcome Home to auction off at the Labor Day wooden boat festival. The charity—which he'd helped fund—in its second year, built tiny rental homes for the homeless, along with providing medical care, counseling, schooling and help finding employment. So there was no buyer. But she didn't need to know that.

"Well." He watched her gather her composure. "I apologize for having taken up your time. Given that you're on such a tight deadline." The sarcasm in her previously perky tone told him that she'd sensed the lie. Not that it mattered.

The important thing was that she wouldn't be invading what, so far, no one in town, even his family, knew had technically become *his* school and shop two years ago when he'd bailed the owner out of debt. There wasn't much of a market these days for handcrafted wooden boats, which admittedly took a lot more upkeep. Most went to collectors and people like him, who'd always loved the one-of-a-kind beauty and were willing to put up with the inconvenience and expense.

He shrugged. "No problem. I was ready for a break anyway."

To demonstrate said alleged break was over, he bent, picked up a board and turned on the saw. Leaving her to walk away, from the shadows of the boat shop into the still bright summer sun.

"WELL, THAT WENT WELL," Chelsea muttered as she walked away from the dim boat shop into the sunshine. One of the things that made up for the long dark winters on the peninsula were the equally long summer days. Although it wasn't officially summer, the sun wouldn't set until after nine o'clock tonight, and the light would linger until just before ten. With its rays glancing off the glaciers at the top of the mountains, today's sun seemed especially bright. "Seriously, you brought up opera with a guy who probably listens to Toby Keith and Trace Adkins?"

She shoved on her sunglasses, which she had to buy every year, because she'd never remember where she'd put them at the end of fall when the rains began, and hoped that Gabriel Mannion didn't think her a total idiot. In this outdoor land of skiing, hiking, mountain climbing and sailing, her personal summer activity of choice was sitting on the front porch with a glass of lemonade and a good book. In the winter the location would change to her overstuffed sofa in front of her apartment's fireplace, with a cup of spiced tea. Which she'd long ago accepted made her different from many Honeymoon Harbor residents.

Although she wasn't one of those stuffy old stereotypical librarians with the wire-rim glasses perched on the end of her nose who was constantly shushing everyone, Chelsea preferred quiet. Order. Having had a lifelong love affair with words, she preferred to choose hers carefully. She did not, ever, chatter away like a magpie on speed.

Until today. From the moment her eyes had adjusted to the shadows in the back of the shop, all her carefully planned words had flown out of her head. She'd remembered the gist, but the point she'd come here planning to concisely make had gotten all garbled, like the conversations through two soup cans and a string the counselors at Camp Rainshadow had taught all the kids to make the summer her parents had sent her away.

After she'd grown up, with the benefit of hindsight, she'd understood that they'd been attempting to give her a respite from the dark, suffocating cloud of gloom that had settled over the Prescott home. What they hadn't realized was how horribly homesick she would be. Or that she'd feel so guilty about escaping such sorrow, she was incapable of enjoying all the sleepaway camp had to offer.

She couldn't allow herself to take part in the boating on the glassy dawn waters of Mirror Lake, the crafts, the marshmallows charred over nightly campfires or even the nature lessons taught by a cute ranger from Olympic Mountain National Park, who all the girls in her cabin had agreed was even cuter than Daniel Radcliffe, now that Harry Potter was growing up. But not her. Because Chelsea's heart, having been battered and tossed around by storms and tides, had lain like a heavy stone in her chest.

The one small, somewhat bright light was when she'd been chosen by her fellow campers to write the skit for the closing night's talent show. It certainly hadn't been due to any popularity on her part. She'd never belonged to any cliques, had never received an invitation to join the In Crowd. The reason she'd been chosen, one of her snarkier tent mates had informed her, was because she was the only one who'd spent every free moment of the summer with her nose in a book.

She'd loved the writing and casting of parts. Just because she'd held back on the outskirts of the groups during activities didn't mean that she hadn't been paying attention to what had been going on around her. She'd been a silent ghost of an observer, learning each camper's personality, which she brought to those pages she'd carefully written on filler paper with a yellow #2 pencil.

The paper and pencil had been given to her by Mrs. Henderson, who'd instructed her to report in weekly about what she'd been reading at camp. In turn, the librarian had written about library and town goings-on. The daily notes were far more than Chelsea had heard from her parents. Which she'd sort of understood. But that hadn't made her any less sad. Or homesick.

The performance was met with enthusiastic applause, the counselors shouting out "Author, author," waving for her to stand and receive accolades. While she appreciated the gesture and their effort to draw a smile from her at least once before she returned home, the recognition only made her regret that her parents and sister hadn't been there to see her literally standing in the spotlight.

"Not going there." Chelsea shook off the bittersweet memory and returned her thoughts to her less than brilliant performance in the boat shop. Her only excuse for her uncharacteristic behavior was that once her eyes had adjusted and she'd seen Gabriel Mannion running the wood through that huge and deadly looking saw, his arms corded with muscles, his raven-black hair falling over his forehead, her heart had stopped, and her blood had heated. Even from across the shop, she sensed the air of distance in him Brianna had warned her about. Over the ear-splitting screech of the saw ripping through the wood, she heard a distant alarm go off inside her.

She could have turned and walked away. Perhaps she should have. But she'd been transfixed by his broad back, and the way those jeans hugged a very fine butt. Not that she tended to go around looking at men's butts, but when it was right there in front of you, well, what was a woman to do?

Seeming to sense her arrival, he'd shut off the saw, turned around and shot her a hard, impatient look through a pair of thick safety goggles.

Which was when her knees had nearly buckled from the impact of the testosterone radiating from him. An olive green T-shirt, damp with sweat, clung to his body, outlining abs that belonged on a Men of Honeymoon Harbor Hunk of the Month calendar, like the one of local hot guys Kylee and Mai had put together and sold to raise money for Project Backpack, which collected school supplies for needy children.

She supposed the theme for his would be *Men of Wall Street*. Not that she could imagine many finance guys were as delicious as Gabriel Mannion. His scruffy jaw was firm, and when he yanked off the headphones and safety goggles, once her eyes had adjusted to the shadows, she could see that Gabriel Mannion's eyes were the dark and dangerous gray of a Pacific storm over the water. The instant they'd clashed with hers, Chelsea knew.

This was *him*. Rhett to her Scarlett. Tristan to her Iseult. Mr. Darcy to her Lizzy. The man she'd been waiting for her entire life. *Maybe fairy godmothers really did exist.*

"That's ridiculous," she scolded herself as she drove to the pub.

Love at first sight was nothing more than lust at first sight. Which she hadn't felt in so long she'd briefly mislabeled it. Obviously she'd been binge reading too many romances. Perhaps it was time to switch to a bloody serial killer thriller. Hadn't she read that the Pacific Northwest had more serial killers than anywhere else in the country?

When Ted Bundy and the Green River Killer came immediately to mind, deciding that might be hitting a bit close to home, she considered horror. While the small town of Forks may still receive vampire tourism, she'd never considered those pasty, chaste, baseball-playing sparkly vampires from Forks the least bit scary. And, by the way, she'd lived through enough Pacific Northwest storms to wonder why none of them had ever been killed by lightning from the thunderstorm hitting their aluminum bats.

"You're digressing again," she scolded her still uncharacteristically distracted mind. Gabriel Mannion might be the hottest guy she'd ever met up close and personal, but he was also the rudest. No way was she going to allow that distressing encounter with him to take her focus off her mission to have the best summer library program ever. "Keep your eyes on the prize." Coincidentally, the anthem of the civil rights movement had been today's inspirational quote on her life planner.

Despite having failed with Grinch Mannion, having already gotten his sister, brother-in-law, parents and uncle on board, she decided to drop into the pub and try one more victim. *Candidate.*

"I've been waiting for you to show up," Quinn said before she'd had an opportunity to pitch her idea of the brewery tours.

"Did Gabriel call you?" Damn. Just saying the man's name caused heat to rise in her cheeks. Chelsea hoped that the light was dim enough in the pub for him not to notice.

"No. Was he supposed to?"

"No. I just thought, since I was at the boat shop before I came here, he might…" She stopped and corralled her whirling, rebellious mind, which, for the first time, had her fully understanding the term *herding cats.* "I thought he might have warned you," she said, punctuating her words with a smile to assure Quinn that all was hunky-dory and she had the situation well in hand.

"You've become one of the main topics of conversation in here over the past few weeks," he said.

"I have?"

"Yep. Would you like something to drink?"

"I'll take a glass of wine," she decided. If nothing else, it might soothe nerves still rattled from her encounter with his brother at the boathouse. "Anything dry and white will be fine."

"You've got it." He pulled a bottle from a fridge beneath the counter, and poured the wine into a glass which he put on a green coaster with *Mannion's* printed in white script in front of her.

She took a sip of the crisp, pale gold Washington State sauvignon blanc and allowed herself a moment of relaxation. "I like it," she said. "So," she forged on. "Please tell me that the conversation is mostly good."

"All good," he assured her. "Want something to eat with that?"

"An order of wings sounds great," she decided, remembering she'd been so busy today, she'd forgotten to eat lunch. And Quinn Mannion was known all over the peninsula not just for his beer, but his wings. "The chili lime ones. With sweet potato fries." A former Olympic athlete from the University of Oregon had opened Honeymoon Harbor's first fitness center in February, and Chelsea vowed to do an extra twenty minutes on the damn stair stepper before work tomorrow morning. That exercise wouldn't make up for the calories, but at least she'd feel a bit more virtuous.

As soon as he put the order in the window behind him to the kitchen, Jarle pulled it off its clip. Which, now that she'd lost the possibility of the ship, had her rethinking her idea to ask the cook if he'd share some Norse tales. But the pub was beginning to fill up with the dinner crowd, and not wanting to interrupt service, she opted to wait.

"Let me guess," Quinn said. "You want me to give your library kids a tour of the brewery and explain the process."

"Only the older kids," she assured him.

"Okay."

"That's it?"

He flashed a devastatingly male grin that didn't affect her nearly as much as his brother's near glower. Having lived through enough drama in her early years, Chelsea had always been attracted to safe, easygoing men. Nice men. Men like Quinn Mannion. His brother Gabriel, she sensed, was not. Yet that hadn't prevented a physical reaction so strong that at first she thought the town might have been experiencing an earthquake. Which, along with volcanic eruptions and tidal surges, was one of the risks of living on the Ring of Fire. At the time she felt as if she'd been simultaneously hit by all three, which had her considering yet again that she may have overdosed on the Brontë sisters.

"That's the plan… You're a lot easier than your brother. He turned me down flat."

His answering laugh was rich and warm and drew the glances of a trio of women who appeared to be a mother, daughter and granddaughter, demonstrating his multigenerational appeal. Easygoing he might be. But like all the Mannion men, he should be required to wear a warning label. "I'm going to take that as a compliment."

"I meant it as one," she assured him. "Though I haven't given up on your brother. I'm hoping, once he learns that you've signed on, he might allow the kids to at least look at the faering. From a safe distance."

"Could happen." His tone was mild, but she saw the skepticism in his blue eyes. "Even without the Viking boat, it sounds like you're going to have a dynamite program."

"I'm trying my best to make it both fun and informative."

Although no one had said it to her face, Chelsea knew that there were those in town who, after she'd spent a year on the job, were still waiting to see if she was living up to Lillian Henderson's decades-long tenure as head librarian. Despite the town having been renamed in the early 1900s to honor European royals who were visiting the peninsula on their honeymoon trip across America, there were many residents, like the annoyingly negative Janet, who steadfastly balked at any idea of change.

Well, Chelsea decided as Jarle came out of the kitchen and placed her wings and crispy browned orange fries in front of her, she was just going to have to drag any resisters along with her.

CHAPTER SEVEN

GABE WAS STILL thinking about Honeymoon Harbor's librarian as he sat back out on his deck overlooking Mirror Lake, as he'd taken to doing after working at the shop. It was a perfect summer evening on the peninsula. The bright blue sky was dotted with just enough puffy white cumulus clouds to keep the temperature in the low eighties, which had brought more people out. A white sailboat with a diagonal rainbow-striped sail skimmed along the water, while two energetic kayakers paddled closer to the eleven-mile shore. Farther out, *The Sea Wolf*, a forty-foot commuter harkening back to the pre-WWII golden age of wooden boats, took passengers on a dinner cruise, leaving ripples in the crystal blue surface as it cut across the lake.

It crossed Gabe's mind that perhaps Brianna had been trying to set him up with the cute, girl-next-door librarian. He might have missed his sister and Seth Harper's engagement party, which caused a tinge of guilt now that he was back home with the family, but falling in love appeared to have her wanting the same thing for everyone else. Brianna had always been a fixer. She'd always wanted to make things better. Although he'd told only Aiden and Quinn about the episode at the funeral, Gabe was aware that he wasn't fooling anyone, that they knew something had happened, but being family, they had decided to let him tell his story in his own time.

He'd been home only a month, but in that time, he'd discovered that he'd lost the art of conversation. Oh, he'd been great at tapping into his inner Irishman and talking a blue streak while buying and selling to make money. Expenses for a driver were one of the perks at his level of success, and he'd remind himself to ask Leo, his long-time driver, how his day was going and offer appropriate comments in response to news of high school graduations of kids he'd never meet, and new grandchildren, who were apparently the most beautiful, smartest children on the planet.

He could go out at night to a bar and talk about the markets until closing with other traders, and if he were in the mood, he could toss out pickup lines that would have like-minded women take him home for no-strings-attached sex. But the pitiful truth was that the give and take of the type people casually and easily exchanged on a daily basis seemed to have evaporated.

He suspected Chelsea Prescott had left the shop thinking him curt. Rude. Which he'd admittedly been. Not that she hadn't been capable of filling any conversational gaps herself. If Gabe had made a list of the top things he was looking to do this summer, playing host and teacher to a bunch of kids definitely wouldn't have made the top ten list. Probably not even the top one hundred.

Fortunately, it was unlikely they'd run into each other all that often. Despite what she'd said about the town being small, the boat school and shop was located on the far end of the peninsula, the library at the other side of town. Plus, the only places he went, other than this rented cabin, were his brother's pub, Cops and Coffee, his family's farm and the shop. "So, no problem."

As he took a pull on the beer he'd brought out with him, it occurred to Gabe that the stock market had been closed for hours. This was the first day that he hadn't felt that inner bell announcing the end of the day's trading. Despite that, he still checked in at least once a day—he was, after all, only human, and it wasn't his money he was playing with—but not every ten minutes like he had his first three weeks back.

That his brother appeared to have been right about the boat-building idea proved a little annoying given that Quinn, being the eldest, had always been the perfect one. He'd been head altar boy, Eagle Scout with the badges to prove it, valedictorian his senior year, and after a stellar career at one of the Pacific Northwest's best law firms, he was now making a beer that deserved all the awards he was winning.

In his rare, introspective moments, like now, Gabe often wondered if he owed some of his success to feeling the need to compete with his brother. The role of perfect eldest was already taken, Aiden had claimed the rebel role and Burke, two years younger, had been the jock. Not wanting to risk juvie like Aiden, or throw rocket passes every Friday night on the Honeymoon Harbor High School's football field like Burke, Gabe had focused like a laser on becoming the wealthiest Mannion brother. And he'd succeeded beyond his wildest dreams.

So what had that gotten him?

And wasn't that the question?

"Just build the damn boat, donate it and get the hell back to work."

Despite his determination to avoid any interaction with Chelsea Prescott, that night Gabe dreamed of Vikings and a goddess of a shield maiden with hair the color of sun-burnished autumn leaves who welcomed him home after a successful raid, passionately rewarding him for the hammered-gold bracelet he'd placed on her bare arm.

When the sun rose the next morning, Gabe woke with an erection and the vivid memory of sailing into port, the single blood-red sail of his faering billowing in the northern wind. And the long night of lovemaking beneath a midnight sun. He couldn't remember the last time he'd experienced a sex dream. Could barely remember the last time he'd *had* sex.

He vaguely remembered picking up an ER senior resident from New York Presbyterian at an Oktoberfest party at a bar, then going back to the place she shared with two other doctors, one of whom, a surgical resident—no lie—had been watching an old *Dexter* episode when they'd arrived at the apartment.

Having not gone out with a woman who had a roommate since college, Gabe had initially been uncomfortable, but neither woman appeared at all fazed. The fact that he and the ER resident—Sonya? Sophia?—hadn't exchanged numbers assured him that they were both merely looking for release, and a brief time of human connection before returning to their workaholic lives.

As he'd left the apartment in the predawn hours, Gabe had already been thinking about the next deal, the next trade, staying ahead of all the hungry younger guys, who, like he'd once been, were racing up the ladder behind him, just waiting for him to slip and fall back into the shark tank.

CHELSEA WAS STILL pondering what to do about Hannah and Hailey the next Thursday as she and Lily Carpenter strolled the aisles of the waterfront farmers' market. She'd been driving them home every afternoon and had seen no signs of problems, and according to the social worker Aiden had spoken with after a home visit, her caseworker hadn't found any, either.

Despite her concerns, she was enjoying the bustle and cheer of the market, the buskers playing their music, the palm reader drawing a long line of customers, the stalls with the shiny fruit and luscious-looking vegetables, the scents of fresh bread and baked goods, and the aromas from all the different restaurant booths floating over all.

"I love this place," Lily said as she paid for a loaf of fresh-baked bread. The cinnamon aroma had drawn them from a neighboring aisle.

"Me, too. I was thinking of bringing Hannah and Hailey down here once school lets out." They'd talked about the sisters on the drive to the market. Lily had also noticed them while shelving books.

"They'd probably love it—who wouldn't?—but, not that you asked for my advice, I'd be careful about getting too emotionally attached."

"I think I can manage that." Chelsea decided to ignore the fact that one of the reasons she volunteered at Harbor Hill nursing home instead of the no-kill animal shelter Cam Montgomery had set up was that she wouldn't be allowed to take elderly residents home. Whereas, if she worked at the shelter, she'd have an apartment filled with cats and dogs which would be problematic given that her apartment had a no-pets rule. Also, a no-children rule, which was illegal but also a moot point, considering that men were part of the baby-making equation and not only was Honeymoon Harbor's dating pool limited, given the population of the town, she didn't know anyone with whom she was interested in having the sex procreation entailed.

They stopped at a fruit stand selling a variety of shiny apples, pears, peaches and Rainier cherries. "I thought I'd slice some of these with peanut butter yogurt dip," Chelsea said as she chose a selection of Braeburn and Fuji apples.

"You've been making a lot of treats lately. Before you left for that weekend conference in Portland, it was oatmeal raisin balls with mini chocolate chips. Not only do

I not recall you being into baking, I haven't seen you eating any of them."

"I test them at home. The oatmeal balls don't need cooking. Neither does the peanut butter dip. I found a book of healthy after-school snacks at Rain Or Shine Books."

"We *do* work in a library."

"True. But I like to support local business. Besides, cooking has never been my forte, as you know, and I didn't want to get chocolate all over one of our books."

"You bought that book precisely to make treats for the kids."

"There was a time when, whatever had happened at school, coming home to fresh-made snacks made me happy. My mother made the best lemon cream cupcakes." That had been before the bad times. Before the snacks and the happiness went away.

"You do realize that at least the older sister doesn't believe your excuse that you just happened to have some left over from your lunch?"

"I knew Hannah would never buy that. But I also knew she'd play along if it made Hailey happy." Because that's what big sisters did.

"You also realize that they're not in the type of home where cupcakes are an expected part of a happy child's life."

"Believe me, I know that." All too well.

"I was a volunteer court-appointed special advocate for kids in family court for a time when I was in Arizona," Lily said. "I have one more word of advice, then I'll shut up."

"Okay." From her friend's tone, Chelsea wasn't sure she was going to like what Lily was about to say, but being totally out of her depth, she was willing to take any advice she could get.

"Kids in the system get moved around a lot. Having

been watching you, out of curiosity, I Googled the stats last night, and the average in Washington State is over five-point-six moves in the first year. It's good that these girls are using the library as a safe zone after school. But if you let them get too attached to you, to think of you as a surrogate parent, like your mom making you those cupcakes, you could be putting them at risk of being even more emotionally and psychologically wounded when they move on. The system's statewide, Chelsea. The kids could end up in any other county next week. And there they'd be, suffering the loss of someone else they'd come to, if not love, depend on for kindness."

Chelsea hated that that made sense. But…

"Surely you're not suggesting I back away? Stop the snacks and putting holds on books for them?"

"Of course not. But after you'd left for Portland, Hailey asked me if you were coming back."

"I assured her I was."

"Given her backstory, I imagine she's lost a lot of people in her young life, so it would be natural to worry that you wouldn't. I'm just saying that perhaps you should make sure you're more the library lady, the way you've said Mrs. Henderson was to you, than a replacement mom."

"Thanks. That's good advice." Chelsea decided not to mention that although she hadn't realized it at the time, the now elderly librarian had not only proven a life raft in the turbulent seas of her life, she'd become the closest thing Chelsea had had to a parent during those difficult years. The one thing she didn't want to do was make the girls' situation worse while trying to brighten their lives a bit.

She was relieved when the topic was dropped as they stood in a line to order a salad made with yellow and red watermelon, green grapes, pecans, feta cheese, mint and balsamic glaze on a bed of fresh greens to split along with glasses of iced tea.

The conversation turned to the upcoming reader adventurers' field trips and a recent meeting, where Janet had continued to rain negativity on Chelsea's reader adventurers' parade. "I have a brother who works in tech in the Silicon Valley, at one of those places that considers their workplace a living laboratory," Lily said. "They're always looking for new ways to keep team members happy. Did you know that diner booths create better work interaction than conference rooms?"

"No." Chelsea glanced over at the glass case of the new Cops and Coffee booth that had appeared last week and wondered how many steps she'd have to do to come close to working that glazed, lemon-filled doughnut off. "But if it's true, perhaps I should try moving our meetings to the diner. Maybe Janet would react better to new ideas."

"Nothing's ever going to get that stick out of her butt. She probably came out of the womb bitching about the light. You'd have a better chance of holding them at the pub. We could order a pitcher of pomegranate margaritas and get her sloshed." Lily considered that as she took another drink of tea. "Though, I'd bet she'd be a mean drunk."

"You're probably right." Chelsea sighed. As much as she needed all the volunteer help she could get, Janet's insistence on arguing every little point took up valuable time they didn't have. "Too bad there probably aren't enough oatmeal cinnamon balls on the planet to get her to bond with me." She and Lily shared a laugh, enjoying the sunshine, the folk singers who were playing on a nearby stage, and their friendship.

CHAPTER EIGHT

THE DAY AFTER her market lunch with Lily, Chelsea had just wrapped up this week's library purchase order with a nonfiction book featuring the nine Native American tribes of the Olympic Peninsula. Along with offering insight into the unique legacy of the groups, whose stories too often went unnoticed or forgotten, the essays, written by members of the different tribes in their own voices, moved beyond the popular romanticized views of American Indians and portrayed real-life experiences.

Lily, on her way out the door, stopped at the desk. "I forgot to ask, how did things go with the Viking boat builder?"

"They didn't." Chelsea rubbed her forehead where a headache had been building all day. "He turned me down. Flat."

"That's too bad. I was having coffee with Kylee the other day. She's going to be taking photos at the scholarship dinner in September, and pointed him out to me as he was leaving with his coffee and a bag of doughnuts. I was going to volunteer for that adventure, just to have an excuse to meet him."

"I suspect you'd be underwhelmed. Brianna warned me not to expect Mr. Rogers, but he's more like Heathcliff."

"That bad?"

"No." Chelsea wanted to be fair. Although she was in the camp of those who'd never considered Brontë's character a proper romantic hero, Gabriel Mannion, while gruff, hadn't shown any signs of being a cruel, sadistic sociopath. "He was nowhere near that. But I could tell that he spells *Trouble*. With a capital *T*."

"Trouble can be appealing in a guy. Not long-term, but as a change of pace from the possible husband material. I'd do him."

"Lily!" Chelsea glanced around, looking to see if there were any patrons still hanging around to overhear her.

"Just saying. Not only is he hot, he's a gazillionaire who made *New York Magazine*'s list of hottest eligible guys in the city."

"You're well-read," Chelsea observed.

"I lived in Manhattan for a year while trying out the ad business as an intern at a Madison Avenue agency. Perhaps it was too much of a sudden contrast in lifestyle, coming straight from the University of Hawaii, but I decided that while the city was a great place to visit, it wasn't for me.

"I did keep up my subscription to the magazine because it's a great mix of politics, culture, food, fashion and gossip. Along with the occasional high-profile society crime, which gives me the same kind of guilty pleasure I get from watching *Dateline*."

"I love the investigative part of that program."

"Me, too, and figuring out the killer from all the suspects, like a real-life *Law and Order*. But then I feel bad that I'm using someone's death as entertainment."

"I'm right with you there. But *Dateline*'s so addictive I have my DVR programmed to record it."

"We should start having watch parties. Its tagline is 'don't watch alone.'"

"I like that idea." Chelsea also liked Lily, who'd become one of her closer girlfriends. "You can bring the ice cream and I'll make the chocolate martinis."

For someone whose family tree, on her mother's side,

included the engineer/entrepreneur who built the Pennsylvania Rail Road and made it, during its heyday, the largest company in the world, and a model for technological and managerial innovation (and yes, Chelsea had researched it), Lily Carpenter was as down-to-earth as anyone in Honeymoon Harbor. Even more so than some, whose roots went back to early founders and felt that gave them some sort of privilege. Such as not paying their library fines. Nor, until Aiden Mannion had become police chief and stopped the practice of police courtesy cards, their parking and speeding tickets.

"Though," Lily said, as she put the strap of her lambskin bag with its iconic double interlocked *C*s over her shoulder, "it does say something about the men in this town that two smart, beautiful, successful women have nothing else to do on a summer night than to sit in front of a TV, eat ice cream and drink alcohol."

"It could also say we're choosy."

"It could. Though it's not as if Honeymoon Harbor isn't populated with hunks. The Mannions are all gorgeous, then there's Seth Harper—"

"Who's taken."

"True. And it's impossible not to like Brianna, so I can't even be jealous. Desiree snatched up that hottie Cajun sax player and chef Bastien Broussard the first day he hit town, but apparently they have a long backstory, so none of us would've had a chance. Still, Quinn's not taken. Nor is Luca Salvadori who could feed a woman well, which is a decided plus. So could Diego Chavez. Is it true he's turning in his taco truck for a restaurant?"

"I was at a town council meeting when he said that even after he gets his restaurant open, he's keeping his Taco the Town to take to various festivals around the peninsula."

"That's a smart business plan… Oh! And let's not forget warmhearted animal rescuer Cam Montgomery and megafit fire captain Flynn Farraday who, having been trained to carry people down ladders, could undoubtedly carry a woman upstairs to bed."

"Over his shoulder. Which isn't exactly Rhett carrying Scarlett up the curving stairs of Tara."

"I'll bet there are a lot of women in town who wouldn't mind if he carried them piggyback, as long as they ended up in the bedroom… Which brings us back to Gabriel middle-name-Trouble Mannion. Since you appear to be the only woman besides his sister who's actually spoken with him since he arrived in town, that gives you an inside track. Maybe you should go back and try again. For the sake of the library, of course."

"Of course. But he's only here for the summer."

"So?" Lily shrugged. "There's something to be said for a summer fling. That's why so many books and songs are written and movies made about them."

"Believe me, he wasn't the least bit interested. In fact, the few minutes I was in the boat shop, he barely tolerated me."

"Then he's a fool," Lily said. "Gotta go. I'm leading the after-dinner singalong at Harbor Hill. Then the readers' group gets another chapter of *The Sorcerer's Stone* read aloud."

"That's an ambitious project for such an elderly age group."

"That's why I chose it. I figure waiting to find out what happens next gives them something new to live for." She waggled her fingers and left the library.

Before turning off the lights, Chelsea retrieved the white bag of treats, paper plates and napkins she'd brought with her that morning from the lunch room. Then went to the children's section, where she found Hannah helping Hailey read.

"Hi, Ms. Prescott," Hailey said. "I'm reading *Dragon Rider*! It's a story about dragons. Bad people are going to flood the silver dragon's special valley, so a brave dragon named Firedrake and Sorrel—she's a girl, like me, but a forest brownie—go on a quest to find a mi-mi-mi—"

"Mythical," Hannah murmured. "That's a magical place called the Rim of Heaven, where the dragons could be safe and live in peace. They meet an orphan boy, Ben, who goes along to help them."

Hailey's cupid lips turned down. "He's like me, too, because he doesn't have any parents. But he's a boy." Despite Hannah's obvious efforts to continue the deception, Hailey had let their foster situation slip last week.

"Tell her about Nettlebrand," Hannah suggested, in an obvious attempt to change the conversation from the fictional boy's orphan status. From *their* orphan status.

"Oh, Nettlebrand is really bad! He's called the Golden One and isn't really a dragon. He has metal scales and was made to kill the last of the dragons."

Her small brow furrowed. "I hope Firedrake and Sorrel find the Rim of Heaven before he finds them."

"I guess you'll just have to keep reading to see." It did not escape Chelsea that the story was about finding a safe home. She was going to have to be more careful about what themes the five-year-old read.

"I am! And I'm almost reading it all by myself, aren't I, Hannah?"

"Yes, you are." The older girl looked at the bag, then up at Chelsea.

"You keep bringing us stuff to eat." She jutted out her slender jaw. "We're not two poor, starving orphans, like from some Hans Christian Anderson fairy tale. We don't need charity."

"I'd never suggest that," Chelsea said mildly. But they did, she believed, need love. And nurturing. "When I was your age, I spent a lot of hours here in the library after school and Mrs. Henderson—she was the librarian before me, while I was growing up—would bring me treats from home. She likes to bake." Something the former librarian still did for the funeral lunch committee at St. Peter's.

"Hannah taught me to make S'mores," Hailey volunteered. "We couldn't make a fire in the backyard, because it would be dangerous, but she knows how to make them in the microwave. They're really good. And gooey."

"I remember doing that with my sister," Chelsea said. When she'd returned home from camp, Annabelle had wanted to hear everything she'd done. Which hadn't been all that much, given her lack of participation, but she had shared stories about the things she'd watched others doing, making it sound as if she'd taken part because it was more than a little obvious that her terminally ill little sister was living vicariously through her at that point.

And since Chelsea couldn't build a campfire in their backyard, she'd made microwave S'mores from a recipe she'd found in a cookbook at this very same library.

"You have a sister?" Hailey's eyes brightened up with interest.

"I had." Damn. Chelsea wished she hadn't brought the topic up.

"Did she go away? I have a friend whose sister went to college."

"No, she died." How did they get into this mine-strewn conversation?

"Oh." Hailey bit her bottom lip as she considered that. "Did she die in an accident?"

"She was sick." For a very long time. But she had managed to get down one of the graham cracker treats and declared it the best thing she'd ever eaten in her life. It also turned out to be the last solid thing she ate, because the next morning she was put on a liquid diet. Before ending up on a feeding tube, which, even with all the drugs the doctors had been throwing at her, still hadn't been enough to keep her from wasting away.

"That's sad." Hailey's teeth continued to worry her bottom lip. "Our mommy and daddy died in a car accident."

"That's very sad, too."

"It was." Her small chest beneath a Big Bird T-shirt expanded as she drew in a deep breath, then blew it out on a long sigh. "We were there, too, but I don't remember it. Hannah rescued us. And then we lived a lot of other places, but now we live here. Not at the library. That would be silly. But in this town, which I like. It's fun watching the ferries come in with the seagulls diving into the water and pulling out fish. We never had anything like that anywhere else we stayed."

Hannah's expression revealed nothing. She stood as still as a stone while her young face could have been carved from ivory.

"But it really doesn't matter where we are, because we'll always be together." Hailey looked up at her silent sister. "Right, Hannah?"

"Right, sprout." The older girl's eyes softened as she looked down into her sister's face, so eager for confirmation of that promise. Then hardened as they turned to Chelsea. "Always."

One of these days, after they'd spent more time together, gotten to know each other well enough that Hannah might begin to trust her, Chelsea was going to steal

her away for a private conversation. Even remembering
Lily's warning at the market, there had to be more she
could do to help than baking and ordering every child's
book on dragons she could find in the catalog.

"Well, I'm not Mrs. Henderson, and I didn't bake these
cinnamon apple bites because they don't even need baking, which is good because cooking has never been one
of my talents. But they're still, in my humble opinion,
just like having yummy apple pie without the crust. Why
don't we go over and sit in the lounge where the coffee
cart is, and you can have some milk with them?"

"Gotta build those bones," Hannah muttered, her tone
dripping with sarcasm.

She was a hard nut to crack, but Chelsea refused to
stop trying. She knew how it felt to lose a family. Her
loss might not have come in one fatal, horrific moment.
Instead, it had taken years of pain before that final blow.

She'd mostly moved passed the survivor guilt of not
being able to somehow save her sister's life and feeling
that somehow, someway, there must have been something
she could've done to keep her broken family together.

If she'd only been quieter. If she'd only known what to
say when she'd feel the explosive energy building up in the
house, the way she'd read that the sky in tornado country
would turn an eerie shade of yellow and you could feel
electricity sparking in the air before the tornado hit and
blew everything away.

If she'd only been able to stop her father from being
so angry. Or her mother so…well…empty. If she only
could've been enough to keep her mother from hurting
so badly, needing to be with Annabelle. If only Harry
Potter and his merry band at Hogwarts had been around
back then to perhaps give her a reason to live one more
day. Then another. And another. Until her mother was

an old lady playing cribbage with Mrs. Henderson and others at the senior center that had been established in St. Peter's annex.

Realizing that Hannah was watching her, studying her, Chelsea shook off the threatening cloud. "You're certainly right about that," she said, in her cheeriest voice.

It was the same voice that she'd used to make plans with Annabelle of all the things they were going to do once she got better. The voice that tried so desperately to bring sunshine into a house where, even in this land of long dark winters, the windows were always covered with closed blinds and heavy draperies.

The voice that, due to nerves, had gotten out of control at the boat shop and probably left Gabe Mannion thinking she was one plank short of a faering.

"We need all the vitamin D we can get, living up here in this rainy part of the country." Which had her wondering if the children were given vitamins. Like nearly everyone else she knew, she dutifully took her tablet of artificial sunshine every day.

The cinnamon bites were as good as the recipe had promised, which she already knew because she'd sampled three of them when she'd made them last night. Merely for product testing. Just because a recipe was on a healthy after-school snack board on Pinterest that promised it was good didn't mean it was. She didn't want to give the girls something that wouldn't taste like love.

After the snacks and more discussion about dragons, she drove them home. Hannah had finally stopped protesting being driven, because, Chelsea suspected, it gave Hailey more opportunity to chatter. To connect with someone besides her sister. Someone who cared.

As she watched the older girl unlock the door and let them both into the house, Chelsea wondered, yet again, how much time their foster mother spent at home. One of these days, she decided, she'd make up an excuse to drop in later in the evening. Just to check.

CHELSEA HAD NEARLY reached her apartment when her phone rang. At the caller ID announcement from the car's speaker, she pushed the icon on the steering wheel. "Hi, Dad."

It wasn't that often her father called her. For a long time after he'd left his family and Honeymoon Harbor for an anesthesiologist's position at Cedars-Sinai Medical Center, it was as if he'd forgotten she'd ever existed. As if she'd died. Like Annabelle had. After a few years, she began receiving postcards, showing palm trees and beaches, yet more proof that he'd left the Pacific Northwest behind in his rearview mirror as he'd driven away from their waterfront home.

It was only later, after he'd remarried—and yes, she had been invited to the wedding, and although it was a little weird, she'd gone—that communication had increased. Not so much in person, but calls on the big holidays, like Thanksgiving and Christmas, and her birthday. Along with cards, actual paper letters with seasonal headers, made up with some sort of publishing software showing photos of the half brothers she'd seen only a handful of times, growing up from infancy to kindergarten graduation. Every card, every letter, had included an invitation to visit anytime.

"Hello, Chelsea."

Although she might not be all that close to his second family, her first thought was concern that someone had been hurt. Or worse. Bad things could happen to anyone. Any day. Without warning. "What's wrong?"

"Why does anything have to be wrong?"

"Well, it's not every day that I get a call from you."

"It's not every day my only daughter has a birthday."

If she hadn't been driving, and didn't want to avoid crashing into cars coming off the ferry, Chelsea would have closed her eyes, taken a few deep breaths and pictured herself lying on a tropical beach while a hot surfer smoothed coconut oil onto her bare back. The meditation technique was one Jolene Wells had learned while working on a movie set in LA and had become a popular start to treatments at her mother's day spa.

"My birthday was last month, Dad. You sent a card. And a box of chocolate truffles." Which she'd taken to the library committee meeting the following day. This call was also yet more proof of what she'd already known. That her stepmother (and wasn't that a strange word for a woman only a few years older than she was?) had sent them.

There was a long pause. "You're right. Of course I did." The laugh was as fake as it was forced. "One of the downsides of getting older is your memory starts to go."

"So I hear," she said mildly. "So, how is Heather? And the kids?"

"The boys are going into first grade in the fall. Can you believe it? It seems like just yesterday they were born."

"Well, you know what they say about time flying."

"True. Look at you, all grown up. Before I know it, you'll be making me a grandfather."

He did not sound exactly thrilled by that prospect, and no wonder that he'd chosen to begin his new life in La La Land, where Chelsea wasn't certain people were even allowed to age.

"I wouldn't hold your breath."

"You're not a lesbian, are you?" he asked. "Not that there's anything wrong with that."

Chelsea laughed, thinking about the wedding she'd taken part in last summer. "No, Dad. I'm just not in the market for motherhood at the moment."

Watching Kylee and Mai with their adopted daughter, she'd seen how much work children could be. You'd think that things would get easier once babies were past the infancy stage, but now that Clara had started walking, nothing in their darling Folk cottage house was safe unless it was locked away or put up high. Though it was, she admitted, fun to watch the speed with which the little girl could run on her tiptoes.

"Heather had a thought she wanted to bring up," he said. "You know we go to Maui every Christmas."

"Yes. I've seen the family photos on the New Year's letter." At first they'd caused a twinge in her heart, but over time, she'd come to realize that they were a sincere effort on her stepmother's part to reach out and invite her into the family. Especially since she was all alone.

No. Not alone. She had friends like Lily who were as close as family. Certainly closer than her father.

"Well, the beach house has three guest rooms and the boys would love to see their big sister. Why don't you give some thought to flying down? I'll pay for the tickets. First class, of course."

"Of course," she murmured. "Tell Heather I appreciate the offer and will think about it."

"Okay. But don't take too long," he warned. "You know how fast flights fill up for the holidays."

"I said I'll think about it." She blew out another breath. "Thanks for calling, Dad. It's always great talking with you. Sorry, but I have to run. I have a meeting." She hit the phone icon, cutting off the call.

Because the stupid tears in her eyes were blurring her vision, she pulled over into the pier parking lot and cut the engine. She'd survived her father walking away. Being young, for a time, although she'd missed him terribly, a stronger part of her was grateful for the quiet that had replaced the yelling, accusations and the slamming of doors. It was only later that she'd realized that silence could be even more difficult, more deadly than domestic war.

The boys would love to see their big sister. Chelsea bit her lip. She liked her stepbrothers. They were smart, funny, rambunctious and had her thinking of golden retriever puppies. She didn't love them. But that wasn't their fault. Or even her dad's or Heather's. It was because she couldn't fully open her scarred heart up again.

After losing her mother while she was in college, she'd gone to a therapist who had, after a few months, convinced her that she had no reason to feel guilty about Annabelle's death. Though Chelsea knew that intellectually, there was still a part of her, a deep-down, instinctive part, perhaps woven into the DNA going back to the beginning of time, that the role of a big sister was to be a stand-in mother. To take care of the younger ones. If that was the case, she and Hannah had definitely inherited that same sister gene.

Usually she was able to brush off her father's benign neglect. To accept it as perhaps having always been his nature, or perhaps, she'd considered during therapy, a way to protect his wounded heart that same way she'd protected hers. No risk. No pain. Whatever, it was what it was. He was who he was.

But that didn't stop her from not wanting to be alone right now. She went through her list of friends… Brianna had a wedding party who'd booked a night's dinner at Herons Landing. Bastien, owner/chef of Sensation Cajun, was catering the meal and Desiree the dessert course, but Brianna was still playing hostess.

Lily was reading *Harry Potter* to the residents of Harbor Hill. And Mai and Kylee had taken Clara to the coast to walk barefoot on the sand for the first time.

She could go to the pub, where she'd undoubtedly find someone to hang out with, but she also wasn't up to all the energy it would take to pretend that things were just hunky-dory. Especially with Quinn being so perceptive.

There was *one* person who could take her mind off herself and get her back on focus.

Of course, she risked being turned away again, but if she could convince Gabriel Mannion that she could keep the reading adventurers from damaging his boat—faering—it was worth another try. Not just for the kids, but, if she were to be perfectly honest, it would give her a distraction from feeling sorry for herself.

"What do you have to lose?" Decision made, she started the car, and headed out of town.

CHAPTER NINE

As SHE DROVE along Lakeshore Drive, Chelsea passed Aiden Mannion heading back toward town. Despite his friendly wave, goose bumps prickled on her skin and her heart hitched. All these years later the sight of the Honeymoon Harbor police shield on the door could cause anxiety. It was as if a slow-burning fuse had been lit at Annabelle's diagnosis. One that had created more and more stress the longer it had burned.

A neighbor had called the police about family disturbances when the fights, while never physically violent, would escalate, and one terrible day, Chelsea's mother had received a DUI after taking Xanax with a glass of wine. The only good thing about her father leaving was that the house had gotten quieter, with the TV providing background ambient noise nearly twenty-four hours a day. After a while, it had gotten so Chelsea hadn't even noticed it. Then, finally, the police had been there on what they'd called a "death investigation."

Blowing out a breath, she continued driving down the road lined with shaggy, towering Douglas fir that cast stripes across the pavement, every so often catching glimpses of the unbelievable blue of the lake. The wildflowers were in raucous bloom and pink, white and blue phlox painted the landscape with sweeping swaths of color, replacing the fading avalanche and glacier lilies. Chelsea rolled down her window, drinking in the perfume, which topped anything that came in the priciest of bottles.

Shortly after turning where her GPS instructed, she found herself facing a tall wrought iron gate with a stone pillar on either side. On the left pillar was a security keypad. She could call Brianna to get his number so she could then phone Gabriel and ask him to unlock the gate. But he might not be willing to do that, which was why her plan, as sketchy as it admittedly might be, was to catch him off guard. She'd already marshalled her argument. Now she just needed an opportunity to present it.

Having run into a literal stone wall, she thoughtfully tapped her fingers on the top of the steering wheel, regretting that she hadn't taken the time to create a plan B. She *always* had a plan B. And C. And, if all else failed, a D. Because life had a way of spiraling out of control, and it was best to always be prepared.

As she saw a security camera on the top of one of the pillars, she realized that Gabriel might know she was parked out here, which would give him time to make up a new argument, because she hadn't believed that insurance one at all. She remembered having lunch one day with Seth and Brianna when they'd taken her for a Sunday sail on his boat. The conversation had come around to Gabe having built the boat. Which then led to more discussion about him having hung around the shop starting back when he'd been in elementary school.

Perhaps the insurance rules had changed. But she'd bet her collection of vintage Nancy Drew books that he'd been lying just to get rid of her.

It was then an idea struck. A sneaky idea. A sneaky, wonderful idea.

After managing to turn around without sliding into the slight ditch on either side of the pavement or backing into a tree, she headed back down the road, around the shoreline, to the other side of the lake.

The bait shack had been there longer than Chelsea had been alive. She'd heard that in the 1950s, there'd been a take-out window, offering sandwiches and sodas to boaters and fishermen. Now, although a café had replaced the take-out window, an old-fashioned red Coke cooler at the door of the boat rental office went back to those early days.

"Well, if it isn't Chelsea Prescott," the elderly man wearing a brown ball cap with fishing flies stuck on the band came out of the office to greet her. "Don't tell me you're out here to collect my library fine."

"Do you owe a library fine?" she asked Bert Carter, who preferred "manly" books by Hemingway and Zane Grey. And the occasional mystery thriller, as long as it didn't have any of those "dirty parts."

"I might have been a bit slow getting through *The Hunt for Red October*," he admitted, stroking his white beard which, if he hadn't been skinny as a beanpole, would've made him a perfect Santa for the annual Christmas tree lighting.

"I imagine you're busier in summer," she said.

"Sure am. Not many willing to go out on the lake in the winter. While winter steelhead's real popular, people like fishing from the bank. I do keep a couple trailers for anyone who wants to take a boat out to one of the rivers for the run, but it's nothing like summer."

"Well, since no one's put a hold on that Clancy book, and you have the extenuating circumstances of your work allowing less free time to read this time of the year, we'll keep that fine between us."

He lifted his hand to the brim of his hat. "I do thank you. Lillian might not have been so accommodating."

"Oh, I'm sure she'd understand your circumstances."

"She might. But she may also still be mad at me for standing her up for the Winterfest dance."

"I hadn't heard anything about that." The Facebook page only went back five years.

"Mebee because it was forty years ago, before she met Ralph. Unfortunately, that woman has a memory like a damn steel trap." He blew out a frustrated breath. "Bygones," he said on what sounded like a long sigh of regret. Which had her wondering. And remembering that he always seemed to show up on Wednesdays, the day Mrs. Henderson usually arrived at the library after her Zumba class at the senior center. "What can I do you for?"

"I need a boat."

"No problem. Kayak, canoe, sail or rowboat?"

"I'll take the rowboat." The kayak and canoe sounded too tippy, and no way was she going to attempt a sailboat. Having watched girls row on this very same lake that summer of her miserable camp year, rowing hadn't looked all that difficult. They'd also seemed to be having fun. Which was why she'd refused to try it. Looking back now, she wished, not for the first time, that she could have written a letter to her younger self, advising her to enjoy happiness whenever she found it because life didn't come with gold-plated guarantees.

"You got it," he said agreeably. "How long do you expect to be out?"

"However long it takes to get across the lake and back." Surely it wouldn't take that long to persuade Gabriel Manning to see the light.

White brows, as furry as caterpillars, disappeared beneath the brim of his hat. "All that way?"

"That's my plan."

"Have you ever rowed before?"

"I'm very familiar with the process," she hedged. "From camp days."

He looked doubtful. But determined not to let anything or anyone deter her from her mission, ten minutes later, wearing a bright yellow life vest, she climbed into the boat, which was more tippy than she'd expected. It had looked so solid. So safe. That thought almost had her laughing since this was additional proof that nothing was safe about Gabriel Mannion.

"It's just like on a rowing machine. You've probably done one of those, right?"

"Of course." At least she'd watched people use them while she'd been riding the stationary bike at the fitness club.

"Great. Sit on the bench seat," Bert instructed. "With your back toward your destination."

"I sit backward?" If she'd known that she'd be doing this, she'd have watched several YouTube videos in order to be well prepared. She was also glad that she'd worn a loose-fitting peasant blouse with a pair of khaki capris and Keds today—which she doubted Mrs. Henderson would have ever worn to work.

"Yeah, because rowing's nothing like paddling," Bert said. "The action of rowing propels you backward, so you need to sit with your back to the bow and face the stern." This time his expressive brows beetled. "I thought you said you know about rowboats."

"I do. The bow is the front and the stern is the rear." Seth had explained the terms the day they'd gone sailing. Which, it was beginning to appear, had little to do with rowing.

"Got it in one." Although he seemed pleased she knew that much, his forehead, weathered by age and years on the water, furrowed, revealing his continued skepticism. "You sure you want to do this?"

"Absolutely," she said, sitting in the center of the wooden bench, placing her feet in the stretchers as instructed.

"Grasp an oar in each hand with an overhand grip," he said.

Again, she followed instructions, listening carefully as he explained the motions of catch, drive, release, recover. Rinse and repeat.

"Got it," she assured him. Piece of cake.

Unfortunately, rowing proved a great deal more difficult than it looked, making her wonder why this type of boat didn't have the same cachet as sailboats. It wasn't as if just anyone could row a boat. She was an intelligent woman with two college degrees, and yet, after Bert had pushed her away from the wooden dock, she found herself going around and around in circles. At this rate it was going to take her until Labor Day to reach the other side of the lake.

"You're only using one oar," Bert shouted through cupped hands. "Keep them both level, turn them to the side, then pull them through the water together."

It took a few more tries, but eventually, Chelsea was on her way. She was soon immensely grateful that the other boaters appeared to realize that she was a novice, because they all took a wide berth as they neared her. Three guys in a powerboat who'd been waterskiing did drift over close enough to ask her if she wanted a tow to wherever she was headed, but even as her hands and calves burned and her back began to ache, she assured them that she was fine.

If she was going to win Gabriel Mannion over, she needed to bring her A game and appear confident and strong. Arriving towed by a boat of cute, puppy dog–friendly college boys wearing board shorts and cutoff frat T-shirts was not part of plan B.

Although she'd put the cabin's address into her phone's GPS app and, every time she checked it, was assured she was headed in the right direction, whenever she looked back over her shoulder, the beach didn't seem to be getting any closer.

Just when she was determined she'd be stuck on this damn lake forever, she came around a slight bend and her breath caught at what had to be the largest, most spectacular log cabin she'd ever seen overlooking the lake from a bluff. Without her GPS, she might never have come across it. There, standing on the deck below the house that three of her apartments could probably fit into, was Gabriel Mannion.

Feeling self-conscious, she was rethinking her decision, but, no, she'd come too far to back out now. There was also the little fact that even if she could turn the boat around, she wasn't certain that she could make it back to Bert's.

"I hate to ask this," she said, as she came closer. "But how do I stop?" The last thing she needed to do was to crash into the dock.

"Feather your oar."

"Like that's a help," she muttered.

"Set it so it's not perpendicular, but not quite parallel to the water, then dig your blade into the water and straighten your arms."

She did as instructed, managing to stop the boat an instant before she rammed the dock. "It worked!"

"It always does."

"Well. Hi." She smiled brightly, as if her rowing all the way across Mirror Lake to his hermitage was nothing out of the ordinary. As if butterflies weren't fluttering their wings in her stomach.

"Hi." He leaned forward and caught hold of the side of the rowboat. "Toss me your lines."

It didn't take a sailor to know those were the ropes coiled at her feet. She watched, impressed, as he tied a line from the bow and stern, and a third from whatever the official term for the middle of a rowboat might be.

"I'm impressed."

"When you spend as much time on the water as I did growing up, things stick with you."

"I imagine so. Like riding the proverbial bicycle." She took his outstretched hand and accepted help getting out of the boat. Even tied to the wooden dock as it was, it still felt a bit too unstable for comfort. "Thanks. I guess you saw me coming up the driveway."

"There's an alarm system that sounds whenever anyone comes up to the gate. I didn't set it up, but since the panel that controls it and most of the rest of the house looks set up to launch satellites into space, I've been afraid to touch it."

"I don't blame you." She liked that he so easily admitted that there was something he didn't know. She also liked his smile, perhaps because, from what she'd seen thus far, it might be as rare as a full eclipse. "I had some friends who went to Hawaii over Christmas." Which had her thinking back on her earlier conversation with her father, which in turn caused her spirits to dip.

"They set the heat to turn off while they were gone. Although the husband thought he'd turned the utilities back on with his phone when they were at the airport on the way home, what he hadn't realized was that a winter storm had knocked out the power, which screwed up the clocks, which, in turn, froze the system the entire time they were gone. They got home from Sea-Tac at two in the morning to a dark, freezing house."

"This place has a built-in generator that turns on if the power goes off for fifteen seconds."

"That would be so handy here." After a storm outage last year, she'd worked two days in a puffy down coat, a knit cap, long underwear beneath her sweatshirt and flannel-lined jeans, and wool fingerless gloves.

"Yeah. Though I don't expect to need it in the summer. The breeze from the mountains and lake provide natural air-conditioning, and if anything did go wrong with the power, the well has its own backup system."

"According to the Facebook page, it's owned by some big tech mogul no one has ever met."

"It is. He's an old fraternity brother. He's thinking of selling it because he never gets over here from Seattle."

"That's a shame. Because it's beautiful." She glanced around at the logs that looked as if they'd been rubbed to a gleaming gold. "A lot of people in town have wondered about it," she admitted. Herself included. "Seth knows it well, because although Harper Construction usually only does remodels, he and his dad spent nearly two years doing finish work. But other than the contractor, subs, decorator and Megan and her Clean Team crew, I don't think anyone else has ever actually seen it."

"Why don't you come in and look around?"

"I don't want to intrude. I just wanted an opportunity to talk with you. Again." She did her best to sound casual. As if driving twenty miles out of her way down a long and winding gravel road, then rowing across a lake to get here was no big deal.

"Well, since you've come all this way, the least I can do is give you the tour."

"I'd love that, thank you."

"How about dinner?" he asked as they walked up the dock toward the stone steps leading to the house.

"Dinner?"

"A noun. Usually used to describe the third meal of the day, unless you live in the South, then it could just as likely be referred to as supper."

"I know what it is. I was just surprised that…are you inviting me to dinner?"

"For some reason my mother seems to believe that despite me going into town every day, I'll starve out here. She's been sending Aiden out with groceries and cooked meals. Today's package included some Alaskan king salmon fresh off one of Seth Harper's cousin's boats. How does cedar plank smoked salmon with rosemary roasted potatoes and grilled asparagus sound?"

"Heavenly." As they reached the expansive three-tiered deck, she paused to look up into eyes that weren't as stormy as they'd appeared in the boat shop. Tonight they were a lighter bluish gray that contrasted with his black hair. It was funny how the Mannion men, father and sons, possessed the same features, but they'd all come together in individual ways. Although they were all stunningly good-looking, none of the others affected her the way this man did. "So, you're cooking?"

"I am. And don't worry." He pushed open a glass wall that somehow disappeared into the walls and literally brought the outside in, just like she'd seen on a *House Hunters* episode. "Mom taught all her sons to cook. She thought it was important for men to know how to feed themselves."

"I'm impressed," she said. "Especially by the asparagus."

"She threw it into the box because, being like most

of her feminine persuasion, she believes in eating green things."

"Asparagus is a superfood. It's filled with lots of vitamins, antioxidants and fiber. And that's just the short label."

"Why am I not surprised you'd know that? As for the potatoes, I was already intending to oil them and throw them on the grill."

"I enjoy cooking, but I learned mostly from following recipes in cookbooks from the library and watching cooking shows on TV." She didn't mention that she'd resorted to learning how to feed herself, and her mother, after dinners had degraded to bowls of cereal every night or, on a good night, sandwiches. "I'm honestly surprised by the invitation."

"That makes two of us," he said.

CHAPTER TEN

"I OWE YOU an apology for being rude the other day."

She shrugged. "I was prewarned. Brianna said you might not be thrilled to see me," she admitted.

"Did she?" Gabe once again considered how open she was. How she seemed to share every thought.

"The words *noncommunicative* and *loner* may have been used."

"Yet you still asked me to take part in your reading adventures. And even after I turned you down at the shop, you rowed across the lake to try again." When he'd seen her coming, he'd felt anticipation curling in his gut. Now, as the lake breeze caught the edge of her blouse, lifting it to reveal a band of smooth skin, that anticipation shot south.

"The worst that could happen is that you'd turn me down. Again. Then I'd row back, and we'd simply concentrate on studying Vikings, and perhaps put on a play. Without any horned helmets."

She had a quick, agile mind, was obviously goal oriented, and apparently relentless since that two-mile trip here wouldn't be an easy one for someone who obviously had never rowed a boat before. Change out her personality, exorcise what appeared to be a warm and generous heart, and she'd make a dynamite trader.

"No one's going to touch the faering," he warned, even as he felt himself caving in.

"Of course not," she agreed. "I'd never forgive myself if something happened to it. Perhaps you could share a short explanation with the children about why you chose to make that type of boat instead of, say, a Spanish galleon."

"A galleon wouldn't fit in the shop."

She laughed, despite it being a lousy joke, but hey, any joke was as uncharacteristic of him as taking even a day, let alone three months, away from The Street. "Scandinavian boat builders still make faerings," he said. "They're popular for fishing and recreation. The lapstrake double-ender is indigenous to the region and the design hasn't changed much in a thousand years." Which suggested to Gabe that when you got something right, there was no use messing with it.

"Now, see, that's even cooler. That it's continued all those centuries."

"There's an elemental simplicity, without the use of a single extraneous piece of wood." He found himself sharing what had him deciding to take Jarle up on his challenge. "There's never been a shape better suited to the sea, oars and wind. Those ancient builders figured out how to fasten together a couple of wide planks in a way that combines a fine underbody with plenty of reserve stability topside."

"Yet more proof of how clever the Vikings were. Farrah, she's the other librarian, would love learning about this." Gabe figured that the woman could probably coax a smile from the tall painted wooden totem a long-ago town council had commissioned from a Quileute woodcrafter in honor of Honeymoon Harbor's centennial. "I probably shouldn't have sprung the idea on you the other day," she said. "But am I making you at all interested?"

Yeah. Gabe was getting more interested by the minute, even as he reminded himself that the librarian with the delicate hands and the bright blue sneakers printed with cheery daisies wasn't his type and the reason for this forced vacation was to have some peace and quiet and to be left alone. No way had he wanted a bunch of kids invading his shop.

"I suppose I could give the project an hour," he heard himself saying against his better judgment. He was leaving right after Labor Day and this was not the kind of woman you had a summer affair with. Chelsea Prescott had white picket fence stamped all over her.

"Oh, thank you!" Her hands crossed over her heart. Which momentarily drew his attention to pert breasts beneath the gauzy blouse that reminded him of photographs of hippies and flower children at Woodstock. She looked as if at any moment she'd begin dancing to Creedence Clearwater Revival's "I Put a Spell on You." He returned his gaze to her eyes, which were practically sparkling with pleasure. Once again his guy brain went to wondering what they'd look like during sex.

"Your family has been wonderful about the readers' experience. I don't know if they've told you, but your parents have invited us to their Christmas tree farm, Brianna and Seth are giving a tour of Herons Landing, your uncle Mike is giving art lessons and even Quinn agreed to give the older kids a tour of the microbrewery." Dimples flashed like the beam of the Honeymoon Harbor lighthouse that warned sailors of breaching onto the rocky shore. Although this was a very different kind of warning, Gabe told himself he'd be wise to heed it.

"He's always liked kids." Which is why, now that he thought about it, Gabe wondered why his older brother had never married. "You're not planning to have Aiden give the kids a tour of the jail?"

"As fine a police chief as he is, I'm not sure… Oh. That was another joke, wasn't it? Now I feel really foolish."

"Don't. It was a lousy joke." Obviously he was as out of practice with telling jokes as he was with casual conversation.

"Still… I'm honestly not as naïve or as annoyingly chatty as I've seemed. I'm just…well, a little nervous."

"You're not annoying." On the contrary, she was temptingly appealing. "Do I make you nervous?"

"You do, a little," she said. "I don't want you to take this the wrong way—"

"Okay."

"I've never been into all that woo-woo stuff, though the jury's still out on ghosts, despite Brianna saying no one has ever heard or seen the ghost supposedly living in Herons Landing, but you have this vibe going on that's a little unsettling."

He surprised himself by laughing. A harsh, rough laugh that sounded rusty to his own ears and probably to hers, as well. "I've heard that before. Lately."

She shrugged. "Well, we all go through moods."

He seriously doubted the woman had ever had a lousy mood. Maybe she'd get a little cranky if a patron brought back a book with the page corners turned down or penned notes in the margin, but it was unlikely she'd ever experienced the kind of stress-related anxiety that had landed him in the ER.

Chelsea Prescott was the antithesis of every woman he'd been with since leaving Honeymoon Harbor for college. She was obviously intelligent, while openhearted, the type of naturally content individual who danced happily through life, a smiling sun shining down on her from a blue sky not a single cloud would dare darken. He could almost envision little cartoon birds flying around her glossy hair.

As an additional warning to keep his distance, Gabe

mentally added a stroller, a pink bike with sparkly streamers, a wooden swing hanging from an apple tree branch and a cocker spaniel to that damn Norman Rockwell painting in his mind. Along with a calligraphed sign out in front, like the ones printed on ancient maps, usually accompanied by a fanciful drawing of a sea serpent, reading *Here there be danger.*

"I think I'll save this visit for last, since it'll undoubtedly be the best part of the kids' summer," she enthused. "You've no idea how much I appreciate you doing this."

"No problem." Now it was his turn to feel uncomfortable. It wasn't as if he'd given her a kidney or anything.

Expressions of appreciation hadn't been part of Gabe's lexicon for a very long time. In New York, he had a job to do. Period. It was his responsibility to perform at the highest level, which, would, in turn, make him more money. Words of praise or gratitude were unexpected and as rare as unicorns in his world.

He was wondering what was wrong with the guys in town that no one had snatched Chelsea Prescott up when he realized his mind had been wandering and he'd missed a question.

"I'm sorry," he said. "What did you say?"

"I was just wondering if it's going to be hard for you to return to New York after being here."

"Not at all. I can't wait to get back to work. I miss the adrenaline rush of trading." That same rush that the doctor warned could kill him. Like it had Carter. But Gabe had no intention of living so far out on the edge.

"I don't think I'd ever be able to leave this house and I haven't even been inside yet. They say money doesn't buy you happiness, but living out here, with all this peace and quiet, would be a good start."

"Away from the hustle and bustle of Honeymoon Harbor," he said dryly.

She laughed at that. "Point taken. But it's still an amazing place. If I had a gazillion dollars, I'd put in an offer right now."

"Well, then," he said, "let's go in and you can see what you'd be buying."

"Good luck with that on a librarian's salary," she said with a laugh.

She was understandably impressed with the interior, oohed and aahed over the kitchen and the high-beamed ceiling, and all the views out to the lake. Especially the master bath that boasted a sleek white free-standing soaker tub. Since Gabe never used it, it still had the little wire tray with a book in a holder and a fragrant candle that had probably been there since the decorator had placed it there.

"Okay," she said. "Correction. I would absolutely never move from *here*."

"Why don't you look at one more room before you make a decision," he suggested, leading her back downstairs.

"Oh, wow!" She stood in the doorway of the library, gazing around in awe at the wood-paneled, book-lined walls, at the towering ceiling and the winding stairs leading up to the second-level catwalk where more books filled the shelves. "I visited the Biltmore Estate in North Carolina once because I'd heard wonderful things about the library," she said. "It has every book George Vanderbilt collected, all twenty-two thousand, many which are rare first editions. My plan, when I arrived in Ashville, was to briefly tour the estate and move on to Savannah to visit all the locations in John Berendt's *Midnight in the Garden of Good and Evil*, but I ended up spending my entire vacation in Ashville, just to read the spines on all those books."

"Now, why doesn't that surprise me?" Her eyes shone like a zealot looking into the face of her god.

"It's one of the greatest private collections in the world," she gushed. "And very eclectic. From English and American literature, architecture, world history, philosophy and religion. He also had two hundred and thirty copies of the French author Honoré de Balzac's works."

"You counted them all?"

"No. It was in the brochure. There were too many to examine them all in only five days. The collection isn't up to Karl Lagerfeld's three hundred thousand, or even George Lucas's twenty-seven thousand, but when you think about how fewer books were published over a century ago than now, twenty-two thousand is amazing. Not many people collect books anymore. They're more into art."

"Probably because art can be more profitable, if you choose the right pieces," he suggested. Carter had, of course, chosen solely for investment.

"Art is important," she said. "The world needs it, just as it needs music. But my heart will always belong to books. You're right. I'd never leave this room."

"Or," he suggested, "you could take a book outside on the deck on days the weather was good. Even when it was drizzling, since it's covered. Then you could have the best of both worlds."

She rewarded him with the same smile the woman in his dream had bestowed upon the Viking who'd brought home that gold bracelet. Gabriel knew, without a doubt, that this woman would prefer a book over jewelry any day. "I like the way you think."

She walked into the center of the room, and slowly

turned around, as if to drink in the entire atmosphere. Although like everything else in the house the library was overdone, he had to admit that it was pretty damn impressive. "I can't imagine owning all these books and not coming here to read them. It's not really that far from Seattle."

"I hate to burst your bubble, but the decorator bought them in packs."

"Packs?"

"Yeah, you know. Crates of them. My mom, who did not decorate this place and doesn't approve of the concept, told me that you can buy them by topic. Or cover— say, like those old leather-bound ones—to impress. Even by color."

"Why color?"

"To match the furnishings."

From the way her eyes widened with shock, he might as well have told her that he was planning to build a bonfire and toss every book in the library into the flames.

"Vanderbilt had all his books sent away to a famous bookbinder, who'd return them bound in Moroccan leather with gold lettering and decorations, but at least he was a voracious reader. I never would have imagined anyone ordering books by color." She walked over to one of the walls, and ran her fingers along a leather book. The colors the decorator had chosen were brown, a deep red and dark blue. "Ordering this way is unthinkable to me, but I guess there are so many that you'd be bound to get a few wonderful books, even if you hadn't intended to."

"Are you always this optimistic?" he asked, then wished he could take the words back. They made him sound cynical, which he admittedly was, but they also hit close to the same type of rudeness he'd impulsively invited her to dinner to make up for.

"There was a time when I wasn't," she said mildly. "But then one day I learned that happiness and optimism could be a choice. So I chose those. Instead of the alternative."

"You make it sound easy."

She gave him one of those long, deep looks that suggested she had more layers than she readily revealed. Had there been a time when the sun hadn't always shone for her?

"No," she said. "It's not at all." The smile was back, but didn't quite reach her eyes. "But nothing worth having should come easily, should it? Otherwise you wouldn't appreciate it as much when you achieve it." She turned away, to continue studying the books. "May I take this one out?" she asked.

He shrugged. "Anyone who buys books by the crate probably wouldn't care what you did with them, as long as they got put back to look good."

She opened the oxblood red book carefully, the way someone might touch an original parchment copy of the Constitution. "Oh, wow. Somehow a 1913 edition of Dickens's *David Copperfield* slipped into the mix." She turned the pages with that same near-religious reverence he'd witnessed when she'd first seen the room. "He's most famous for *The Christmas Carol*, which became iconic, but this was his most autobiographical book."

"Is that so?" He wasn't all that interested in the book, but he was definitely interested in the woman who *was* interested in it. Which made it a second-degree interest.

She nodded. "The headmaster's sadistic brutality and the grim, run-down atmosphere of Mr. Creakle's establishment were taken from his two dreadful years spent at Wellington House Academy. Dickens was very much alone in the world during his early years. And very poor, which gave birth to his affinity for the working class."

She carefully, as if holding a delicate piece of glass, put the book back on the shelf. As he watched her fingers run lingeringly down the book's worn spine, Gabe remembered waking up with the imagined touch of the Viking woman still warm on his chest.

"I wish the reading adventurers could see this," she murmured. "So many of them don't have the money for any books, which is why it's so important to keep the library well-funded, to make reading available to everyone. Some of the children probably don't even have the concept of a personal library, collected just for the love of the stories."

"You could bring them here," he heard himself saying, even as a voice in the back of his mind was screaming *What the hell are you doing?*

She blinked. Slowly. Seriously. Like that owl he'd heard again last night before falling to sleep. "You're suggesting I bring them here? To this house?"

"After the boat shop," he suggested. "If you can keep them from running wild all over the place."

Her spine stiffened as she lifted her chin. "The reading adventurers are very well behaved," she said. "Granted, they have a lot of energy because they're children, after all. But they certainly know library manners, which they will demonstrate at both your boat shop and here, if you're serious about the invitation."

"I am." He found himself smiling. "You know, for a moment, you reminded me of Mrs. Henderson when she had me dusting shelves to pay off my library fines. But you're a helluva lot better looking."

"She was very beautiful when she was younger. I've seen a photo of her on her honeymoon. When anyone mentions my looks, which isn't that often, it's more along the lines of cute, which annoys me. Baby elephants are cute. Puppies and kittens are cute. But I suppose it's better than the other description I read in the *Honeymoon Harbor Herald* when I was appointed to take over Mrs. Henderson's head librarian position."

"What was that?"

"The girl next door." Her brows furrowed, and her mouth drew into a tight line. "Why would the reporter even feel the need to mention that in the article? Especially when they didn't bother to mention my BA in Literature and MLS? That's blatant sexism."

"There's a lot to be said for the girl next door."

"I wasn't fishing for compliments." She waved his words away. "You've already let me into the house, shown me this magnificent library and are cooking me dinner. Fresh-off-the-boat salmon, no less. I'd say you've definitely made up for however rude you may have been."

"None of that's a big deal," he said with a shrug.

Now *that* was a lie. Because every minute he spent with this woman, he was becoming more and more intrigued. And not just because she *was* beautiful, inside and out.

"It will be a very big deal to those kids," she said. She studied him again. Deeper. Longer. "You know, you and your father couldn't have chosen more opposite lifestyles. Him growing Christmas trees, you making money hand over fist in a city which, as the song goes, if you can make it there, you can make it anywhere."

"I can't argue that." Wasn't that what he'd planned for as far back as he remembered? He loved his dad. Respected him. But he'd wanted a larger life. A richer life, and not just in wealth, but experience.

"Yet at heart, where it counts, I suspect that you're both a great deal alike."

That was a surprise. His father had spent two years in Tibet in the Peace Corps, teaching people sustainable agriculture. After receiving dual degrees in business and agriculture, he'd stood up to his father and turned his back on a career working in Honeymoon Harbor's first bank, established by a Mannion, to grow Christmas trees. Because they made people happy. In that way, he'd broken with family tradition, yet he'd also, like many Mannions before him, taken on the job of mayor. The *unpaid* job.

While Gabe made money. More than he could spend in a lifetime. Which was why he'd started investing in small startup businesses, like his soon-to-be sister-in-law's skin care line. And the mobile pet-grooming business of a former Iraq veteran who'd been so successful that Gabe figured he'd be able to start selling franchises within the next five years.

"You don't believe that," she said, when he didn't immediately respond.

"Not really."

Her smile lit up her face and, again, touched that well-guarded place inside him. "Well, the way you helped Jolene's business get off the ground, and letting the adventurers come here, plus the fact that I read on Facebook that you're generously putting the faering up for auction for Welcome Home tiny houses, when you could probably sell it for a tidy profit, is proof that you're wrong."

"Since my mother taught me enough manners not to argue with a guest, how about I get you a glass of wine, then start on dinner?"

"I'm impressed at how deftly you changed the topic. And thank you, I'd love a glass of wine."

CHAPTER ELEVEN

WHEN THEY RETURNED to the deck, the lake was putting on quite a show, its water still as glass, with only the sudden splash of a fish here and there to disturb the mirror image of the mountains. He opened a wine cooler that was next to the sink on the outdoor kitchen and took out a bottle of a Washington chardonnay, uncorked it and poured it into a glass.

When she reached for it, he pulled back the glass and set it on the table between the two chairs. "Why the hell didn't you say anything about your hands?"

"My hands?"

He grabbed hold of one and turned it over. "You have blisters."

"Undoubtedly because, not having had any urgent reason to row lately, I didn't build up calluses." Chelsea flinched a bit as she glanced down at her palm. Sometime on her seemingly endless trip across the lake, as her calves had burned, and her back and arms had begun to ache so badly, the pain in her hands had faded into the background.

"These need to be cleaned and bandaged. I saw a first aid kit in the kitchen. Stay here."

Since his gruffness seemed to come from concern, she decided not to point out that he'd just spoken to her as if she were a dog who was expected to roll over, sit and stay on command. "I'm not going anywhere until I get the apology salmon."

His lips quirked in something close to a smile. Gabe

Mannion smiling, wine, seeing that amazing library, the beautiful view and a grilled salmon dinner were all worth the blisters. Though she still hadn't figured out how she was going to get the boat back to Bert's.

He was back in less than three minutes, and taking hold of her wrist, so as not to grab her injured hand, led her over to the outdoor sink, where he carefully washed both her hands, then dried them with a clean white linen towel he'd brought with him. His touch was gentle and soothing, and for a moment took her back to a long-ago time when she'd fallen off her bike when it had gone downhill too fast and she'd scraped her knees. It had been before Annabelle began having those stomachaches that had taken away her appetite and mystery bruises had started appearing on her pale skin. When Chelsea had arrived home, limping and crying, pushing her bike up the driveway, her mother had run out of the house, given her a big hug, dried her tears, dug the gravel out of her knees and treated her with much the same care as Gabriel was doing now.

Despite the burn in her palms, Chelsea liked the feeling of his hands on hers. And wished she could feel them on other parts of her body. Like all over.

Gabriel Mannion was turning out to be one surprise after another. Granted, all Chelsea knew about the world of New York finance were movies like *Wall Street*, where Michael Douglas pronounced greed to be a good thing, but if that plot was even partly true, Gabriel would have had to become city hardened to survive.

Which, she considered, as she sat back down, careful of her bandaged hands as she sipped her wine, and watched him grill the salmon and vegetables with an ease that was another surprise, may have been why he'd seemed so uncomfortable by the comparison to his father. All his family were generous in their own way. His father

serving as mayor and giving the town such a wonderful
Christmas festival every year, which the Mannions certainly didn't need to do to sell trees.

Aiden, whom she remembered behaving in rebellious
ways that these days would be called *acting out*, had not
only gone on to serve his country with multiple deployments, but was now serving Honeymoon Harbor as chief
of police. And Brianna, who'd left a high life of travel
and glitz and glamour to rescue a landmark Victorian
from crumbling to dust.

Then there was Quinn, who'd also been living what
must have been a wealthy, high-powered life in Seattle,
but was now brewing beer, serving the people of the
town, giving them a welcoming place to gather. And he
probably had more people confessing at his bar than Father O'Malley had at St. Peter the Fisherman.

She'd found Quinn to be a natural listener, never judg-
ing, and while never offering direct advice, still gently
steering a person in the right direction. She'd certainly
talked things over with him on more than one occasion,
and last year, he'd been the one to call a cab to drive her
home when, against his advice, she'd drunk too much
on an anniversary that years later continued to break her
heart. She hadn't been falling-down drunk, though she
was admittedly perhaps too tipsy to drive. Along with her
outward extraversion she'd learned to put on each morning
before leaving her apartment, she'd always had a strong
amount of self-discipline. Except for once a year.

So, try as hard as he might, Gabriel wasn't going to
convince her that his generosity wasn't part of either his
upbringing or DNA. Perhaps, she decided, it was probably equal parts nature and nurture.

"I envy you," she heard herself saying her thoughts
aloud. Damn. That was the problem with living alone.

You tended to get into the habit of talking to yourself. Perhaps she ought to get a cat. Though wouldn't an unmarried librarian with a cat be a stereotype?

"Me?" He gave her a look over his shoulder. "I'm guessing not because I live in New York. Or have money."

"No. Although," she added on second thought, "it must be nice to have enough that you can change people's lives. That part would be lovely."

"I get more back than I give."

"I can understand you believe that. And, although I certainly hadn't planned to bring it up, I envy you your family. My younger sister died of leukemia when I was eleven. She was seven."

HELL. GABE HADN'T been expecting things to turn so serious. "I'm sorry." Which sounded like a cliché, but what the hell did you say to someone who'd dropped a bombshell like that on you?

"So was I," she said. "Then my dad left six months later. Some marriages are made stronger by a child's incurable illness. Others break apart. My parents were the second kind. By the time he packed his clothes and drove off to accept a new position at a hospital in California—he's an anesthesiologist—it was so shattered there was no picking up the pieces."

"That's tough." And wasn't that an understatement? "I don't really know what to say," he admitted.

"You don't have to say anything. I didn't mean to bring it up. To be honest, I never talk about it. Although, of course, a lot of people knew. Fortunately, there wasn't a Facebook page back then to chronicle the life and times of the Prescott family cancer journey.

"Although," she considered, "if social media had existed back then, Annabelle probably would've become one of those small-town celebrities. The darling, brave little girl who spends too much of her energy trying to cheer everyone else up… The kind who sometimes make the final segment of the nightly news. Then there might be an update when she died, but probably not, because hey, that's supposed to be the feel-good segment of the evening, right?"

There was an edge to her tone, one that had him understanding why she'd purposely chosen happiness and optimism. It also had him wondering how long she'd lived with the pain.

"We don't have to talk about this if you don't want to."

"No." She polished off her wine, then held out the glass. "It's okay. But I think it's going to be a two glasses of wine night." She glanced down at the boat bobbing beside the dock. "Though I won't be able to row back if I have another one."

"You won't be able to row back with those hands anyway."

As he took the glass and refilled it, she glanced down at her bandaged palms. "Good point. A guy I went to school with has a taxi business. I can call him."

"Or you could stay here. It's a big house with two wings. You wouldn't have to worry about me jumping you in the dark."

That drew a hint of a smile. "Too bad." She took another drink of wine. "I have a position of responsibility in town. I'm sort of a role model to the kids. I don't want to end up on the Facebook page as having spent the night with you." She held up the bandaged hand that wasn't holding the glass. "And before you try to assure me that news flash wouldn't happen, you haven't been home long enough."

"Yeah. Bert would probably mention you coming out

here to someone. Then it'd be all over town. I'll give him a call after dinner and ask if he can come over with his grandson, take care of getting the boat back to the marina, and driving your car back to your place. Then I can drive you home."

Her lips curved in a faint smile. "Thank you, that's a very sensible solution."

"That's what I get paid for. Solutions."

"I suppose you do… Looking back on it, I realize that Mom and Dad tried to keep up a positive front. At least in the beginning. But then Dad started spending more and more time away. I suspect being a physician who couldn't cure his own child must have left him with terrible survivor's guilt."

"Cancer wasn't his specialty."

"No. But still, how would you feel?"

"Exactly the same," Gabe admitted, knowing that even if he worked on empathy until doomsday, he probably wouldn't ever truly know the pain her family had suffered.

"He did have a doctor friend prescribe Mom Xanax. And antidepressants."

Gabe was starting to feel like when he and his brothers, sister and Seth would break into Herons Landing, creeping through the night shadows in the long-abandoned Victorian house, waiting for something or someone bad to leap out at them. It was usually only a mouse or bat, but there'd also been a raccoon who'd decided to have her babies in a pile of old rags in what had been, at that time, the kitchen. When he and Aiden had stumbled across the raccoon nursery, she'd made it perfectly clear with a snarl that showed surprisingly sharp teeth that she was prepared to do anything she had to to keep them safe.

Which, in turn, had Gabe wondering who'd been keeping Chelsea Prescott safe.

She glanced down at her wine, as if seeing those difficult days in the straw-hued depths. He thought about how devastated he would've been if he'd lost Brianna when he'd been as young as Chelsea had been.

"Unfortunately, as we know from all those PSAs, drugs and alcohol are a deadly combination." She took another drink of wine. "Mom overdosed my freshman year of college. It was ruled accidental. I choose to believe that's true."

"Hell. I'm so sorry."

"Me, too. And I've no idea why I'm telling you all this. While it's not a secret, it all happened so long ago, no one talks about it anymore. Though I did get some comments from my parents' generation when I first came back. Apparently they were pleased that my miserably broken life had turned out well." That edge was back in her voice.

"This town can be a fishbowl. Quinn told me that after a too-close-and-personal encounter with Mildred Marshall while shopping at the market, he started buying condoms online."

She laughed at that, as he'd meant her to. Then he turned serious again as the unexpected turn in conversation demanded. "The positive thing is that people care enough not to indulge in harmful gossip. And mostly tend to be supportive."

"I don't know what I would've done without Mrs. Henderson. And your sister went out of her way to be nice when we lost Annabelle."

"That's Brianna's nature."

"I know. I suspect it's why she ended up owning that B and B. She can make everyone's visits here better. She'd already left town when my mother died."

"What about your dad?"

"He didn't come back for Mom's funeral. He said it would just be too hard for him. He does keep in touch. Not regularly, but a few times a year. He remarried, has twin sons and calls me every year on my birthday." She looked out over the water and appeared to be miles away.

"In fact, he called today, as I was leaving the library, to wish me a happy birthday."

"Oh. Well, hey, happy birthday. If I'd known you were coming, I'd have bought a cake." Okay, that wasn't very funny, either. But at least he was trying, right?

"The thing is…" She took another, longer, drink. "My birthday was last month."

"I'm sorry," he said again, not having any answer for that. How could he? Her life experience was the polar opposite of what his had been. He'd been fortunate to have grown up in a warm and loving family. One whose parents still held hands when they watched a movie, or walked through the rows of fir and pine trees on long summer evenings, when he suspected they often were remembering that day his father had proposed to her on that very same farm.

She shook her head. "I'm sorry for being such a downer. It was just a bad day, and I wanted to be with someone, but everyone else I knew was busy, so—"

"You worked your way down the list to me."

"You could put it that way. But I honestly did want to try again to convince you to let the reading adventurers see your faering. I didn't plan on rowing across the lake."

"Whatever your reason, I'm glad you did." And, despite his determination to keep his distance, that was the absolute truth.

CHAPTER TWELVE

CHELSEA WAS RELIEVED WHEN, as if by unspoken agreement, after the call to Bert had been made, including offering a payment probably more than the man made in a month, the conversation shifted to more typical dinner talk—the Mariners' chances of getting to the World Series, the upcoming Fourth of July celebration, her reading adventurers group, which she was always eager to talk about, the changes in Honeymoon Harbor since he'd been away, and the upcoming double wedding of his sister to Seth Harper, and his brother Aiden to Jolene.

"You weren't kidding when you said your mother taught you to cook," she said. The salmon was dark pink, flaky and delicious. Grilling it on a cedar plank, which she'd only ever had in a restaurant, had added a smokiness and enhanced the herbs he'd put on it. He'd also taken advantage of the outdoor kitchen to make rosemary roasted potatoes, grill the asparagus his mother had included in the basket, then toss it with a light vinaigrette.

"I haven't for a long time."

"I've watched New York City real estate shows and most of the kitchens I've seen would probably fit in this place's pantry, and you're unlikely to be able to grill outdoors."

"My apartment has a balcony, but city fire codes don't allow cooking on it, which is actually reassuring since I wouldn't want anyone burning the building down. But the real reason I haven't cooked is that I work long hours, and it's not worth the trouble shopping and cooking for one person."

Did that mean he didn't have a girlfriend waiting for him in Manhattan? Or perhaps he did, and if they ate in, they'd have dinner at her place. "With all the amazing restaurants, I imagine going out is more practical."

"Mostly I stick with takeout."

"Me, too," she said. "I will admit a weakness when it comes to your brother's wings."

"He started making those back when we were kids."

"Then I guess it's not such a surprise he left the law to open a brew pub."

"It was at first, because of all of us, he'd always known what he wanted to do when he grew up. And then, once he'd achieved it, he tossed it all away to brew beer and cook for a living."

"But he only cooked for the first few months, when he was getting started. Then Jarle came to town and they formed a perfect partnership."

"Seems so. Tell you what though, I sure as hell never would've bet Aiden would end up police chief."

"You're not alone. Word around town was that your dad put some pressure on him when he came back to Honeymoon Harbor."

"So he said. Dad's sneaky that way. You can see my mom's motives coming a mile away. You remind me a lot of her."

"Oh?" It couldn't be a good thing that he was comparing her to his mother, could it? Then again, all the dating advice columns advised that a man who was good to his mother would be good to you. The problem, a pesky little voice popped up in her mind, was that she didn't exactly want him to be good.

"I don't want you to take this the wrong way."

Had any comment starting out that way ever turned out well? "Okay."

"She's known in our family as the velvet bulldozer. You might as well cave or she'll roll right over you."

Oh, no. That wasn't at all good. "You're comparing me to a bulldozer?"

"Only in a good way," he assured her. "Answer me this… Has anyone else in town turned you down when you asked them to participate in the reading adventurers' activities?"

"Well, no. But that's because Honeymoon Harbor's citizens have always been strong supporters of the library."

"I get that. But they agreed for the same reason I did."

"And that was?"

"You're impossible to turn down."

"Yet you tried," she reminded him.

"I did, indeed," he agreed. "But resistance was futile." She laughed at that, even as he continued his explanation. "On the other hand, Dad has mad ninja skills. He appears out of nowhere, and takes you down. Which is what Aiden said he did to him."

"It must have been horrible for Aiden, losing his partner and nearly getting killed in that shootout in LA." Of course, she only knew what she'd read in the *Honeymoon Harbor Herald* and on the town's Facebook page.

"From what I've been told, it wasn't a picnic. But hey, it brought him back here, where he not only got a job he likes, but a woman he loves."

"And once again, the town lives up to its name," she said.

"So it seems."

As the gloaming sent a soft rosy lavender drifting across the blue sky and gilding the clouds, Chelsea realized how right her impulsive decision had been to come here. Getting to see inside the house was a treat—the scenery and complete peacefulness of the setting had taken away the sting in her heart from her father's call;

the dinner had been as good as anything she'd had in a three-star restaurant in Seattle, and—here was the biggest surprise—just sitting here on this deck with Gabriel Mannion was the nicest evening she'd had in a very long time. Maybe, she considered, ever.

The temperature was dropping. She knew he'd seen her shiver when he suggested going inside.

"Let me help," she said after they'd taken the dishes into the kitchen.

"Megan Larson's Clean Team comes tomorrow morning," he said. "They'll take care of it."

"It must be nice to have your own private elves," she said dryly. Wealth did, indeed, have its privileges.

"As you undoubtedly noticed, this is one big ass house. Megan is an entrepreneur. If I did my own cleaning, she'd have one less client, and I wouldn't get the faering done before I had to leave."

"She's expanding to Port Townsend and Sequim, so I guess I can see your point." For not the first time, Chelsea wondered what it would be like to have so much money you never, ever had to worry about it. She could tell he hadn't stopped to think of what to pay Bert. He'd just pulled a number out of the air. Or, perhaps it was the going rate in New York City for odd jobs. She also wondered what all he could possibly buy with it. With the work hours he'd described, it didn't sound as if he spent a lot of time jetting around the world. "You could probably buy the entire town."

"As it happens, I'm not in the market for a town. And this one has been chugging along just fine on its own for nearly three centuries. I'll tell you what. Since you've turned down spending the night with me—"

"At this house," she corrected. He had, after all, mentioned a separate wing, which would preclude them sleeping together.

"At this house," he agreed. His tone was so even, she couldn't tell if he was at all disappointed as a very strong part of her was.

"I suppose I'd better be taking you home."

If her defenses hadn't already been down, she never would have ended up here in the first place. So, if anything was happening between them, and she wasn't certain of that since she definitely wasn't sure of her own feelings, let alone his, calling it a night would probably be the most sensible idea. The problem was, she hadn't been feeling all that sensible since she'd climbed into that rowboat to cross the lake.

"It is getting late," she said. Though she doubted she'd get any sleep. "So, that's probably best."

He shrugged a wide shoulder. "Your call."

It *was* her call, Chelsea reminded herself as they reached the door. She paused, and as they stood there, less than a foot apart, her looking up at him, Gabe looking down at her, she could read the naked hunger in his eyes. Okay. So, something *was* happening, and she wasn't the only one feeling it.

"I think I'm getting nervous again."

"Join the club."

"This wouldn't be a good idea. "You and me…being together that way."

"You're not going to get any argument from me. But you want to tell me why it feels so damn right?"

"It's the night. It's been beautiful. And the food was perfect, and there was wine, and me sharing a story I never tell created an intimacy that might color what seems to be happening."

"That doesn't sound so optimistic."

"Maybe not. But it's being careful… A friend of mine, you wouldn't know her, told me earlier this evening, before I'd even thought to come here, that I should have a summer fling."

"So you were already thinking about it?"

"Yes. But only as a hypothetical."

"You're not the only one. But my thinking wasn't so hypothetical. But here's the deal, Chelsea. That's all I can offer. The summer. And everything tells me that you're not the type of woman to have a summer fling."

"I never have." Nor a spring, fall or winter fling, but he didn't have to know that. "Though there's something to be said for new experiences."

He shook his head as he ran the back of his hand down her face, his knuckles grazing her skin. "You're not making this easy."

"Perhaps things worth having—"

"Aren't supposed to be easy," he repeated what she'd said earlier. "Like you said, I'd better take you home now."

"I think so." It wasn't her first choice. Nor his, from both his words and tone. But it was, Chelsea reminded herself again, the wise, sensible thing to do.

As much as she was tempted, she wasn't sure that she wanted to be his summer girl, the one he slept with before going back to his women in Manhattan. Sleek, polished, sophisticated women in designer suits who lived in the fast lane. Women like him.

She was, she considered, a novelty. Although he'd grown up here, the same as she had, unlike Quinn or Brianna, who'd slid right back into small-town life, it was more than a little apparent that he'd left Honeymoon Harbor far behind. Whatever had brought him home for the summer—and wasn't she now dying to know the reason?—he'd made it clear that once his sister was married and his faering done, once the Labor Day wooden boat festival and the last of the fireworks signaling the official end of summer had faded away, Gabriel Mannion would be on his way. Back to his real life. The one he'd chosen. The one that she'd never fit into. Not that she'd want to.

But, heaven help her, she wanted him.

He'd just taken hold of the door handle, when she reached out and covered his hand with hers. "You know how you said, earlier, that if you'd known it was my birthday, you would've bought a cake?"

"Sure."

"I just realized what I'd rather have for my belated birthday."

"What?"

She lifted her arms, and combed her fingers through his hair. "You."

A dangerous flame flared in the smoky depths of his eyes as he slowly trailed his thumb along her bottom lip. Her breath caught as she waited. As impossible as it was, it felt as if the earth had stopped turning on its axis.

Slowly, deliberately, giving her time to back away, he reached up and took off her glasses, placing them on the marble-topped foyer table. Then, just when Chelsea feared she'd pass out from a lack of oxygen, he spun her around, with a fast, practiced move that told her this was not the first time, backed her up against the door and took her mouth.

His body was hard and hot. His mouth clever and hungry as he took the kiss deeper, his hands beneath her blouse, scattering sparks everywhere he touched. He filled his hands with her breasts, that same thumb that had her parting her lips, teasing her nipples to hard points. Then they went lower, skimming over her rib cage. When he unzipped her capris and eased them down her hips, Chelsea learned something she'd never known about her own body—that her stomach could actually be an erogenous zone. All it took was a light touch of a fingernail tracing an excruciatingly slow trail down her abdomen and pressing his thumbs on that tangle of nerves below that set off an explosion of tiny fireworks. That place where she wanted him. Before she could change her mind because if they stopped now, she could possibly die.

She'd heard of people dying during sex. But as his fingers continued their sensual journey she wondered if a woman could actually die from becoming too aroused without release. Someone should do a study, she thought as his tongue tangled with hers and the wickedly clever hands stroked slick flesh.

"Kick off your shoes." His voice was low and rough.

It was more order than request, but one, that at this extraordinary moment in time, she was all too willing to follow. She toed them off, then, after he'd shoved the capris the rest of the way down her legs, she managed to step out of them without falling down only because of his hold on her.

Their bodies were pressed so closely together she could feel him reach between them to unbutton his jeans, which was followed by the hiss of zipper.

Somehow, without her noticing through the fog of arousal clouding her mind, he'd gotten hold of a condom that he put on with a quick, practiced move.

There was no seduction. No soft murmuring in her ear. No tenderness. It was rough and raw, and exactly what she needed. Because if he'd carried her off to bed for candlelight and soft, slow romance, she might change her mind. She might realize how insane this was. She was a librarian. Maybe not one of those sexless, dried-up old maids that seemed to be the flipside stereotype to the naughty librarian, but still…

Ms. Prescott did not have hard, hot, up-against-a-door sex with men she barely knew. Ever.

But she *was* having it. And it was amazing.

Her breasts were pressed against the hard wall of his chest, their bodies so close together she couldn't tell whether it was his heart hammering she felt, or her own. With just his hands and mouth, with no movement on her part except to hang on for dear life, he brought her to the brink. Every nerve ending in her body was electrified. Waiting.

Finally, when he pressed down on that sensitized nub, Chelsea cried out in a voice that she didn't even know had been hiding inside her. One she'd never heard before.

She was trembling. Everywhere. Her bones were turning to water and once again, he knew exactly what to do, bracing her up with one wide hand while using the other to guide himself into her. This time her cry was half moan, half strangled laugh. How could she possibly laugh at a time like this?

But there was no time to figure that out because his hips began jackhammering against hers. He took her. Filled her. Claimed her. And after a few long strokes, the earth that had only moments before seemed to have slowed on its axis, suddenly and violently tilted, throwing her into a dark, swirling void.

It could have been minutes. An hour. Years. But when she was once again capable of thought, she was sprawled on her back, naked from the waist down.

"I think I may be blind," she managed to say.

Life was filled with trade-offs. Chelsea suddenly heard her father's voice back when she was seven and he'd still lived at home, pointing out that the reason she was on her knees on hard tile, throwing up into the toilet, was that she'd ignored his warning not to eat all the county fair junk food. There was a good chance that had she known ahead of time that such rough, raw sex with Gabriel might cause something to explode in her head, costing her her sight, she might just have accepted that trade-off.

"Try this." He lifted her melted arm away from where it had been flung over her eyes and laid it down next to her with a gentleness far different from their fast and furious lovemaking—not lovemaking, sex—they'd just experienced.

"Better?" he asked.

She blinked and found herself looking directly into his eyes. Which had turned unnervingly unreadable. "I owe you another apology," he said.

"You already cooked me dinner." *And gave me not one, but two orgasms within seconds, something that had never, ever happened before.*

"I knew we were going here as soon as I saw you rowing that boat across the lake," he said, trailing a hand down her side. At any other time, with any other man, she might have felt embarrassed to be lying half-naked, while the man who'd just rocked her world was braced on one elbow, looking down at her. Touching her. But this was not any other time. And Gabriel Mannion was not any other man. "But that's definitely not the way I'd imagined it going down."

"I've never done anything like that before," she murmured. And wasn't that a staggering understatement? "That woman wasn't me."

His lips quirked. "You could have fooled me."

She turned onto her side. As thrilling as the sex had been, now that the fog was drifting from her mind, she wished they'd made it to the bed in that stunning master suite she'd seen earlier. Because if he was finally going to open up and initiate a conversation, it would have been nice to be able to cover herself with a sheet.

"I never have sex with men I don't know. Especially,

well—" she waved her hand, toward the door "—against-the-wall sex."

"You know me."

"Not really. We both may have grown up here, but I only actually met you at the boat shop."

"True. But technically it was against the door."

"I'm well aware of that. And thank you for avoiding the door handle. And for having a condom so handy." Not to mention thinking of using it, when she wasn't sure, with all those explosions going off, she would have thought of it. Another thing that was so not her.

"One thing I took from Boy Scouts is the motto 'be prepared.'"

"You were a Boy Scout?" While nowhere near the rebel Aiden had once been, she couldn't imagine Gabriel putting on a uniform and marching in lockstep down Water Street in the Fourth of July parade.

"For a while. I had this dumb need to try to beat Quinn's troop merit badge record. Which, by the time I was fourteen, I realized was impossible, so I dropped out and let him be the only Eagle Scout—well, besides my dad—in the family. Quinn was always the superstar. At everything. Which was why him deciding to brew beer was probably the last thing any of us would have expected. Though," he said, seeming to think about it for a moment, "Mom didn't seem all that surprised."

Apparently having sex had opened him up. Chelsea was surprised that he'd given her that private glimpse into the Mannion family dynamics. As successful, as wealthy as he was, could he possibly still not feel as if he measured up to his eldest brother?

"He seems very happy."

"As a clam," he agreed. Although his tone was easygoing enough, his shuttered eyes revealed the topic closed.

"I suppose we should get you home. Unless you're up for round two?"

She felt the change, like a wind from the winter sea blowing over them. Chilling her skin. And, she recognized, that portion of her heart that had, for those few minutes, flung open. Being with this man was not easy. And she'd always done easy. Now she wanted to ask the real Gabe Mannion to stand up. Was he the gruff boat builder? The genial host who'd given her a tour of the house and cooked her dinner? The masterful alpha male who'd just taken her against the door?

As tension strung between them, Chelsea reminded herself that her heart had nothing to do with what they'd just done. She hadn't heard that he'd been out with anyone since he'd returned to town, so, having gone without sex for these past weeks, he undoubtedly needed to scratch an itch. And then she'd conveniently shown up in that damn rowboat and lost her mind.

"I really do need to get home," she said, ignoring her hormones, which had an entirely different idea.

"Your call," he repeated what he'd said earlier.

As he left the foyer to dispense with the condom, Chelsea hurriedly scrambled to dress before he returned, shoved her glasses on her face and told herself that if they'd been in New York, and happened to have ended up at the same bar, he wouldn't have looked at her twice.

As long as she remembered that, she'd get past this embarrassing episode and be fine.

While they drove in silence through the night, the North Star rising in the sky directly ahead of them, Chelsea thought of all those ancient sailors, including, undoubtedly, the Vikings, who'd used that very same star to navigate.

Wouldn't it be lovely if only life came with your own personal star to guide you through the storms to a safe harbor?

CHAPTER THIRTEEN

ALTHOUGH SHE REMAINED quiet on the drive back to town, Gabe could practically hear the wheels busily turning in her head. Was her mind tempting her, as his was him, with thoughts of what else they could be doing right now rather than driving through the darkening night? That hot Viking plunderer dream came back. After the last half hour, it was no longer merely a memory, but a probability.

Unlike Aiden, who'd always seemed to go out of his way to be the polar opposite of their eldest brother, growing up, Gabe had always asked himself, *What Would Quinn Do?* Partly because he'd admired his brother's goal to achieve success in a larger arena than what their small hometown offered. And he'd considered, during these past weeks, a very strong streak of sibling rivalry he hadn't realized was still lurking inside him had wanted to not merely equal, but surpass his elder brother's success. He'd never been surprised by Quinn's swift rise to legal heights, but as impressive as that career climb had been, as much money as he'd probably been making, as booming a market as Seattle had become, it wasn't, and never would be, New York City.

Of course, Gabe suspected that most Seattleites would be quick to point out that their beloved Emerald City on the Sound was far superior, in all the ways that counted, to Manhattan. Yet, every time he saw the towering skyline as his plane came in for a landing at JFK, he recalled the lyrics Chelsea had brought up about how if you could make it in New York, you could make it anywhere.

Well, he'd damn well made it. In spades. Another few years, and he could even top what Carter—who'd spent more time screwing and drinking these past years than working—had achieved. Of course, why should Carter Kensington have bothered with work when he'd had Gabe to bring in accounts for him?

Gabe knew that the board had a senior partner's seat to fill. He was also well aware that they'd turned a blind eye to Carter's reckless behavior for a very long time because of him having worked double duty for all these years. So, despite taking this summer off, Gabe was the logical, the *only* real choice.

By the new year, he'd have achieved the goal he'd had in his mind when he'd accepted Carter Kensington's job offer. It wasn't as if he hadn't had other choices. Despite his small-town Pacific Northwest roots and lack of decades-long East Coast business and social connections, several top firms had bid for him before he'd left Columbia. But none of them had come with a mentor, he'd realized before the interview was over, that he could someday surpass.

Which was why he'd worked longer hours than anyone at Harborstone. Why he'd given up any semblance of a personal life. Why he'd never returned home for holidays, birthdays, anniversaries and even his only sister's engagement party. Why he'd put his own ego aside not only to let Carter take credit for much of that work—knowing that the senior members of the board weren't blind to what was going on—but had also been willing to play babysitter to an adult man who'd never grown up.

His first month on the job, Gabe had drawn two red lines in the sand. The first one was that he'd never overlook or cover up any illegal or unethical business act

Carter might do. The second was that he would never serve as an alibi for Carter with any of his wives.

Not that he'd wanted Carter to drop dead. That had never, not once, entered his mind. His timeline had been to rightfully claim his place with that elite school of big fish at the top of the food chain within the next two years. But Gabe couldn't deny that by Carter's passing, he was now on a fast track to achieving his goal.

"And what—" he heard the doctor's damn voice echoing in his mind again "—has that gotten you?"

I'm not done yet, he mentally answered it back.

Although he hated to admit it, Gabe had come to the reluctant conclusion that the snarky doctor had been right about him needing a break. When he'd spilled his guts about the funeral episode, Aiden, who'd done multiple deployments and had gone undercover to take down bad guys in LA, had pointed out that stress was stress. "If work causes you to pass out," his brother had said, "you're probably doing it wrong."

So, he'd take this time to recoup. Then, once the summer was over, he'd come roaring back, stronger than ever.

As SOON AS they pulled up in front of the house, Chelsea opened the door of the SUV to get out, intending to escape, but Gabriel caught her arm.

"My dad taught me to always walk a girl to the door after a date."

"This wasn't a date."

"We had wine. Dinner. We talked. Had sex, though I'm hoping for a do-over to demonstrate that I have better moves than your average caveman."

With her mind still spinning, there was no way she'd been going to admit that apparently she had a thing for cavemen. Who knew?

She found herself wishing, as they walked up the steps to the double front door of the olive green, gingerbread-trimmed Victorian, that she hadn't blistered her palms. Not because they were beginning to burn again, but perhaps, just maybe, otherwise, he'd have held her hand.

And wasn't that high school thinking? Next she'd be wanting to wear his letterman's sweater. After their encounter in the boat shop, despite every bit of common sense she possessed, she'd looked up the Honeymoon Harbor yearbook online for the year he'd graduated and had seen along with the young entrepreneurs' club, the Future Business Leaders club, and Boys' State, he'd also run track. Not hurdles, relays or sprints, but long-distance, which, she thought, suited him. It was one of the few sports she could think of that required you to be part of a team, while still allowing you to be an individual.

She'd seen students running on trails in the woods, at the lakeshore, and one April Monday when she'd had lunch with Jolene, Farrah and Lily at the park. They'd been enjoying a lunch of clam chowder and smoked coho salmon BLTs in the historic Roosevelt dining room at the Lake Quinault lodge as the runners had passed by the windows, looking a bit like ghosts in the mist and fog rising from the lake.

Chelsea wondered if he still ran. Which, despite New York having a marathon, seemed as if it might be impractical with all those long hours he'd mentioned. Unless he never slept.

And why was she even thinking about this? Why did it matter?

Because, she admitted, if they spent too much more time together *he* could matter. And then what?

"Thank you for the lovely dinner," she said. Then cringed inwardly. Who spoke like that these days? She

may as well have been returning to Downton Abbey.
Which, in turn, brought to mind Elizabeth Bennet's feelings after dancing in circles at Netherfield with the frus-
tratingly enigmatic Mr. Darcy. For the first time since
reading *Pride and Prejudice* (she'd also watched many of
the movie adaptions and the miniseries with Colin Firth,
who'd always be her true Darcy), Chelsea finally understood exactly how Lizzy could be both attracted to and
frustrated by the man.

His lips quirked again. Not in a smirk, but amusement.
She was wondering if he was laughing at her when he put
his arm around her, low on her hips, and drew her close.

With the confidence of a man who'd probably kissed
more women than he could count, this time he didn't
rush. His lips teased hers, lingering, tasting at their leisure in a lengthy exploration that instead of engulfing her
in flames as his earlier kisses had, trapped her in gauzy
layers of sensation.

His other hand gathered up her hair, which had fallen
loose around her shoulders while she'd been rowing
across the lake. Once again, he was taking control, but
once again, she liked it. A lot. His teeth nipped at her bottom lip, just hard enough to send desire surging through
her like a bolt of lightning from a summer storm. Someone had trembled.

Him?

Or her?

What did it matter, when, despite already having two
(!) orgasms, she was so desperately hungry, and Gabriel
so blatantly aroused? Knowing she'd had the same effect on him as he did on her was proving an aphrodisiac
in itself.

Was he actually turning her around and around? Or
was that spinning, dizzying feeling just in her head? Be-

fore she could decide, he lifted his head, and with a touch as gentle as one of the rare snowflakes that had fallen on Honeymoon Harbor last Christmas, he ran a fingertip over her still-tingling lips. "I knew you'd be trouble. As soon as you walked into the shop."

No one had ever referred to her that way, but instead of being insulted, she decided she rather liked it. It made her sound dangerous, like some femme fatale wearing a sexy, body-hugging dress, killer heels and dark lipstick who'd sashay into a film noir detective's seedy office and get him mixed up in murder while searching for a missing black bird.

"One more. For the long, lonely road home," he said. Then kissed her again, a light touch of lips that promised so much more.

As he strolled back to the Range Rover that undoubtedly cost as much as, if not more than, she made in a year, Chelsea had an urge to call him back. One she managed, just barely, to resist.

AFTER A RESTLESS night reliving her time at Eagles Watch with Gabriel Mannion, tossing and turning, achieving—according to her wrist Fitbit—a total of three hours' sleep, Chelsea woke with a headache, stuffed-up nose, sinuses that felt as if they'd been stuffed with an entire roll of cotton batting, and a throat that felt as if someone had taken a sandpaper block to it. Which didn't help as she started hacking like a cat trying to throw up a fur ball.

"Oh, great." She recognized the drill, having had one cold a year for most of her life. And unlike during the cold and rainy winter season when it would make sense, hers always hit in the middle of the summer. Which also happened to be her busiest time at the library.

The only good news was that today was Monday.

Forcing her aching body out of bed, she brushed her teeth, washed her face, tossed down two Advil, gargled with salt water, and warmed a rice-filled sinus mask in the microwave. Then dragged her body back to the bedroom and climbed under the covers.

As she lay there, hoping the padded warm mask over her eyes and nose would help clear her head, she thought back on last night. Her hands were still slightly blistered, but not punctured, which, she'd read on the web, meant that new skin was already growing.

So, along with not being expected at work today, she was on a roll. If only she knew what to do about Gabriel Mannion.

All night long, her thoughts had kept spinning back to him and that conversation they'd had after dinner. Unlike a lot of men, who'd keep you agonizing and wondering, he'd been honest and straightforward with her, telling her that nothing would come of their shared attraction except a summer affair. Which was tempting. Even after that wham-bam-thank-you-ma'am door sex. Which, right there, should be enough to have her running in the opposite direction.

But as much as she'd tried to tell herself that it had been all about sex, the inescapable truth was that it had been more. Although she knew she was nowhere as experienced as Gabriel, she hadn't spent the years since high school in a convent. She'd had sex. Granted, not raunchy, dirty sex like she'd had last night. But no man had ever suggested she was a dud in bed. She'd read *Cosmo*. She knew the ten things most likely to turn a man on. She could spot seven ways to know when your man wanted sex (besides the obvious one), and an article in the far more scientific *Psychology Today* claimed that, on average, males thought about sex nineteen times a day.

Which, if true, suggested that there were very few times they wouldn't want sex.

She knew that hot, wet kisses made a man horny (duh), even knew how to do a lap dance, though she seriously couldn't imagine ever actually performing one.

And if there was anything last night had proven, it was that she now also knew that she could avoid freaking out when she came out of a sex coma and found herself lying on the floor, half-naked, next to a fully dressed man.

Chelsea knew all that and more. But she'd never known a man, been with a man, who'd possessed the power to crash through those walls she'd spent most of her life building. To give her a view, however fleeting, of all those feelings she'd run from for so many years. For the first time since she'd been eleven years old, a year younger than Hannah was now, she'd allowed herself to be vulnerable, to release the reins of control that she'd always held on to as if her life had depended on it.

And nothing bad had happened. In fact, those few minutes against that tall, wide wooden door had probably been etched into her memory banks for life. If only she'd stayed...

"You've got a stuffed up head," she muttered on a cough. "You're not thinking clearly."

Unfortunately, other parts of her body, unaffected by invading germs, hadn't gotten the memo.

Now, looking back, she wondered if having had no one to take care of her but herself for most of her life was why it had felt so glorious to let loose and hand those reins to someone else. If only for a few stolen moments.

Even as wretched as she felt this morning, the memory of that door sex sent streams of warmth flowing through her. Unless she had a fever, which would be preferable. Fevers could be gotten rid of by taking some aspirin.

She feared getting rid of the imprint Gabriel had left on her body and her mind would be a great deal more difficult. Taking off the eye mask, which had cooled, she retrieved her Kindle from the bed table, scrolled down the list of books and decided yet again that she really had to widen her reading.

The majority were historical, contemporary and YA teen romances. Or biographies.

The romances were too dangerous, given that Gabriel had taken up residence in her fuzzy mind, and if she wasn't careful, she'd end up thinking about sex nineteen times a day. And how distracting would that be? How did men get anything done?

She'd never dated in high school, never had a boyfriend, never attended a prom. So, although she couldn't personally relate to the YA stories filled with teeming emotion and angst, she definitely saw herself in the ones about teens growing up in dysfunctional families where dying siblings, alcoholic parents and divorce were common threads. Along with never fitting in. Those hit too close to home today.

Not being in the mood for reading about real lives, all of which would undoubtedly make hers seem excruciatingly boring by comparison, she clicked on the TV and resumed her binge watching of *Grey's Anatomy*.

Four hours and half a box of tissues later, she'd gotten to the episode where, after a difficult heart transplant, after finally asking Izzie to marry him, while all alone in his hospital room (except for all the viewers, including her, who had fallen in love with the sweet, smart, hot, handsome patient for weeks), Denny succumbed to a stroke and quietly breathed his last.

As Izzie threw herself on the bed next to him, crying her eyes out, refusing to leave the room, Chelsea sobbed right along with her. Even knowing the story, there was some part of her that believed that it was somehow all a mistake, and that he'd come back to life.

The phone rang as she reached for the last tissue. Between the cold and Denny's death, she'd gone through an entire box.

"Hey," the familiar voice said. "I had an idea I wanted to talk over with you, but when I called the library, I found out it's not open today."

"We're closed on Mondays and Thursdays." A tear trailed down her cheek. She swiped it away with the back of her hand.

"Yeah, I got that from the recorded message. Are you okay?"

"I'm fine." She blew her nose with a loud honking sound that would put the wild geese that summered on the peninsula to shame. "I just have a cold." And was currently heartbroken.

"I'm sorry."

"It sounds worse than it is." No way was she going to admit that a fictional character on a repeat of a TV show had turned her into a basket case. "There's an incubation period. I may have given it to you."

"I live in Manhattan," he reminded her. "There's probably not a virus I haven't been exposed to after all these years. I'm pretty sure that I'm safe."

"But they change. Mutate. The incubation period is three to five days, so you won't know until then."

"If I do catch it, I promise not to hold it against you."

"I think it's better if I just spend the day in bed." Izzie was now being lifted off Denny's bed and carried out of the room, which triggered a whole new stream of waterworks.

"Are you sure you're all right?" he asked after she

couldn't cover her mouth fast enough to stop the sob from escaping. Which, in turn, set off another bout of coughing.

"It's just a code." Huh. Apparently she'd lost the ability to say the letter *l*. "No biggie."

"Okay. I guess I'll see you later."

"Okay. We can set up the meeting. Thanks for calling." She quickly ended the call before she started wailing like a baby.

This is what happened when you give your heart to someone, she warned herself as Izzie had a total meltdown. *It ends up being broken.* It could be your sister. Your dad. Your mother. Or a wonderful fictional transplant patient who'd already been through so much that he deserved to live and have his much deserved happily-ever-after with the woman he loved.

Not that Chelsea believed Izzie to be the right woman for him, but Denny had been convinced, so she gave him reluctant credit for knowing best.

"He's not real," she reminded herself. "He's merely a character out of Shonda Rhimes's imagination."

Yeah. Try telling that to her heart, shattered pieces of which were scattered all over the top sheet along with a blizzard of crumpled tissues.

Twenty minutes later, after turning off the TV because she just couldn't take any more of the aftermath episode of Denny's death in the fragile state that sadistic television writer had left her, Chelsea had just gone into the small kitchen to see if she had any honey and lemon for her sore throat when the doorbell rang.

Not expecting any deliveries, and certainly not wanting anyone to see her looking like this, she ignored it and kept digging around in the cupboard, where she was certain she had a jar of local honey from one of the hives on Blue House Farm. This particular hive was set in a field of lavender, which gave it a faintly floral taste with hints of mint and rosemary, herbs Jim Olson had told her lavender was related to.

The bell rang again. Seconds later, she heard her cell chiming from the bedroom. And ignored it. "I know I bought honey the day I was with Lily at the market." She pushed aside a bag of flour, thinking that perhaps it was hiding behind that. No luck.

Apparently giving up on the bell, whoever it was began knocking. Didn't they get that she wasn't going to answer? Her annoyance rising, she was pulling the bag down when it slipped from her hands onto the counter, split apart and sent flour flying everywhere. At the same time her landline, which she kept because cell signals were iffy in this part of the country, began ringing.

CHAPTER FOURTEEN

Frustrated, and covered in flour, she snatched the receiver from its base on the counter, not recognizing the number. "Who is this?"

"It's me."

Just that. No name. Not that she needed one. She'd dreamed of that voice crooning sweet nothings to her while they made love in a Viking faering anchored in Serenity Cove.

"I'm sorry, but I'm a bit busy here." She sneezed, creating a new cloud of flour.

"Can you take time to open the door?"

"Why?"

"Because I'm outside."

"No. I can't let you in. I already told you, I'm contagious." She was also wearing pajamas printed with ice cream sundaes. Not to mention the flour all over the front of them, in her hair and undoubtedly all over her face.

"I'll take my chances. I come bearing soup."

"Soup?"

"Chicken noodle from Luca's. It's his nonna's recipe."

Damn. The man didn't fight fair.

"I also have cold medicine. And the 50th Anniversary DVD of *Charade*."

"Where did you find that?" Blockbuster had closed years ago, there was only a single rack of rentals at Marshall's Market and she sincerely doubted he'd brought the romantic suspense comedy with him from New York.

"After Brianna told me it was your favorite movie, I

called my mom. She always made us watch old movies when it was her night to choose. I figured she'd have this. Because it's a classic."

"Wasn't that handy? Did you ever think your sister's trying to set us up?"

"It occurred to me." She could hear the shrug in his voice.

"And you're not bothered by that?"

"Not particularly. I'm only bringing soup, cold medicine and an old movie. I'm not asking you to wear my class ring."

It wasn't a letterman's sweater, but it was close enough to have her uneasy that they were thinking along the same lines. He'd be so much easier to resist if he were more like horrid Greed-Is-Good Gordon Gekko.

She heard voices, a brief conversation, on the other side of the door. "That was your neighbor," he said. "Wanting to make sure I wasn't harassing you. If you don't let me in, we'll start drawing a crowd."

"Or you could leave."

"But then you wouldn't have the chicken soup. Which is supposedly not only good for your soul, but also for colds."

"I'm beginning to understand why you're so successful."

"Because I'm always right?"

"No." She sneezed again. A second time. Then a third. "Because you won't take no for an answer."

"That's because I'm always right."

Before she could answer, she heard another voice, this one a female's. Then his baritone response, followed by a girlish giggle.

"That was your landlady," he informed her of what she'd already figured out. "*She* thinks I'm very sweet. And a hottie. Her words, not mine."

"Mrs. Moore is in her eighties. And I don't want to burst your bubble, but while you may be good-looking, in a Black Irish way, she also hits on the UPS guy when he's wearing his brown summer shorts. Along with the college kid delivering pizzas to earn college money. She's an equal opportunity flirt."

"I imagine it helps keep her young. My grandparents have been married for decades, but I dropped by the house one morning and noticed that my grandmother had put on fire-engine red lipstick before going out to Luca's pasta making class at the senior center. But I'll take your compliment."

"It wasn't a—oh, damn." Realizing that he wasn't going to go away and they were definitely going to soon be drawing a crowd, she marched over to the door and flung it open. And felt that same skip of her rebellious heart and those butterflies start fluttering their wings again. But since last night, they'd turned into great blue herons like the ones that nested at Herons Landing. "You might as well come in."

"Thanks." Her already-tiny foyer seemed to shrink even more when he entered. He also took the air out of the room, making it difficult to breathe. Even dressed in jeans, a black Mannion's Brewery T-shirt and work boots, the man radiated a masculine charisma that probably drew women to him like a magnet.

Don't think of that! Blaming her stuffed-up head for that uninspired simile, as those gray eyes swept over her, she remembered what she must look like. "I had a flour bag mishap while searching in the cabinet for honey." She combed her fingers through her bed head in an attempt to somewhat tame it, which only succeeded in sending up another cloud of flour.

"I could go to Marshall's and get a jar."

"No. It's in the cupboard somewhere. I bought it at the farmer's market with Lily. She's a friend and library volunteer who's in charge of marketing at the college. But you don't need to know that."

Some women would undoubtedly be struck speechless by such male beauty. And yes, Gabriel Mannion somehow managed to be beautiful and manly at the same time, which really wasn't fair. But for some reason, he had the exact opposite effect on her because her mouth kept getting ahead of her brain whenever she was around him.

"Are you laughing at me?" His lips were doing that quirking thing again.

"Did you hear me laughing?"

"No. But you could be doing it on the inside."

"I could be. But I'm not. I was thinking you look cute."

"I'm not certain I believe that. But even if I did, do you happen to recall me mentioning that cute is not my favorite description?"

"Sorry." His gaze skimmed over her flour-dusted pajamas. "How about sweet? And tasty."

She suspected none of the women he'd been with in New York wore ice cream sundae pajamas. Which made her wonder, yet again, if she merely represented a summer novelty to him. Which was even worse than being cute.

"I wasn't expecting company."

"Neither was I last night. Yet there you were at my dock. And here I am at your door." His eyes drifted to her lips. Then darkened as if she wasn't the only one who remembered him kissing her senseless. "Why don't you go back to bed," he suggested. "I'll bring you the soup, some tea, and clean up the kitchen."

Wanting, *needing* to maintain equal power in whatever this relationship they seemed to be developing turned out to be, Chelsea was about to inform him that she'd been doing just fine by herself, thank you very much. But the aroma of Luca Salvadori's nonna's chicken soup, and the idea of having someone else clean up that dreadful mess she'd made proved unreasonably tempting.

"Thank you. Though, if you catch this cold, you can't say I didn't warn you."

"I'll take my chances. And if I do catch it, maybe *you* could bring *me* soup."

"I suppose I could do that. But only if you give me the gate code. Because I'm not rowing across that lake again."

"It's a deal. I don't suppose you happen to have one of those white nurse's outfits with the lacy white stockings handy? Just in case."

She rolled her eyes. "That is so outdatedly sexist."

"Ouch. I think you just called me old."

"The word I used was *outdated*."

"That's even worse. It makes me sound as if I've passed my sell date. So I take it that's a no?"

"A definite no."

He sighed. Dramatically, the hand that wasn't holding the bag covered his heart. "I'm crushed."

Despite her stuffed-up sinuses, her burning eyes and sandpaper throat, Chelsea was almost enjoying herself. "I'll tell you what." She patted his scruffy cheek. "If we're ever in Paris and you rescue me from a would-be metal-handed assassin, like Grant does Hepburn, I may, just possibly, consider the nurse outfit. Meanwhile, what you see is what you've got."

Changing the teasing mood on a dime, his gaze moved slowly from the top of her white-dusted hair, down to her fuzzy black-and-white whale slippers. Then back up to her face. "I like what I see just fine. Including the slippers."

Oh, damn. She would have to be wearing those. "We

had a slumber party for preschoolers at the library last month. I bought these on a whim because I love our orcas and they fit the theme of the day."

He didn't say anything for a long moment, making her wonder if he found them as silly as, despite his compliment, her pajamas. Why, oh why wasn't she wearing something lacy and sexy from The Dancing Deer's lingerie department? Oh. Maybe because she didn't *own* any lacy, sexy underwear. If she was going to indulge in a summer fling, she'd definitely have to do some shopping. But as much as she believed in supporting local business, she'd have to buy online, rather than risk the news that she'd bought a barely there lace thong and push-up bra showing up on the town's Facebook page.

"Do you have a TV in your bedroom?"

"I do, despite the fact that they're supposedly bad for sleep."

"Good." He handed her the DVD. "Get into bed. I'll bring in the soup and medicine."

His tone had turned almost tender. Like when she'd told him about her dad's call, and all the backstory behind it. Heaven help her, he was getting to her. And not merely because after last night's caveman sex, even on the brink of possible death from a cold virus that could be mutating into pneumonia at this very minute, she had an urge to jump his bones.

The undeniable truth was that he'd touched something inside her. And wasn't that far more dangerous than his ability to hand out orgasms as if they were dark chocolate truffles and he was the candy man?

"Damn. I just realized that I forgot to buy tea," he said. "Mom and Brianna always drank it when they got sick. I imagine they still do."

"I have tea." She pointed toward the set of tea tins

formed to look like old books she'd received from Mrs. Henderson as a graduation gift upon receiving her MLS.

"Super. What kind do you want?"

Despite a head filled with cotton batting, Chelsea felt reckless, as she too often did around him. "Surprise me."

That challenge hanging in the air, she raced back to her bedroom and began madly gathering up the blizzard of Kleenex. Deciding she didn't have time for a shower, she stepped into the stall just long enough to brush the flour from her hair and pajamas onto the tile floor and decided that she could wash it down later. Hopefully the mix of flour and water wouldn't turn to library paste and clog up the pipes. Her heart sank as she looked in the mirror and saw that she looked even worse than she'd feared. After brushing her teeth for the second time that morning, she washed the flour off her face, then tugged a brush through her tangled hair, which was sticking out as if she were auditioning for the role of Doc in a *Back to the Future* sequel.

"Well, at least you're not going to have to fight him off," she told her reflection. "Even a cave-dwelling Neanderthal probably wouldn't be turned on by you right now." She considered putting on lipstick, but decided she didn't want him thinking she'd gone to extra trouble just for him. But a little pink-tinted ChapStick wouldn't hurt, right?

After smoothing out the sheets that had tangled during her erotic dream, she stuck the DVD into the player and managed to climb into bed seconds before he arrived in the doorway.

"Okay if I come in?"

"Could I stop you?"

He shook his head. "It always surprises me that women don't know how much power they have over us lesser, mortal men. Which, in turn, leads me to wonder why you haven't taken over the world yet."

"*Yet* being the operative word. How do you know that we're not planning the ovarian uprising as I speak?"

"You sure as hell couldn't do worse."

As he entered, carrying a tray, Chelsea couldn't remember the last time she'd had a man in her bedroom. Oh, wait. It had been after last year's public employees' Christmas party in the Friendship Hall when, not wanting to be totally alone for the holidays, she'd allowed a cute rookie fireman to talk her into letting him come over afterward. Not that it had taken that much talking. He'd been fun, ridiculously fit and energetic, and she'd enjoyed herself enough to go out with him two more times. Then, when he'd shown warning signs of getting serious, she'd broken it off. Fortunately, he'd bounced back quickly. A week later, she'd seen him playing darts at Mannion's with the owner of Rain or Shine Books.

Chelsea knew from therapy that her unwillingness to commit stemmed from having lost the three most important people in her life during such formative years. But the head and heart weren't always the same and although she understood, intellectually, that the odds of everyone she might ever love leaving or, worse, dying on her were slim, the protective stone walls she'd built around her heart were tall and thick.

Or they had been. Until she'd walked into that boat shop and felt the first crack appear in the mortar. Okay, it was more than a crack. Because she'd known he was *The One*. Which wouldn't make any difference, unless he felt the same way about her. Which he obviously didn't. Before he'd blasted through that wall last night, sending stones flying, he'd been up-front about his plan to leave at the end of the summer. That he was not interested in a long-term relationship. She'd gotten that message loud and clear.

Now she just had to decide if she wanted to settle for

a summer romance. And not a sweet Lifetime movie romance where the couple strolled through wildflower meadows with birds chirping and little hearts circling their heads as the soundtrack from *Beauty and the Beast* played, but a down and dirty hot summer fling.

She knew what her friends would advise her to do. Brianna Mannion had loved Seth Harper most of her life, only to watch him marry her best friend Zoe, after which she'd left Honeymoon Harbor for years. Then Zoe Harper had tragically been killed in Afghanistan and two years later, Brianna had returned home and made the brave choice to take a chance on a man who, at first, had appeared as if he'd never move past the loss of his first wife. And now Chelsea was going to be an attendant in their wedding.

Desiree Marchand had also caved the day her former lover had shown up in town. Supporting the claims of many that there was something in the water of Honeymoon Harbor that made it impossible to resist love.

Lily had already told her to go for the fling.

And if last night was any example, the sex would be amazing.

So, maybe…

He was carrying a tray she kept on the top of the refrigerator for entertaining, with utensils placed on a quilted place mat. He'd poured the delicious-smelling soup into one of the oversized white mugs she'd bought in the gift shop section of Cops and Coffee, a plate of buttered bread slices and tea in her *I'm a librarian. What's your superpower?* mug. If that weren't enough, he'd put a fresh peach-hued rose from the backyard garden in the Waterford cut crystal bud vase Kylee and Mai had given their wedding attendants.

The only other time she'd had a meal delivered to her

in bed was when a hospital food services employee had brought her a watery salad, rock-hard roll and a lump of some gray mystery substance claiming to be meatloaf. And she'd had to have her appendix taken out to get that.

"Okay, I'm both surprised and impressed by your plating."

She felt as if she should be wearing a froufrou bed jacket like Scarlett O'Hara had worn the morning after Rhett had swept her off her feet and carried her up that staircase. Once she was older, Chelsea had come to realize that iconic scene was actually incredibly rapey, but in her impressionable youth, she'd thought it to be the most romantic scene ever.

"Even before Mom started taking decorator classes, she was big on presentation. We boys didn't get the flower, like Brianna did, when we were sick. But we always got a bed tray. And a Hot Wheels car, Star Wars figure, or comic book she kept stashed away for the occasion."

"That's very special." Chelsea felt another of those uncharacteristic twinges of envy. "No wonder Brianna ended up a top-end concierge and now runs a bed-and-breakfast. It's either in her genes, or she learned well."

"Probably a bit of both. She was born a nurturer." He fluffed up her pillows—something else he'd learned from Sarah Mannion?—and set the tray on her thighs. "I couldn't count the number of imaginary tea parties with her dolls and stuffed animals we boys had to sit through."

"That was nice."

"We took turns at the tea table. Because she was our little sister." And didn't that say it all? Chelsea thought. "After Santa brought her an Easy-Bake Oven for Christmas, instead of pretend food we got miniature chocolate cakes," he said. "With milk in tiny flowered china cups."

"When she and Seth have those children she's been talking about, those are going to be very lucky kids."

"That would be true."

"You do realize that you paid your rudeness penance with that dinner last night." And the orgasms.

"That's good to hear. But I've been told I need to work on my attitude."

"How's that working for you?"

"To quote Alan Jackson, I'm a work in progress. The bread is olive rosemary that Luca bought from the bakery this morning," he said, deftly changing the subject. "Apparently Desiree Marchand supplies all his bread."

"She does. Also for Sensation Cajun, which makes sense since she's engaged to the chef. They had Seth knock a hole in the wall between the buildings so they could share the same space." The fragrance rising from the bread was as delectable as everything Desiree made.

"I hope Earl Grey is okay. I unearthed the honey behind a box of Rice Krispies, and added it and a squeeze of lemon for your throat."

"I appreciate that." Though it was starting to freak her out, just a little, at how nice he was being. She wanted to ask him what he'd done with the surly boat builder/ caveman ravisher. "Well, thanks so much for dropping by. It was really sweet of you."

"You know how you feel about cute?"

"Yes."

"Well, that's how guys tend to think of being called sweet."

"I'm sorry. Would you prefer I return to rude?"

He shook his head. Folded his arms. "I never would have figured you for a black-or-white-view woman."

"Touché."

She hit Play on the remote. "Again, thanks. It was very manly of you to play male nurse."

She saw the spark in his eyes and realized that her innocent words had suggested a gender twist on his naughty nurse suggestion.

"Seriously. You really don't have to stay," she said, feeling her cheeks heat up. Hopefully, he'd think the color was from a fever.

"I told you, Mom always made us watch these old flicks. What she didn't know was that despite all our moaning and groaning about wanting cowboys or action movies, we kind of liked them. Even Aiden, although he'd probably rather eat sand than admit it. There's a reason this one's a classic. It's a trifecta of Grant, Hepburn and the best Hitchcock movie Hitchcock never made."

Damn. Which was why it was *her* favorite. It made her even more uneasy to have anything in common with him. Instead of leaving, he sat down in the overstuffed flowered chair by the bay window that looked out onto the backyard garden where he'd obviously found the rose.

"I thought you had a boat to build."

"It can wait a couple hours." He stretched out his long jean-clad legs, making himself right at home.

Despite having seen the romantic comedy/spy thriller so many times she could probably quote all the dialogue, Chelsea was still transfixed by the fabulous French scenery, the suaveness of Cary Grant—did that man ever look less than perfect?—and the radiant beauty of Audrey Hepburn, who it was easy to tell had been Givenchy's muse. And then there was that dialogue that managed to be both crisply snappy and sexy at the same time.

Finally, one hour and thirteen minutes later, Hepburn's sexy, mysterious ally with the multiple aliases had finally revealed his true name and offhandedly suggested putting it on a wedding certificate, which may be the worst proposal in any movie ever, but Hepburn hadn't hesitated to accept.

She'd finished the soup and bread, both of which were unsurprisingly delicious, and the tea with the lemon and honey he'd added had actually helped ease her sore throat. Also, sometime during the romantic caper, the cold medicine seemed to have worked on her sneezing and those coughs that had made her sound like a plague victim.

"They don't make movies like that anymore," Chelsea said on a sigh. It did not escape her that both Elizabeth Bennet and Audrey's Reggie had fallen for impossibly hard-to-read men. Men like the one currently sprawled in the chair she'd found at Treasures antique shop.

"You're not going to get any argument from me. Grant set a high bar for the rest of us."

And didn't that have her wondering what Gabriel was like in Manhattan? All she'd seen him wearing were jeans, T-shirts and work boots or sneakers. But she imagined him standing in front of his skyscraper office, in a crisp shirt, silk tie and an Italian suit surveying his realm. Glancing over at him, she decided that he might just give Grant a run for his money.

"How many suits do you own?" she asked.

"I'm not sure. I've never counted. Why?"

"No special reason. I was just wondering. Do you own a tux?"

"I work too many hours a day to have the kind of social life that requires a tux."

She was thinking that she preferred that answer to the previous one, when he threw her another curveball.

"You remind me of Hepburn."

Her short, sharp laugh set off a coughing bout that made her sound—and feel—as if she were about to hack up a lung. So much for the miracle cure pill.

"In what universe?" she finally managed to ask once she got enough air back to talk. If Hepburn had ever coughed, Chelsea was certain that she'd done it discreetly, into a lace-trimmed white linen handkerchief. Embroidered with her initials in a flowery, feminine script.

"This one."

"I don't look anything like her." Audrey was spectacularly one of a kind, with her sublimely perfect bone structure, wide, Bambi-brown eyes, a swan neck, a figure made to wear designer clothes and incredible grace.

While Chelsea was all too aware of being, well, average. She wasn't tall and willowy. Nor short, and lushly round. Her hair was an ordinary brown and her eyes were a color that couldn't decide, on any given day, whether they were blue or green, and while her other features fit together pleasantly enough, even when it wasn't covered in flour her face wouldn't stop traffic.

There'd been a time when she'd been much younger, probably the age Brianna had been when she'd been hosting those tea parties, back when her mother had enjoyed watching old movies, Chelsea had decided that when she grew up and got married, she was going to wear a dress just like the tea-length white gown Audrey Hepburn had worn in *Funny Face*. She'd forgotten that until last year while shopping at The Dancing Deer for her dress for Kylee and Mai's wedding, Dottie and Dorothy had shown her a photo of a knockoff of that exact dress that they'd sold a bride at their previous store in Shelter Bay, on the Oregon Coast.

"This would be the perfect dress for you someday," bubbly Dottie had told her.

"It does suit," her sister Dorothy had agreed.

At the time Chelsea had wondered if the two elderly twins possessed some psychic gift that allowed them to know that it had, once-upon-a-time ago, been the dress of her heart. What they hadn't realized was that they'd never be ordering it for her, because in order to pledge your forever-lasting, until-death-do-you-part love to someone, it was necessary to also pledge your heart. And hers had never been available. Until, maybe, just possibly now.

Wasn't it ironic that the very man who was beginning to free her tattered and broken heart was the very same man who'd made himself very clear that if offered, not only did he not want it, he wouldn't accept it?

Fate, she'd learned early in life, could be a mean-spirited bitch.

"The reason I first called you," he said, breaking into her thoughts, "was that I had another thought about you bringing the kids to the house to see the library."

"Oh." She felt her spirits sink, but put on the brave smile she pulled out whenever she felt an emotional hit coming. "That's okay if you've changed your mind. I understand that Eagles Watch isn't your house, and it would only be natural for you to be concerned—"

"I'm not concerned about that. Why don't I fund a personal library for the kids?"

"You're going to give the reading adventurers a library?" He couldn't possibly mean that. The cold medicine must have gone to her head.

"Not exactly. I was thinking more along the lines of a book club, like Dolly Parton's Imagination Library. Where I'd provide the seed money, then the community would get involved to keep it going, so kids could receive their very own book every month. You'd need to select a group of key people, the most important being someone to co-ordinate the program, though, having gotten a handle on how you work, that would undoubtedly end up being you."

"Are you serious?"

"I'm always serious when I'm talking about business and money. I can help you set up a nonprofit. Or better yet, Quinn, since he's undoubtedly written up that type of paperwork while practicing law."

"That would be a huge undertaking," she said, even as her mind whirled with glorious possibilities.

"Like I said, you'd need people with the right skill sets to help you run it."

"You're talking about more than the library advisory board."

"You may want to put one or two of those people on the team. That'd be up to you. But you'd need to keep them separate entities to avoid breaking federal nonprofit finance laws."

"I'm sorry." She rubbed her temple, where a headache was threatening. "I can't quite process all this."

"I'm not surprised. I had all last night to think about it, then sprang it on you when you're feeling bad. Not to mention being under the influence of a cold medicine. Why don't you think more about it, and if you're interested, we can drill down to more detail once you're feeling better."

"In other words, when I don't look like a cast member from *The Walking Dead* wearing a Rudolph nose?" Could her bid for a compliment be any more transparent?

"Since you brought it up…" He pushed himself out of the chair, came over to the side of the sleigh bed and gave her a long look. "You should see your face."

Even recognizing Grant's line from the film, she instinctively lifted a hand to her cheek. "What about it?"

"It's lovely. But you have circles beneath your eyes." He swiped a finger beneath each eye, one at a time, this touch unnervingly tender. "And your nose is definitely not a Rudolph one, but it is a bit pink." He skimmed a fingertip down her nose, which, unlike Hepburn's, tilted up a bit. "And you are pale."

Damn. Definitely the walking dead. "It's the Pacific Northwest. We don't tan here." The old joke was that Pacific Northwesterners didn't tan; they rusted. "And I prefer to think of myself as fair."

"My Fair Lady," he murmured. "Another movie Mom would make us watch. If you're still stuck in bed tomorrow, I'll bring it by."

"I'd rather you didn't. That happens to be a very misogynistic retelling of *Pygmalion*."

"Granted, but Rex Harrison has to grovel to win Hepburn back. I thought your kind liked that in your fiction."

"He didn't grovel nearly enough. Especially considering that George Bernard Shaw intended Eliza to leave Higgins at the end. And what do you mean by 'my kind'?" Chelsea was surprised when even arching a brow hurt.

"Romantics."

"I'm not a romantic. I'm very much a realist."

"Okay." His gaze drifted meaningfully over to the stack of paperbacks on the bedside table and the bookshelves lining the small room, the well-worn spines of all those romance novels looking like a brightly colored kaleidoscope. It was obvious that she had not chosen her books by the crate.

"They're entertainment," she pointed out, glad to feel the spark of annoyance steamrollering over her earlier heady feeling of attraction. "Not a guide to real life. Just because I enjoy them doesn't mean I can't tell fiction from my actual life. The same way you can read thrillers without feeling a need to go blasting away at bad guys with automatic weapons and snapping necks with your strong, bare alpha man hands. At least I hope that's not one of your fantasies."

He laughed at that, a bold, rich sound that caused those awakened body parts to do a happy dance. Not a happy dance, she corrected. A mating dance. Like the ones on all those nature documentaries Larry Franklin from the hardware store was always checking out. Whenever the sixty-something widower returned them, she was forced to listen to a play-by-play of various courtships.

"Point taken," he agreed. "And I apologize for sounding sexist."

"You wouldn't be the first," she said. "As a reader, and a librarian, I've always found it interesting, albeit annoying, that women who love the romance genre help put those male writers on all the bestseller lists because we're very eclectic readers. But men who eat up blood-and-guts thrillers like beer nuts would die before even picking up a romance novel."

"As it happens, I had the same conversation with my sister, back when she was in college."

"And how did that go?"

"It was a long time ago, but I seem to remember her claiming that men were cowards, afraid to explore our emotions."

Chelsea was thinking that was pretty much on the money, when he surprised her yet again. "I didn't disagree."

"At least you're honest."

"Unlike Cary Grant's undercover spy character with all those aliases in the movie, I never lie. In the first place, my mother had this saying about spiders and lies."

"'What a tangled web we weave, when first we practice to deceive.'"

He nodded. "That's it. Dad weighed in and pointed out that if you always tell the truth, you never have to remember what you might have told someone. And even more important, in my business, getting caught lying can end you up in federal prison."

"As I've seen on the news."

The depressing shift in topic hadn't calmed her re-awakened body. Which brought her unruly mind back to where his too-appealing laugh had caused it to drift.

"There's this patron… Larry Franklin, owner of Franklin and Sons Hardware. After being widowed last year, he got hooked on watching documentaries. He'll watch any one I order, then gives me a detail by detail review. He was in the other day to tell me all about the courting techniques of birds."

"Sounds riveting."

"You'd be surprised. There's this songbird in New Guinea and Australia, called a bowerbird, who has a very complicated courtship ritual. It begins with the males building nuptial bowers—a tower of sticks which other males try to destroy. If they can protect them from being torn apart, they decorate them with exclusively blue objects. They'll steal anything blue, often from other bowers. It doesn't matter what the object is. It can be natural, like a flower, or a ribbon or even a piece of plastic. So long as it's blue. After they're finished, the female will go around and inspect them."

"Pressure time."

"Like being a contestant on *Cake Wars*," she agreed. "But instead of $10,000, you're out to win sex."

"Those are really high stakes."

"Indeed. But even then it's not over. If the female approves of the blue bower, the male has to dance for her."

"Proving once again that females of all species hold the power. I wonder if they line up and compete like avian Chippendales?"

"I don't know." She laughed. "Probably not, because

Larry would have definitely mentioned that. But he did tell me that there's some sort of selection process going on because researchers tried putting red objects on the bowers and every time the females chose the males who removed the red items."

"So while the bird wars suggest the survival of the fittest selection process, the females were choosing the more intelligent ones."

"They seem to be."

"Thereby giving an entirely new meaning to bird brain. And remind me never to play Trivial Pursuit with you."

She smiled and tilted her head. "You're turning out to be very different from the man I met in the shop."

"Like I said, I'm supposed to spend the summer finding my Zen. Which is going a lot better at the moment than it was before I came over here."

"That's what I love about old movies. They provide an escape from real life."

"That's what my mom would say. But in this case, I think it's more the company."

"Just because I'm a small-town girl doesn't mean you can get away with a line you'd never try on a New York woman."

"That's because I've met very few New York City women with a Zen vibe."

"I can't decide if that's a backward compliment, or you just called me boring."

"The one thing you could never be would be boring." He leaned over, and although for an instant, she was hoping he'd risk the plague and kiss her again, he merely picked up her phone on the bedside table and clicked in some numbers. "I'll take this tray into the kitchen. Now that you have my number, you can call me later if you want another delivery for dinner."

What Chelsea really wanted him to deliver was another orgasm. Or two. No. Bad, bad mind! Apparently the cold medicine was making her as loopy as the time she did tequila shots at a going away party for Fran, who'd left town for the sunshine beaches of Costa Rica after selling her bakery.

Why on earth did she bring up bird sex? Oh… Her mind must've circled back to her ovaries doing the mating dance, which had, in turn, brought up Larry. And once again, as so often happened around Gabriel, her thoughts had gone directly from her head to her mouth, without passing through a filter first. She'd really have to work on that.

"I'll be fine. And thanks again. That was more than I usually eat for lunch."

"Okay. Get some sleep then," he said. "I'll call tomorrow, and if you're feeling better, we can discuss ideas for the personal library book club plan."

"Hopefully I'll be at the library tomorrow."

"Tomorrow evening, then. I haven't had Cajun food for years. How about we discuss it over dinner?"

"Are you asking me out on a date?"

"Do you want me to ask you out on a date?"

"No." Now she was as big a liar as Cary Grant in *Charade*. "It just sounded as if you might be."

"We could call it a working dinner. You have to eat. I have to eat. We can kill two birds with one stone. And Cajun spices should be good for your cold."

"I think this is where I tell you that I need to take a step back."

"Okay. How big a step back?"

"I don't know…just a step. Maybe two. Do I have to be so specific? It's just that I wasn't planning…"

"How about I promise no door sex?"

"I'd think that's a given, considering we'd be in a public place and I doubt you'd want your brother arresting us."

"Good point. How about I swear not to have sex with Chelsea Prescott during or after said business dinner at Sensation Cajun?" He lifted his right hand.

"You left out before."

His laugh was short and definitely more amused than she was feeling. "Maybe you'd be happier with Quinn. You both think like lawyers."

She'd been quite happy with Gabriel. No. That didn't come close. Ecstatic? Euphoric? More like intoxicated. And wasn't that part of her problem? She needed him to be with the stepping-back program because she couldn't entirely trust herself.

"How about kissing you good-night at your door afterward?"

"There's a logistical problem with that idea because I'd be driving myself home in my car. Which would be parked out in front of the restaurant."

"Since I suspect you don't want to be caught kissing on a public street—yet—I could follow you home in mine."

She frowned, considering the idea. "Now you're starting to sound a little stalkerish."

"We do happen to live in the part of the country with the most serial killers. I wouldn't want anything to happen to you on the way home."

"I live three blocks from the restaurant, with streetlights all the way. Yet... I suppose, since my house is on the way out of town, meaning you'd be passing it anyway, a kiss would be okay." There was that quirk again. Chelsea folded her arms. "I'm glad I'm proving to be a source of amusement."

"Make that enjoyment and I'll cop to it. Because I can't think of anything I don't enjoy about you, Ms. Prescott. Especially when you talk like a librarian. It gives me ideas of ravishing you in the stacks."

"There will be no ravishing." Hadn't he already done that? "Even bringing up that word isn't helping."

"Okay. I'm here for the summer. And you're not going anywhere, right?"

"I couldn't if I wanted to. Because of the—"

"Reading adventurers. So, we've plenty of time for you to decide whether or not you're up for a fling."

The sensible thing to do would be to cancel the entire idea of the boat shop visit and just stay on her side of town and away from Mirror Lake. But Chelsea had spent her entire life being sensible. And wasn't sensible a close cousin to boring?

"Why don't you call me tomorrow afternoon?" she suggested. "I may just come home and collapse."

"You need to take care of yourself," he said agreeably. "For all those reading adventurers."

"I'm not going to let them down."

"Of that I have no doubt. Lock the door behind me."

With that he took the tray into the kitchen. Chelsea heard water running. Then the dishwasher open and close, then start. Finally, the door to her apartment closed.

Since she had the feeling that he wouldn't leave until he heard the click of the lock, she climbed out of bed, padded into the living room on her orca slippers and turned the lock.

"There's also a deadbolt," she heard him say.

"We're not the city."

"I grew up here," he reminded her. "With a brother who also happens to be police chief and who told me all about the multi-county-wide manhunt last winter."

She thought about asking if Aiden had also mentioned that said manhunt happened to be due to a domestic abuse arrest warrant, which wouldn't have proven a danger to her. Then decided it wasn't worth arguing about.

She turned the handle for the second lock.

"That's better."

She was just about to go back to bed when she heard another voice drifting up the stairs. Mrs. Moore, her landlady again. The deep baritone responded with something that had the woman laughing again.

The man was a chick magnet. Which so wasn't her type. On the rare occasion she did date, she preferred easygoing men. Like that cute fireman, who'd only been up for fun times. Or Duane, the county auditor who droned on about analytical procedures, compensation balance and lockboxes from the appetizers through dessert. Or Bruce, the county's IT guy who'd gotten the library's computer system going again after last winter's storm. He was cute, trending toward hot, but her mind had started drifting after twenty minutes of tech talk. The last two had proven boring. All three had been safe.

Gabriel Mannion was neither.

He was the type of man a woman might have a fling with. Which was becoming more and more seductive. It *could* be a once in a lifetime experience. Something she'd still remember when she was an old white-haired centenarian, rocking in a chair on the porch of Harbor Hill, waiting for a volunteer to read her *Harry Potter*.

He'd already warned her that, just like Cinderella at the ball, her romance would come with a countdown clock. Or more specifically, a countdown calendar. As long as she could remember that she'd be okay.

CHAPTER FIFTEEN

WHAT THE HELL was he getting into? She wasn't his type. At all. But the thing was that, damn, he liked her. Not only in a want-to-drag-her-off-to-bed caveman style and keep her there until September, which, yeah, he did. Even when she was wearing ice cream sundae pajamas covered in flour.

The attraction had been near instantaneous when she'd walked into his shop, which was one reason he'd been so rude to her. He'd known that if he searched Manhattan for a decade, he'd never find any woman less his type.

He was city. She was happy in a hometown so small it had all of three stoplights. And one didn't count because it existed only to direct traffic boarding the ferry. His work was his life and his life was his work. Since landing on Wall Street, there'd never been any distinction between them, and although this forced time off wasn't turning out to be as excruciatingly boring as he'd feared, Gabe knew that as soon as his plane landed at JFK, his phone would explode with texts and calls. Catching up with work, especially after Carter's death, would require even longer hours than before the funeral.

In stark contrast, Chelsea Prescott, who was as dedicated to her work as anyone he'd ever met, still somehow managed to have time for a life outside those library walls. Not only had she created the reading adventurers, he'd skimmed through the photos on the town's Facebook page and saw her auctioning off books to raise money for school supplies, packing boxes of holiday food at the food pantry and delivering library books to patients at the hospital, along with creating a library at Harbor Hill nursing home. Factoring in all her volunteer work, she probably worked as many hours a week as he did. But her time actually made a difference in people's lives. While he made money.

"Which is important, too," he reminded himself. It wasn't as if he hoarded his wealth like Scrooge. He was a firm believer in philanthropy, and if it weren't for people like him who made the money in the first place, how could the recipients of his charities ever have their scholarships, hospital wings and school computers?

If there were times that it occurred to him, especially when he considered the number of homes, yachts and cars of those whose net wealth equaled more than the GDP of many countries, that a more equal distribution of that wealth would be a good thing, Gabe assured himself that when he reached that lofty level of what many were, not precisely wrongly, referring to as modern-day robber barons, he'd be different. He'd never been in it for the money. It was all about keeping score. No different from Burke's football rankings.

That was his story, and he was sticking to it. Even though he had a niggling feeling that Honeymoon Harbor's librarian might disagree.

Which brought his uncharacteristically wandering mind back to Chelsea. It was hard to imagine what she'd gone through. His family was intact, and although, except for Quinn, he and the rest of his siblings hadn't come home as often as his parents probably would've liked, every single one of them knew that they were always welcome at home. When Dr. Doogie had strongly suggested him taking some time to regroup to save his life, rather than escaping to some tropical island, or going summer

skiing in France, Gabe knew that like the swallows signaling the return of spring every year, this lush green
land with its towering trees and impossibly blue lakes—
formed more than ten thousand years ago, as the last Ice
Age receded—was precisely where he'd needed to be.

Despite his plan to hole up at the cabin for the prescribed three months, he'd ended up having to engage
with regular people, like the guys at Cops and Coffee,
locals he'd run into at the bar at Mannion's—a part of the
relaxation thing he hadn't considered along with Honeymoon Harbor's slow pace.

Then there was also Megan, owner of The Clean
Team, who insisted on supervising her team to ensure
that the cabin was left as clean as the fir- and salt-scented
peninsula air. He and Megan had dated for a few weeks in
high school, but had an amicable breakup because he was
determined to make his fortune in New York, while she'd
chosen to remain a hometown girl. Divorced after what
she'd casually brushed off as a bad choice in husbands,
she occasionally brought her three-year-old daughter to
work. Although he wasn't usually all that into kids, he
had to admit that the little girl with the double blond po-
nytails was pretty cute. And well-behaved.

After Jarle and Quinn had pressed him to tackle the
faering, he'd set up shop in an old storage building on
the school's property, and reconnected with men who'd
known him since he was a kid. Guys who'd taught him
how to cut chines and inwales from the same pieces of
timber to ensure that both halves bent with the same uniform pressure, to patch every screw rebate and even the
smallest space with epoxy putty and that he could never
do too much sanding.

Just like the anxiety attack that had been the impe-
tus for this journey home, Chelsea Prescott had hit like

a lightning bolt from a clear blue sky. Even as every instinct kept warning him that the cute girl-next-door librarian was trouble, Gabe knew that he wouldn't be able to stay away from temptation.

"It'll be okay," he assured himself. "Be honest about your intentions, only take it as far as the lady wants to take it, and you could have one helluva summer to remember."

ALTHOUGH HER HEAD still felt stuffed up, and she was drinking gallons of honey and lemon tea from the coffee cart to soothe her throat, Chelsea was feeling much better Tuesday morning. Although Friday should have been the last day of the school year, Monday and Tuesday were school makeup days lost to a surprise February snowstorm. Not much stuck on the ground in this part of the country, but neither parents nor school district employees were willing to send children out in buses on icy roads. Especially when so many of those roads were deeply shaded by trees, unwarmed by any winter sun that might manage to break through the clouds.

She stayed busy all day, catching up on acquisitions, ordering from the requests list and also some of the books that had gotten good reviews and looked like ones readers would enjoy. Following Mrs. Henderson's lead, she also chose a number of both fiction and nonfiction books by writers with different voices. While Washington might not lead the nation in diversity, her mentor had argued forcefully at town council meetings that a well-educated population needed to read about cultures other than their own. In full agreement, Chelsea had continued that policy and was proud of the fact that many books in Honeymoon Harbor's library were routinely requested by others through the state's interlibrary loan program.

Gabriel had, as promised, called at three, to see if they were on for dinner. "I have something to do after work," she'd told him. "But I could be there by seven."

"I'll have Bastien hold a table," he said. "Inside or out?"

The outside courtyard, with its aged stone floor, lush plants and fountain in the center was lovely. Quiet. And, she warned herself, romantic.

"Outside," she said before she changed her mind. "It'll be more quiet and make it easier to talk."

Even as she heard the words leaving her mouth, she knew that she wasn't fooling either of them. Nor, she suspected, would the dress she'd brought to change into before leaving work. It was carnation pink, sleeveless with a V-neck with just enough show of cleavage that she'd brought a cardigan to put over it in case she chickened out, and a short flounce skirt. She'd bought the dress on impulse after seeing it in the window at The Dancing Deer last year and, until this morning, it had still had the tags on it. Throwing caution to the wind she'd also left a pair of royal blue heels in the car. It had been so long since she'd had any occasion to wear heels, she hoped she could walk from the car through the restaurant to the patio without falling over.

"Outside it is," he agreed.

"Hot date?" Farrah asked on her way out, after Chelsea had changed clothes in the staff restroom.

"It's a working dinner," she insisted, not fooling either of them.

"Well, whatever you're after, you're going to definitely get it in that dress." She blew Chelsea a kiss, then breezed out the door.

The library closed at six thirty on Tuesday, and that half hour would allow her to take Hannah and Hailey home. Which reminded her that she'd been so buried in work, she hadn't come out of her office to check on them as she usually did when they'd first arrived after school.

"And wouldn't you make a great mother," she scolded herself, wishing she could blame cold meds for her inattention, but she hadn't taken any due to that warning about operating heavy machinery. No point in taking any chances. "You'd be the type who'd leave children behind at a rest stop on the way to Disneyland."

Yet another reason child rearing was better left to women like Kylee and Mai. And Brianna. And Sarah Mannion, who'd somehow managed to raise all five of her children to adulthood without losing one of them.

When she found the children's library nook empty, she decided they must be at the coffee cart, getting the milk she'd always encouraged them to drink every day, which was certainly better for them than the soda Hannah had been buying at Marshall's on the way from the school to the library.

Nothing.

Starting to feel a prickle of panic, she checked the restrooms, finding all empty. She went through the building, calling out their names. No one answered.

"It's a lovely day," she reassured herself. "Maybe they walked home."

She called Farrah who, after giving it a thought, said that she hadn't seen them, either. Assuring herself she was overreacting, Chelsea drove over to the house, and, finding that the bell didn't work, knocked on the door. At first lightly, then more heavily.

Nothing.

She left the porch and was about to go around to the back of the house, when a next-door neighbor came out of his house headed toward a truck with an attached boat trailer. "You looking for Marlene?" he asked.

"Yes." Chelsea had already learned the foster mother's name from Aiden. "And the girls."

"She told me she was going away for the weekend to the coast. She probably decided to stay there a few extra days."

"But Hannah and Hailey had a snow makeup day today."

He shrugged. "I went to school with her back in the day and she was never in the running for a perfect attendance award. I can see her keeping them out if they were having fun."

"Okay. Thanks." While it wasn't the most responsible thing to do, at least hopefully the girls would be having fun.

"No problem. Have a good evening. Nice weather we're having, isn't it?"

"It's been perfect," she agreed, her mind flashing back to the salmon dinner Gabriel had cooked her on the deck of that amazing lakeside home.

"That's why I'm going fishing. Gotta take advantage of the couple months of summer Mother Nature gives us. Six months from now, we'll all be wondering why the hell we stay here."

"Because there's still nowhere better?" she suggested.

"There is that," he agreed cheerfully. Then tipped his fingers to the brim of his Bert's Bait Shack cap, climbed into his rig and headed away, out of town toward the public dock at the harbor.

Feeling somewhat reassured, and deciding to check back tomorrow morning, she continued on to Sensation Cajun. Bastien had painted the restaurant in a deep rose, which had been a popular color during the Victorian era in New Orleans. It hadn't been that typical in the Pacific Northwest but, as Desiree had explained to Lily, Brianna and Chelsea during a Monday lunch at the restaurant, along with assuring the building stood out as people came into town on the ferry, Bastien wanted diners to feel as if they'd been whisked away to The Big Easy. The green-and-white awning and black scrolled iron grill added to the ambiance.

Although at first Desiree had been skeptical when Bastien wanted her to paint her bakery the same color, she'd caved in order to visually connect the two businesses. Seth had done such a good job with the remodel, you never could've told that it had once been two separate buildings.

The patio was lovely, with weathered stone underfoot, lush plants and a fountain in the middle. She thought it odd that Gabriel was the only person taking advantage of the lovely summer evening. Then she had a second thought.

"Tell me you didn't buy out the patio."

"What's the point of having money if you can't have fun with it from time to time? I could have booked one of the private dining rooms upstairs, but the night seemed too nice to spend indoors. And you don't have to worry. I asked Bastien and he assured me that no one had called in with a special occasion request."

"Still, as lovely as the inside is, the restaurant is nearly full. There must be people in there who'd rather be out here."

"I've no doubt. And they can dine out here next time. This time I want to be alone with you. Unless you'd rather have someone putting our plans for the kids' library book club on the Facebook page before we even get them finalized."

"That's coercion."

"It's sensible," he corrected, standing up and pulling out one of the wrought iron chairs for her. The cushions were covered in a striped print that matched the awning. "And if you're still feeling guilty, consider it saving diners from catching your cold."

"Impossible," she muttered as she nevertheless sat down.

"If it's a virus and not summer allergies, like you said, you could be contagious."

"I'm not talking about that. I'm referring to your ability to always turn an argument your way."

"Says the woman who wrapped a simple good-night kiss into miles of red tape. I always thought Quinn was a master, but you could hold your own with him. Which is saying a lot given that he would've been state high school debate champion if one of his teammates hadn't cheated and gotten the team disqualified."

"Well, that sucks."

"That's what Quinn said at the time. But a great deal more colorfully. He claims to be over it, but if you want my opinion, I suspect that despite going on to be a big shot lawyer who got paid to debate, he's still pissed."

"I'd certainly be." Chelsea shook out the white linen napkin and put it on her lap.

"Really? I wouldn't have thought you'd be a woman to hold a grudge."

"I'm not. But I also wouldn't ever want to be accused of cheating. Even secondhand."

"Now see, there's another thing we agree on." He handed her the wine menu. "There was a guy at Harborstone who was stealing from his accounts. Auditors caught him before the feds did, but there are still times when I go in a finance bar and wonder how many people are wondering if I was in on it with him. Wall Street thrives on gossip, which is also how people get caught inside trading, because someone will have one or more drinks too many and talk about something he's not supposed to know."

"I can't imagine anyone thinking that about you," she said. "And I had no idea there are such things as finance bars."

"They're not really designated that way, but they've morphed into them over the years. Like sports bars. Or cop bars."

"I like the idea of library bars," she decided. "We could all have intense conversations and arguments over books, like Robert Benchley, George S. Kaufman, and all the others of the self-named "Vicious Circle" who had lunch at the Algonquin Hotel. They had a game, where they had to make a sentence from a word. When Dorothy Parker got *horticulture*, she came up with "You can lead a horticulture, but you can't make her think.""

He laughed. "Clever. Though you seldom find finance guys talking about books. Unless they're business ones. And those are usually audio books listened to in cars or on the train."

"That's rather limiting."

"Yeah, well, you have to understand that Wall Street's like a fraternity, in that it feeds on people's insecurity and need to fit in. So, if the conversations all revolve around trading, then that's what you've got to be able to talk about."

"I can't envision you ever being insecure."

"You should've seen me when I landed at Columbia. I was thrown into the pool with all these students who'd grown up with fathers in the business, so they were light-years ahead of me. Not just on contacts, but knowledge they'd learned growing up."

"But you caught up."

"Sink or figure out how to swim," he agreed. "Would you like a glass of wine? The menu suggests pairings."

"That's helpful," she decided. "Last time I was here I had the gumbo, which was delicious. I think this time I'll have the étouffée. According to the pairing notation," she read, 'a German Riesling has balanced acidity and sweetness that goes well with the spice of the dish.' Not that I'd honestly notice," she admitted.

"Ah," a voice behind her said, with that familiar bayou accent that had more than one woman in town regretting that Bastien Broussard had put a ring on Desiree Marchand's finger the same day he arrived in town. "That's the point of a good pairing, *chère*. Wine and food are supposed to go so well together that you never think about it. If you had, say, a pinot noir, or a boldly oakey chardonnay, you'd undoubtedly notice something off about the meal."

Chelsea smiled up at the chef who'd moved to Honeymoon Harbor solely to follow his long-ago sweetheart and singer for his former blues jazz band. And didn't that gesture cause more than one romantic heart to flutter? What must it feel like to have a man love you so much that he'd give up a famed generations-old New Orleans restaurant and a singing career and travel to this far corner of the country just to be with you?

"I'm going to take your word for it," she said.

"One étouffée and a Riesling for the lady. And the gentleman?" he asked, drawing a laugh from Gabriel.

"It's been a long time since anyone's called me a gentleman. Maybe never."

"You've been hanging out in the wrong places," the chef suggested.

"You're probably right." Gabriel closed his menu. "I'll have the gumbo. And a beer."

"The gumbo's spicy," Bastien said. "Some people might go with a heavy ale, but my recommendation would be your brother's Good Vibrations. The light hoppy flavor will balance out the spice."

"Sounds good to me."

"Any appetizers? One of the Harpers brought in some fresh oysters today, so we're serving local fresh shucked oysters grilled over an open flame with a cayenne garlic butter. Served with a French bread Desiree made this morning. Or, we can serve them raw on the half shell."

When Gabriel gave her a "your choice" look, Chelsea said, "I think I'll have them the way they're meant to be eaten."

"*Bien*. Raw it is." Bastien took the menus. "The server will be out with your drinks and oysters right away."

"You're adventurous," Gabriel said as the chef stopped at various inside tables to greet diners on his way to the bar.

"I grew up here, the same as you did. I know people who can tell what beds oysters have been pulled from by the taste of the brine, but my palate isn't that refined."

"The meal choices in town have definitely improved since I left," Gabriel said. "Not that the diner wasn't good, especially for breakfast, but it's still—"

"A diner. I waited tables there in high school and summers from college. Although you're right about the improvement in choices, the diner's still the best place in town for breakfast, unless you want a doughnut with your coffee. But you're not going to get all that many fishermen stopping by Cops and Coffee for a latte before going out on their boats early in the morning. It's also the only place around still serving an old-fashioned club sandwich on toasted Wonder Bread."

"Gotta stay with tradition," he said as their drinks arrived, along with a plate of oysters on a bed of rock salt, a quartered lemon, cocktail sauce the server warned them came with a kick of Cajun Tabasco and small loaf of herbed bread with butter formed into the shape of a Louisiana crawfish.

After they were alone again, Gabriel lifted his bottle of beer. "To our partnership."

"It's your money," she said, even as she lifted her glass.

"True. But it can't do anything without a team to administer it. Which is where you're going to come in, if we can come up with a workable plan. That, to my mind, makes us equal partners."

As the rim of her wineglass touched the neck of his beer bottle, it occurred to Chelsea that whatever happened with her possibly potential fling, she and Gabriel wouldn't entirely be going their separate ways at the end of the summer. Not with the children's library book club between them. But that would only be business.

"So tell me more about Wall Street," she said. "Is it as cutthroat in real life as it is in fiction?"

"You want the truth?"

"Of course."

"Honestly, a lot of days it's worse. Thus the finance bars that, unfortunately, are what help keep the white male patriarchy so strong. The way you get into the group isn't necessarily due to intellect or merit, but whether or not people want to hang out with you."

"It seems that would make it an even more difficult world for women."

She took the time to tip an oyster into her mouth, enjoying the bite of brine. Many years ago, her father had taken her out to an oyster farm and taught her that the proper way to eat oysters fresh from the water was to eat the first one naked, so you could get the full taste before adding anything to it. After she'd placed the shell upside down on the rock salt, and caught the intense way Gabriel was looking at her, she wondered if choosing raw oysters had been a tactical mistake.

"Yeah," he said after a long pause. "There aren't many women at Harborstone, or any of the others firms I know. I remember reading a study a few years ago that put them at eleven percent in leadership positions."

"So it's a boy's club."

As he slurped down an oyster, it occurred to Chelsea that if you weren't accustomed to raw oysters, they might not be the best first date appetizer. Eating them wasn't at all dainty. It was, in a way, primal.

"Pretty much," he said once he'd swallowed.

"I wonder if that gender gap isn't because women aren't getting hired, but because they're not given the opportunity or encouragement to succeed once they get there."

"Believe it or not, I've thought about that ever since the study came out, and suspect it's mostly because, due to the lack of women ahead of them, they're less likely to find a mentor when they're starting out. Like I had."

"What's he like?" she asked. "Your mentor?"

"He died recently."

"I'm sorry." Chelsea wondered if that death had something to do with Gabriel's out-of-the-blue return home, but decided against prying.

"Yeah. I was, too. Carter Kensington was brash, bold, taught me the ropes and promoted me at board meetings, which resulted in my being given larger and wealthier accounts to handle in the early days, while I was out scrambling to bring in my own. That's what's probably needed."

"It sounds like it. Leaning in is all well and good but it seems as if it would be difficult to do without strong mentoring. Mrs. Henderson not only encouraged me to become a librarian when I was young, she was also a wonderful mentor while I was in school and especially when I came back and took over from her." She squeezed a lemon quarter over her second oyster and added a dab of the red sauce and tipped it back. "Wow, the server wasn't kidding. This sauce will definitely clear my sinuses." She took a long drink of ice water, which didn't do all that much to put out the flames.

"It's hot, but good," he said, having taken another one as well. His hands were large, with roughened calluses that he undoubtedly didn't get from pushing paper in New York, but from here, working with dangerous-looking tools. And wood. Although it probably wasn't safe to go there, she couldn't help remembering how his fingers had felt trailing down her rib cage and over her stomach and beyond.

"True," she agreed, shaking off the erotic memory. "I've always found regular cocktail sauce boring… Why couldn't you be one?"

"One what?"

"A mentor."

She could tell that thought hadn't occurred to him. Which undoubtedly had a great deal to do with the dismal lack of women in leadership roles in financial firms. Which was counterintuitive, since a good number of the patrons who came into the library looking for help balancing their overdrawn checkbooks or with managing their credit card debt were men. She couldn't remember ever having a man show up for the January workshops on how to make and maintain a yearly family budget.

"I don't know," he admitted. As he considered her suggestion, he began stroking the neck of the bottle in a way that had her transfixed. "It's a big firm, but off the top of my head, I can't think of any woman other than receptionists who work on my floor."

"Sounds a bit as if you all are stuck in the *Working Girl* movie mentality," she murmured. "Isn't that a suggestion that finance has a strong institutional culture supportive of conformity?"

"I can't argue that. But, playing devil's advocate, aren't the majority of librarians women?"

"White women," she allowed. "And you've no idea how often that disparity is discussed and argued about especially because when there are men, they're often promoted over better qualified women, proving that sexism is alive and well. Diversity is admittedly a problem as it is in so many occupations. But I've found the most successful librarians are innovative and forward thinking."

"Like your reading adventurers."

She felt the color rush into her cheeks at the compliment and bet his sophisticated, Armani-wearing New York women never blushed. Giving herself time to collect her thoughts, she polished off her third and last oyster. "I suppose that qualifies. But my point was that, from what you've told me, Wall Street requires you to give up anything in your personality that makes you unique. So you can stay on a direct track of focusing solely on making money."

Before he could answer, the busser arrived to take away the oyster plate and was immediately followed by the server, bringing their meal.

"I have a suggestion," he said after declaring the

gumbo the best he'd ever tasted. Better than any he'd had in New York or New Orleans.

She took a bite of the étouffée and nearly moaned, but held back because she didn't want to sound like a minor league version of Meg Ryan's fake restaurant orgasm. "Okay, what is it?"

"Just talking about The Street isn't helping with my Zen. Since I'm in a beautiful place, with a beautiful woman, eating food that tastes as good as it looks, what would you say to tabling the business planning for a day or two, since it's not something we can put together all that fast anyway."

All day she'd told herself that this was merely a working dinner. But now that she was here, sitting across the small table from him, close enough that if she just stretched her leg a bit, it would be touching his, it was beginning to feel more and more like a date.

And Chelsea was okay with that. Mostly.

"How about you tell me the basics for your idea and that way I can get a handle on what you're suggesting. The library's staff is already limited."

"That's why you're going to need a new team. I'd suggest getting the local business owners, city council, whatever county government officials would be suited for the work, and other nonprofits on board. You'll need to begin with a chairperson—someone to coordinate the effort. I know your initial impulse is this is something you should do. But you need to think of the project like a business. Your key job is to keep an eye on the big picture, while the other people are answerable to that chairperson. Or you'll have everyone taking up all your time with unnecessary stuff that can be dealt with lower down the chain."

She liked that he hadn't insisted on entirely changing the topic. Wizards of Wall Street were undoubtedly accustomed to getting their way. "Okay. You're right. I'm a control freak. But…you know your Zen project?"

"Sure."

"That's how I am about surrendering control. I'm a work in progress."

He took hold of her hand, turning it over, and traced an infinity design on her palm. The blisters had, fortunately, turned out to be only hot spots and there were times today when she'd forgotten all about them. Until now, when an entirely different type of heat seeped into her blood. "You did a pretty good impression of surrendering control the other night," he reminded her.

His low, husky voice, along with the memory, had the rest of her warming. After dithering for days, Chelsea decided that she had two choices. She could spend the rest of her life looking back with regrets and wondering "what if."

Or she could take a leap into the unknown, only to find out that what she was feeling was merely due to that initial jolt of attraction. How could that be a bad thing since there'd be no need for regrets, because she'd have more fantastic sex in the meantime?

Looking at it that way, there was only one choice: leap.

"It wasn't an imitation. And perhaps next time we could see how well *you* can pull it off," she suggested from beneath her lashes in the same way Hepburn had outrageously flirted with Grant. Something she'd never, ever done before.

And from the way his eyes had darkened with emotion, she must have pulled it off. "You're on," he said.

When she was tempted to leap across the table, she dragged her unruly mind back to the book club proposal. "What's next?" she asked, pulling out her planner and turning to a blank page in the back.

"Here." Obviously stifling a sigh, he reached down beside his chair, retrieved a portfolio that some alligator had given its life for and pulled a piece of paper from it. "I printed out a copy."

"That's very efficient." Of course it was. It's what he did for a living.

"Thank you. As you can see, I'm suggesting a fund-raiser to identify and collect local funds."

"I know a county auditor. He'd probably be perfect. He's very efficient, although a bit stodgy."

"All the better. He's less likely to run off to Rio with the funds."

She laughed, remembering her seemingly centuries-long date. "No, Duane would definitely not do anything that involves foreign food." Some men were meat and potatoes guys, the meat usually meaning a steak. Or ribs. Duane had been a meat loaf and mashed potatoes man.

"Next, a person to plan where and how to enroll the children, oversee the registration, create and distribute brochures and create marketing plans."

"I'm close friends with the college's marketing director who volunteers at the library. She'd do it in a heartbeat."

"Terrific. Then you'll need someone to enter the new registrations, accept pending online registrations and update addresses."

"That person shouldn't be hard to find. Maybe a student from the college. What else?"

"Community outreach to collaborate with other local organizations and coalitions."

"Again, Lily from the college would be great. And perhaps your father would help us reach out, being that he's mayor."

"He and Mom would both be in. And finally, you'll

need family engagement, which means coming up with ways to encourage parents to better engage their children through books and to read more often."

"We're already doing that at the library. Mrs. Henderson did it for years before I took over. I'm firmly convinced that's why Salish County always ranks so high on state reading comprehension tests."

"Sounds as if you're off to a good start."

"You make it sound, well, not easy, exactly, but doable."

In the boat shop, she'd seen a craftsman who cared about his work. While he'd been making her dinner, bringing her chicken soup and watching that old movie with her, she could see him as Sarah Mannion's son. But now she was looking into the steely eyes of a Wall Street Master of the Universe.

"Aiden told me that one of the mottos Marines live by is that failure to plan is a plan for failure," he said. "But failure is not an option. So, yeah, we're going to make it work and it's going to be great."

If anyone else had told her that, she'd have reason to doubt him. But with all Gabriel's success, she doubted that he was familiar with failure.

"Well, that's encouraging and you've given me a lot to think about." But for now, sitting here with a gorgeous man on a patio that reminded her of a secret garden, she was going to put the topic aside, as he'd suggested, relax and enjoy the evening.

She was surprised once again at how easily the conversation flowed between them. She told him of the other excursions the reading adventurers would be taking around town and he told her more about the faering, and how Jarle had advised him to name the boat *Freya*.

"The daughter of the god Njord, and the goddess of love and beauty," she said.

He lifted the bottle in a salute. "It's true. You librarians really are the original Google."

"I can't remember if I told you—" her mind had been fogged by pheromones during her visit to the boat shop "—but we're studying the Scandinavians during the adventure. So I bought a book on Norse myths. Freya's beautiful home was called 'field of men' because, although her husband had gone missing, it was always thronged with merry men."

"Sounds like she was the party girl of goddesses."

"She supposedly was always given her choice of captured warriors, with the remainder being sent to Odin. She also reportedly slept with all gods and elves, which I've no intention of sharing with the kids. But she did miss her husband. Every night she'd weep herself to sleep, but she was so lovely, her tears were pure gold."

"Jarle also mentioned that she's the goddess of war and death."

"I read that in a few papers about her, but others don't mention it. Which doesn't really matter since I'd leave that part out, too, because war and death aren't exactly child summertime fun topics."

"Perhaps men warred over Freya. And thus the deaths." He told her Jarle's claim about Norse blood being passionate.

"I normally think of them as having a cooler blood, but the bloody myths and Vikings disprove the stereotype, so wars for love could be a possibility. If you believe classical epics, the Trojan War was waged over Helen of Sparta's abduction to Troy." She took another sip of wine and tried not to imagine Gabriel abducting her. Right now.

"Yet, it's difficult to take them as historic fact since

so many of the main characters in the tales are direct off-spring of gods. Helen, after all, was fathered by Zeus, who disguised himself as a swan and raped her mother. While long sieges were historically recorded in those days, it's hard to buy the idea of wars between various competing gods...

"But I digress. Yet again. So, getting back on topic, are you going to name the faering that?"

"Your side trips through conversations are one of my favorite things about you," he surprised her by saying. Before she could come up with a response, he continued as if he hadn't complimented her for the very same thing she'd been beating herself up over. "I haven't decided yet. I'm not keeping her, so I'll probably leave it up to the new owner."

"That's sort of sad that you're going to spend the entire summer building a boat you're never going to sail."

"I'll give her a test run. Then donate her to Welcome Home to auction off as a fund-raiser."

"That's very generous." And less surprising than it would have been only a few days ago. They'd just finished their meal when the server came to clear the plates and ask if they'd like dessert. Before either could answer, Chelsea's phone chimed. She frowned as she noticed the caller ID. A call from the police was never a good thing.

"Aiden?"

"Yeah," Aiden said. "About those girls you asked me to look into, I thought you'd like to know that the fire department was called to the address."

"Oh, no! Do you have any more information than that?"

"Not yet. The truck just rolled. I'm headed there now and will keep you updated."

"I'm on my way." She hit End, stood up and grabbed

her purse. "I'm sorry, Gabriel, but I have to go. There are these girls…Hannah and Hailey, they're foster children who stay at the library every afternoon, and I bring them treats. Which you so don't need to know." In her panic she was rambling again. "A neighbor told me they were at the coast, but Aiden just called to tell me that the fire department is on the way to the house."

"I'll drive you."

"That's not necessary."

"You're white as a sheet and you're shaking. And you've had wine."

"You had a beer."

"Yeah. But I outweigh you by probably sixty pounds. And I'm not the one with the shaky hands." He pulled his wallet from his jeans pocket, took out some bills and tossed them on the table. "Sorry," he told the server. "But an emergency has come up. Please tell Bastien that the meal was excellent. One of my best ever."

"I'll tell him." The server, a woman who looked to be in her forties, sent Chelsea a look filled with sympathy. "Good luck, hon."

While she appreciated the sentiment, Chelsea didn't answer because she was already racing through the restaurant.

CHAPTER SIXTEEN

"IT'LL BE OKAY," Gabe told her as they drove to the address Chelsea had given him.

"You have no way of knowing that." She was squeezing her hands together so tightly her knuckles were white.

"No," he admitted. "I don't. But let's try to stay positive until we have some more facts."

"People die." Her voice was even shakier than her hands. "Innocent *children* die."

Damn. While anyone would be concerned, he thought of what she'd told him about her sister and realized that for her, little girls dying was not a hypothetical.

"I went by the house after work." She was leaning forward toward the dash, as if she could get them there faster. "I was concerned, because they *alwa*ys come to the library after school, and normally school should be out for the summer. But it's a snow makeup day. Damn! Three lights in this stupid town and this one has to turn red."

"I'd run it," he said. "But there's all the traffic leaving the theater parking lot." *The Secret Life of Pets* appeared to have filled the late 1920s art deco building. Which, Gabe figured, made sense since it sounded like a movie you could take kids to. Not that he knew a damn thing about kids, but he remembered his parents being pretty choosy which movies he and his brothers and sister could see.

"I should have asked more questions when the neighbor told me that they were probably at the coast. Dammit, I should have called social services."

He put his right hand on her leg. Not to seduce, but to calm. "The office would have been closed."

"Don't you dare be reasonable right now," she snapped. But did not, he noted as the light finally turned green again, knock his hand away. "I could have called Aiden. He'd have a way of contacting someone. Or I could have knocked on more doors. I should have done *something*!"

"Sounds as if you've already done more than most people would."

"But still not enough." She drew in a deep breath. Let it out. Drew in another. Let it out. Gabe recognized it as one of the anxiety-easing exercises listed in the pamphlet he'd received when he was discharged from the hospital. "Thank you," she said quietly. She may not have made it all the way to Zen, but she sounded calmer. "For driving me. For being with me."

"Happy to," he said. Then inwardly cringed. "Not actually happy, but—"

"I know what you mean," she said as she spotted a red pumper truck parked in front of a small house, its engine running. Aiden's black Honeymoon Harbor police SUV was parked behind it.

"Wait until I stop to jump out." He grabbed her arm when she went to open the door. "It won't help anyone if you fall and break your leg."

Not wanting to get in the way of the firefighters, who were coming out of the house dressed in full turnout gear, but with their helmets off, he pulled over to the other side of the road and parked while she was taking off those sexy heels she'd sashayed into the restaurant on. "Okay."

As she ran barefoot across the street, Aiden, who was talking to one of the firemen, spotted her and headed toward them. Although he raised a brow and gave Gabriel a questioning look, he didn't ask what the two of them were doing together. And why she was all fancied up, but without shoes. "They're okay," he assured Chelsea.

"Where are they?" She grabbed his arm. "I need to see them."

"Flynn Farraday—he's the fire chief who's new since you left," he told Gabe, "says they're next door. It wasn't anything major. The house is old and the microwave shorted out and filled the place with smoke. The neighbor was walking her dog, heard the detector blaring and called 911 at the same time that the older girl did. She took the kids home with her."

"I need to see them," she repeated.

"It's fine with me."

"What about the foster mother? Is she there, too?"

"No sign of her. Flynn said the kids were on their own. The older one—"

"Hannah."

"Okay. Anyway, she was nuking some S'mores when the thing shorted, smoke came billowing out and set off the alarm. She got her little sister out right away."

"Of course she did," Chelsea said. "She's a big sister."

It would have been impossible to have missed her having to push that second part past the huge lump that appeared to have settled in her throat. Gabe wanted to assure her that she hadn't been responsible for keeping her sister alive, but this was neither the time nor the place. So, instead, he merely put his hand on her lower back. "Let's go check on them."

Just as he didn't know anything about kids, Gabe had no way of guessing how old the two girls were. One was obviously older than the other. Her lips were pulled into a tight line, while the little one was holding a stuffed dragon tight against her bony chest.

"Hi, Ms. Prescott," she said, seeming none the worse

for the experience. "That's a really pretty dress. Like what a princess would wear. Pink is my favorite color." She took a breath. "We almost had a fire. The alarm went off and there was a lot of smoke, and Hannah made me go outside. Then Mrs. Lawler brought us over here. And gave us chocolate chip cookies."

"I baked today," the elderly woman, who appeared to be about Gabe's grandmother's age, said. "There's a funeral at St. Peter's tomorrow and Lillian Henderson and I bake for the lunches. I always put an extra amount of love into them to hopefully make someone's very sad day a little bit better."

"I could taste the love!" dragon girl said.

Her older sister had not yet said a word. Just stood there, one hand protectively on her sister's shoulder.

"Are you both all right?" When Chelsea bent and gave the little one a hug, thin arms went around her neck and clung.

"We're okay. I didn't do anything," the older one said defensively. "I just turned on the microwave the way I do every night."

He could tell that captured Chelsea's attention. She glanced up at Aiden, who gave a slight shake of his head.

"An electrical wire shorted out," Aiden said. "It would have happened to anyone."

Gabe had a feeling it was the first time the girl—Hannah, he remembered—noticed Aiden, because the color suddenly drained from her face. As he watched, she straightened her shoulders and folded her arms. Because of his uniform?

"What happens now?" she asked. Her voice sounded both angry and resigned at the same time. This obviously wasn't her first rodeo.

"We find your foster mom," Aiden said.

"She's on the coast. She got a gig last weekend at a casino dealing blackjack that pays more than both her jobs here."

"This is Tuesday." Chelsea's voice was calm, but tight. He knew Hannah had heard it too, when her arms tightened.

"She was offered a few more days. Then some more, so she decided we should take the bus back here."

"It took forever," the younger one said.

"We had to keep stopping for all these other people to get off," Hannah said.

"That's why it was so slow. Mrs. Hayes said the tips are awesome," Hailey piped up. "Maybe we'll go out for ice cream when she gets back."

"Who's taking care of you in the meantime?" Chelsea asked. Gabe knew she was keeping a tight rein on her emotions when her voice turned to an ice he'd never heard. Not even when he'd been purposefully rude to her in the shop to make her go away.

Hannah shrugged. "Me." More squaring of shoulders as if she were mentally preparing for a cage match. "I've done it before. It's no big deal."

"You're a wonderful big sister," Mrs. Lawler said. "And Hailey's fortunate to have you taking care of her, but as happy as I am to have you visit, you girls really do need an adult. One a little younger than me. Not that I feel that old, but I suspect I don't quite make the qualification age cut."

Hannah shot Aiden a hard look far older than her young years, whatever they were. "Hailey," she said. "Maybe you and Mrs. Lawler could go get another cookie and a glass of milk."

"What a great idea," the older woman said, immediately catching on. Gabe figured at one time she'd had kids and could pick up on the signs. She took hold of the younger girl's hand. "Do you think you can help me plate them to take to the church tomorrow? I can't decide which would be the best one to put them on."

"Okay. Do you have a plate with dragons? That would be the best."

"I'm afraid I don't. But I do have several decorative ones with flowers. I even have one from my wedding." Her cloudy eyes turned a little dreamy. "Truth be told," she leaned down and said, as if sharing a secret with the child, "fifty years ago, my mama and daddy said we'd never last.

"But we showed them. I only lost my husband in January of this year. My favorite plate has a painting of Lake Crescent Lodge on it, with pink roses around the rim. My Joe bought it for me when we were honeymooning at the lake and my bouquet had been made of pink roses. Back in those days, Blue House Farm wasn't growing flowers so they had to be brought in all the way from Portland. Do you know it's called the Rose City?"

"No."

"Well, now you do."

"I also didn't know people got to eat cookies at funerals. I don't remember Mommy and Daddy's funeral," she said as they left the room. "Hannah told me it was really nice, though. With lots of flowers. I like flowers. Hollyhocks are my favorite, because if you turn them upside down, you can pretend they're princesses wearing colored gowns and make them dance."

Once the swinging door to the kitchen had closed, Aiden addressed Hannah's question. "I have a night number for social services. I'll call and they'll send someone to get you settled."

"We're not going anywhere if they try to separate us."

"I'm not sure that's your choice at the moment," he said gently.

"Yes." A sharp young chin shot up. "It is. Because if anyone tries to put me in a different home than my sister, I'll run away and come get her. Then we'll both run away to someplace where I can take care of her without anyone moving us around all the time."

Chelsea dragged her hands down her face. When she took them away, Gabe could see the tears shining in her eyes.

"Honey, as much as I understand your feelings, that truly is a very dangerous idea and I know your first priority is keeping Hailey safe."

"Yeah. I sure did that tonight," she said.

"Not your fault," all the adults in the room responded.

"So," Chelsea suggested, "how about them staying with me?"

"You?" Aiden and Hannah asked in unison. Having come to know Chelsea Prescott, Gabe wasn't surprised at all.

"I'm employed. I have room in my apartment. The girls could take my bed and I could sleep on the couch. I've lived here forever and everyone knows me. Aiden, surely if you, and your mom, and perhaps Mrs. Henderson, could vouch for me, I'd be given some sort of temporary foster designation. Because of this being an emergency situation."

"One of my deputies tried to rent an apartment in your building," Aiden said. "And was told kids aren't welcome."

"So Mrs. Moore told me when I rented the apartment. But the Fair Housing Act makes that illegal," Chelsea pointed out. "He could have fought it."

"That's what I told him. But he decided he didn't want

the hassle. It worked out. He's now in one of those re-stored Craftsman bungalows in the former mill housing neighborhood. In fact, he lives two doors down from Jolene and me. His wife and Jolene are already plotting to have our daughter, if we have a girl, and their son get married someday."

"I live by my planner," Chelsea said, another thing that didn't surprise Gabe much. "But planning that far in advance seems a bit excessive... Is Jolene pregnant?"

"Not yet. But it's not for the lack of trying." He im-mediately looked up at the ceiling. Then rubbed his hand across his brow. "Sorry, TMI."

"Don't worry. I know all about sex," Hannah said. "One place I was in, one of the foster parents' sons tried to have sex with me when I was feeding the horses in the barn."

"Oh, no!" Chelsea gasped, looking stricken. She was a grown woman. Undoubtedly she'd heard stories, same as he had. But having one hit so close to home was ad-mittedly a shocker.

"What did you do?" Aiden asked casually in what Gabe figured had been his good cop voice when he'd been working LA's mean streets.

"I put a pitchfork against his chest and told him that if he ever tried that again, with me or my sister, I'd run him clear through with it. And if that didn't kill him, then I'd call the cops. Though I'd rather have had him die slowly. And painfully."

"I can understand the impulse," Aiden said. "But if it ever happens again, call 911 first. Because you wouldn't be of any help to Hailey if you ended up in juvie."

"Yeah. Like cops are going to help us. We're the in-visible forgotten kids in the system. Some families are nice, like Mrs. Hayes, though she's not real dependable.

But that's because she's been having a rough time making ends meet after her husband ran off with a woman he met in rehab."

It occurred to Gabe that the girl knew more about the dark side of life than any child should. He tried to think back on Brianna around this age and vaguely remembered slumber parties and boy band crushes.

"Sometimes, like on that farm, we're taken in to be free workers. It's a better deal for the foster parents because the state pays them for us to be there. We kids share stories. And lots of times, even if a kid does complain to the social worker, they believe the family. Because it's easier, and less paperwork on everyone's part." She shot Aiden another look. "Including the police."

It was *his* turn to fold *his* arms. And return her hard look with one of his own. "Not my department."

The stare down lasted probably thirty seconds. Then Gabe could tell when Aiden had won her over. Or maybe she was just understandably worn out from trying to be the adult. The defiance left her expression, her tight arms unfolded, and the ready-to-fight stance relaxed a bit.

"Maybe you're different," she allowed. "So, hey, if they don't approve Ms. Prescott, maybe you can let us bunk on the cots in your jail cells." It was snark. And a challenge.

One the former marine and undercover big city cop ignored. "And have you taking up bunks I might need for actual criminals? Sorry, kid, that doesn't really work for me."

"You don't talk like a cop."

"Sometimes I don't feel like one, either," Aiden said. "It's a new gig, so I'm still finding my own groove, so to speak."

"They could stay at the cabin," Gabe heard himself

saying. "I'm not doing anything except building a boat. Since you're my brother and have known me all my life, you could vouch for me."

Aiden's brow furrowed. Gabe suspected Honeymoon Harbor's former bad boy had never imagined being responsible for the entire town and everyone in it. He wondered how many times his brother had had to make a possibly life-changing decision. "I'm not sure that'll fly with social services," he said. "Two young girls staying alone with a guy. Even one I could and would vouch for."

"I could stay with them," Chelsea said. "It's a big house. I imagine there are a lot of bedrooms, right?" she asked Gabe, her innocent expression not revealing that she'd already been there.

No point in letting people think they were becoming a thing, Gabe silently agreed. Two adults who might have hot sex on the kitchen counter while impressionable kids were sleeping in the house might have trouble making the approval list. Though, he considered, once everything settled down, that counter idea had potential.

"There are two separate wings," he said. "It was designed for a kids' wing and an adult wing."

Aiden rubbed his jaw. "I'll call and have someone come over here and we'll see what we can work out."

"We're not going to be separated," Hannah insisted yet again.

"As one of five kids, I get that," Aiden assured her. "Let's wait to burn that bridge until we've crossed it." He went outside to make the call. Less than three minutes later, he returned to the house.

"Your social worker's on her way. Mrs. Douglas was a substitute teacher at the high school for about twenty years. Which is a good thing, since that means she knows Gabe's and my mom really well."

"Why?" Hannah asked.

"Because my mom's been principal for nearly forever."

"I'll bet that sucked for you."

Despite the seriousness of the situation, Aiden laughed. "You'd be right."

It didn't take long for a blue SUV to pull up outside the house. Having declared the building safe, Flynn and the other firefighters had taken off. Gabe recognized the woman with the short gray bob immediately. Mrs. Douglas hadn't been one of those subs who'd let kids get away with murder, or hand out passes for supposed restroom breaks so they could wander the hallways the rest of the period. She'd been tough. But fair.

"Hello, Hannah," she greeted the older girl. "I hear we have a slight situation."

"The microwave burned up when I was making S'mores for Hailey."

"So Chief Mannion told me. He also said that you handled it very well, getting your sister out of the house right away."

"Duh. Knowing to get out of a smoke-filled kitchen doesn't take that many brains."

Gabe was getting a handle on the kid. The more frightened she became, the tougher she got. In a fight-or-flight situation, she'd always fight.

"Well, I'm still glad you did. Now we need to find emergency placement until we work out a long-term plan." Apparently knowing Hannah pretty well herself, she lifted her hand to forestall the argument every adult in the room knew would be coming. "I attempted to reach Mrs. Hayes, but apparently her phone is either off or she isn't answering. And, before it comes up, I do realize that you don't want to be separated from your sister."

"Mrs. Hayes got a new job working at the casino on the

coast. And I *refuse* to be separated," Hannah corrected. Gabe exchanged a glance with Chelsea that told him that once again they were thinking the same thing. That not only was Hannah intensely loyal to her younger sister, it was a shame that she needed to be the caretaker at such a young age.

"Well, the bad news is that we don't have any licensed homes that can take in two children at the moment. However," she pressed on before the girl could state her refusal yet again. "Fortunately, having foreseen the problem of limited foster homes, the state allows, in the event of a sudden unavailability of a child's primary caretaker, that emergency placement in the home of a private individual can be granted. Which includes neighbors, friends, relatives or an individual the child or, in this case, children feel comfortable with."

"Ms. Prescott's okay," Hannah said. "She brings us treats in the library, makes sure Hailey drinks her milk and drives us home in the afternoon."

"I can vouch for her," Aiden said. "She's good friends with Brianna, and Lillian Henderson would definitely give her a recommendation."

"Well, then, it seems we have our solution. I can temporarily place you with Ms. Prescott until further arrangements can be made." She turned toward Chelsea, appearing unfazed by her lack of shoes. "There'll be both a state and national criminal check, and you'll need to be fingerprinted within fifteen days or the placement will be rescinded."

"I was fingerprinted when the town council hired me to take over Mrs. Henderson's job as librarian," Chelsea said. "Also when I received my TSA Precheck. But I have no problem with having it done again."

"Fine. They'll be in the national database, so there's no need to repeat the process."

"As for placement, that gets a little complicated," Chelsea admitted.

She went on to explain about her landlady's no-children policy, to which Mrs. Douglas in turn informed her such a policy wasn't legal. To which Hannah jumped in and said that she and her sister didn't want to be anywhere they weren't wanted.

Which was when Gabe repeated what he'd said earlier about the house and the separate wings, and that he and Chelsea Prescott were merely friends who were working together on a book program for the county's children and a reading adventurer visit to his boat shop. And he'd also stated that he'd been fingerprinted for both his TSA Nexus and securities license.

As Mrs. Douglas appeared to be considering that latest twist, Aiden assured her that he, as well as both his parents, would of course back up Gabe's sterling reputation. Which, thankfully, the former substitute teacher remembered.

"You're only here for the summer, correct?" she asked him.

"Yes, Mrs. Douglas," he responded in his most polite tone.

"We're both adults now," she said. "You can call me Adele."

Gabe considered that. "I'm sorry. But I think you'll always be Mrs. Douglas to me."

She sighed and half rolled her eyes. "You've no idea how often I've heard that. Sometimes I think that when I retired from teaching I should have moved to Port Townsend. Or Gig Harbor. Anyplace where kids

I'd taught didn't live. At any rate, I'm sure we'll find a more permanent solution before Labor Day."

She turned back to Chelsea. "My granddaughter is one of your reading adventurers. Meggie Lancaster."

"I know. She's told me she's most looking forward to seeing the Whistler mural at Herons Landing."

"She wants…no, make that *intends*, to be an artist when she grows up. She decided that life goal when she went to SAM on a school field trip in kindergarten. She loves the Family Fun Workshops. I swear, I believe if her family and the museum would let her, she'd pack up her sleeping bag and move in."

The Seattle Arts Museum was the premier center for the arts in the Pacific Northwest. Gabe's mother had often dragged them up there a few times a year for various exhibits. All he remembered was being captivated in the eighth grade by a huge, fifty-four by forty-one inch painting of numbers *0* to *9* all superimposed over each other in different-colored bold sweeping brushstrokes. His parents had bought him a print of the Jasper Johns painting for Christmas. A print he'd carried with him to UW and Columbia and was now hanging on the wall of his Manhattan apartment.

That little exchange of chitchat over with, Mrs. Douglas got down to business again. "Are you and Gabriel dating? I only ask because I need to know the dynamics in the house."

Gabe guessed she wouldn't be asking that if he were Chelsea's husband.

"As Gabriel said, we're working on those projects together," Chelsea hedged. It wasn't technically a lie. They *had* discussed business.

"There's a housekeeper's cottage on the property,"

Gabe said. "Since I don't have a housekeeper, I can stay there while the girls are in the house."

"That sounds appropriate enough. Well, then." She glanced down at her watch. "Since it's not getting any earlier, even though the girls don't have school tomorrow, they've obviously had an eventful day. So, I'll get the paperwork and one of the extra booster seats I keep in the trunk, just in case of emergencies like this, and we'll make things official so they can get to bed."

She turned toward Gabriel after the paperwork was signed, sealed and back in the woman's portfolio. "I forgot to mention, we're going to need a home visit to assess the situation." She opened the calendar on her phone. "I need to complete it within thirty days."

"We'll make any date work," Chelsea assured her.

"No problem," Gabe said at the same time, wondering what the hell he was supposed to do with two young girls in the house for possibly a month. Brianna's tea parties had been a very long time ago. First things first. They needed to get the girls to the cabin and into bed.

They all watched her drive away.

"Hannah," Chelsea said, "why don't we go over to the house and pack up some things for you and Hailey?"

Hell. Gabe hadn't even thought of that. He knew how to chart an advance/decline line, could spot when a market maker was painting the tape, and had been able to define the Dow Theory in detail by his freshman year of high school. But he knew squat about kids.

"Don't worry," Aiden assured him as Chelsea and Hannah crossed the yard and into the house that had to be smelling of smoke. "It can't be that hard."

"Says the guy who has no kids."

"Not yet. But Jolene quit taking her pills last month, so who knows? And look at it this way. That foster mom set a really low bar when she took off and left those girls to fend for themselves. It'd be hard for you to have a bigger fail."

"Thanks for the vote of confidence," Gabe muttered, flashing him a one-finger salute.

"Anytime." In the flash of Aiden's grin, Gabe saw a remaining spark of bad boy still residing in the responsible adult police chief.

Once Hannah and Chelsea had returned with two large heavy-duty trash bags (*Seriously?* Gabe thought), and Hailey had handed them a Tupperware container of chocolate chip cookies, they decided that Gabe would drive Chelsea and the girls to the restaurant, where she could pick up her car. Then he'd go to Eagles Watch while they stopped at her apartment to pack a suitcase for herself, then they'd meet him at the cabin.

Watching Chelsea buckle the little one onto the booster seat, and seeing how the older girl appeared to be letting her guard down more around her had Gabe once again picturing that damn picket fence. *You should've kept your distance,* the voice in his head said. And didn't he already know that? But it was too late now because he'd opened his big mouth and invited the three of them to stay at the cabin.

At least, by moving to the housekeeper's cabin, it'd be a helluva lot easier to take that step back she'd asked for.

Good luck with that, pal, the damn annoying voice mocked.

CHAPTER SEVENTEEN

"Wow," HAILEY SAID as she pulled up in front of the large Victorian house. "Is this where you live? You must be rich."

Despite the seriousness of tonight's situation, Chelsea laughed at that. "Librarians don't make enough to afford all this. I rent one very small apartment in the house."

"If she owned the whole thing we wouldn't be having to stay with Mr. Mannion," Hannah pointed out, a bit more sharply than the comforting way Chelsea had always heard her talk to her sister, revealing that she was under even more stress than usual. As bad as things had gotten in her family once Annabelle had gotten sick, Chelsea had never had to carry all her possessions in a heavy-duty Glad bag. She could, however, relate, in a way. Back when she'd essentially been taking care of both herself and her mother, if anyone had tried to put her in a foster home, she might well have taken the ferry to Seattle and lived on the street with the runaway kids she'd seen in a television documentary.

Not wanting to leave the children alone in the car, even for the few minutes it would take her to toss a few necessities into an overnight bag, she brought them both inside, well aware of how exhausted they must be by now. As bad as things admittedly were, at least they'd soon be settled into that palatial mansion everyone, in the understated way of Pacific Northwesterners, referred to as a cabin.

She'd just entered when Mrs. Moore popped out of her door. The very same woman who Gabe had made giggle like a young girl, swept a stern, hard look over these girls.

"Have you forgotten that I have a strict 'no children' rule, Chelsea?" she asked.

"They're only going to be with me a few minutes," she said. "I'm packing a bag, then we'll be on our way."

"Well, then." She huffed out a breath. Then wagged her finger. "Just see that it doesn't turn into an overnight visit."

"That's against the law," Hannah said.

"What did you just say?" Her landlady's mouth gaped open like a hooked steelhead trout and her eyes turned googly in obvious surprise at being talked back to by one of those children she apparently didn't like. At all.

"I said," Hannah repeated, biting off each word, "that the Fair Housing Act prohibits a landlord from refusing to rent to people with children. If Police Chief Mannion knew what you were doing he could arrest you and have a judge fine you a lot of money. Maybe even put you in jail."

"Well," Mrs. Moore huffed, her face turning as red as a boiled Dungeness crab. "I never." This time her stern look was directed at Chelsea. "You need to speak to that child about her smart mouth."

"She was merely stating a fact," Chelsea said. "But it's a moot point because, as I told you, we're only going to be here for a few minutes." Wanting to end this confrontation before it escalated, Chelsea ushered the girls upstairs and into her apartment and, although she had an impulse to slam the door, firmly closed it behind her.

"She's a real bitch," Hannah said.

"A bitch," Hailey echoed loyally, though Chelsea suspected she had no idea what she was talking about. That she adored her older sister was obvious. The fact that the feeling was returned was, as well.

"She was unpleasant," Chelsea allowed. "But that's an impolite word I'd rather none of us use."

"Okay," Hannah muttered. But Chelsea knew she was still thinking it. She wasn't alone.

It didn't take long to throw a few clothes and toiletries into a bag and they were back in the car in under ten minutes. As they passed by her landlady's apartment, Chelsea noticed that the door was opened a crack in order to make sure they left, and decided that once this situation was settled, as much as she loved her cozy little apartment in the beautiful landmark building, she was definitely going to move.

Unsurprisingly, Hailey fell asleep in the booster seat Chelsea had bought after that first day driving the children two blocks to what, until tonight, had been their foster home.

"I'm very proud of you," Chelsea told Hannah as they headed out of town.

"Why? For nearly burning down the house?"

"Captain Farraday told you that it was the wiring. It could have happened to anyone. No, I'm talking about how well you handled things and what a strong support you are for your sister."

"I'll bet you weren't proud when I called that old lady a bitch."

Chelsea shrugged. "It's not a nice word, and you do need to set a good example for Hailey, who's going to copy everything you do because she looks up to you, but I can't argue the sentiment. No, I was talking about how you argued with Mrs. Moore about the law."

"You're the one who said it was illegal."

"True. But when I was your age, I never would've had the nerve to speak up."

Dark had finally fallen, their's was the only car on the road, and when a light night rain began to fall on the windshield, it added to the intimacy of the moment. "I told you my sister died."

"Yeah. That sucks. I'd want to die if I lost Hailey. We've been all each other have had most of her life."

"I know. Aiden told me."

"How did he know?"

"I had him look you girls up after I took you home that first afternoon."

She could feel the sharp look directed her way. "Because you wanted to see if we were kids like the ones who end up in juvie? Were you afraid we'd steal something from the library?"

"No. I was worried about you and when you didn't seem to have anyone looking after you, I asked him for information. Granted, that was a violation of your privacy—"

"You think? I'll bet he could get in trouble for that."

"Perhaps. I'm not sure. I suspect checking on calls about concern for children's safety falls under his jurisdiction. But here's the thing, I just want you to know that I sort of understand. Because, whatever happens, whatever foster home you and Hailey might be moved to, from now on, you'll always be in my life."

"I've heard that before." There was a lot of pain underlying the cynicism.

"I'm sure you have. I'm certain a lot of adults have failed you. But they weren't me… My sister was sick for three years. From the time she was two until she was Hailey's age. It was hard on my entire family. Her last summer, my parents sent me to a camp at Mirror Lake. I realize they were trying to protect me, but it only made things worse."

"Because they separated you."

"Exactly. So, that's only one reason I totally get where you're coming from, and believe me when I say that will not happen."

"Like you could stop it."

"Yes. I could." Of this, Chelsea was perfectly sure. "And I will, if it comes to that. I've no idea how, but it's not going to happen. So, that's one thing you don't have to worry about anymore."

"Okay." This time her voice sounded small. And near tears, reminding Chelsea that although Hannah might appear tough as nails, she was still just a child, trying to do the best in an impossibly difficult situation.

"Anyway, my sister, Annabelle, passed away shortly after I got home from camp. I hadn't wanted to go and it took a lot of years before I could forgive my parents for causing me to miss her final weeks. But I held my anger in because they'd already been through so much and the three years had taken a terrible toll on our family. Annabelle's death was like the final blow."

"Mom and Dad's death was the start of ours."

"So, you had a good life until then?" Chelsea had been afraid to ask.

"Yeah, it seemed great. Up until Dad slept around with the mom of a girl on my soccer team."

Ouch. She hadn't seen that coming. "You were young," she tried to smooth things over. "Perhaps you misunderstood."

"They started drinking a lot and I'd hear them fighting through the wall to their bedroom. I started putting my earbuds in to try to shut them out. Then Dad got into a fight with the other girl's dad. Right there on the soccer field. We were playing a team over at the coast for the divisional semifinals. I was so embarrassed I thought I was going to die."

There was a long pause, the only sound the hiss of tires on wet asphalt and the swish of the wipers. "Mom was yelling at him on the way home. He was yelling back that she was so busy with us kids she fell asleep as soon as she went to bed every night, so it wasn't his fault he had to go somewhere else to find comfort."

Suspecting that was a direct quote that had deeply embedded itself in a little girl's memory, Chelsea felt her eyes welling up.

"I'm sorry." And wasn't that both the truth and an

understatement? And undoubtedly did nothing to ease Hannah's still-fresh pain.

"Yeah." She sighed heavily. Swiped at her own eyes with the back of her hands. "Me, too." Without saying a word, Chelsea reached into the console and took out a small pack of tissues and handed them back between the seats.

"Thanks." She blew her nose. Chelsea was so in over her head here. Why had she started this conversation? She wasn't a professional therapist, which both girls, but especially Hannah, undoubtedly needed. Another thing she added to her to-do list.

"They were fighting when a deer ran in front of them. Dad tried to miss it and drove over the cliff. It was raining…like tonight. When the car finally stopped rolling over, I realized that Hailey and I were all alone and it was up to me to take care of her from then on."

"For someone who was so young, you've done a remarkable job. If I'd met Hailey any other way, I never would have realized all you two have been through."

"Thanks." Again the voice was small and choked with tears.

"I like to think that I'd have done everything I could for Annabelle. But I don't believe I'd be as strong fighting the bureaucracy. I took a psychology course in college, where they determined personality types from our answers to a questionnaire. I turned out to be a friendly helper type, which, according to whoever created the test, essentially meant that the more stressful things get, the friendlier I get, trying to smooth things over."

What she didn't say was that the negative part of that personality was those times when helpfulness had come from an underlying central fear of worthlessness.

Obviously her own father hadn't found her worth staying around for. He'd walked away from the rubble of his marriage and shattered family and began a new life, with a new wife and children in California, where his sun-filled days were the exact opposite of Washington's gray skies and rain. He still didn't remember her damn birthday.

She understood her mother's pain. Within a few short months, she'd not only lost a daughter, but her husband. Which would have been bad enough if it had been in an accident. Like driving over a cliff. But by the time of his desertion, she'd been worn down to a fragile shell of the pretty, laughing woman she once was.

And, although Chelsea had tried and tried to make up for that loss, she hadn't been enough to keep her mother from spiraling down until she'd finally overdosed on alcohol and pills. The medical examiner had declared the death accidental, but even if it had been, Chelsea had always viewed it as a slow, years-long suicide.

She shook off the pain that was always lying beneath the surface, something rising up like a troll from beneath a bridge, reminding her that no matter what she did, no matter how hard she tried, she'd never be nice enough, good enough, worth enough. Having gone through therapy, she understood that her insecurities were illogical. Yet, emotions were, by their very nature, often illogical. She could tell herself all day long that she shared a personality type with Alan Alda and Bishop Desmond Tutu, but the other side of that coin was *Gone with the Wind*'s mealymouthed, overly self-sacrificing Melanie.

Hannah had fallen silent. When she seemed to be taking a very long time to respond to something Chelsea had never shared with anyone, she looked into the rearview mirror and found that she, too, had fallen asleep.

CHAPTER EIGHTEEN

GABE HAD LEFT the light on and was waiting out front as Chelsea pulled into the semicircular stone driveway.

Hannah roused as she cut the engine, but the soft snoring showed Hailey was out like a light. Assessing the situation, Gabe gently unfastened the buckles and lifted her from the booster seat and carried her into the house.

As Chelsea and Hannah followed behind, Hannah came to a sudden stop in the foyer that was as large as Chelsea's entire apartment and stared up at the thirty-foot ceiling. The wrought iron wagon wheel chandelier appeared to be six feet across and had three tiers of lights.

"Wow," she said to Gabe, "you must be really, really rich."

"I'm only borrowing it from a friend for the summer." Chelsea noted he evaded her comment about his wealth. "Come on in and I'll get you and your sister settled."

"They'll need to eat," Chelsea said. "At least Hannah." She glanced over at Hailey, whom Gabe was holding over his shoulder. "Maybe we should let Hailey sleep."

"We already had a frozen pizza before the S'mores. And she's a superdeep sleeper. It would take a jet plane landing in here to wake her up," Hannah advised. Then looked around the great room. "Though one would probably fit in here."

"It was built for a big family," Gabe answered. A bit defensively, Chelsea thought.

"Then why aren't they living here?"

"It's an uninteresting story for another day. Let me

show you your room before we get you some supper. I'm guessing that you want to sleep in the same room as your sister. At least for tonight?"

"Duh." As distressing as the second half of what had begun as a special evening had been, Chelsea almost laughed at the exaggerated eye roll. After years of what had to have been a chaotic existence, the girl had somehow managed to remain far more normal than a lot of kids would be.

They followed Gabriel up the stairs, and down a long hall lined with art depicting Northwestern scenes and Native people. Chelsea wondered if they'd been chosen by the tech mogul, perhaps from his personal collection, or, like the books in the library, bought by the crate load. What must it be like, she wondered, yet again, to have more money than you could possibly spend in a lifetime? She imagined many would think it freeing. While others might feel burdened by the responsibility. From the way he'd been able to take an entire summer away from work, she'd begun to wonder if perhaps Gabriel had found a sweet spot somewhere in between.

When he opened a door at the end of the hallway, Hannah audibly gasped. She was not alone, although Chelsea managed to keep her amazement inside.

It wasn't merely a bedroom, but an entire suite with two single canopied beds covered in a pink-and-cream bedding that matched the wallpaper (which even covered the ceiling) and curtains held back with silk sashes edged with crystals. From the center of the ceiling hung a large chandelier with pink crystal butterflies cascading down from an antique white iron double frame. The twin wooden dressers were painted antique white with pink crystal butterfly knobs, and small tables with antique wooden tops and pink tulle skirts had been placed on either side of each bed. Enough stuffed animals to stock a Build-A-Bear store and a mountain of throw pillows covered much of the beds. A white ballet barre was fastened along one wall, although Chelsea thought it would be difficult to practice dance on that thick white fluffy rug.

Through an archway was a room which, if designed for an adult, would be a large sitting room, but here had again been decorated with a young girl's taste in mind. Dolls that looked too fragile to play with perched on antique white shelves alongside more stuffed animals, and against one wall was a dollhouse nearly as tall as Hailey. The dollhouse furniture, which included a glossy white baby grand piano, like the dolls, looked too delicate for any typical child to play with. There was also an open white armoire on wheels, where clothing hung on a white metal rack. In case one couldn't figure it out from the pink boa and sparkly princess gown that the clothes were meant for play, *Dress Up!* had been painted along the top in pink script.

A Snow White mirror hung on the wall over a scaled-down dressing table. The pièce de résistance was a raised white half-circle stage in the corner, framed by the same pink-and-cream-striped curtains, with a pink microphone and stand in the center. And natch, Chelsea thought, looking up at the ceiling, a spotlight was trained to shine onto the stage. As if whatever little girls might live in this room wouldn't already live in a spotlight.

"I guess your friend has a daughter," Hannah finally said.

"No, actually, he doesn't. A decorator he hired did all this. My guess is that maybe she only has sons and had always wanted to design a room for a little girl."

"This would be the same decorator who did the library?" Chelsea asked under her breath as she tossed the pillows and stuffed animals onto the floor and pulled back the covers on one of the beds, revealing—what else—Disney princess sheets.

"How did you guess?" he murmured back.

"It's really, really pink," Hannah said, continuing to look a little stunned. Chelsea didn't blame her.

"Like a truckful of Pepto-Bismol bottles exploded," Gabe suggested.

For the first time since Chelsea had met her, a true, full smile broke out on Hannah's face. Along with something that sounded like the beginning of a laugh. "Hailey will probably love it," she said.

"That's a positive way to look at it," Gabe said as he lay Hailey on the bed Chelsea had prepared. "Meanwhile, you get extra big sister brownie points for risking color overload while staying in here."

"I don't see any pajamas," Chelsea said, digging through one of the bags. Who has children carrying their possessions in garbage bags?

"That's because we don't have any," Hannah said, a bit of her usual protective challenge sneaking back into her tone. "We've always slept in our underwear."

"Me, too," Gabe said easily, even though Chelsea doubted he wore anything. Not that she'd be finding out anytime soon.

"There's nothing wrong with that," Chelsea said. "But I'm a big fan of pajamas. My favorites have ice cream sundaes on them."

Hannah's eyes narrowed. "You're making that up."

"Why would I make something like that up? They're not exactly proper adult nightwear, but they make me happy. And if you go to bed happy, you're more likely to have good dreams."

"Really?" Even as she could hear the skepticism, Chelsea also sensed Hannah wanted to believe it to be true.

"There have been studies done confirming that," she said, airily waving her hand. "I'm a librarian. I know these things. We'll go shopping and get you both some." While rifling through the bag, she realized how little clothing the children possessed and how worn and obviously well used those pieces were.

Which had her remembering Jolene telling her at the wedding, while doing her makeup, how hard it had been having to wear the better-off girls' donations from Goodwill. They'd agreed that since both of them had been loners, it would've been nice if they'd been friends back then. These days it had given them a special bond she doubted Brianna or Lily, as good friends as they were, would ever understand.

"I wouldn't mind some pajamas," Hannah said. "But not with ice cream sundaes on them."

"We'll find you the perfect ones that you love," Chelsea promised.

After Hannah had brushed her teeth and both girls were tucked away in the blindingly Barbie-pink princess room, Chelsea took her things into the small suite across the hall that appeared to have been designated for a nanny. Then she and Gabe went downstairs to the kitchen.

"Well," Gabe said, as he got himself a beer and Chelsea a glass of wine. "This night didn't turn out how I saw it going in my mind."

"Mine, either." Chelsea sat down on one of the kitchen stools. "Thanks for stepping up. I don't know what would've happened to those girls if you hadn't." Once again he'd surprised her. If there was one thing she never would have imagined Gabriel Mannion doing, it would be to take in two orphaned girls.

"I'm happy to help. Well, not happy about having a reason for them needing the help, but this place was the obvious choice."

"It's funny how one action sets so many others in motion," she said thoughtfully. "If Brianna hadn't told me about you building a Viking boat, I never would have gone to the shop. And if I hadn't met you, you wouldn't have been there when Aiden called me. And if you hadn't been there, Hannah and Hailey wouldn't have this safe place to stay. Unless Brianna had two rooms available at the B and B. Which would have been a less than satisfactory solution and I'm not certain Mrs. Douglas even would've agreed to it. Hannah's right about them needing to be together. As wonderful as this house is, they can't stay here until a new foster family is found. So I'm going to start looking for another apartment. One that'll take kids."

"It sounds as if you're thinking of this situation being long-term."

"You heard Mrs. Douglas. She said she was hopeful to find someone to take them by Labor Day. You obviously came here to be alone." She still wasn't sure of the reason, but figured he'd tell her when he was ready. "Having two little girls and me descend on you couldn't have been further from your plans."

"You can descend on me anytime. For now, maybe we should take it one day at a time," he said. "You never know. The perfect foster family could pop up any day."

"They'd have to at least be somewhere in the approval system or Mrs. Douglas would have mentioned them."

"Good point. But worrying about it isn't going to make it any easier."

"I'm not worrying." She took a sip of the wine. "I'm considering different scenarios. Right now getting a new apartment or rental house seems the most viable."

"You don't have a lease where you are now?"

"It'll undoubtedly cost some money to break it." Especially after that earlier showdown with her landlady. "But it's not as if I'm planning to blow my savings on a Greek island cruise anytime soon. And besides, after the way Mrs. Moore acted toward the girls, I couldn't keep renting from her even if I were alone."

"All this is awfully sudden," Gabe said. "And unexpected. I've always found things look clearer after you sleep on them. After all, you probably didn't work out the logistics of your reading adventurers in a flash of inspiration."

She studied him over the rim of her glass. "Do you know what's annoying about you?"

"Undoubtedly many things. Which one are you referring to?"

"That except for that day in the boat shop, you're too often right."

"You would've come to that same decision on your own. And changing the topic to a more pleasurable one, I have this fantasy…"

"Let me guess—the nurse with the crotch-length dress and neckline cut to the navel, wearing white lacy stockings, and white stilettos."

"Don't forget the starched white cap," he said. "I'm not old enough to remember them, but they definitely add to the appeal. But that's not the fantasy I was talking about. I was thinking how it'd be to take you here. On this counter."

She held up a hand. "That's definitely not stepping back like you promised."

"I also promised honesty," he reminded her. "So, I thought I'd mention it in the name of full disclosure. For sometime down the road. Meanwhile, it gives you something else to sleep on."

He put his empty beer bottle in the recycling bin built into the kitchen island, took her wineglass from her hand, set it on the counter that she'd never think about the same way again and gathered her into his arms. "If I'm not stepping over a line, I'd like to kiss you now. Then have you kiss me back. Then I'm going over to the housekeeper's cabin and dream about all the places and all the ways we could make love before Labor Day."

She shook her head, even as she lifted her arms to twine around his neck. "You so do not fight fair."

"I didn't realize we were fighting."

"We're not. It was only...you know...an expression," she said on an unsteady breath. "Just a kiss," she reminded him.

"Just a kiss," he agreed. Then bent his head and closed the distance.

The stirring started, slow and deep. And sweet. Achingly, wonderfully sweet, and so different from the fiery passion of the last time she'd been in his house. With scintillating slowness, using only his mouth, he drew her into a languor that clouded her mind even as her body warmed to a radiant glow.

Then, too soon it was over. She murmured a faint protest as he lifted his head.

"Just a kiss," he reminded her as he outlined her tingly lips with a thumb. "Sweet dreams."

And then he was gone. No, Chelsea thought with a long sigh as she climbed the stairs to the nanny's room. While this definitely wasn't the night she'd been expecting when she'd pulled this flirty pink dress from the depths of her closet, it was the night she'd gotten. And, given the opportunity, she wouldn't do anything differently. She'd had no choice. But she honestly didn't know how things would have ended if Gabe hadn't offered this spectacular, if over-decorated, home for the girls to stay in.

Not only had he provided much-needed moral support, he was also, hands down, the best kisser she'd ever kissed. Now that she was alone in a room much more simply decorated than the princess/pop star bedroom, the emotional roller coaster of her day came crashing down on her. And the cold, which she'd kept at bay, was attempting to make a comeback. After washing her face and brushing her teeth, she took another cold pill, and dragged her body into bed.

The night silence was broken by the lonely hoot of an owl. Although it was foolishly romantic, the thought of Gabriel hearing it while lying in his bed made her feel even closer to him.

With that thought making her smile, Chelsea fell into sleep.

"Ms. Prescott, wake up!"

The small insistent voice was like a siren, jerking Chelsea awake. Hailey was standing beside the bed, clad in a pair of white underpants. "Guess what?"

"What?" Chelsea sat up, momentarily confused to find herself in a strange bed.

"I have a princess bedroom." Her eyes were as wide as saucers. "It's amazing! Do I get to stay forever? Because I never want to leave it."

Hannah, who'd obviously paused to yank on a T-shirt and shorts, followed her sister into the bedroom. "It's temporary, sprout," she said. "Like all the other places we've stayed. Just fancier. Don't get used to it."

Chelsea lifted a brow, unsurprised, but a little disappointed that the girl with the hard, protective shell had made a comeback.

"What?" Hannah challenged, reading her expression. "We all know we're going to be leaving, like we do everywhere. If you let her get her hopes up, she'll only have her heart broken again."

"Maybe we can stay," Hailey suggested. "If Ms. Prescott marries Mr. Mannion, then they could adopt us and we could all be a family."

Hannah momentarily closed her eyes. When she opened them again, Chelsea had no problem reading the angst in them. A young girl, not even yet in her teens, should not have to deal with this.

Last night's idea to get them out of this situation into a new place where they could stay at least through the summer still seemed like the logical solution. Perhaps she could find one of those cozy Craftsmen, like Aiden and Jolene's, to rent. Without all the creepy cat old-lady wallpaper they'd spent the past months steaming and scraping off.

Admittedly, she couldn't duplicate that over-the-top designer princess room, but she could buy pink paint. And the library undoubtedly had books on how to make bedding and drapes. Perhaps Sarah Mannion could help. The idea was sounding better and better the more Chelsea thought about it.

"We'll figure out something," she told both the girls. "I promise," she told an openly skeptical Hannah. "Just give me some time… Meanwhile," she said, this time to Hailey, "why don't we go downstairs and have breakfast?"

"You really do have ice cream sundae pajamas," Hannah observed as Chelsea got out of bed.

"I told you I did," she said mildly. "I may not know

how we're going to manage this," she said honestly. "But the one thing you can depend on is that I never say anything I don't mean, I always do my utmost to keep my word and I never lie."

Hannah shrugged as only an adolescent girl could pull off. "Fine."

There was no missing the naked hope behind that faked flat tone. *Do not screw this up,* Chelsea told herself after taking a moment to rid herself of morning mouth and brush her hair. She called the library and left a message about last night's events, telling Farrah that she wouldn't be in today. Then, deciding that Gabriel had already seen her at her worst, and in these very same pajamas, she went downstairs with the girls. Since Aiden had been bringing food from their mother, surely there was something in the kitchen she could make for breakfast.

CHAPTER NINETEEN

A DELICIOUS AROMA drifted up the stairs. "It smells like cinnamon rolls!" Hailey shouted.

"Bacon," Hannah said.

"I think it's both," Chelsea said. Surely Gabriel hadn't gotten up early and made breakfast? He must have had someone come in. Possibly Brianna, who, last time they'd talked about the breakfast menu of her B and B, was up to one hundred recipes she rotated around. She hoped it was Brianna. She'd hate for a stranger to see her in ice cream pajamas.

But it proved to be neither Brianna nor a stranger. They entered the kitchen just as Gabriel was taking a casserole dish out of the oven.

"Good morning," he said, greeting them as if it was merely a normal day and nothing was out of the ordinary. While in reality, nothing was ordinary. "I called Brianna and got one of her easier, quicker recipes that worked with stuff already in the house," he said. "It's baked French toast."

"I love French toast!" Hailey said. "One of our nice foster moms used to make it for us. But then she was going to have a baby, so we had to go somewhere else where there was more room."

It broke Chelsea's heart that this vagabond life was the norm for Hailey. A thought occurred to her as she saw the way Hannah was looking at Gabriel. Remembering how she and all her friends had crushed on him back in middle school, she belatedly realized that Hannah was at that same age, with a heart just as vulnerable as hers had once been.

Had she made a mistake bringing the girls here? As tough as Hannah appeared to be on the outside, in many ways, she was the more vulnerable one. Even before the accident, she'd lost so much that wretched day with her father's affair coming out in front of both friends and strangers. As distant and neglectful as her own father had become, he'd had never gotten in a physical fight. In public. Remembering times when she'd been furious at her father, Chelsea couldn't imagine how much survivor guilt she would have suffered if he'd died while she'd been angry, never having had a chance to make up.

She was going to have to warn Gabriel about not letting Hannah fall in love with him. Which, she was discovering herself, was far too easy to do. But if she could find a new house sooner than later, there'd be no reason for him to be in the girls' lives long enough for them to make an emotional connection. She didn't need the perfect place. Just one suitable for now.

"It looks and smells wonderful," she said. And from the glance he shot her, she knew that he'd recognized her fake, cheery, everything's-just-fine-and-dandy-what-makes-you-think-I'm-nervous voice from her boat shop visit. "You certainly didn't have to go to all this trouble, but I'd never turn down French toast. Or bacon." If she kept eating like a lumberjack, she was definitely going to be getting her money's worth from her gym membership. "What can I do to help?"

"You can pour some of the OJ that's in the fridge. And milk for the girls. I made coffee for us."

"That gets you sainthood in my book," Chelsea said. Although she'd been exhausted when she'd fallen into bed last night, she felt nearly as tired this morning.

"Hannah and I can set the table," Hailey piped up. "We've done it at lots of houses we've stayed at. I even know which side of the plate the fork goes on."

"Then you're ahead of me," Gabriel said. "I still get them mixed up." He took a handful of cutlery from the drawer and put it on the table, along with some beautiful linen place mats that Chelsea wasn't sure were actually designed to be used, especially by children.

"That's okay." Hailey flashed him one of her bright melon-slice smiles. "I can teach you."

As much as she was happy that the little girl seemed to have gotten through last night with flying colors, Chelsea also realized that Hannah wasn't the only sister who'd already begun to make a connection with him.

"It's the adrenaline," he murmured as he handed her a mug of coffee. "There's sugar on the counter and cream in the fridge."

"I drink it black," she said. "What do you mean, it's the adrenaline?"

He put his hand on her back, leading her into the adjoining butler's pantry, where they could have some privacy while still keeping an eye on the girls. "Adrenaline is why you have those circles back beneath your eyes." He skimmed a finger along the shadows she'd cringed at while brushing the snarls out of her hair before putting it up in a high, messy tail. "It can create a helluva buzz, which messes with sleep."

"Sounds as if you're familiar with that."

"Sweetheart, you just described my life. If you let it, it can become addictive."

Yet another reminder that he wouldn't be staying in slow-paced Honeymoon Harbor where the most excitement was the annual Christmas boat parade and the time a longhorn Angus bull had gotten loose from Eldon Manning's ranch and gone running through town during the Fourth of July parade, creating havoc like, well, a bull in a china shop. One of the cowboys riding in a rodeo association group toward the back of the parade had finally raced his quarter horse down the street, just like something out of a Western movie, and lassoed the bull, putting a stop to the excitement.

"I'll take that as a warning."

"As it was meant. I also called my mom," he divulged.

"Oh?" He'd certainly been busy while she'd been chasing sleep.

"Yeah. I figured she might have some ideas. She suggested putting the kids in day camp. Apparently they have all different age classes, and not only would that keep them busy, it sounds like a fun way to spend the summer. And those are two kids in serious need of fun. Which is an oxymoron now that I think of it, but you know what I mean."

"I do. And that's a perfect solution. But is there still time to enroll them with school already being out?"

"It was sold out last month. But don't worry, that's taken care of. Although I can't remember her ever doing it before, she used Dad's clout as mayor and got them in. It starts next Monday, so we only have to figure out what to do until then and how to tell them."

The first thing that struck her was that he'd said *we*. As if they'd become a team. Which, by default, they probably had. Still, he could've just let them stay at this house and left it at that. There'd been no reason for him to get involved.

"I should feel sorry for people who don't have your family's influence," Chelsea murmured, watching as Hailey chattered away while the girls set the wooden table in the breakfast nook. Like seemingly every room in the house, it boasted expansive windows offering a spectacular view. It was a waste, she thought, not to have a family living in this stunning home. "But I'm not going to."

Chelsea couldn't remember the last time she'd eaten breakfast with anyone other than librarians at an out of town conference. She and Brianna *had* shared that doughnut at Cops and Coffee, but it wasn't the same thing as sitting around the table, almost like a family. No. Exactly like a family, she considered, watching Hannah devour the stories Gabriel was telling about his days growing up in Honeymoon Harbor. She was definitely going to have to find a new place sooner rather than later.

AFTER TELLING THEM about the camp, Hailey was over the moon, but Hannah was unsurprisingly skeptical. "What do you do at a camp?"

"I've only ever been to a sleepaway camp," Chelsea said, refusing to allow her own dismal experience to color her conversation. "But I think they have lots of fun arts and crafts stuff. And probably singing."

"Will I get to color?" Hailey asked. "I *love* coloring!"

"I'm sure you will. And I'm sure the events will be age appropriate," she assured Hannah.

"If I don't like it, do I have to stay there?"

"Of course not. But you might want to give it a chance, in case your sister wants to stay. But here's the deal—you cannot take off on your own. If you decide to leave, you have to promise to call me to come get you."

Hannah shrugged. "I guess I can do that."

"Then it's settled. I was thinking that we should go to Seattle and get you some new summer clothes, but it's getting a little late in the day to get there and back. So, how about you put on some swimsuits and we'll go down to the beach and build a sandcastle?"

"We don't have any swimsuits, either." When color rose in Hannah's cheeks, revealing embarrassment, Chelsea wanted to bang her head against the nearest hard surface. From the lack of pajamas, she should have guessed that. So far, her mom skills were not exactly stellar.

"I want to build a sandcastle," Hailey shouted, just in case her big sister was going to shut the plan down.

"Sandcastles are for kids."

Hailey put both small fisted hands on her hips. "I am a kid."

"They're not just for kids," Chelsea said. "Long Beach's SandSations Sand-Sculpting Competition was named as one of the top ten best sand-sculpting competitions in America by *Coastal Living* magazine.

"People *compete* to build sandcastles?" Hannah still wasn't convinced. But she was intrigued enough to take the bait.

"They do. There are different skill levels, so beginners have a chance to win, and there are even classes beforehand."

"There are not."

"It's true. We can go online and I'll prove it. Meanwhile, shirts and shorts will be fine until we can buy you suits. I'll gather up some measuring cups and whatever else I can find to make shapes, then we'll go down to this cove's beach and see what we can come up with."

"If you're going to drag us to that sandcastle contest, I'm not going to compete in front of strangers," Hannah warned her.

"Did I say you had to? Watching's fun, too. And did I mention there are free hot dogs?"

"I don't like hot dogs. They're gross."

"We'll pack a picnic, then. Or pick something up at a food booth or restaurant when we get there. It'll be fun."

"You have to come, too," Hailey insisted, looking up at Gabriel, showing that she did, indeed, possess an inner princess accustomed to bossing people around. "That way we'll look like a real family."

Damn. Wasn't this what Lily had warned her about? Chelsea exchanged a look with Gabriel, who looked as trapped as she felt. "We'll see. If Gabriel has time. He has work to do this summer."

"What kind of work?" Hailey asked, showing a bit of her older sister's distrust of any adult's promise.

"He's building a boat."

"Like a model?" Hannah asked. She didn't use the word *stupid*, but from her tone, it was implied.

"No," Gabriel said. "A real boat. Like you sail in a lake. Or the Sound. Or even along the coast."

"It's a faering," Chelsea jumped in. "Like the Vikings used. But smaller."

Hannah's eyes widened, and for the first time since they'd met, she looked like a normal twelve-year-old excited about something. "I never knew anyone who built a boat before. Can I see it?"

Gabe exchanged another of those *WTF do I do?* looks with Chelsea. They just kept getting in deeper and deeper. She shrugged.

"Sure," Gabriel said. "We can go down there after building the sandcastle. And get something to eat in town. Do you like tacos? I get them from the Taco the Town food truck most days so I don't take a long break from the boat because I need to get it done before I go back to New York City."

"You live in New York?"

"Yep. That's where my job is. I've racked up a lot of vacation time, so I decided to take the summer off."

"Oh." Chelsea watched Hannah digest that subtle warning. "Yeah. Okay. I like tacos."

As they unearthed measuring cups and various-sized mugs to use as molds, Chelsea realized that she and Gabriel would have to have a discussion about what to do about the fact that not only did the two of them have a connection, but right now, at this moment, they were behaving a lot like a family. Which could only end in heartache when Mrs. Douglas moved the girls to their new home.

CHAPTER TWENTY

AFTER BUILDING WHAT they all agreed wasn't a bad first effort, they stuck a flag Chelsea had made from a cocktail pick into the top of the tallest turret of the castle. As they walked back up the steps to the house, Gabe realized that somehow, when he hadn't been looking, during that sandcastle project, he'd actually felt a flicker of something that felt like Zen.

One advantage to a house this size was that with so many bathrooms, it didn't take long to get everyone cleaned up and into the SUV and on the way to town.

At the shop, Hannah appeared duly impressed and asked him a lot of questions about the building process of the boat, which then led to more. From the way she paid attention to every word, he suspected she was a human sponge, a lot like Chelsea must have been at her age.

Hailey's attention span, on the other hand, appeared to be somewhere under five minutes, so Chelsea took her out to the water's edge to search for agates. "Look what I found," she said, when she came back with her small hands filled. From the way she was holding them, they could have been diamonds. "Chelsea says that we can polish them and make them shiny."

"In a rock tumbler," Gabe agreed. "I got one for Christmas when I was a little older than you. It was fun."

She looked up at Chelsea. "Can we get one?"

"Sure. We might find one at a craft store here. If not, I know there are places that have them in Port Townsend."

"Yay!" Her bright gaze turned to Gabriel. "You can teach me."

He tipped an imaginary hat. "Of course, Princess Hailey." He thought it was funny that despite the fantasy bedroom with more toys than any little girl could possibly need, she'd gotten the most excited about common beach rocks. It reminded him of the times his parents would claim they could've saved a lot of money if they'd skipped buying their five kids toys, and just wrapped the boxes they came in.

She beamed. "This is turning out to be the best day ever!"

"Don't get used to it," Hannah, the voice of doom, and, unfortunately, experience, muttered.

"I'm impressed by how far it's come along," Chelsea said in an obvious attempt to lift the mood again as they drove to the food truck. "It actually looks like a boat."

"Then I'm on the right track because it's *supposed* to look like a boat.

"I had no doubt, but I couldn't envision that flat chalk drawing in 3-D form, and those boards didn't have any shape yet."

"It's hard to envision if you don't actually do it," he said. "Yet Hannah certainly caught on quick."

"That's great." Although she didn't say it aloud, Gabe suspected Chelsea was as surprised as he was by the enthusiasm the older girl had shown. He guessed she'd enjoy sailing, but decided to wait until he was alone with Chelsea to suggest it. It was a tricky tightrope they'd unexpectedly found themselves walking on. How not to get the girls' hopes up, while trying to make their lives brighter for this short window in time.

Diego greeted them with his usual smile when they arrived at the bright red-and-yellow food truck's window.

Noticing Hannah's brow furrow as she studied the menu, Gabe realized many of the specialty items would be foreign to her. He also suspected she wasn't going to risk embarrassing herself by asking what any of them were.

"How about I order a bit of everything to share?" he suggested. "Then we can go up to the park and have a picnic?"

"A picnic!" Hailey shouted, obviously on board with the idea. And, from the yearning in her eyes, Gabe suspected that Hannah, too, secretly liked the suggestion. But from the shadows in those wary brown depths he also wondered if she was perhaps thinking back to another time when her family was happy and whole and summer days had included picnics at Olympic National Park, which had always been a popular spot with locals, who felt it was *their place*. Though, since they brought a lot of money to town, visitors were tolerated.

After getting enough food for an army, they drove to the park, and up the twisting, winding road of Hurricane Ridge.

"We used to come here with our parents," Hannah murmured as they passed the visitor center.

"Me, too," Chelsea told her.

"I don't remember," Hailey said.

"You were too young," Hannah said. Chelsea couldn't tell if this had been a good idea or one that might trigger memories of that day the girls had lost their parents. If only children came with an instruction manual. "It was fun times, though." Hannah sighed, and glancing back in the visor's mirror, Chelsea thought she could see the moisture in her eyes.

"It's good to remember fun times," Chelsea said. "Memories keep them alive."

"Yeah. I guess so." Hannah didn't seem convinced, but Chelsea hoped they'd made progress.

She'd gone online last night before falling asleep and read that there wasn't any timetable for bonding with a foster child. Each situation was different, each child unique, as she was already discovering with Hannah and Hailey. She wondered if, perhaps, because she'd lost her parents at such a young age, Hailey wasn't feeling the loss as strongly as Hannah.

Once at the picnic site, Gabriel opened all the boxes and put them in the center of the wooden table while Chelsea got out the drinks. Milk for Hailey and fresh-squeezed lemonade for Hannah. Both Chelsea and Gabriel had nixed the idea of cola, which apparently most of their previous foster parents had allowed. Chelsea had gone with iced tea, while Gabriel had chosen coffee.

It was a glorious summer day, with only high, puffy clouds in the sky. "This was a great idea," Chelsea said. She hadn't realized how stressed out she'd been by last night's events until she felt herself begin to relax.

"A great idea!" Hailey bit into a crunchy corn taco with emphasis. "Why do they call it Hurricane Ridge? Will a hurricane come?"

"No," Gabriel assured her, leaning over to wipe a bit of sauce off her cheek. "But the winds do blow really hard up here in the winter. They can get up to seventy-five miles an hour and the snow can be thirty-five feet high."

"You mean inches," Hannah said.

"He means feet," Chelsea told her. "One year it hit a record sixty-two feet."

"That's higher than a house."

"It is. But it makes for good skiing and snowboard-ing. Also, the winds and all that snow are hard on trees, which helps create all the meadows. That and the wind scraping the snow over them all winter."

"Do you ski?"

"I never have, but we'd come up and play in the snow when I was little," Chelsea said.

"The last time I skied was Christmas break my senior year in college," Gabriel said.

"Skiing looks scary," Hannah said. "But I was watching snowboarding on the Olympics and it looked really cool."

"You can get hurt," Hailey said. "And maybe die."

You would have had to have been deaf not to hear the worry in her thin voice. "I don't think you can die just regular snowboarding," Hannah assured her. "Or even get hurt. I wouldn't do all those flips and flying tricks." She ruffled her sister's hair. "But you don't have to worry because I'll probably never do it, anyway."

Chelsea was about to suggest that they could try it next winter, then immediately remembered that the girls wouldn't be with her then. Although she might not have been through foster parent training, she knew interfering in the next family's life with the girls would be the entirely wrong thing to do.

"Look!" Hailey had left that worry behind as a herd of tame deer came out of a stand of trees into the meadow and came toward them. "Deer!"

"Great," her sister muttered, reminding Chelsea that a deer had been inadvertently responsible for her landing in the situation they were in. Not wanting to get into such a discussion here, Chelsea reached out and linked fingers with Hannah's icy ones.

"Can we feed them?" Hailey was obviously unaware of the tension surrounding her.

"The sign says not to," Gabriel said. "Because people

food is bad for them, and although they're used to people, they're still wild animals and should stay that way."

"Like dragons," Hailey decided.

"Exactly," he answered.

He had an easy way with children. Chelsea had seen adults, parents with children of their own who volunteered to read on story night, not be nearly as comfortable. Another thing she never would have expected from that surly Gabriel in the boat shop.

"Look!" It was Hannah's turn to point up into the blue sky where a bald eagle was riding on the thermals. They all watched for a time, then she said, "I wish I could fly."

"I suspect you're not alone. When I was a little girl, about your age, Hailey, I'd tie a towel around my neck, like a cape, and jump off a box, trying to fly because Peter Pan said that thinking happy thoughts will give you wings. It never worked."

"That's because you probably didn't have any pixie dust," Hailey said.

"You're right." Chelsea hit her forehead with the heel of her hand. "How could I forget that?"

It was about that time that the lone cloud overhead, which had been getting grayer during the lunch, floated over their way and began sprinkling rain on them.

"I guess we'd better go," Chelsea said, a part of her wishing they could just freeze this moment in time. "Wait a minute. We need a picture." She pulled her phone from her bag, then had Gabriel and Hailey come and sit on the bench with Hannah and her.

"Say pickles," Gabriel said, drawing giggles from Hailey and an actual true smile from her sister.

"Perfect!" Chelsea said, showing the others the photo.

"That is one good-looking group," Gabriel said.

Chelsea could not argue that. If she hadn't known better, she would have thought that they were a real family.

"Hashtag Great Day," she said.

Fortunately, the library was closed the next day, when Chelsea took the girls shopping in Seattle. No way was she going to send them to that day camp in the obviously well-used clothing they'd packed into those garbage bags.

Wanting to crowd as much as possible into a busy day, she'd called ahead to Nordstrom and arranged for a personal shopper who'd already had a selection of possible clothes and shoes set aside for the girls to try on when they arrived.

"I've never heard of a personal shopper," Hannah said, as they tried on clothing from the racks that had been wheeled into the oversized dressing room.

"It's handy for saving time," Chelsea said. "I know my favorite departments, but I have no idea how to find things in the girls' section."

"It's like when Cinderella's fairy godmother made her a beautiful dress for the ball." Hailey twirled in front of the three-way mirror holding her flowered skirt out as a ballerina might a tutu, in what Chelsea remembered as being demi second position from her four years of ballet classes with Mrs. Petryka, who'd immigrated here from Ukraine with her fisherman husband.

Chelsea had started classes when she was about Hailey's age. Of course, eventually, she'd had to stop as Annabelle's leukemia took precedence but she still remembered how her sequin-adorned tutus had always made *her* feel like a princess. She knew the little girl would love lessons. Just as she knew, despite one of her former classmates now teaching a new generation of young Honeymoon Harbor ballerinas, that the chances of that ever happening were slim to none.

After the girls had changed into new outfits to wear for their day on the town, she saved out the light jackets they'd need on the Space Needle's windy observation deck, then left the rest of the bags to pick up later.

The two-minute monorail ride there might not be all that special to most, but Hailey declared it "just like Disneyland!" Hannah, unsurprisingly, pointed out they'd never been to Disneyland, but Hailey blithely ignored her, refusing to allow anyone, even her adored big sister, to spoil her special day. Her eyes widened as they approached the elevator line. "We're going to go all the way up there?"

"I thought it would be fun," Chelsea said, worried by the furrowing of Hannah's forehead. She should have thought to ask if either one of them had a fear of heights. It certainly wasn't uncommon. Her father had taken their family one time, when Annabelle had still been a plump, healthy toddler, and he'd started hyperventilating before the elevator had reached the lower level. "Unless either of you would rather not. The stairs aren't really an appealing option. The brochure says that it's nearly six hundred feet to the top, which works out to ninety-eight flights and eight hundred thirty-two steps."

"I want to take the elevator!" Hailey raised her arm and started waving it around as if she were in kindergarten and was the little girl who was always eager to answer the questions. Just as she had been. It occurred to Chelsea that she could recognize a bit of herself in both girls. Hailey was the before; Hannah, the after.

"Sure. Why not?" Hannah said. Despite her words, Chelsea saw the seeds of worry in her eyes. Damn. If she were a mom, she'd probably know what decision to make.

Or, perhaps not. The difference, Chelsea considered, was when you started out with a newborn, you could build your own history and relationship. Instead of trying to guess what all could be in these girls' backgrounds.

After passing through security, they stopped to have their photo taken, which could be downloaded for free when they came back down. Obviously that option hadn't been available when Chelsea had last come, but she did have a faded Polaroid of her parents on their honeymoon at the top of the tower, before her father had begun his residency at UW Medical School. They'd looked so young. And happy, oblivious to what their future held. She'd decided over the years that it was better not to be able to know your future. Annabelle had been the best of them at living in the moment, celebrating joy whenever and wherever she'd found it.

Hannah closed her eyes on the ride up and her cheeks paled a bit, but she didn't look about to pass out. When Chelsea took hold of her hand, she did not pull away.

"This is weird," Hannah said, as they got out on the lower level with its glass floor.

"Don't look down," Chelsea advised.

"I kind of want to." Taking a deep breath, Hannah looked at the floor, which revealed the city laid out at their feet below. "Okay." She blew out the breath. "It's still weird, but kind of cool, too."

"It's like walking in the sky," Hailey said. "We're like that eagle." She held out her arms, bending back and forth, the way the bald eagle had while flying over Hurricane Ridge.

After walking around the lower level, they went up to the top, where glass benches leaned against a tall glass wall that tilted away from the tower. "It's supposed to make you feel as if you're sitting on a cloud," Chelsea read from the brochure.

They stood there, watching as people got up the nerve to try it. "I don't need to sit on a cloud," Hannah decided.

"Me, neither," Chelsea agreed. Unlike her father, she'd never had a fear of heights, but this might test her limits.

"I want to!" The soles of her new sneakers flashing, Hailey raced to the bench and flung herself down, causing Chelsea to gasp and instinctively reach out for her as, without hesitation, she leaned backward.

"Welcome to my world," Hannah said. "She has no fear."

"Apparently not." Chelsea wanted to close her eyes as Hailey leaned back against the glass wall, over the edge of the towering building. "You deserve a medal."

"I love her," Hannah said simply.

"Take my picture, Chelsea!" Hailey called out.

"I'm not certain we should show this one to Mrs. Douglas," she murmured as she snapped a series of photos with her phone.

"What she doesn't know…" Hannah agreed.

As they shared a conspiratorial smile, Chelsea decided to stop worrying about bonding. Because it was happening anyway, and if it was what Hannah needed at this moment in time, she wasn't about to deny her.

After her heartbeat had settled to normal, they walked around the platform that offered a spectacular 360-degree view. "There's downtown, where we just were." Chelsea pointed out the Nordstrom and the short monorail. "And that's Elliott Bay." Despite it being a workday for most people, there were several pleasure boats on the water. "That's Mount Rainier."

"It looks as if you could reach out and touch it," Hannah said.

"Doesn't it? We're lucky she decided to come out today. Some days she hides behind the clouds she makes."

"The mountain can make clouds?" Hailey asked.

"It's so tall it blocks the air that has to rise up over it. As the air cools, it makes water droplets that form into clouds." That was a hugely simplistic answer, but she was, after all, talking to a five-year-old. "Other times there are circular clouds that look like flying saucers. In fact, a lot of times the police get calls about them. But they're just what's called lenticular clouds."

Chelsea heard Hannah murmur it to herself, as if to learn the word. Wasn't that exactly what she'd done growing up? Unfortunately, she knew more words about cancer and chemo than she would've chosen to remember.

"See those mountains," she said, pointing toward a range of towering, snow-capped mountains, wanting to get those negative thoughts out of her mind. *Live in the Moment.* Which, she admitted to herself, was what that uncharacteristic, first-time-ever door sex had been all about. "Those are the Olympics. They're the same mountains you can see from town, and where we had our picnic yesterday."

"Wow," Hailey breathed in awe. "They're really far away, but we can still see them!"

"Thank you," Hannah said quietly.

"For what?"

"For everything. But especially for bringing us here. It makes you think differently about things."

"How?"

"How small we are when compared to this city full of people, and the water and mountains. Even when things get bad, we can still find something to feel good about. And to maybe make a difference in someone else's life." She looked up at Chelsea. "Like you have. Whatever happens, wherever we end up, Hailey's going to remember this day for the rest of her life… Me, too."

"Look what *you've* done," Chelsea complained, as she ran her fingers beneath her eyes. "You've made me cry."

"I'm sorry." Although she was an expert at hiding her emotions, Hannah's young face turned openly distraught.

"No, don't be." Chelsea gave her a big hug. "They're happy tears, and I'm going to remember it forever, too."

Although they had official photos waiting at the base of the Needle, she took a selfie with the girls, wanting to document this day. "Hashtag Making the Best Memories."

"So," Quinn asked Gabe, who was sitting at the bar, eating a pulled pork sandwich with fries and coleslaw, "how does it feel to be a family man?"

"It's temporary. The girls needed an emergency place to stay and I have way more rooms than I need."

"That's what Aiden said." Quinn squeezed some limes into a pitcher of margaritas for a table of women undoubtedly in town for a wedding. "He also said you were staying in some housekeeper's cabin?"

"Yeah." Gabe took a drink from the bottle of Surfin' Safari, a pale ale with a zing of Meyer lemon that not only continued his brother's seeming salute to the Beach Boys, but, like his Good Vibrations, tasted like summer and was made for barbecue. "Trust Mr. Perfect to make a nonalcoholic beer that doesn't taste like piss."

"Thanks. I think. So, I guess there's nothing going on between you two?"

"Why would you think that?" Gabe hedged as he took a longer drink from the pilsner glass. He'd decided that since he was responsible for kids, even for the short term, it'd be more adult not to drink during the day. Not that he'd ever had a drinking problem, like Aiden had said he had the first weeks he'd come home, but Mrs. Douglas, who might hear it through the grapevine, wouldn't have any reason to know that.

"I don't know." Quinn hit a button on the blender. "Maybe because she rowed across the lake to the house? And you were at her apartment. You also bought out the patio for dinner at Bastien's place. Which, I have to admit, is a more romantic date place than here."

"Word gets around."

"Always does. I suspect you remember that, or you wouldn't be ordering a nonalcoholic beer that doesn't taste like piss."

"To answer your question, Chelsea and I aren't *together* out at the house, because—hello?—there are currently kids living there."

"If Mom and Dad had subscribed to post-child celibacy, I'd have been an only child."

"Yeah. I've thought of that. And I'd ask them how they did it, but…well, hell…it's complicated. Especially since I'm going back to Manhattan after Labor Day."

"And Chelsea Prescott isn't a booty call woman."

"No." Though there had been that door sex. Which, if the kids stayed until Labor Day, might be the only sex he got all summer. "It's also different here. There's no such thing as anonymous sex."

Quinn laughed as he turned off the blender, poured the frozen margaritas into four salted glasses, then the rest into the pitcher.

"What?" Gabe asked.

"You might want to talk to Seth about that. He and Brianna were foolish enough to believe that they'd hidden their affair. But the fact was, the whole town knew. But Seth had had such a hard time after Zoe's death, everyone wanted to give the two of them some privacy to see if it was going to work out. As it was, he wasn't exactly with the marriage program until he just about lost her and saw the light."

"He's always been a friend but if he'd made our baby sister cry, I would've had to come back here and beat him up."

"Don't feel like the Lone Ranger." Quinn placed the pitcher and glasses onto a tray and took them over to the table.

"That is something I never thought I'd see," Gabe said when his brother returned and ran a wet towel over the bar.

"What?"

"You waiting tables."

"It's different when it's your own place."

"That's another thing I don't get. You spent your entire life preparing to be a lawyer. Don't you ever miss it?"

"Not for a heartbeat," Quinn answered without hesitation. "Maybe it would've been different if I'd decided to be a prosecutor and put bad guys behind bars. Or a defense attorney seeking justice for the wrongly accused. But all I did was push around mountains of paper, figuring out ways for the one percent to get even richer." In the kitchen behind him, Jarle put a half order of ribs and a baked potato in the window. "After a few years, I felt as if I needed a shower when I got home at the end of the day."

As he watched his brother deliver the ribs to one of the Cops and Coffee guys who was sitting at the end of the bar, Gabe felt an unwelcome twinge of recognition at Quinn's description of his former career. His wasn't the same thing at all, he assured himself as he polished off his beer, tossed some bills on the table, waved to his brother, who was now taking a meal order from the margarita women, and returned to the shop.

When he got a text that Chelsea was on her way home with the kids, he packed it up for the day. Feeling good about the progress he was making, he drove back to the lake house. He'd lost some work time, but not having experienced any unforeseen glitches yet, he should have the faering back on schedule and finished in time for the Labor Day wooden boat festival. He'd already had people coming by the shop to see it, and apparently word had spread on wooden boat message boards because he was also getting email inquiries from all over the country and Canada. All of which boded well for the Welcome Home auction.

As he punched the code into the gate of what could only honestly be referred to as a log mansion, Gabe thought back on what Quinn had said about his dissatisfaction with the law.

"It's not the same thing," he assured himself again. "If you weren't making money, you wouldn't have any to give away."

He also wouldn't have been able to provide a shelter for those girls.

"Nope. Not the same at all."

If you keep telling yourself that, a nagging little voice in the back of his mind piped up again, *you might just start believing it.*

CHAPTER TWENTY-ONE

"GABRIEL!" HAILEY BURST into the house like a tiny blond hurricane. She was dressed in—surprise—pink leggings, a purple T-shirt with a unicorn jumping over the Space Needle, and a pair of pink sneakers that flashed colors as she ran. "Chelsea drove the car right up onto a big boat! And we got to go stand outside, and I thought I saw a whale, but it turned out to be a dolphin."

"That's still great," Gabriel said. "I grew up here, but don't remember ever seeing one."

"Well, I did today! Then we drove to Seattle and I went way up in the sky and sat on a cloud!"

"The walls on the upper deck of the Space Needle are now glass." Chelsea who'd just walked in the door with Hannah, both of them laden down with large shopping bags, caught him up on yet more changes that had occurred since he'd left Honeymoon Harbor. "They slant outward, so you can sit on glass benches and lean backward beyond the tower base."

"Not me," he said, taking the bags off their hands and moving them to a couch in the great room.

"Me, neither," Hannah agreed. "Chelsea didn't, either. Hailey was the only one crazy enough to do it."

"It was fun! And we got lots of clothes and rode on a monorail, and I ate a...a..."

She turned toward her sister.

"Crêpe au fromage," Hannah told her. "A cheese crepe."

"That's it! A crepe! It's kind of like a grilled cheese sandwich," she explained to Gabriel. "But the cheese is inside a pancake instead of bread."

"Sounds great," he said.

"And we saw men throwing really big fish!" She stretched out her arms to demonstrate. "Oh! And I forgot to tell you that when we were way up high on the Space Needle, I could see all the way to the mountains where we had the picnic. And there were lots of boats. And Mount…" She looked over at her sister again.

"Rainier," Hannah supplied.

"Yes! And we were lucky because she wasn't making clouds today. Did you know that sometimes the clouds look like flying spaceships?"

"I've seen them."

"There weren't any today, but that was okay because I saw *everything else*!" Again she threw out her arms. "Maybe even to the edge of the world."

"Sounds like you had quite a day."

"We did! And we bought this T-shirt and space pasta, and astronaut ice cream Chelsea said we should save for dessert tonight."

"Where did you find that?"

"At the Space Needle!"

He glanced over at Chelsea. "Freeze-dried ice cream," she explained. "And the pasta is in the shapes of planets, rocket ships and the Needle."

"Cool," he said. "I've never had either of those."

"Astronauts eat it in space," Hailey informed him. "It floats around in space. But you don't have to worry, because it won't here. Because we have gravity."

"That's reassuring." He glanced over at Hannah. "I like the outfit." She was wearing distressed jeans, a red sleeveless hoodie with the message *Girls Are Powerful* repeated in white all down the front, and high-top red sneakers. "And you got some sun."

When Hannah lifted a hand to her cheek, Chelsea remembered the insecurity of adolescence.

"It looks good on you," he said, demonstrating that she needn't have worried about Gabriel understanding that. Then again, she reminded herself, he had grown up with a sister he and his brothers all had tea with.

"Thank you." Hannah ducked her head as her cheeks blushed even brighter.

"Show Gabriel your bracelet," Hailey urged.

Hannah held out a slender arm displaying a silver bangle bracelet with four Space Needle–themed charms.

"Pretty," he said.

"It's so she'll always have a memory of today when we leave here," Hailey said.

"Why don't we go upstairs and hang up your new clothes?" Chelsea suggested, desperate to change the subject.

"But Gabriel hasn't seen them," she whined. It had been a long, eventful day. Maybe too long. Perhaps a real mother would've had enough sense not to cram so many things into so few hours. But she'd wanted to make memories for the girls to take with them. Now, as she thought about them leaving, Chelsea felt on the verge of tears herself.

"I have an idea," Gabriel suggested.

"What?" Hailey asked with a dramatic sniffle.

"You go upstairs with Chelsea and hang them up, then tomorrow, after breakfast, you can give me a fashion show. On your stage."

"Can I turn on the spotlight?"

"Of course, It should be shining down on you just like a pop star. Did you get new pajamas?"

"Yes. The store didn't have any with ice cream sundaes like Chelsea's, or with dragons on them, so I got unicorns."

"They sound amazing."

Her expression brightened. "They are! Wait 'til you see them!" She ran toward the stairs, shoes flashing.

"Why don't I boil up that pasta," he suggested. "There just happens to be a jar of my mother's organic tomato sauce in the cupboard."

"Hailey just likes butter," Hannah said.

"Then that's what she'll have," Chelsea said. She looked at Gabriel, thinking, yet again, how grateful she was for him. Which didn't preclude him being really hot. He was turning out to be maybe something as rare as one of Hailey's unicorns: a near perfect man.

Dangerous thinking, she warned herself as she headed with the girls up the stairs.

BY THE TIME the pasta dinner was over, before they'd even gotten to the astronaut ice cream sandwiches, Hailey's eyes were at half-mast.

"I know exactly how she feels," Chelsea murmured. "It was a fun day, but a long one. What would you all say if we skip the night baths and go straight to bed?"

"That sure works for me," Hannah said. Although she'd seemed to enjoy herself, Chelsea realized that habit would have had Hannah as concerned about her younger sister as Chelsea had been. And undoubtedly worn out by the unrelenting whirling dervish energy.

Twenty minutes later, Hailey, wearing her unicorn pajamas, and Hannah, wearing a blue *Live Your Dreams* camisole over plaid pajama shorts, were tucked into bed.

"Good day?" Gabe asked Chelsea after they'd settled down in the library, which was, needless to say, her favorite room in the house. His arm was around her shoulders, and she'd nestled into him in an easy, familiar way that felt all too right.

"It was long. And I'm surprised at how exhausted I am, but it was fun. Hailey's enthusiasm, as wearing as it can be, is contagious."

"Which brings up a question I've been pondering the past couple days."

"What?"

"How the hell do parents ever have sex?"

Chelsea nearly spit out her wine. "I don't know. But I was wondering the same thing driving home and decided they must be so continually exhausted they don't miss it that much."

"They must have some way. Or else they'd stop after one child."

"True," she said. "Maybe when the kids are asleep. Like they are now... That wasn't an invitation." She sighed and dragged a hand through her hair. "I know I said I wanted to step back, but I may be reconsidering."

"That's the best news I've heard all day. As much as I enjoyed the caveman door sex, I want more. I want to do it right. I want to spend the night with you."

"Me, too. Sometimes adulting is really, really hard." She combed her fingers through his hair, then linked them together at the back of his neck. "This *is* a big house," she pointed out. "There are a lot of rooms."

"All of which hold numerous intriguing possibilities." His lips plucked at hers. Tasting, teasing, nipping, creating that familiar warmth. "Have you ever had sex in a library?"

"Of course not!" But the idea had her trembling. Just a little, as her lips opened to invite a deeper kiss.

"Okay," he said against her mouth. "We'll put that third on the list."

"Third?"

"First is to get you in my bed." He nipped at her lower lip. "Then that decadent master bath tub built for two.

"Then for the hat trick—"

His mouth had trailed down to that hollow in her

throat, where she knew he could feel her pulse pounding hard and fast.

"The library," she agreed breathlessly.

It was clear he wanted her. And she wanted him. Her need to not risk being caught having sex by two impressionable foster girls tangled with all the erotic images stimulated by his words flashing through her mind like the beam of the Honeymoon Harbor lighthouse, warning her of danger, while at the same time blinding her to anything and everything but this man.

Just when she was ready to throw caution to the wind, to live in the moment once again, he broke the kiss, drawing a whimper from somewhere deep inside her.

"Say good-night, Chelsea," he said.

She couldn't remember ever being with a man who could make her laugh, even as he made her ache. "Good-night, Chelsea."

His answering rough laugh was as regretful as she was feeling as he took her hands and pulled her lightly off the oxblood leather couch. "I think I've hiked every trail in this state," he said. "Including Hannegan Peak on Mount Baker and up to the top of Olympus. But the hardest hike I'm ever going to take is the one back to that lonely cabin."

"I know." She touched a hand to his cheek. "That group meeting of foster moms Adele Douglas told me about while we were filling out all those papers and I'd agreed to go through the licensing process is tomorrow night. Maybe I can learn the secret."

He kissed her again. Quick and hard. "Take notes."

"I HAVE AN IDEA," Gabe said the girls' third morning in the house after serving up blueberry pancakes, which Hailey declared the best ever. Though, by this point, Chelsea suspected he could make her sardine pancakes and she'd declare them wonderful.

They'd left the girls having breakfast and were having a rare private conversation in the library. "I know you need to get back to work with the adventurers—"

"Well, I wouldn't put it precisely that way. But yes, that's admittedly how I'm feeling."

"But you want to. Because it was your idea. Your project. Your ass on the line."

"All true. But I also understand priorities."

"You don't have to prove anything to me. Here's the thing… Weren't you taking them to Herons Landing today?"

"After a trip to the museum to learn about Honeymoon Harbor's Victorian era. And why the buildings on Water Street are now stone and brick due to fire that swept through town and destroyed all the wooden ones back in the 1900s." Those up on the bluff and set farther back from the harbor had been saved. "How did you know?"

"You told me the schedule over dinner at Sensation Cajun."

"You remember that?"

"It's important to you. So, sure, of course I remembered. After Bri there's a five-day break, then you go to Blue House Farm."

"Okay. I'm impressed."

"I don't know why. I'll bet dollars to those doughnuts the cops make that you memorized everything I told you about wooden boats."

"Well, of course, but…"

"You're smarter than me?"

"That's not what I was implying at all. It's just that I didn't know anything about them, so it was interesting to me."

"In case you haven't noticed, I'm extremely interested in you. So, it only stands to reason that I'd be interested in what interests you."

He was not making this fling plan at all easy, even if they could ever get it off the ground. Despite their short time together, they'd been forced into a domestic situation that didn't allow for pretension. Chelsea still didn't know what had brought him back to town, but she did know what kind of man Gabriel Mannion was. Her first instinct had been right. He really was The One. Which, despite that set-in-stone timetable she'd agreed upon, she was already teetering on the brink of falling in love with. The slightest nudge and she'd go tumbling over.

"Well. Thank you."

She was going to think about his unexpected declaration later. And undoubtedly drive herself crazy delving for hidden meanings, clues that he might be open to changing his mind, too. Sure. That was going to happen. Because there were so many openings for a billionaire stock trader here on the peninsula. And as much as she loved visiting New York, Chelsea knew she could never live there.

"You're very welcome. Want to hear my idea?"

"Of course."

"Take Hannah with you to work. You know she belongs with the adventurers."

"I do know that. I just couldn't figure out what to do with Hailey while Hannah was off having adventures."

"That's solved. She's visiting the farm."

"Your family's farm?"

"Well, I could have called Jim at Blue House Farm, but I figured my family made more sense. And before you worry, I called Mrs. Douglas yesterday to see if it'd be okay, and she approved it without a second thought, which didn't surprise me. I would've mentioned it last night, but we got sidetracked by Hailey the dervish, then trying to decide what to do about our sexual drought."

Despite her tangled nerves, Chelsea laughed at that. "Wow. If you call this a sexual drought, you must really be looking forward to getting back to New York and your regular life."

"There's sex and then there's more," he said. "This is more."

Once again it was as if he'd read her mind. Yet, *more* could mean a very different thing to him than it did to her.

"It is," she agreed, waiting to see if he'd elaborate.

"So, what do you think?"

"About Hailey going out to the farm?"

"Unless you're open to me ravishing you here on the couch, that would be the topic on the table."

"You're making fun of me."

"Never." He bent down and touched his lips to hers. As light, as short, as the kiss was, it still set off sparks.

"I think it's a wonderful idea," she said. "Please thank your mother for me."

That problem taken care of, thirty minutes later, she and Hannah were on the way into town to the library, where the adventurers were meeting. "Are you only taking me because you feel sorry for me? Or because I'm staying with you and Gabriel, and you don't know what else to do with me until camp opens or Mrs. Douglas finds us a new family?"

It belatedly dawned on Chelsea that Hannah would have seen the posters about the program, along with stacks of signup sheets. How could she have not felt left out?

"You should know better than that, by now," she said mildly. "You and I have come a long way since that first day when you had to decide whether or not I was a child trafficker."

"I didn't really mean that I thought you were going to sell us to pervs. I just need to be careful that Hailey stays safe."

"I get that. But, and this is one hundred percent the truth, I couldn't figure out what we could do with your sister. Can we both agree that there's no way she has the patience or maturity for the adventurer program? Which is only open to middle school through high school anyway." Although, unsurprisingly, she hadn't had any high school age readers sign up. She might have spent her summers in the library, but she'd been well aware, even back then, that she was an anomaly.

"But now that Gabriel's taking her to his family's Christmas tree farm, the problem's solved."

"I remember getting a tree at the farm once," Hannah said. "They were having a festival, with music and cocoa and cookies. It was a lot of fun. There was a sleigh, but it was on wheels because there wasn't any snow that year."

"I remember that. My family went once, too."

Hannah sighed. "Sometimes life really sucks."

"You're not going to get any argument from me. Which is why we have to grab hold of special moments and hold them tight, so they're always there to brighten up suck-fest days."

"Like at the Space Needle."

"That, too," Chelsea said. "But I was thinking of now. Just the two of us, having some quiet time together." Like a mother and daughter. Which, Chelsea considered, was even more dangerous than her thoughts about Gabriel.

CHAPTER TWENTY-TWO

THE DAY TURNED out to be even more of a success than she'd hoped. The group of a dozen adventurers had liked the museum's Victorian display, although the girls had admittedly been more interested in the women's cumbersome clothing, especially those corsets and bustles, while the boys had liked the idea of a giant fire roaring through the town. Chelsea knew they didn't want Honeymoon Harbor to go up in flames, but she'd been a librarian long enough to know if a topic had anything at all to do with explosions, boys would eat it up.

They'd enjoyed the painted balsa wood models of early buildings and seemed excited about visiting one that was much the same as it had originally been, albeit updated. They'd all been suitably impressed by the enormous mural painted on the high arched ceiling of the foyer, although—no surprise—none of them had heard of James Whistler.

Rather than going with the mythological figures popular at the time that Herons Landing had been built, Whistler had painted scenes of the peninsula—from the cliffs and crashing waves, to the glaciers of Mount Olympus standing tall over Hurricane Ridge, to the towering hemlock and Douglas firs, fields of lavender farms, the Juan de Fuca Strait leading to Puget Sound, and, of course, the dazzling blue bay that Honeymoon Harbor had been built on.

Scattered throughout the quadrants were the Native American original settlers; the tall ships, including Admiral Vancouver's *Discovery*; and fishermen and builders like Seth Harper's family. Unsurprising, given that the Victorian house had been contracted by a wealthy timber baron, loggers claimed the center. Many of the adventurers' families' occupations were represented in the mural, which made the excursion even more relatable.

"That was fun," Hannah said on the way home.

"I'm glad you enjoyed it."

"I don't usually get to hang out with kids my own age."

"Well," Chelsea said easily, even as those words sliced another little piece off her heart, "that's one reason to look forward to camp next week."

"I guess so. At least none of the kids today made fun of me for not having parents."

"That's not as rare as you might think, these days. Though you do have a far more challenging situation than most." She wondered if there were any other foster children in the county Hannah's or Hailey's age and made a mental note to ask Adele Douglas. Perhaps they could arrange meetups.

"Do you have any Dickens books in the library?" Quotes from Dickens about Victorian times had been part of the museum display.

"Absolutely. There's one, appropriately titled *Charles Dickens*, that includes some of his personal letters and takes you right into Victorian England, so you feel as if you're experiencing his horribly difficult life as a boy growing up. By reading it first, to get some background, you'd probably enjoy *David Copperfield*, which is a wonderful story, even better than *A Christmas Carol*.

"Dickens based it on his own life and it has many dreadfully wicked characters and tells about wretched times for poor David, who was a fictional version of Dickens, as a boy. It also has some humorous parts. I've always felt that Dickens was the best writer ever at bal-

ancing comedy and tragedy. I know there's an edition
of *David Copperfield* in Eagles Watch's library, but we
could go back to the library and get the other one."

"That's okay," Hannah said. "You have that meeting
with the other foster moms to go to. And you said you
wanted to bake brownies to take to it."

"Mrs. Douglas said it was a coffee and cookie type of
thing, so I thought bringing some to the meeting would
be a good way to break the ice." She hoped her nervous-
ness about attending didn't show. She could have picked
up a box of delicious macaroons at Desiree's bakery, but
homemade felt more appropriate for this situation.

"That's a good idea," Hannah said, unknowingly echoing her thought. "Everyone likes brownies. Maybe you
could bring the book home tomorrow?"

Home. Hadn't that become a charged word? "Absolutely. It's also somewhere in the house library, but the
books aren't catalogued, so I've no idea how long it would
take to find it."

"Maybe you could catalog them."

"That's an idea." The task would definitely take longer
than the remaining time she'd be living at Eagles Watch.
Although she'd been looking at Realtor listings on Zil-
low, she hadn't found anything even halfway appropriate. Honeymoon Harbor, she was discovering, was not a
bustling real estate market.

"Thank you," Hannah said quietly.

"No need to thank me. I'm a librarian. Nothing makes
me happier than sharing books, especially when I can introduce a reader to one of my favorite authors."

Okay, if she had to be perfectly honest, sex with Gabriel would top book sharing. But although she and
Hannah were getting along better each day, that was
definitely too much information.

"ARE YOU SURE you'll all be okay?" Chelsea asked before leaving for the meeting at the library with the other foster mothers. With Hailey helping with the sifting, she'd made two batches of brownies. One for the meeting and the other to leave at home for Gabriel and the children.

"Positive," Gabriel assured her. "I've got things all planned. After we're done playing with matches, we're going to run down to the beach with scissors."

"Matches aren't funny." Hannah folded her arms. "I've already been through one almost fire."

"You're right," he agreed. "That's my bad. How about we all jump off the roof?"

"You are so *not* funny," Chelsea scolded.

"I believe we've already determined that. Don't worry. We'll do great," he assured her. "We'll get a pizza and watch a movie."

"I love pizza!" Hailey said with her usual enthusiasm, which Chelsea found rather amazing given what all she'd been through in her young life. Then again, she'd always been able to count on Hannah for taking care of them. Meanwhile, it appeared Hannah hadn't had anyone to take care of her for a very long time.

"I don't want mushrooms," Hannah said. "Or pineapple."

"I can live without mushrooms," Gabe agreed. "And you're absolutely right about pineapple, which is a heresy and disrespectful to pizzas everywhere."

"Can we watch *Mulan*?" Hailey directed puppy dog eyes, which Chelsea doubted anyone could resist, up at him. And heaven help them all, she could even flutter her lashes. "She's my favorite Disney princess. Because she has a dragon for a friend. And she ends up saving China!"

"But she's technically not a princess," Hannah pointed

out. "Her father was a commoner and she marries a captain in the army."

"You go argue that with Disney," Gabriel suggested.

"Maybe she became a princess when she got the Emperor's Medallion," Hailey suggested.

"Maybe." Hannah's tone was doubtful. "Whatever, I have to admit that she's a kick-ass girl who proves that being smart is just another way to be strong. The best part is when after shunning her for being a girl, the soldiers have to dress like women to help her rescue the emperor."

Chelsea didn't have a clue about the movie, but this was something she could bring into the conversation. "There's a Norse myth like that. An evil Jotun—they were the enemies of people and the gods—stole Thor's hammer and wouldn't give it back until the goddess Freya married him. So Thor and Loki, Odin's blood brother, dressed up like a bride and a bridesmaid to trick the Jotun at the wedding, and get the hammer back.

"It's in a book of myths that Hannah and I could read you. But," she said on afterthought, remembering Jarle's comment about Norwegians being a passionate people, "they might be a little violent."

"There are battle scenes in *Mulan*, and the armies burn villages and kill people," Hannah said. "I think she could handle it."

"Well, all right, then." Chelsea decided that the movie princess franchise had definitely moved on from Snow White whistling while she worked and Cinderella attending the ball in a pumpkin coach. Though Snow White's evil stepmother had made Chelsea cover her eyes when she'd been Hailey's age. "I'd better get going. Have fun, guys!"

"You, too," Gabriel said. "We'll save you a piece of pizza."

He walked her to the door, bent his head and brushed his lips against hers. "Maybe you'll find out how people with kids have sex."

She wrapped her arms around his waist. "I hope so."

"Me, too." His brief yet heartfelt kiss suggested a promise neither of them was prepared to make.

THE MEETING WAS about to start when Chelsea arrived. A group of ten women, ranging in age from midtwenties to, perhaps, fifty, all wearing stick-on name tags, were helping themselves to coffee and cookies. Chelsea recognized most of them as library patrons. Many had brought in children over the years that she never would have guessed weren't their own.

"Hi," she said. "I'm Chelsea Prescott."

"I think we probably all know you from the library," a tall redhead, whose tag read Julie, said.

"Are those brownies?"

"They are."

"Oh, yum. Now we're even more happy to have you come tonight."

"I sort of threw myself into the deep end before learning how to swim," Chelsea admitted. "I'm hoping for some tips that will keep not just me but, more importantly, the kids afloat."

"That's a good analogy," Susan, the branch manager of the Mannions' family bank, said. "And don't worry, even with the licensing classes, we all were you on our first day."

"Especially if you come in through the kinship program, like you and my husband and I did," a woman Chelsea recognized as their server from Sensation Cajun added. "We had no clue what we were doing when we took in a child who was in my daughter's Girl Scout troop after her mother went to jail for shoplifting three hundred dollars of clothing from the Walmart outside town. It turned out to be a third-degree felony that comes with a possible maximum jail time of three-hundred sixty-four days and up to a five-thousand-dollar fine. She probably could have gotten off with a fine, but because she had a record for the same crime in Portland, the judge gave her sixty days in jail. He did waive the fine if she agreed to attend six weeks of counseling classes.

"Still, two months away from your mom is a very long time for a child, so it wasn't easy. We've received a lot of help from this group, but we've also discovered that every child brings his or her unique set of challenges."

"Especially when they come with traumaversary," Laura, a silver-haired woman in her fifties who managed Michael Mannion's art gallery, joined in. "We'd been fostering for a few years when we took in a young boy who'd been removed from his family on Memorial Day weekend after a murder/suicide domestic situation. We were blindsided when he became angry and particularly disruptive while we were camping in the park. Although we were his third family in a year, no one else had reported that kind of behavior, and while we knew the date that he'd first entered the system, Memorial Day is one of those holidays without a consistent date like Halloween or Christmas, so we didn't make the connection. That, of course, can happen with any child, but it's especially important to know with foster kids."

"I'm not a child," Chelsea said. "But I'm personally familiar with anniversary triggers. This year was the first year since I was a freshman in high school that I didn't get drunk on the anniversary of my sister's death. It started as a way to connect with my mother, who became an alcoholic after we lost my younger sister to cancer and my dad left the family. But, even with therapy, it became a destructive pattern."

"How did you break it?" a woman, whose tag introduced her as Karen, asked. "Or is that too personal?"

Chelsea was surprised she'd even brought up the topic she never talked about. But now that she had…

"It was a small thing. Last year I woke up feeling okay and decided that it was time to quit beating myself up over something I'd had no control over. Fortunately, it was a super busy day, which helped me hold the urge at bay. Then I stopped at Mannion's and had chocolate caramel martinis on an empty stomach. Quinn tried, unsuccessfully, to talk me out of the third one, then cut me off. He called the single cab in town to drive me home after I threw up in the restroom.

"Sitting in the back of that cab I still felt the loss I know will never completely go away, but not only was my behavior embarrassing, if the bartender had been anyone else but Quinn, I could have ended up driving home drunk and possibly having an accident and causing another family the same horrible grief my family had been through. So, I guess you could call it being scared straight. This anniversary I went out for dinner with friends after work, stuck with water, then went home and watched *Gladiator*."

"That's an odd choice," the scout leader said. "I think I would've chosen a more upbeat romantic comedy."

Chelsea shrugged, surprised at how she was already feeling a kinship with these women. "If you can't feel better looking at a young, hot Russell Crowe in a tunic, you should check your pulse, because you're probably dead."

The group laughed, then settled down in chairs that had already been arranged in a circle, and began sharing how the past two weeks had gone. On the occasion of less than perfect incidents, empathy and advice were offered. Meanwhile, Chelsea madly wrote every bit of information she was gleaning on the blank pages in the back of her life planner. Then one thing struck home.

"The first thing I need to say is these are the best brownies ever," a mom named Jess said. Which earned unanimous agreement. "I have a degree in child psychology, so I foolishly thought I'd be a natural. I already knew that we humans don't bond or love generically. We bond to a specific person. Or, in the case of a family, persons. Many of the children are coming from very damaged families. Which makes it only natural that they'd bond with the first family that makes room for them, not just in their homes and lives, but their hearts.

"So, keeping that in mind, imagine you've been happily married for a few months when some kind and caring person, through no fault of your own, has inexplicably been put in charge of every aspect of your life. And that person, whom you've never met before, announces that it's time to pack all your things because you're going to go live with a different husband. And don't worry, he's a very nice man and lives in a very nice home."

"That would be terrible." Chelsea didn't need to be a child psychologist to tell where this was going.

"Isn't it? Yet that's no different from telling a foster child that they'll be moving to a new placement."

"They don't allow a child to stay in a situation where she—or he—is thriving?"

"That's the ideal," Susan said. "But the system is so strained at the seams that it's not a guarantee. If a child from Yakima, to use an example, is fostered here due to lack of local space, then a family suddenly opens up in Yakima, that child will be moved back across the mountains. Because, typically, especially for reunification, placement near the original home is preferable.

"My husband and I often take in kids with special needs. So, if we have a child who's finally doing well, if a new boy or girl with serious problems comes along, there'll likely be a rotation. So our child will move out to make room for the more needy one."

Chelsea thought about what Hailey had said about their constant moving. Her own roots were so deep in the glacial till and sand beneath Honeymoon Harbor, she was planted for life. But children like Hailey and Hannah were like tumbleweeds, blown across an arid desert by the wind.

"I have a question," she said, as the allotted time wound down, all too soon to her mind. "It's kind of embarrassing."

"You've already told us about getting drunk every year," the gallery owner, whose name was Diana, said. "Let me guess… Since you're living with Gabriel Mannion out at the lake, and rumor has it Gabriel bought out the entire patio at Sensation Cajun so you two could have a private dinner on—"

"Which was *so* romantic," Jess gushed, earning affirmative nods from everyone present

"You're wondering how to have sex with kids in the house," Diana guessed.

"It takes some management skills," the mom with the Memorial Day boy said, after Chelsea had admitted that had, indeed, been her question. "One thing you're going to have to embrace is quickies."

"You'll be surprised how erotic having sex hidden in the closet can be," Karen said.

"Just make sure you lock the bedroom door first," Julie advised. "Kids never recognize a closed door. We've taught ours that sometimes we just need some Us Time. Then stick in a video for them to watch."

The list continued. Chelsea dutifully noted them all. Wearing sexy underwear to get in the mood, the same way you did when you dated. Which brought her back to really needing to buy some sexy underwear. Whispers and blanket tents could be every bit as sexy as headboard banging. Playing music to get you in the mood can also muffle noise.

"A sound machine," Julie advised. "After a few weeks, I could almost orgasm by myself walking on the beach at the coast, because I identify the sound of ocean waves with sex." Everyone, including Chelsea, laughed at that.

"If you have a home office with a guest bed, every parent knows it's really a sex bed," Susan said.

More suggestions followed. Making out in the car like you did back in high school. Chelsea had never had an opportunity to do that, so hey, maybe it was time. A camper or travel trailer, which drew some heartfelt votes from several women. Locks on every door. Appointment sex.

"You'd be surprised at how sexy anticipation of a scheduled time can be," Teri, a county prosecutor, said. "I put fireworks stickers for sex days on my planner and just looking at the page while I'm at the office can turn me on."

Nooners while the kids were at school or day camp. Something she and Gabriel could easily do.

Flirt with him. "Squeezing my husband's butt while we're in the kitchen cooking dinner always works for us," Diana said. "Also, get a long tablecloth for warmups. Like playing around on date night in restaurants." Another thing Chelsea had never done, but if Sensation Cajun had had tablecloths on the patio tables, given that they'd been all alone out there, she might have been up for that.

"A special word. Like a bat signal, to let your partner know you're up for some sexy time," another woman suggested.

Sex in the pool at night while the kids were sleeping. Sex without taking your clothes off. As she wrote that one down, Chelsea felt the heat warming her cheeks. She could definitely check off that box.

"And," Susan wrapped up the discussion, "the most important reason God created baby monitors was so parents…"

"Could have sex!" everyone shouted together, causing much shared laughter to ensue.

As she left the meeting, thanking everyone and promising to be back in two weeks if the girls were still fostered with her, Chelsea was feeling much more confident. Also, just imagining all those scenarios while driving back to the lake had her ready to jump Gabriel the minute she walked into the house.

She found them in the library where Hailey was sitting on a couch with her stuffed dragon next to her, a library book she'd brought with her from their previous house on her lap. "After my princess bedroom, this is my favorite room," she told Chelsea. "It's just like the library that the Beast gave Beauty. I'm reading Daisy a book about dragons. So she'll know where she came from."

"What a good idea," Chelsea said.

"She's really not reading," Hannah said, looking up from an antique table where it appeared Gabriel was teaching her chess. "She's memorized it from all the times she's made me read it to her."

"That's a good start," Chelsea said. "You all seem to have survived without me."

"We did great," Hannah said. "The movie was okay. But I could live in this room."

"Me, too." Chelsea decided against telling her about the books having been bought by the crate. "I never learned to play chess."

"I'm going to be a writer when I grow up," Hannah said offhandedly. "And Gabriel could teach you chess. Though since you're an adult, he might not let you capture his pieces so easily." She diagonally moved a white pawn, taking Gabriel's black off the board.

"Hey, that was great strategy for a beginner," he argued, causing the girl to roll her eyes.

"So," Chelsea said, "you want to be a writer?"

"Yeah. I have all these emotions that sometimes feel like they're going to explode inside me, you know?"

It was a rhetorical question, but Chelsea answered it anyway. "Very well."

"But when I read books about girls like me, I realize that I'm not alone."

"That's one of the wonderful things about books. While they can take you to faraway places, sometimes they speak to something about ourselves."

"That's what I want to do. I want to write stories to help other kids like me."

"That's a wonderful goal," Chelsea said. Hadn't she been that same lost, lonely girl at Hannah's age? And hadn't books been a lifeline? "I'll be so proud to have your books in my library."

That earned a rare smile, the first Chelsea had seen that lit up the girl's eyes. "That would be so cool," she said. "Having a book I wrote in a library."

"Even better than cool," Chelsea agreed. "Even though I'm surrounded by books every day, I don't get to meet many writers, and when I do, they've already written their book. But I'd be able to tell people that I knew you when you first decided to become a famous writer. That would give me some serious cred in the library world."

That earned an even brighter smile than the first.

"Break time," Gabriel said. "Why don't you practice some of your moves, Hannah, while I talk with Chelsea about her meeting."

They'd decided, after the sandcastle excursion, that Mr. Mannion and Ms. Prescott were too formal for their situation. Although Hannah had learned at the meeting that some foster parents choose to go with *mom* and *dad*, especially when there was no chance of reunification with their birth parents, that didn't feel quite right for the short-term.

While Hannah studied the beginner chess book Gabriel had somehow managed to unearth in the color-coded library and began experimenting with moving different pieces, Chelsea moved with him into the hallway.

"How did it go?" he asked.

"It was great. Everyone was very open and sharing and I came home with some helpful information that will help with the girls. As to that other topic we were discussing, I have a list."

"A list?"

She took her planner from her bag and opened it to the relevant page. One ebony brow lifted as he read his way down the list. "Excellent." His eyes, dark with intent, moved down to her lips. "Your room. Tonight. Ten thirty."

"You've got yourself a date." As her body warmed beneath his smoldering gaze, Chelsea decided that there was, indeed, a lot to be said for anticipation.

CHAPTER TWENTY-THREE

WHAT WAS SHE supposed to do? Take off her clothes and get into bed? Or wait and let him undress her? And why, oh why, didn't she own anything better than a pair of pale pink Jockey French Cut panties and a smooth pink T-shirt bra? Although the white on pink polka dots looked cute in The Dancing Deer, now she wondered if she didn't look as if she were wearing something childish. More suitable for a training bra for Hannah. Which, she made a mental note, they were going to have to go shopping for if the fostering lasted a few more months.

She was standing beside the bed, mind whirling, when Gabriel opened the door, took the time to lock it, then crossed the small room and stood in front of her. "You're on time," she said, trying for humor that fell flat.

"That's because I've been pacing the deck for the last ten minutes. I figured timing was important for appointment sex." He kept his voice low, both of them all too aware of the hopefully sleeping children across the hall.

"Planning feels a little more awkward than door sex," she whispered.

"Only if we let it." He framed her face in his hands, then lowered his head. The kiss was as soft as thistledown against her mouth. It was only a kiss, she told herself as his tongue traced a damp, beguiling pattern across her lips. The feathery brushing of lips, the slow stroke of his tongue, the gentle nip of his teeth on her bottom lip was more temptation than a proper kiss. More promise than pressure. But that didn't stop it from weakening her knees.

He unbuttoned the white blouse that she'd worn that day to the boat shop. She'd always felt the crisp tuxedo style made her look, perhaps not sophisticated, but polished. And definitely confident, which was why she'd worn it to the shop, and again tonight when she'd been admittedly nervous about meeting the other moms.

But as he slowly opened it, one button at a time, Chelsea didn't feel starched and crisp. As her skin warmed beneath his touch, she felt sexy. And desirable. Any man who radiated such sexuality—a potent power she'd experienced herself, downstairs in this very same house—would've had plenty of opportunity to perfect his technique. What was coming as a revelation was that such a meltingly soft touch could create such scintillating heat.

His mouth tempted. Enticed. Seduced. As rich liquefying pressure flowed through her, Chelsea let out the breath she'd been holding on a soft, shimmering sigh and twined her fingers together behind his neck. God, she loved his mouth. Loved. It.

Finally! He slid the blouse off her shoulders, where it fell to the floor. "Nice," he murmured as his fingers grazed the sides of her breasts, dipped in at her waist, and lower, over her hips. If he'd been fantasizing about silk and lace, he didn't appear the least bit disappointed. "I've been imagining this," he murmured as his lips skimmed up the side of her face before returning to her mouth. "Dreaming of it."

"Me, too."

She felt his smile curve against her lips. "I'm glad to know that I wasn't the only one suffering."

He wrapped his arms around her and drew her into the cradle of his thighs. "But this is even better than my dreams."

Chelsea sighed her pleasure. "Mine, too." He continued to kiss her lovingly, lingeringly, until her entire world became focused on his mouth. She'd never known it was possible to feel so much from just kissing. She'd never realized a kiss could make you fly.

She had no idea how long the delicious time had gone on when he took her hands from around his neck and placed them against the front of his shirt. "I think we're wearing too many clothes."

"It's your turn to take something off."

"I thought you'd never ask." He pulled the T-shirt over his head and threw it across the room where it landed on an ivory velvet-covered slipper chair.

He was so beautiful. Entranced, she ran her hands down his chest, over his tight abs, and lower, following a crisp black happy trail down to the button on his jeans.

Slowly, as if they had all the time in the world, they took turns. And when every bit of clothing had been discarded, he lifted that sexy brow, and said, "Didn't that list mention blanket fort sex?"

She nodded. "It did."

"Good. Because I'm beyond ready to capture the fort."

He yanked back the quilt, the blanket and the sheet, had her tumbling onto the bed with him, then, as they lay there, legs tangled, flesh to flesh, he pulled the blanket over his head, and captured her quick laugh with his mouth. "We have to be very quiet," he said.

"Yes," she whispered back, surprised how it felt as if they were in their own private cocoon.

It was the last thing either of them said for a very long time.

"WELL, THAT WAS more fun than I expected," she said, snuggling up against him. Although he was accustomed to getting right up and out, Gabe found himself in no hurry to move.

"Next time I'm going to bring a flag," he decided.

She pressed a kiss against his chest over his heart that was settling down to a normal rhythm. "Oh, I think you planted yours just fine."

"Why, Ms. Prescott, did you just use a dirty euphemism?"

"I thought I'd try out being a naughty librarian on for size."

"You proved very naughty."

"If you're going to do something," she suggested, her fingers playing idly—or teasingly, he wasn't certain which—in his chest hair, "I believe it should be done correctly."

"Mrs. Henderson taught you well."

"I know." They lay there together, listening to the now familiar owl hidden somewhere in the trees. Finally, after a long silence, she sighed. "As much as I'm starting to love this place, which is a big surprise to me, I'm really going to have to step up my search for an apartment. One that'll take the kids."

While Gabe wasn't exactly an expert on postcoital conversation, considering he hadn't been with that many women who'd either expected or seemed to want it, this was definitely not the norm. "Still thinking of this being long-term?"

"You heard Mrs. Douglas. She said she hoped to find someone to take them by Labor Day. What are they supposed to do in the meantime? Live in a tent up at the park? I have a friend who used to be a child court advocate who told me that foster kids in Washington State's system have over five-point-six moves in the first year. I looked up the statistics and on any given day there are between nine and ten thousand foster children needing homes and, as we've already found out ourselves, a serious dearth of beds, which is increasing every year. I'm thinking that perhaps I could take the training and be a permanent foster mother, actually a guardian, so they could stay with me until they age out at eighteen."

He frowned, taking time to parse his words carefully. "How could you do that and work?"

"I don't know. Maybe the way millions of working moms manage every day? And by the way," she flared, "the 1950s just called and want their 'women should remain barefoot and pregnant in the kitchen' slogan back."

Obviously, from her uncharacteristic reaction, his attempt at parsing had failed.

She closed her eyes for a long, silent moment. Having been working on finding his own Zen, Gabe could recognize the struggle within her. "I'm sorry. It's just that the more time we spend together, the more worried I become about them."

"Of course you are. And there's no need for you to apologize. I feel the same way. It was a stupid, knee-jerk, sexist thing to say and I should know better. My mom managed to raise all of us while working at the school."

"Your parents could have juggled," she allowed. "Your dad's mayor position is voluntary and most of the town council meetings happen in the evenings, or are planned way ahead of time. I'd admittedly be at a bit of a disadvantage being single, but until summer vacation, and the S'mores incident, they'd already stayed at the library after school. And I do have two days off a week."

"There are probably day care places in town." Thinking about it, he realized everyone he knew with kids either had au pairs or nannies. Sometimes one for each child. "Or you could go old-school and hire a sitter."

"That's not a bad idea," she said thoughtfully.

"Maybe Mrs. Lawler. She was certainly good with

Hailey. And didn't hesitate to take care of them when she saw that smoke."

"True. She might not be able to be a full-time foster mother, but she's not so old she couldn't watch them a few hours a few days a week," Chelsea mused.

"It wouldn't hurt to ask. All she can do is say no. Perhaps she knows someone who'd be perfect for the job."

"I'll do it," Chelsea decided. "I'll call her tomorrow."

"Good plan. Meanwhile, you know what your moms' group said about quickies?" They'd already done the whispers and blanket fort thing. Which had turned out to be surprisingly hot. And had him looking forward to the surreptitious closet sex.

"It would be hard to forget since I only wrote it down a few hours ago."

"How would you feel about crossing that item off that list?"

She laughed softly as she rolled over on top of him. "Well, imagine this," she said as she felt his renewed erection. "You already have a head start."

From the way she'd begun to move her hips, there'd be no problem ticking off the quickie.

"Perhaps you could catch up," he suggested as she slid down his body.

She looked up at him, her eyes on his as she curled her fingers around his length. "I can do that," she said.

Then lowered her head.

"Since today's not an adventurers' day, can I go to the boat shop instead of the library?" Hannah asked over breakfast the next morning. "I'd like to see how far it's come along."

Chelsea looked up from her omelet. Gabriel had been working his way through his sister's menus and it occurred to her that if he ever gave up Wall Street, he could probably get a job as a personal breakfast chef.

"The shop?" She glanced over at Gabe, who shrugged.

"It's okay with me," he said. "I'm putting fiberglass on the hull today and could always use an extra hand."

Hannah's eyes widened. "You'd let me work on the faering?"

"Would you like to work on it?" he asked easily as he refilled Chelsea's coffee cup.

She appeared as surprised as Chelsea was. This was quite a turnaround from the man who'd made her swear no adventurer would touch his boat. "I guess. Sure. But I don't know anything about boat building."

"That's why the school is there. To teach people. I wasn't born knowing how to build boats. I spent summers as a kid hanging around the shop learning from the guys who'd learned the ropes from guys before them. It's one of those crafts that's passed down over generations. When the town was first founded, there was a big business in wooden boat building and repair, but that dwindled off after World War II. Then, about the time my dad was in middle school, one of the Harpers decided to bring the place back to life. And it's grown since then."

"How did I not know that?" Chelsea asked.

He grinned. "If we ever play *Jeopardy!*, it sounds as if I might actually beat you at the boat category."

"I suspect watching me row across the lake to this house gave you your first clue."

"You rowed across the lake? All the way?" Hannah asked.

"I did. And, FYI, rowing is not nearly as easy as it looks. I think, if Gabriel is up for it, going to the shop with him sounds like a very cool day."

"Then it's settled." He skimmed a glance over Hannah, who'd dressed in her go-to-the-library clothes. "You'll want to change into some old clothes," he said. "This stage can be messy."

"I'll be right back!" She jumped up from the table, put her plate in the dishwasher and ran out of the kitchen. A minute later they could hear her running up the stairs.

"Thank you," Chelsea said, as Hailey went chasing after her big sister. "That's very generous."

"She's seemed interested, but I remembered what you said about attachment—"

"I think that ship sailed a long time ago. But you've made it clear that you're only here for the summer, so her being happy probably outweighs the risk."

Chelsea paused, wondering if she should share what she'd been thinking. "And it's not as if you're going to another planet. Or even another country. Maybe this year you might be able to get away to spend the holidays with your family. And, if I get appointed a guardian, maybe you could visit them. As a friend. Or maybe more like a favorite uncle."

"Sounds like a plan. I know my parents and grandparents would be happy, and I could probably get away given that Christmas is on Wednesday this year, so the markets will close early on Tuesday, then remain closed on the twenty-fifth. I could come home on Tuesday, take the red-eye back Christmas night and be at work on Thursday."

"Do you always know the dates of the holidays?"

"Sure. The market may not be that easy to predict, but it does have some trends. The days between Christmas and January 8 are typically the most positive market days of the year, due to the so-called Santa Claus rally, so although the gain isn't that much, it's still a good trading time."

"May I ask you a question without you thinking I'm being judgmental?"

"Sure."

"When was the last time you went to the Christmas tree lighting at Rockefeller Center?" It was something Chelsea had always wanted to experience. While Honeymoon Harbor had two very wonderful lightings, one in the park, the other at the harbor, to her New York was the quintessential holiday city. Or, perhaps she'd seen *Miracle on 34th Street* and *When Harry Met Sally* too many times.

He sighed. "I'm going to disappoint you."

"I don't have any expectations one way or the other." That was the deal. No strings, no expectations, on either of their parts. "I was just curious."

"I haven't seen it lit." He held up a hand. "And before you ask, no, I haven't gone ice skating there, either. But I have driven past it many times. Why?"

On the way home from his office, she suspected. During those few hours he'd sleep before starting all over again. Chelsea loved her library. She thought about it every day. But she'd still achieved a good work-life balance. Which would be expanding even more over the upcoming years with the girls. Although Gabriel had certainly proven to be a far nicer man than Scrooge, his entire life, by contrast, appeared to revolve around making money.

"It's no big deal." She gave him a reassuring smile. "I just always thought it would be wonderful to see in real life."

"Maybe someday you could come to New York," he suggested, appearing to have forgotten their summer-only fling rules.

"Maybe," she said, even as she knew that the chances of that happening were about the same as a white Christmas here in Honeymoon Harbor, which had occurred all of eight times in the past one hundred twenty-one years. And since they'd been gifted with one last year, Chelsea wasn't going to hold her breath.

CHAPTER TWENTY-FOUR

IF ANYONE WOULD have told Gabe two months ago that he'd be building a Viking faering with a twelve-year-old apprentice, he would have asked what they'd been smoking. He'd also have guessed he'd be doing that in one of the lower rungs of hell.

But to his surprise, as much as he'd been enjoying getting back into the groove of boat building, Hannah's open enthusiasm made a good day in the shop even better.

"I don't understand," she said as she helped him smooth out the fiberglass cloth he'd draped over the overturned hull. "Why would you put fiberglass on a wooden boat?"

"Because while this might look like white burlap, it's made of very fine strands of glass woven into the cloth. After we bond it to the hull and deck with epoxy, we'll have a tough skin that'll help minimize dings from rocks that aren't visible, or from dragging it up onto a rocky beach. It'll also make it more watertight."

"But then it won't look like a wooden boat."

"Sure it will. We're using a low-viscosity epoxy, which will make it invisible beneath either paint or varnish."

"Are you going to paint it?"

"No, I'm going with a clear varnish. To show off the grain." He smoothed the cloth outward from the middle, pleased with how easily it conformed to the shape of the hull.

"What did the Vikings use?"

"They'd seal the cracks between planks with moss and/or animal hair, then cover that with a mixture of oil and tar called boat soup."

"The moss wouldn't be so bad. But I'm glad we're not using animal hair."

"Me, too." After mixing up the epoxy, he brushed it lightly onto the cloth, handed her a pair of gloves and a squeegee, then covered her hand with his. "Now we're going to smooth it carefully, not too hard so we don't get air bubbles. This first coat will turn the cloth from white to nearly perfectly clear, but the weave will still show."

"What if you used more to cover it better the first time?"

"Then it could float off the boat. This is just to attach it. The next coats will start filling in the weave."

"How many?"

"I like three on the hull. Two inside. Larger boats you might want more."

They worked in companionable silence for the next hour. She caught on quickly enough that he'd given her her own squeegee.

"You did great," he said once they'd finished. "You're a lot more diligent than I was at your age. And I'd been hanging around the shop for a few years by then."

"Really?"

"Really." He pulled off his gloves. "And, for future reference, I never say anything I don't mean."

A soft pink colored her cheeks as she followed suit, taking off hers. Then she looked down at the chalked plan. "Can girls ever be boat builders?"

"No reason why not. Come with me."

He led her over to the boat-building school office, where the walls were lined with photographs of boats and their builders. "See this one?"

She studied it. "That's you. And some lady."

"Not just any lady. That's Mary Brice, from Maryland, who came here as a guest teacher the year before I went to college. She taught me how to make that Northeaster Dory, which I sold to a surgeon from Seattle to help pay for college."

"That's kind of sad. That you had to sell it. It's really pretty."

"Thanks."

"But it's epic that a woman taught you."

"She's famous in boat circles," he said. "Her family has been shipwrights going back to colonial days. So, to answer your question, yes, women can most definitely be professional boat builders."

"I still want to be a writer when I grow up," she said. "But maybe I could make boats between writing books."

"Sounds like a plan. Like me building this one during a break from work."

"Before you go back to New York."

"Yep." It was important that everyone remember this visit was temporary. He and Chelsea had been walking a tightrope with the girls from the beginning. Chelsea appeared to have come up with a plan for herself, while he felt as if he were now blindfolded on that tightrope, over a bunch of alligators while juggling flaming torches. "Are you hungry?"

"A little." He'd noticed she'd begun to eat more than she had when she'd first arrived at the house and wondered if that was due to no longer being flooded with the stress hormones he'd read about in that anxiety booklet.

"What would you say to a burger at my brother's pub?"

"Don't we need to put on the second coat?"

"It needs to set up enough to be tacky, which gives us plenty of time for lunch."

"I'm not sure Mrs. Douglas would approve of me going in a bar."

"It's not that kind of pub. It's a restaurant that also serves beer my older brother makes."

"Your brother makes beer?"

"Yeah. And it's really good."

"Cool."

"Quinn is definitely cool. And he has this cook who'd probably love to tell you more about Vikings and faerings. It was his idea I build this one."

"Okay." Her casual tone and slight shrug belied the light that had brightened her eyes again. It also tore a hole in his heart.

"Quinn used to be a lawyer," Gabe said casually as they drove to the pub. "In Seattle. A couple years ago he came back home and fixed up a building that had housed our ancestors' pub. It'd been in the family going back into the 1800s, but got shut down during prohibition, and they never started it back up. Prohibition was a short time when it was illegal to drink alcohol."

"That could've been a good thing," she murmured. Remembering how her parents had died, Gabe decided not to give her a little history lesson about most of the country flaunting the law. "Your family has really lived here since the 1800s?"

"Yep. Another ancestor's name is on the cornerstone of the courthouse. He was mayor at the time it was built and one of the Harpers—Seth Harper is marrying my sister, Brianna, this summer—built it."

"That's epic, that your family has lived here so long. Why did you leave?"

"It's complicated." How to explain he wanted to make a lot of money to an adolescent girl who carried her clothing around in a black garbage bag? And what message did that bag give the kids about their self-worth? Gabe had a feeling that Hannah was, in great part, responsible for her sister's apparent belief that she could do anything. Even sit on a cloud.

"Mostly," he said, as he realized she was waiting for an answer, "I had other things I wanted to do. Things I couldn't do in a town this size."

"I like the size of this town. If I could, I'd live here forever."

What she had no way of knowing—yet—was that if Chelsea had her way, that could well become a reality.

"So," Lily asked over a Mediterranean mezze platter at Leaf, "how's living with Gabriel Mannion going?"

"I'm not living *with* him. He's staying in the house-keeper's cabin."

"Sure he is. That's why you've been glowing lately. Either Jolene has created the most amazing skin care product ever, or you've been having dynamite sex on a regular basis."

"The latter," Chelsea agreed. "But although we've been very careful and discreet, I'm not sure Mrs. Doug-las would approve."

"She'd probably be envious," Lily said as she spread some roasted red pepper hummus on a torn piece of pita bread. "But one look at you and she'll probably know anyway."

Chelsea's hands rose to her cheeks. "Is it that obvi-ous?"

"Honestly, not to someone who doesn't know you as well as I do," her friend reassured her. "I was just kidding. But it appears you decided to go for the fling."

"More a summer romance," Chelsea said quietly.

"Oh, hell." Lily pointed the knife across the table. "You've fallen for him, haven't you?"

"A little."

Lily folded her arms. Waited.

"Okay, more than a little. A lot. But it doesn't mean

anything, because he's been very clear that he's not looking for a long-term relationship."

"That could change."

"No, it couldn't. It's obvious that his place is in New York. And my place is here."

"Having lived in Manhattan during a brief Madison Avenue gig I decided didn't suit me, I can't argue that," Lily agreed. "You could try a long-distance relationship."

"Taking in the time it takes to get to Sea-Tac, it's at least a nine-plus-hour trip from here to JFK. And that's before the cab ride into Manhattan."

"Interesting that you researched that. And the trip from the airport would be at least forty-five minutes on a good day. Though you could always take the train, then AirTrans."

"And undoubtedly get lost and end up in Maine." She squeezed lemon over a dolma made with rice, onion, currants, pine nuts, parsley and mint beautifully rolled up in a grape leaf. "Besides, he works impossibly long days. A hundred-hour week. He wouldn't have any time to play tour guide."

"There are professionals who do that," Lily said. "And lots of double-decker buses that are admittedly touristy, but then again, you'd be a tourist. However, I doubt walking all over the city is what the man would have on his mind if you did go there."

"It's a moot point because if I become a permanent foster mother for Hannah and Hailey, there's no way I'd leave them. At least not until we're all settled in and they feel secure."

"He could come here."

"That wouldn't make the trip any shorter. By the time he got here, he'd have to turn around and fly back." She hadn't found his abbreviated Christmas visit idea at all encouraging to any future. "Plus, he hasn't come home to see his family for ages. The man even missed his own sister's engagement party, for Pete's sake."

"There is that," Lily agreed.

"I've almost decided he's a bit like Dr. Jekyll and Mr. Hyde." She stabbed a kalamata olive with the small fork. The olive's brine was as sharp as her disappointment that there was another side of Gabriel Mannion she'd probably never reach.

"Oh? How? Don't tell me he's violent—"

"Oh, no!" Chelsea almost choked on that idea. "It's just that he's so caring with others, like bringing me soup, which admittedly could have been a seduction ploy, but not only did he offer his house on the spot so the girls could stay together, he's been marvelous with them. He listens to Hailey's long monologues about dragons, and seemingly every other topic under the sun that flits through her active mind. He's been teaching Hannah chess, and, as we sit here eating lunch, they're at the boat shop where he's letting her work on the faering."

"Get out. You had to promise none of the adventurers would so much as touch it to get him to agree to them visiting."

"True. But that's changed for her, which could also be a problem when he leaves, but for now, I'm taking my blessings where I find them. You should've seen her face when they left for the shop. She could've lit up this town for a month."

"If this is the Mr. Hyde part, you need to reread that book."

"No, it's the good, Dr. Jekyll part." After studying the platter that looked as if it should be hanging in Michael Mannion's gallery, she chose a cherry tomato, mozzarella cheese and basil leaf skewer. "The bad part is that he's so fixated on making money. I'll bet he even thinks about it while sanding that boat."

"Did you ever think he might be using that boat *not* to think about work?"

"I suppose that's a possibility. But I really believe profit is his default."

"Like the library is yours? And changing the topic for a moment, this tabbouleh salad is delicious. As good as any I had during my six months in Greece."

"Touché about the library," Chelsea said. "And is there anywhere you haven't lived?"

"There are a bunch of places on my bucket list. But I'm happy here for now. So, your main problem with Gabe, when you get right down to it, appears that he's über rich."

"That's simplistic, but I guess so."

"I'm rich. In fact, to paraphrase my accountant, I'm loaded. And, unlike Gabriel Manning, I lucked out with having a bunch of ancestors make it for me."

"I know. But you're so normal, I forget about that."

"Thank you. I think."

"Besides, although you could be living a party girl life, jetting around the world and hanging out on yachts, you work full-time at the college. You also volunteer at the library, you read to the seniors at Harbor Hill and you deliver food for Meals on Wheels."

"I like to keep busy," Lily said mildly. "Plus, Gabriel is philanthropic. Sure, he expects to make a profit from his investment in Jolene's skin care business, but she told me that the deal was so generous, she should be able to buy him out within the next five years. And you can't discount the children's book club plan."

"No, that's a huge thing," Chelsea agreed.

"Then there's the scholarships, not to mention—"

"Scholarships?"

Lily was suddenly paying a great deal of interest to the char-grilled slice of eggplant on her plate. "Forget it, that was a slip. Besides, since the two of you have obviously gotten so close, I'd have guessed he'd told you."

"You guessed wrong."

"I promised him confidentiality."

"You're my best friend. Plus, you've already let it slip, and you know I'm not going to immediately post it on Facebook."

"Okay." Lily sighed, then took a drink of the cucumber-flavored water. "Gabe gave a generous amount of scholarship funds to the college. More than twice what the foundation gets from all other sources combined in an entire year."

"That's impressive."

"True. But he did it through an LLC to keep it anonymous."

"Which it still will be," Chelsea assured her.

"Thanks. He's not our only anonymous donor, so I'd hate for word to get around that I let this slip or others might be less willing to contribute. Anyway, since I'm already in this deep, I'll admit I got a little curious and looked up the LLC's holdings."

"And?"

"It seems to exist solely to fund a foundation that makes lots of donations around the country, including clean water projects and school funding on reservations. He also funded that new pediatric trauma wing at the hospital years ago after Mrs. Henderson's son died due to the peninsula not having one. If all that weren't enough, he gave a computer to every kid in the Salish County school system who can't afford to have one at home. With funding to continue in perpetuity."

"Gabriel did all that?" The hospital wing, she considered, certainly hadn't been named after him. Which, she decided, was because ego had never been the reason for his generosity.

"He did. And that's just what I could find with a public search. I imagine if I dug deeper, I probably could've unearthed more."

"We *have* talked about his money," Chelsea allowed. "Making it appears to be his superpower."

"One he apparently uses for good."

It didn't matter, Chelsea reminded herself. Gabriel might be The One. But what Lily had just told her was even more evidence that he wasn't the Forever-After One who'd settle down in Honeymoon Harbor and build a life and family the way his parents had. But perhaps with fewer children than the Mannion five. He was The One for Right Now. She'd known that going in and since he'd proven a man of his word about everything else, there was no reason to believe he wasn't leaving on that ferry after the Labor Day fireworks had died out.

It wasn't as if she hadn't recovered from much greater loss. As Lily returned to the college, and she returned to the library, Chelsea reminded herself that the smart thing to do was treat Gabriel like a Pacific Northwest summer. Savor the short season to the fullest while it was here, then enjoy the memories made in those sun-filled days through Washington's long, gray winter.

CHAPTER TWENTY-FIVE

"It's as if the days are flying by on wings," Chelsea complained five days later as she sat out on the deck with Gabe after the girls had gone to bed.

"Probably because they've been so busy. You're going to have to see Hannah with Jarle. I think he's replaced me as her favorite man in town." Which Gabe didn't mind in the least. She also had, no surprise there, hit it off with Quinn, so it wouldn't be as if he was abandoning her come September.

"I hope he's keeping it clean."

"He's been the soul of discretion."

"Maybe I will have him talk to the adventurers, then" she mused.

During the past days she'd gone to work, while Hannah, who decided to opt out of the day camp idea, split time between the boat shop and the library. Hailey was spending mornings at the camp, where she'd, unsurprisingly, already gained a number of friends. Afternoons Gabe would take her out to the farm, where, from all accounts, she was having a wonderful time with his folks. His dad had taught her how to shape a Christmas tree, his mother had her playing with fabrics and paint chips and creating color palettes with crayons, she'd baked a pie with his grandmother, and his grandad had even taught her to fish on the creek running through their property.

Hannah had not appeared the least bit impressed that her little sister had touched a worm. Not that it slowed down the younger girl's minute-by-minute report on her day.

After spending this morning at the boat shop, Hannah had gone to the library, where she'd helped the volunteers put the finishing touches on the library's Fourth of July parade float.

Although he'd taken this house to be out here on his own, Gabe was getting a kick out of the girls and Chelsea had definitely made his evening deck time much more enjoyable. Of course, the best thing, hands down, was working their way through the list every night.

"I don't understand how Realtors make a living in this town," Chelsea said, as he was pondering the idea of buying a motorhome so they could check off that box. "There's nothing on the market."

"That's because developers are only building vacation rentals. And a lot of people are taking campers and motorhomes over to the coast and renting out their houses for the summer."

"Well, that's just wrong," she muttered.

"It's business."

"Like dollars are worth more than two little girls finding a home?"

He'd never seen her seethe until tonight. Which made him glad that she hadn't seemed to spend a great deal of time considering what, exactly, he did for a living. Which entailed making more money for people who might already have a dozen homes, all like this one or larger, scattered around the world and private planes to jet between them.

"I'm going to buy this one," he said. "And since I have no intention of playing landlord, even through some property management company, it's going to stay empty."

She glanced over at him. "Then why are you buying it?"

"For the investment."

It hadn't sounded that crass when he'd told Aiden

about his plan. She fell silent as she appeared to take a serious interest in the sky filled with stars overhead. You sure as hell never saw stars like this in the city. Then again, the only bright lights in Honeymoon Harbor were from the lighthouse and the green and red lights on the buoys. Trade-offs, he considered.

"We studied stars in the sixth grade," he broke the chilly silence. "But I've never been able to see the different constellations at night."

Crickets. Actual, real ones from somewhere out in the woods.

"Is that Mars?" He pointed toward a bright light in the deepening sky.

"That's the North Star. Which you undoubtedly already know since you and your brothers supposedly spent a lot of time sailing." If her voice held any more disinterest, he'd have thought he was talking with Hannah, her first couple days at the house. Although he could still sense the older girl's wariness about her situation, she'd begun to remind him of a flower after a drought, blooming in a way Mrs. Douglas, when she came for their home visit, couldn't help but see.

"Mars is the red one."

"Now I remember."

She didn't even bother to acknowledge that conversational ploy with a response.

The silence settled over them again, broken only by those crickets, the croak of frogs in a nearby marsh and the splash of a jumping fish breaking the night-still water.

"Do you like your work?" The change in subject surprised him. Yet, on some level it didn't, given that they'd been talking around the edges of how he'd made what could, admittedly, been seen as an obscene amount of money.

"I wouldn't do it if I didn't." Who didn't like something they did well? Some people created symphonies. Others wrote novels. Then there were those who could build a skyline that defined a city, or take a broken-down heart out of a chest and replace it with a new one. Gabe made money. Lots of it. Not just for himself, but others.

"I suppose being able to help people must be a wonderful thing." She was looking out over the water, which was beginning to deepen to indigo. "I try to make a difference, but there are so many times when it would feel so lovely to simply write a check to make the problems go away."

"Money doesn't necessarily buy happiness." Great. Now he was sounding like an internet meme.

"No, it can make lives easier."

Gabe felt uncomfortable whenever anyone outside his field brought up the topic of money. He felt even more so hearing it from this woman who, from what he'd seen, lived a life of service every day. He also knew what she clearly wasn't saying: that she couldn't approve of his plan to buy this house only to have it sit empty when so many others were homeless.

"I went to a party last summer," he said. "At this beachfront mansion in the Hamptons."

"As one does," she murmured, the smile she slanted him taking any censure from her words.

"It would make this place look like a cottage. It had two swimming pools, one for kids, the other for adults, tennis courts—plural—a lawn that an entire crew of gardeners kept as perfect as a putting green, and gardens where I doubt a single weed was allowed to sprout. The furniture had been made especially for the house in Italy. It had taken two years. The double front doors had come from a thirteenth-century French abbey, the arched ones to the stables from an Italian winery."

"They allow horses in the Hamptons?"

"East Hampton, I'm told, has always had a history of horses. They have a lot of horse shows."

"We have barrel racing and draft horse pulls at the county fair, but I suppose that's not quite the same thing."

"You'd suppose right."

"I'll bet we have as much fun. The peewee sheep riders are absolutely darling."

"I remember those." He also had fond memories of sharing kisses with girls on top of the fair's Ferris wheel during high school. Maybe he could relive the experience with Chelsea.

"Why did you go to the party?"

"Because it was an annual event hosted by my best friend. Most of the year he lived an hour north of Manhattan, but summers were spent on Long Island."

"Sounds as if he's a lucky man," she murmured.

"Not so lucky. He was the mentor I told you about."

"The one who died?"

"Yeah. I was a pallbearer at his funeral."

"Oh, I'm so sorry." She put her hand on his, the gesture meant to comfort stirring entirely different emotions. He knew, if not now, then later, she'd figure out the dates and suspect Carter's death had something to do with his return to Honeymoon Harbor.

"Yeah. I was, too." Because she hadn't taken her hand away, he turned his and linked their fingers together, the gesture feeling as natural as breathing. "He was forty-six."

"Oh, my. That's young."

"Yeah. But there's a saying that Wall Street years are like dog years, so maybe he wasn't so young."

"Did he have children?"

"Four. Ranging in age from three to eighteen."

"That's so sad."

"Here's the thing." Once again he was going to tell

her something he hadn't told anyone else. Something he hadn't even entirely admitted to himself. "I looked around this spectacular thirty-five-million-dollar estate—"

"Thirty-five million? For a house?"

"For a ten-acre estate," he corrected dryly. "The house was eighteen thousand square feet, with twelve bedrooms and a professional spa. There was also a six-bedroom former carriage guesthouse with its own pool, and a caretaker's cottage at least three times the size of the one I'm staying in."

"You were definitely in Great Gatsbyland."

"I was." He decided that it wouldn't add anything to the conversation to reveal that despite all that money, Carter had turned out to be underwater on both houses and, even with secret bank accounts scattered all over the Caribbean, had left debts that would probably take months, if not years, to unravel.

"But I kept looking around, knowing that my friend had incredible skill and expertise at what he did. He was a true Master of the Universe. And not the comic book kind."

"He sounds as if he could have been a character in *The Bonfire of the Vanities*."

"He would've fit right in. I read the book while I was at Columbia."

"You told me you don't read much fiction."

"I don't. But that wasn't really fiction."

"You read it as a primer," she guessed. "An instruction manual."

"Yeah. I did." And how crass did that sound?

"To decode, understand and hopefully fit into the world you were planning to enter."

"Exactly." She got him. Maybe it was because, coming from the same small town, she could imagine the culture shock he'd experienced. And how he'd always felt as if he had to work harder, faster, longer. "So, getting back to the party, I couldn't help wondering if the world would be all that much better, or worse, if Carter Kensington, that was his name, hadn't been born. Had he really made any difference? Driving back to the city the next morning, I thought how great it would be if we could live in a culture where the people who got to live in those houses, or even my apartment, used all their knowledge, skill and experience coming up with ways to help others. And not just those who need it the most, but also ordinary, everyday people who, if they just had a hand up, could reach their full potential."

"Thus the student computers," she said quietly.

He wasn't that surprised she'd learned about that. She was a librarian. She could probably find anything online.

"I wasn't snooping into your business," she assured him. "Lily thought I already knew about the scholarships, and accidentally mentioned them at lunch. Then, well, the conversation moved on to the hospital and the computers."

Gabe wasn't annoyed by Lily Carpenter's slip. Honeymoon Harborites didn't live their lives as guarded here as they did in New York. Probably because so much of what you did was already out in the open. Not wanting to embarrass her, he hadn't told Chelsea that Quinn had spotted Bert and his grandson delivering her car to her house after her first visit to the lake. The night of the door sex, which could still make him hard just thinking about it. And had him deciding the motorhome would be worth the cost. Hell, they could even take the kids to the coast in it. If Chelsea didn't want it after he left, he could possibly donate it to Welcome Home.

"It's not any big deal," he said. "A few computers aren't going to change the world."

"But they're going to change lives. Maybe one of those lives they change will be that of someone who goes on to change others' lives, and even the world."

"I wouldn't go that far." He was getting uncomfortable again. Outside the office and those finance bars, where competition reigned supreme, Quinn didn't talk about money. It was, after all, only a way of keeping score. And yes, trying to make a difference. Perhaps now that she knew about his donations, she wouldn't view him as a Carter clone.

Although Gabe was still pissed at Dr. Doogie's attitude, there was ultimately a chance The Street perhaps *had* contributed to Carter's death. Would he have lived to see all his children grown if he hadn't become addicted to the rush?

"I've come to the conclusion that the old system of for-profit businesses being driven by the need to make money, while leaving nonprofits to focus solely on good works, creates a false disparity. Even nonprofits have to make money to stay active, which is why I've become interested in impact investing."

"Which is?"

Gabe's first thought was that this was a lousy conversation to be having beneath a starry sky while the girls were upstairs sleeping. But he knew she'd keep turning it around and around in her busy mind and he wanted to show her that he wasn't one of those modern-day robber barons who kept making the news. Many of whom people outside their privileged world only heard about when they were headed off to prison.

"It's an out-of-the-box form of crowdsourcing. While angel investing, which is what I've been doing, tends to be focused on startups—"

"Like Jolene's skin care business."

"Exactly. Impact investing is social venture capitalism, where investors allocate a portion of their portfolio to investments providing social or environmental benefits. Instead of the old model of philanthropy, where donations go directly to nonprofits, investors can receive a return on their investment and socially conscious groups receive funding to grow and do more good, which in turn makes them an attractive investment. So, then you've got a situation of circular cumulative causation."

"But won't you be drawing contributions away from nonprofits, making it more difficult for them?"

"Nonprofits are already finding it more and more difficult to raise the money to stay afloat. Instead of having to scramble for competing dollars for some project that will help people from individual sources, struggling to create the program piecemeal as small amounts of funds trickle in, or putting it off entirely until they've collected enough, which could take years, they receive a large-enough influx of money from a philanthropic equity campaign to fund the project's success."

"How do the investors get paid back?"

"As an example, take a project that builds housing and a support network for recovering addicts being released from prison. Unsurprisingly, there's a high recidivism rate in that population. If there's a measurable decrease in the number of beds needed for returning inmates, the state pays part of the money it's saving. Not all plans work that way, but most investors aren't doing it so much for profits, but because it addresses their belief system. They typically tend to reinvest any profits earned."

"That's what I do with Kiva. I love the ability to invest online in entrepreneurs and students around the world. Over the years I've tended to invest in a lot of cows and hair salons. Not that they have anything in common, but they're usually successful and it makes the recipients, their customers, clients and me happy."

"That's an important aspect of charitable giving. Millennials, especially, want to make a difference in the world. But well-meaning investment boycotts of 'bad' companies only represent a drop in the bucket of the world's financial system. Thinking of for-profit businesses as bad and non-profits as good creates a false disparity. Instead of holding dollars out of the market with boycotts, by investing in philanthropic equity programs, you can address the human need to do good in the world, but also make money for those organizations and companies so they'll continue to exist."

"It *is* getting more and more difficult for everyone to find funding," Chelsea agreed. "At almost every monthly public town council meeting, someone will stand up and insist that libraries are outdated now that everyone has Google and Wikipedia."

"Because everything you read on the internet has to be true."

"Thank you." Her pique apparently gone, she leaned over and kissed him.

"Honeymoon Harbor is a good town, populated by generous people. Yet, not a month goes by that I don't have to defend the library's budget from draconian cuts, never mind the fact that our founding fathers established America's first lending library. Can you believe even comparing libraries to the buggy whip industry has been brought up?"

"I'd like to say I'm surprised. But I'm not."

"Did you know that public and academic librarians answer nearly six-point-six million questions every week? And if everyone who asked a question formed a line, it would span all the way from Miami to Juneau?"

"No, I wouldn't have guessed that, in this computer age."

"That's exactly how people usually respond! But it's a statistic. Librarians were the original Google before anyone had thought to invent the internet.

"And don't get me started about them being funded by taxpayers' dollars, because I hear that every damn month.

Taxpayers get so much more than they give. At a library, it doesn't matter if you're an out-of-work fisherman looking for job-training information, or Bill Gates. Every resource in every library is free. Not just books, but internet access and educational training programs, along with help filling out résumés, job applications and government forms. Everyone in a community can count on their library to provide them with the resources needed to succeed. We also provide a safe shelter for the homeless and others in need."

"Like two little foster girls who don't have a home to go to after school."

"Exactly." She was on her feet, beginning to pace, energy radiating from her like crackling electricity. "We're a gathering place for the community and so many don't realize how much we do, because libraries have always been part of their lives, so they take them for granted. Although I understand that feeling, and try not to take it personally, they have no idea what the world would be without libraries, because along with everything else the most important thing they do is preserve history. And in turn, truth." She blew out a breath as she wound down.

"You didn't have to convince me," Gabriel said mildly.

"Sorry." Color rose in her cheeks. "It's admittedly a hot button. Sometimes I tend to get carried away."

"I like it. It shows passion. Which brings up another question… What would you say about checking the pool sex off our list?"

She glanced up at the darkened bedroom windows. "It'd have to be quick."

Gabe stood up, grabbed the back of his T-shirt neck, pulled it over his head and tossed it onto the deck chair. "That works for me."

CHAPTER TWENTY-SIX

"GUESS WHAT, CHELSEA," Hailey said after coming back from a Sunday at the Mannion farm. "I get to ride in the Fourth of July parade on the Christmas tree float tomorrow!"

"My mom said *if* Chelsea agreed," Gabe reminded her.

"Oh. That's right. I forgot." Chelsea did not believe that for a moment, but having researched typical behaviors for both girls' ages, she'd learned that children tended to tell the most lies between five and eight years old, mostly to test what they can get away with.

"Next time try to remember invitations," she said. "It's easier for adults to make decisions about whether or not to grant permission."

Blue eyes widened. "Are you going to say no? I'm sorry I forgot."

"Thank you for the apology," Chelsea said. "Now, maybe Gabriel can fill me in on the details."

It was exactly as Chelsea remembered. John and Sarah Mannion always had a float in the parade with a Christmas in July theme. When she'd been younger, the Mannion kids had dressed up in what had to have been sweltering winter outfits, throwing fake snowballs at each other while Christmas music played from hidden speakers. As each of the boys, then Brianna, dropped out of the annual event, they'd been replaced with children from the community.

"Tell her about the snow!" Hailey insisted, tugging on his shirt.

"Oh, yeah. Dad got together with a tech kid at the college and they invented a portable snow machine that uses water and shoots snow into the air. They never used fake snow in the past because it'd make a mess, but this stuff is made from water and melts when it hits the ground. I saw it work today. It's pretty cool."

"It's cold!" Hailey corrected.

"That, too," Gabriel agreed.

"That's why I have to wear a parka and a knit cap. And you're invited, too, Hannah."

"That's really nice," she said. Chelsea guessed that she'd rather jump naked into the harbor on the New Year's Polar Bear Plunge than have any peers from school see her tossing fake snowballs with her little sister. "But I'll stay on the sidewalk and cheer as you go by. And take lots of pictures, which I couldn't do if I was on the float."

"Oh. That makes sense," Hailey decided. And the topic was dropped.

SOME TRADITIONS NEVER CHANGED, not that anyone in Honeymoon Harbor would want them to. That was what traditions were all about, residents would tell you. As Chelsea watched the Shelter Bay High School band march down the street, proceeded by teenage girls in sparkly outfits twirling batons, she could see Hannah watching them carefully.

"I tried to twirl a baton once," Chelsea said quietly.

Hannah turned toward her. "How did you do?"

"I dropped it while practicing in the living room, which I wasn't supposed to do, and it fell on a vase that had been a wedding present to my folks from my grandmother Prescott." Who'd died of a stroke when Chelsea was Hailey's age, so she couldn't remember her very well. But she did have a very clear memory of the pieces of porcelain vase scattered all over the carpet.

"Did you get in trouble?"

"Not as much as I could have. I just had the baton taken away for a weekend, which wasn't any big deal because I'd already decided that I could practice all day long every day and probably never get as good as the girls in the parade because my coordination was off. Years later I learned that my mother and grandmother had never gotten along, so I suppose that was why she wasn't overly upset about the broken vase."

"It doesn't look that hard," Hannah mused as the band, led by a high-stepping drum master in a tall Mountie's-type hat, began playing an enthusiastic, only slightly off-key rendition of a Sousa march.

"You'll never know unless you try. We could find one online."

"It's silly."

"It never hurts to try." Chelsea waved to John and Sarah Mannion as they cruised by in a land yacht of a 1960s red Cadillac DeVille convertible donated by a member of a Port Townsend classic car club. The mayor was always designated grand marshal, and since John had been mayor as long as Chelsea could remember, Sarah had had many years to perfect her regal windshield wiper wave.

Behind the car came the local veterans, marching along with Boy Scouts and Girl Scouts carrying flags. While the girls had marched during those two years when Chelsea had worn the green uniform, they hadn't been allowed to carry flags. Which, she thought, made this one major change for the better.

The vets were followed by floats, pulled by decorated trucks representing businesses and service groups from the community. This was Bastien and Desiree's first year and their red, gold and purple colors brought a New Orleans flair to the Pacific Northwest. The chef/sax player stood on one side of the float, the baker/singer on the other, tossing Mardi Gras beads to the crowd lined up on the sidewalk as hidden speakers played their new album, a musical tribute to, and a soundtrack of, their native city.

And then, finally, toward the end, right before the Mannions' Christmas tree farm float, came the library float that Chelsea, Farrah, Lily, and even Janet and the other volunteers had been working on part-time for months. On the backdrop of the float, they'd painted a large mural of familiar Dr. Seuss characters; on the front was another board with large wooden letters Seth had cut out with his jigsaw which had been painted in bright crayon primary colors reading "Oh, the Places You'll Go!"

On the platform, sitting on boxes painted to look like stacks of books, were the reading adventurers and members of the younger readers group. Chelsea had asked Hannah if she'd like to join them, but, again, she'd declined.

"Maybe next year," Chelsea had suggested.

"Maybe," the girl had answered. "If I'm still here."

And wasn't that the problem that hovered over everything like a threatening storm cloud?

The Kiwanis had already started their annual holiday barbecue and the scent of grilling meat greeted the parade participants and viewers alike as they reached the park.

The music, provided by the high school pop choir, was wonderful, the company even better, and the fireworks, lighting up the sky over the harbor and reflected in the water were, Hailey declared, "The best fireworks ever!"

"That was a good day," Chelsea said to Gabe as they drove back to the lake.

"I think Hailey nailed it," he said.

"Your parents' snow machine was a big hit."

"Yeah. Dad was worried about it working, but it was a great ending to the parade."

"I think the adults enjoyed it as much as the kids. And speaking of kids, we've lost Hailey." And Hannah had her head against the window, looking as if she was about to fall asleep.

"It's been a long day."

"But a good one," Chelsea said. "I know it can be considered old-fashioned, but I really enjoy our small-town holiday celebrations."

"You won't get any argument from me on that."

AFTER THEIR LATE NIGHT, the girls both slept in. Fortunately, with the library being closed on Monday, Chelsea was able to enjoy the slow morning after having spent almost an entire night with Gabriel. He still left before dawn, though with the girls having been so exhausted, they'd taken the chance on him staying over. But had been sure to lock the bedroom door and open the closet one for a quick hiding place if necessary.

They were out on the deck, enjoying the morning birdsong while Hannah read in the library, and Hailey drew pictures of yesterday's adventures at the kitchen table, when Chelsea's phone rang.

"Good morning, Mrs. Douglas. What can I do for you? The girls, by the way, enjoyed yesterday's celebrations."

"So I heard," the social worker said. "I happen to have a family to visit on the other side of the lake today, and thought, while I was out here, I might as well kill two birds with one visit, so to speak."

"That's fine. Gabriel can open the gate for you."

As soon as she ended the call, she said, "You know

she did this last-minute inspection on purpose! To catch us off guard!"

"That'd be my guess."

"I need to change!" She was wearing her *I proudly contribute to the literacy of minors* red T-shirt with a pair of leggings, and no shoes.

"I think you look great. And it's not as if you're lounging around in ice cream pajamas."

"But it's an official investigation! At least I should put on some makeup. Or lipstick, or…oh my god, did the girls make their beds yet? I haven't looked."

"They're kids. Besides Monday is like our Sunday. A day of rest. Still, I'll just… Damn." They heard the car coming up the road. "Too late," Gabe said.

"What if she finds something that will make me unsuitable?"

"I can't think of anyone more suitable. Besides, if that woman they'd been living with had been approved, you can't possibly have anything to worry about."

"Try telling that to the giant condors in my stomach."

She took a deep breath as the doorbell rang and grabbed his hand. Hers was ice-cold.

"I suppose we ought to let her in," he said. "I'll send the girls upstairs." Chelsea thought, not for the first time, that for a man who claimed not to know anything about children, he possessed very good parenting instincts.

"I guess we don't have any choice."

"Hello, Chelsea. Gabriel," Adele Douglas said. "It's good to see you again, in more pleasant circumstances." She took in Chelsea's shirt. "I like that message."

"Thank you." Chelsea ran a hand down the front of her shirt. Maybe casual was okay. After all, the moms who brought their kids into the library for story hour didn't dress for a formal tea at The Mad Hatter. "Mrs. Henderson was always so well turned out, but that's not really my style. I have found that both adults and kids respond to the T-shirt messages." This one was definitely better than her *Crazy Book Lady* or *Librarian by Day. Ninja Demon Slayer by Night* ones hanging in the upstairs nanny's room closet.

"Spreading the gospel of libraries and reading is always a good thing," Mrs. Douglas said. "Where are the girls?"

"When I opened the gate, I sent them upstairs," Gabriel said. "In case you wanted to talk alone with us first."

"I do. Where would you like to conduct the interview?" Chelsea realized that her nerves might have shown for a moment, when the woman who held two little girls' lives in their hands backtracked. "Interview can sound more daunting than it is," Adele Douglas said. "I'm going to make notes for my report, but mainly I'd just like to have a conversation about how things have been going, and if you've considered any plans, Chelsea."

"Why don't we go into the great room?" Gabriel suggested. "That way the girls can know where we are if they come downstairs."

She smiled approvingly. "That's an excellent idea." As they led the way, Chelsea considered that Gabriel was batting a thousand. Perhaps she ought to just let him handle this.

The great room looked as if the decorator had been channeling Ralph Lauren. While impressive, Chelsea remembered an HGTV designer proclaiming that there was a thin line between sublime and clichéd. While she was certainly no decorator, having seen what Sarah Mannion had done with both Mai and Kylee's Folk Victorian and Herons Landing, she had no doubt that Gabriel's mother could come into this room, remove a few things, change others around and immediately make it more homey.

More as if a family lived in the house, while at the moment it appeared to have been staged for a photo shoot. Which, thinking about it, she guessed that it was now probably front and center on the decorator's website.

"This is quite the house," Mrs. Douglas said.

"I'm just borrowing it from a friend for the summer," Gabriel said.

"Yes, you mentioned you'd be leaving."

"Would you like some coffee? Or tea?" Chelsea asked.

"No, thank you. I'm fine." She opened her notebook to a page Chelsea noticed already had been written on. The woman had probably made contemporaneous notes that first night. While details were still fresh in her mind. That's what she herself would do.

"You mentioned going to the parade yesterday."

"We did. They both had a great time. Hailey wore herself out, but that was probably partly due to dancing to 'Jingle Bells' all the way down Water Street on the Mannions' Christmas farm float."

"So I saw on the Facebook page." She made a note. "How did that come about?"

Damn. Chelsea had forgotten all about checking that page. She spent the next few minutes explaining about the picnic, the trip to Seattle, the sandcastle building, Gabriel taking Hailey to the farm, which the social worker already knew because he'd called her ahead of time to make sure it was okay, and Hannah's days at the library. "She'd already spent every day there after school, so she felt comfortable and safe."

"Both good things," the woman said with a decisive nod.

"She's also been working with Gabriel at the boat shop."

"Oh?"

"I'm building a faering," Gabriel said. "It's a smaller version of a Viking boat. I'm auctioning it off for Welcome Home during the boat festival."

"I remember you making some lovely boats," Mrs. Douglas said. Then wrote some more.

"So, Chelsea, although you're staying here for the time being, you're still renting an apartment in Edna Moore's house?"

"For now. But I'll be moving."

The slight lift of a brow was unreadable. "Will you be staying in town?"

"Oh, yes. Absolutely. I just thought it was time for a larger place."

"Any particular reason?" The pen poised over the lined paper again.

Knowing this woman hadn't been born yesterday, and had shown herself to be very good at her job, Chelsea didn't try to hedge. "I was hoping that I could be approved to be a foster parent. Rather than merely an interim placement."

"I see." She didn't seem the least bit surprised. Merely made a notation in the notebook. "And, I assume, from what I saw of your relationship to the girls the night of the incident, and heard from Sarah Mannion and Mrs. Henderson, that you might be a candidate for guardianship."

"They've already moved so many times for such young ages," Chelsea said. "I know all about growing up in a less-than-stable environment. I wouldn't want that to be their future. So, yes, I've considered it."

"It's not an easy process," the social worker warned.

"It shouldn't be. Not with children's lives in the balance."

"A child or children must be in a proposed guardian's

home for six months prior to any guardianship being established."

"I'm not going anywhere."

"You'd need to participate in a shared planning meeting."

"Planning meetings are a normal part of my life," Chelsea said.

"You'd also have to understand that you'd be making a commitment to the children until adulthood with the intention of a continued lifelong relationship. This is nothing like bringing a puppy home from the shelter."

Chelsea was about to object to the idea that she would consider the situations at all similar, then decided against challenging a statement that felt like a test of some sort. "Absolutely, I'd make that commitment."

"Yet it seems a bit impulsive."

"I can see how it could appear that way." Chelsea didn't allow herself to look at Gabriel, who she could feel intently watching her. "Sometimes you know things are right. You don't just know it in your head. But also in your heart." She covered her own heart, which was currently beating like a snare drum playing Sousa. "I felt an immediate connection to both Hailey and Hannah within minutes of finding them in my library. *The* library," she amended, reminding herself that although it might feel like hers, officially it was Honeymoon Harbor's library.

"Perhaps it was because I recognized my younger self in them. Perhaps the bond, which has grown since then, was merely fate. Something inexplicable, but meant to happen. All I know is what I know. And I know I can give Hannah and Hailey the home they need. The home they deserve."

"That's very heartfelt," Mrs. Douglas said as she

began writing again. "And sincere. I do have one additional question."

"Okay."

"Guardianship is typically considered when reunification isn't possible and adoption is not in the child or children's best interests. As in the case of permanently separating siblings. Is there a reason you haven't considered adopting?"

"I have considered that." The idea had circled around and around, like a leaf caught in an eddy since that night they'd brought the girls home from Mrs. Lawler's. "But I assumed that I'd have to prove the ability to be a good guardian first."

"Well, yes, that's the case. Why don't we keep things as they are for now, and get you through the guardianship process while you give additional thought to a more permanent relationship."

"My relationship will be permanent whatever its official status. But if adoption is open to me, I'll definitely take it. If only to make the girls, especially Hannah, feel as if they've found their forever home."

She cringed inwardly, realizing that statement sounded like all those shelter adopt-a-pet TV commercials and videos that were always showing up in her Facebook timeline, but Mrs. Douglas merely continued writing. Then finally slipped her pen into the holder on the side of the notebook.

"I believe I have enough for today," she said. Then turned to Gabriel. "Now I'd like to speak with Hannah and Hailey. Alone."

"Of course." He stood. "I'll show you to their rooms.

CHAPTER TWENTY-SEVEN

DESPITE HAVING NO reason to expect things would go wrong during the social worker's interview with Hailey and Hannah, Chelsea's nerves were buzzing like electrical lines in the fog.

"You're going to pace a path in this rug," Gabe advised. "Not that either the current owner nor I would care. Just saying."

"It's nerve-racking."

"Obviously. You sure threw a curveball there. Adoption is quite a jump from considering trying to become a permanent foster mother."

"Not as much a jump as it seems. The friend who gave me those foster care statistics warned me against getting too involved with the girls. Or letting them get too involved with me, because they'd start seeing me as a mother figure, which in turn would make them feel the loss so much harder when they moved on. Which can happen several times a year."

"Hard to get your feet under you when the ground keeps shifting."

"Exactly. I was trying to walk a line between being just the library lady and a friend and mentor. Like yours was in New York."

The absurdity of that comparison almost had him laughing, but Gabe knew that she was dead serious.

"That's a difficult line." The one thing that the two situations had in common was that Carter and he had blurred their line from his very first year at Harborstone.

"It's been getting narrower and blurrier every day. It took the fire and seeing what their lives really were, what they might never be, perhaps until they aged out of the system at eighteen. And even by then, they could be so messed up, the entire rest of their lives could be affected."

"Possibly. But it wouldn't be your fault."

"Wouldn't it?" She stopped pacing in front of him. "Answer me this… If you were driving across the Tacoma Narrows Bridge, and you saw someone standing there looking as if they were going to jump, would you just drive on by and risk the chance of them jumping, or stop and try to help?"

"I'd call 911." When her eyes narrowed, he lifted his hands. "And okay, although I see where you're going, of course I'd stop. *After* I called 911. Because first responders are professionals. They know what to do."

"That argument isn't going to work for me, because what the admittedly overworked and underpaid professionals can do under these circumstances is shuffle kids around from home to home to home. It's not their fault, because they can only work with what they have and I looked on their website and they're trying a lot of outreach to prospective foster parents. But even if they get more, you and I both know that the opioid epidemic, which doesn't appear to be going to disappear anytime soon, will only increase demand for homes. For beds. Meanwhile, two innocent young children might spend over half their lives without parents, stuck in a never-ending revolving door. And the most important reason I want to adopt them is that I love them."

"I can't deny you didn't have a strong point before you got to the close. I also can't think of anyone who'd be a better mom. Despite your attempt to walk that tightrope, it's obvious that the kids have bonded with you. You've even managed to put cracks in Hannah's protective shell."

"So have you."

"Even if that's true, it's a moot point. Because I'm not going to be here to deal with future problems. Not that you asked for my advice, but I say go for it."

"Thank you." She blew out a breath, surprising him with her obvious relief. "I had serious doubts I'd ever have kids," she admitted. She shook her head. "I don't know why I keep telling you these things I never tell anyone else."

"Maybe because I'm a safe sounding board because I'm not sticking around that long and I sure as hell don't have any reason to tell anyone."

"I will admit that from what I've seen from friends, raising children isn't easy. And it's serious. The past days have proven that it's going to be tricky balancing work and life as a single mom. But my hours are more flexible than most, and as you said, I have a strong support system, like your mom who thought of the day camp and welcomed Hailey into her home, your dad who pulled the strings to get them in the camp, and Brianna, who gave you all those recipes so you can make the kids a special breakfast."

"That's the easy part. I told you my mom taught us all to cook."

"You also opened up your house, and not just as some sort of temporary hostel. By teaching Hannah chess and sitting through Hailey's seemingly never-ending fashion show, you made it feel like a home to them. That's made a big difference."

Since he had no answer, other than point out, yet again, that his part in the girls' care would last only a few more weeks, Gabe didn't say anything at all.

AFTER THE MEETING with the girls, Mrs. Douglas left to pick up another child she'd just received notification about.

It had gone through Gabe's mind as they'd waited for the social worker to come back downstairs that the girls' presence hadn't affected his work. While he'd set himself a tight deadline, he couldn't work on the faering 24/7. He could continue to help out with the girls. Like taking them to the park. Or crabbing off the pier, like his dad and grandfather had done with him. Hailey had enjoyed her time at the farm, and he'd bet Hannah would too, although she might not readily admit it.

The idea was sounding better and better, until he remembered what Chelsea's friend had told her about being careful about bonding. What if they started thinking of him as a potential father? Chelsea might be in for the long-term, but he was leaving before the swallows and Canada geese.

He'd have to try to keep his distance.

"Good luck with that," he muttered.

THE NEXT WEEKS WERE, hands down, the happiest of Chelsea's life. She'd always known that having her family disintegrate like a sandcastle at high tide had left a hole inside her that she'd never expected to ever fully fill. Unlike her mother, who'd simply faded away until she'd finally died, Chelsea had, as she'd told Gabriel, chosen to be happy. She'd learned to fill her time with friends, civic activities, and ambitious projects like the reading adventurers to always keep active, never giving those cold dark shadows a chance to catch up with her.

She'd found once she handed Farrah more responsibility, the librarian was proving to be exactly what the town, the library and Chelsea needed. Farrah's first idea was to set up little free libraries around the county, where people could "take a book, leave a book." Not only had she gotten the entire community involved in the idea, to build enthusiasm she'd devised a competition with various categories of designs. The most popular design was, unsurprisingly, Victorian buildings. But there were also whimsical ones, like the bright red Snoopy doghouse outside Cameron Montgomery's veterinarian office, the Cat in the Hat's tall red-and-white-striped hat and, almost earning its own category, the large fish-shaped box Bert had set out at his café.

It did not escape Chelsea's attention that Bert had sought Lillian Henderson's advice on his project, which had apparently required many meetings. Including one where they'd supposedly been discussing which books to stock the wooden fish with over lunch at the Lake Quinault Lodge. Some enterprising Honeymoon Harborite had taken a photo of them together and not only sent it to the Facebook page, but also to the *Honeymoon Harbor Herald*, where it had ended up on the "Around the Town" page. Which had her thinking back on Bert's mention of having stood Lillian up for the winter dance, before she'd met the man who'd become her husband. Seth's parents, along with Gloria Wells and Michael Mannion, had already demonstrated that romance wasn't just for the young. Why shouldn't Bert and Lillian—him in his early seventies, her in her late sixties—have a second chance at love?

It hadn't originally been easy giving up control, but while picking up Hailey at the Christmas tree farm, when she'd asked Sarah for advice on how to juggle both family and work, the most important thing Gabriel's mother had told her was learning to prioritize and delegate. "No one expects you to be Wonder Woman, dear," she'd advised.

Chelsea thought about that all the way home, as Hailey chattered on and on about the two Australian shepherd mixes Mulder and Scully, and how she'd loved to have a dog of her own "more than anything!" The next day Chelsea had told Farrah, the assistants and volunteers that she'd be taking some time off this summer for personal reasons, but would certainly be taking part in the adventurers' program.

"Why can't I come to Mr. Mannion's brewery?" Hannah had complained. The more comfortable she'd become, the more she'd started challenging authority. Which either meant that she was beginning to feel more comfortable now that the girls had been told Chelsea was on the list to begin her foster parent classes in September. Or, perhaps, she was pushing to see if Chelsea's love had limits. If she'd someday decide that kids were too much trouble and send them away. Which wasn't going to happen, but Chelsea had, nevertheless, made a series of appointments for all three of them, each by themselves, then in joint sessions, with a counselor in Sequim to help ease the transition.

"Because you have to be fourteen years old. Which you're not."

"Gabriel is Quinn's brother. That should count for something," she complained, looking directly at him.

"Sorry, kiddo," Gabriel said. "Quinn's always been a stickler for rules. And you wouldn't want Aiden to have to arrest his own big brother for breaking liquor laws."

"No. But it's still not fair," she huffed.

"We can take Gabriel's shiny new motorhome down to Oregon and tour Tillamook," Chelsea suggested. He had, indeed, decided that there was no point in having a list if you didn't work through all the items, and although she found the motorhome to be an extravagant waste of money, they'd taken it to various places along the rugged Washington Coast, and once to Long Beach for the SandSations sandcastle competition where, after some practice here at the cove with the proper tools, they'd taken second place in the amateur category. "That's supposed to be fun."

"It's a cheese factory."

"You like cheese."

"Yeah. Some cheese. But I don't need to see it being made."

As she'd hoped, Gabriel's Viking boat proved to be the most popular with the adventurers. She'd already had them read selected stories about the Vikings, and, by the time the boat shop came up on the itinerary, Gabriel had just finished the red canvas sail. While it wasn't yet ready to go in the water, he did invite all the adventurers to watch its maiden voyage at the Labor Day wooden boat festival.

"It's not really going to be her maiden voyage, is it?" Chelsea asked the night after that adventure.

"That's always been the plan," he reminded her. "But if you want, we can take it out here on the lake before the festival."

"The girls would love it," she said.

"I've been thinking the same thing. Hannah, especially, after all the time she's spent at the shop."

"She's sincerely interested in the faering. But I suspect she's also got a bit of a crush on the boat builder."

"Does she? Is there anything I should do?"

"Just keep doing what you're doing. I looked it up and it's a normal part of adolescence. The more she gets to know you, the sooner it'll wear off."

"Familiarity breeds contempt?"

"Not contempt. But she's got you on a pedestal, and eventually, it's going to crumble."

"Well, hell, that makes me feel a lot better."

She laughed and patted his cheek. "Meet me in the motorhome at midnight, and I'll make you feel a whole lot better."

"You're on. That's turning out to be my best investment ever."

He wasn't going to get any argument from her on that count. Chelsea thought of the foster mom who could nearly climax merely by walking on the beach, and hoped she wouldn't get to the point where she'd have an orgasm every time she followed a motorhome, which, since that happened to be every day in summer, would be exhausting.

CHAPTER TWENTY-EIGHT

CHELSEA COULD FEEL fall coming. It didn't arrive in a dazzling blaze of autumn color but with cooler nights, and each day the sky grew darker just a few minutes earlier. While people in other parts of the country might not notice such small incremental daily changes, here in the Pacific Northwest, where summers were short, and never got too hot, residents wanted to hang on to them as long as possible.

"Are you getting nervous?" Chelsea asked Brianna as she, Jolene and Lily had lunch at Leaf.

"Only because I want to get it over with," Brianna said, picking at her salad. "No, rewind. I didn't mean it that way. It's just that I fell in love with Seth when he shared his Ding Dong with me in the first grade, and I finally want to be married."

"Me, too," Jolene said. "Though I didn't fall for Aiden until high school. Then we spent all those years apart, so we were very different people than we are now. I was also wary of commitment, but your brother's a hard man to resist," she told Brianna.

"I'm probably biased. Okay, I am. But all my brothers are special in their own individual ways."

"Seth is no slouch," Lily said.

"He's the closest thing any woman could ever find to perfection for me," Brianna agreed. "And maybe it's a hormonal thing caused by so much sex, but I am so ready to start our family."

"When you do, I'll give you my list," Chelsea volunteered.

Jolene, who'd been watching the ferry coming in to dock, turned her full attention to Chelsea. "What kind of list?"

"A sex list."

"You have a sex list?" Brianna, usually the model of public propriety, asked loudly enough to have people at nearby tables turning to look at them.

"I was going to type it up and save it for your baby shower gift, but now that you've seen fit to broadcast it, yes, I do have a list I got from women at my foster mom group on ways to have sex with kids in the house."

"I'd never thought of that problem. But I guess it's a thing."

"Believe me, it's a thing," Chelsea said. "If you're not careful, you're going to find yourself in sexual drought-land."

"Well, that saves me from asking whether or not you and my brother are having sex," Brianna said. "I suspected it, but except for that dinner at Sensation Cajun, I haven't seen any suggestion that you two were getting it on out at the lake house."

"Thanks to the list, the sex has been sensational. Some of it's a bit unconventional, but it's surprisingly hot."

"I so want to wash my brain out with Clorox at the thought of my brother getting naked and having unconventional sex—"

"You don't always have to get naked," Chelsea said with a Cheshire cat smile.

"No!" Brianna covered her ears and shut her eyes. "Now I'm never going to be able to unsee that and it's all your fault."

"You did bring up sex," Lily reminded her.

"I did not. I brought up having a baby."

"Which involves sex. Unless you've had a visit from an angel bringing you tidings of great joy recently," Chelsea said. "So as not to upset your apparently delicate sensibilities any further, I'll just put this out there and let you decide if you want to explore it. Did you ever make a blanket fort when you were a kid?"

"Of course. It's a long winter and there are a lot of days when we kids couldn't go outside, so…oh!" She covered her mouth.

"Let's just say your brother is very, very skilled at capturing the fort. And planting his flag."

"I am never going to be able to look at him again without picturing that."

"Picture Seth instead and I'll bet it won't bother you so much. In fact, why don't you try it out on your honeymoon. *Wargame* it, so to speak."

"I still can't believe they gave you a list."

"I only wrote down what they were saying. It wasn't a *list* list until then. You'd be surprised at the ways and places you'll be able to ensure your first baby won't be your last."

"OMG. *That's* why Gabriel bought that fancy new motorhome. None of us could figure it out since he's going back to Manhattan, where he definitely couldn't drive it around the city."

"I can neither confirm nor deny."

"You don't have to. It's written all over your face." Brianna stabbed a fresh strawberry with her fork, which stopped halfway to her mouth. "Wait a minute. Does this mean he's not going back to New York?"

"Oh, he's going, right after Labor Day. Just as he said."

Brianna sobered. "I'm so sorry."

"Me, too," Jolene said.

"Me, three," Lily chimed in.

"You were the one who suggested a summer fling," Chelsea reminded Lily.

"Exactly. A fling. As in a short, intense version of friends with benefits. You're not supposed to fall in love with a fling."

"I did," Jolene volunteered.

"With a guy who wasn't going anywhere. In a town where you can't go out for milk and eggs without running into a dozen people you know. You don't have a fling with a man you're still going to see every day when it's over. Flings are for long weekends at a winter ski lodge. Or a Caribbean cruise. Two ships passing in the night. Or, in the case of a small-town girl and a guy who's got a short shelf life, before he goes back to the city."

"It's just sex," Chelsea insisted, ignoring Lily's knowing look. "Summer fling sex."

If she could only make herself believe that, everything would be hunky-dory.

"Okay," Brianna said. She glanced down at her watch. "Let's table this discussion because Chelsea, Jolene and I have ten minutes to get over to The Dancing Deer and try on our dresses."

"And I have to get back to work on the new semester press release and invitations for the scholarship reception," Lily said.

"But," Brianna said to Chelsea as they left Leaf after paying the bill, "we all still want that list."

As if wanting to give her own wedding gift to the brides, Mother Nature had turned benevolent, bringing back a perfect day of late-summer blue skies and clear air that allowed the mountains to glisten for as far as the eye could see.

Brianna, who'd once planned a formal wedding for a pair of dogs with a six-figure price tag, had decided she wanted a casual ceremony and reception at the Mannion Christmas tree farm to celebrate her marriage. Since she was marrying a Mannion brother, Jolene had readily agreed on the venue.

It was a family affair, with Caroline Harper, Seth's mother, who'd become an ordained minister last year, performing the ceremony. Chelsea was attendant to both brides while Quinn was groomsman to his younger brother and the man his sister had loved since childhood.

Bastien and Desiree provided the music, as they had last summer for Kylee and Mai's garden wedding. It was that wedding which had brought the two former lovers back together.

Brianna had chosen an understated ivory slip dress, a single pearl on a platinum chain and white ballet flats that wouldn't sink into the turf of the back lawn as she welcomed guests in the reception line. Jolene, wearing her favored '50s vintage style, had gone with a knee-length backless dress with a full skirt that swayed like a bell when she walked. Around her neck she wore a simple heart made from a piece of aqua sea glass found on the peninsula on a white gold chain. Aiden had given it to her one summer night, back when they'd still been in high school, before he'd gone off to Marine boot camp.

Despite the casual atmosphere, the grooms waiting at the head of the white satin runner were handsome in black tie.

Life had taken both couples down separate paths for many years until they'd ended up back here in Honeymoon Harbor. In this place, on this day. Unlike the last wedding they'd all attended, when Kylee and Mai had written their own vows, today's words were simple, complex and timeless.

To love. Honor. Cherish. For better or worse. Richer or poorer. Forsaking all others. Until death we do us part.

Rings were exchanged, and as Caroline Harper pronounced both couples married, everyone in attendance stood up and applauded. Then as the couples walked up the aisle to Bastien and Desiree singing "Signed, Sealed, and Delivered," the guests began dancing in the aisle behind them.

THE MOOD WAS festive as toasts were made; Seth and Brianna and Aiden and Jolene danced for the first time as married couples, then some guests joined them on the dance floor as others dug into the barbecue ribs, burgers and all the trimmings prepared by Jarle, a sous chef borrowed from Luca, and two line cooks hired from the college's culinary arts school.

Chelsea, Gabe and the girls had just sat down at one of the round tables when his phone rang. He glanced at the screen, then told Chelsea, "I'd better take this." Before she could argue that business could wait while he was at his brother's and sister's wedding, he was gone.

"I'M IN THE middle of something, Phil, so this better damn well be good."

"If you want that senior slot, you'd better get back here ASAP," Phil Gregg warned him. "Hendricks has been trying to poach your accounts and he's definitely playing hardball politics, suggesting that having taken this break so soon after landing in the ER, you're not up to the job. That maybe you're too emotional over Carter, or maybe you're burned out. You've got a lot of guys in your corner, but I've got to tell you, Gabe, I'm not sure we're going to be enough to stop the coup by ourselves. You need to be on the scene before you lose everything you've worked for."

Which was something Gabe had no intention of letting happen. Barry Hendricks was a trust fund baby, hired more for his social good-old-boy connections going back to the cradle. He'd been playing lacrosse and tennis at Groton while Gabe had been running cross-country track at Honeymoon Harbor High. He'd gone to Harvard while Gabe had received an excellent education at UW that had gotten him into Columbia, but a West Coast public school didn't carry equal clout in East Coast boardrooms. But Gabe was smarter and tougher. And a better trader because people trusted him. Which couldn't always be said for Hendricks.

"I'm on my way." It took one call to arrange for a jet to be waiting at Sea-Tac to fly him back to Manhattan. Another for a car. Those details taken care of, he went in search of Chelsea. She wouldn't be nearly so easy to manage.

HE FOUND HER on the dance floor with Hailey and Hannah. The two girls had gotten new dresses for the wedding. Hailey was wearing—what else?—pink, with one of those puckered-up tops. Smocked, he remembered Chelsea calling it during another fashion show the girls put on beneath the spotlight. Hannah was wearing a short turquoise dress with a white collar and cuffs. And looking frighteningly mature.

"Is Hannah wearing a bra?" he asked after he'd gotten Chelsea off the dance floor. The girls were now dancing with a boy who looked to be about Hannah's age. "And who the hell is he?"

"Yes, to the bra. It was time. Girls are maturing earlier

these days. As for the boy, he's Ryan, a Harper cousin. His parents seem like very nice people."

"Isn't she too young to be dancing with boys?"

"It's a wedding, Gabe. Kids dance at weddings. It's not like he's asking her to go to the movies."

"To which you'd say no, right?"

"Seriously? This is what you want to talk about? Why don't you fill me in on what that phone call was about?"

"I have to go."

"Where?"

"Back to Manhattan."

"Well, I know that. You've been very clear about your plans to return after the boat festival."

"No, I mean I have to go back now."

"Now?" She combed a hand through her hair. "I'm confused. Are you talking about after the reception? Or right now this minute?"

"I have a plane waiting for me at Sea-Tac. And a car on the way here to take me there."

"I see." She folded her arms as both her voice and eyes turned to frost. "I'm surprised you didn't hire a helicopter to land on the center of the dance floor and whisk you away to the airport so you don't have to suffer that inconvenient ride in a limo."

"I deserve that," Gabe said, feeling whatever Zen he'd manage to achieve in the past weeks going up in flames around them.

"Yeah," Quinn's deep voice behind him said. "You do."

"Once again, you're right. But it is what it is. If I don't get back there ASAP, everything I've worked for all these years could go down the drain."

"I'd suggest that's an exaggeration," Quinn said, his

eyes and mouth hard. "But you're obviously not ready to hear that."

"Our situations are different," Gabe argued. "You didn't enjoy your work anymore and found your niche making great beer and running the pub. And as happy as I am for you, bro, that's not me."

He turned back toward Chelsea. "You can take the Range Rover back to the house. And feel free to use it while you're staying there."

"Gee, thanks bunches for the offer, but I like my car. As for the house, did you already buy it?"

"No, but that doesn't matter."

"It does to me. The girls and I aren't staying alone in a house owned by someone we don't know."

"We'll pick up your stuff," Quinn suggested. "Then I'll take you to the farm. You can stay there while we figure out a plan."

"I hate to impose." She dragged an unsteady hand through her hair again. Gabe hadn't just blown up his Zen. Chelsea and the girls were turning out to be collateral damage. *Like the sex fog was too thick for you to have seen that coming?*

"I have a situation to fix," he said. "Then I'll be back as soon as possible. Quinn's idea is a good one. You can stay at the farm. We can still have the rest of the summer."

She lifted her chin. If looks could kill, he'd be six feet under. "Surely you're not serious."

"It's just a glitch."

"And this is your sister's and brother's *wedding reception*. But your glitch apparently is more important. Remember the night I rowed across the lake? When I told you about my messed-up family and said that I envied you yours?"

Gabe saw it coming and decided there was nothing he could do but take the hit. "I do."

"I still envy you for them. But here's a newsflash—" she pointed a finger at his chest "—you don't deserve them. Now, since there's nothing else to say to each other, we're done. And I'd like to go back to dancing with my soon-to-be adopted daughters."

"Well," Quinn said as they watched her march away. The smile she greeted the girls with was nothing like the steely look she'd given him. "You sure as hell screwed the pooch on that one."

"I don't have a choice. If I don't get back to New York right away, I'm not only going to lose my chance to be the youngest trader at Harborstone to make senior partner, I could well be out of a job. Because once people find out I let some piece of shit rich guy undercut me, my reputation will be shot and all those places that recruited me when I got out of Columbia won't want me."

"First of all, may I point out that you, too, are a really rich guy. So, using that as an epithet isn't exactly your best use of words. And second, it's just as well that you forced Chelsea into a corner where she had no choice but to break off whatever it was you thought you had going. Because you know what she said about you not deserving your family?"

"She was angry."

"She was *right*. And here's another newsflash, baby bro—you don't deserve her or those kids, either." He shook his head. "I never realized you'd turned into such a dumbass. Now, I'm going to go have barbecue with the terrific woman you let get away. Then I'm going to dance with the three of them, and later take her to that house you're going to buy, which you don't, in any real-life scenario, need except to turn a damn profit from.

"Then, once they're packed, I'm taking them to the farm. Where they'll be treated like they deserve."

That said, Quinn walked away.

Gabe watched Chelsea talking to the girls. Hannah shot him a look, then turned toward him and although Chelsea obviously tried to stop her, she shook off the restraining hand and headed his way.

"You said you weren't leaving until after Labor Day."

"That was my plan. But something came up."

"Chelsea already said that. Did someone die?"

"No. You wouldn't understand. It's a work thing."

"You're wrong. I *would* understand because I've heard all the excuses. Yours is one of the weakest though, it's not even original because we've already had two families where the dad got a work transfer and they decided we weren't worth taking along. So, yeah, I get it. I'm just mad that I was stupid enough to think you were different."

Her eyes swam and her lips, which he noted had been tinted a pale pink, quivered. Then she squared her shoulders, which she hadn't done since those early days, and resolutely blinked the tears away. Except for one that managed to escape, which she furiously swept away with the back of her hand.

"So go back to New York City to your fancy job in your fancy office and your fancy apartment in some fancy skyscraper and enjoy making all that money. Because we don't need you."

That said, she spun on a heel and went running back to Chelsea and her sister. Leaving Gabe just as he'd been for all these years since leaving home—alone.

CHAPTER TWENTY-NINE

CHELSEA WAS JUST coming to see if the girls needed any help when she heard them talking.

"Why did Gabriel go away?" Hailey asked her sister, as they packed their things so they could move. Again.

"Because he got tired of us."

"Was it because I was bad?"

"No." Hannah went down on her knees and drew her sister into her arms. "Some people like kids okay, but don't want to be around them all the time. He's said all along he was going to leave once summer ended."

"But summer isn't ended yet." Hailey's bottom lip was quivering, a sign she was about to burst into tears. "We haven't gotten to go for a ride in the faering. And he's going to miss the boat festival."

"He knows that. And I'm sure he's feeling really bad about leaving. But he's got important work to do."

Hailey wiped the back of her hand between her nose and mouth. "Do you think he'll come back?"

"I don't know, sprout. But even if he does, we won't be here. You like the farm."

"I do like it. It's fun. But I hate moving." She threw her unicorn T-shirt into the small pink polka-dot suitcase Chelsea had bought her in Seattle. "And I hate Gabriel."

She'd done this, Chelsea told herself with a sinking heart. She'd put these two girls at emotional risk just so she could have a damn summer fling. Why couldn't she have seen this coming? Because, she admitted, she'd fallen in love with Gabriel, which had allowed her to believe, deep down, that he'd decide to stay. To help her create a family. A family, ironically, like the one he'd grown up in.

She could do this. She'd overcome loss before. She could do it again, if not for herself, for Hannah and Hailey. Her soon-to-be daughters. And they might not be as large a family as the Mannions, but two children would never be more loved.

And maybe, when she was a very old woman, the pain she was feeling today would have eased. She hoped.

As ALWAYS, QUINN was right. Gabe had screwed the pooch and as he sat in the back of the black town car—which was a far cry from the limo Chelsea had probably had in mind—he thought about his parents and the story he'd heard about their rocky courtship.

His mother had been the first in her family to go to college, and her parents, whose family had been fishing in these waters for over a century, had wanted more for her than small-town life. Which was what they'd feared she'd *settle for* if her teenage romance with John Mannion was allowed to blossom. But they'd been too late to stop it, and, as the story went, the high school sweethearts often sneaked out to be together that last summer before Gabe's dad had gone off to UW and his mom went east to college. But even then, his dad had worked extra jobs while at school, making money for the trips across the country so they could be together.

It was difficult at the best of times to keep a long-distance relationship going. His parents were young and made mistakes, more his than hers, his dad always insisted, which was when his mom would jump into the conversation and point out that if she'd only been honest and brave enough to speak her mind, they wouldn't have lost those years apart.

During which time, they both would say, looking into each other's eyes like the love-besotted teenagers they'd once been, neither had ever stopped thinking of the other.

Then fate had brought them back together and in a whirlwind twenty-four hours, she had decided not to return to Oxford, where she'd been accepted into a PhD program, and he'd revealed his plans to become a tree farmer rather than a banker, and proposed at the very farm where they lived now.

And so they'd married, with the blessing of her parents, who, it turned out, had only ever wanted her to be happy, had five children, his father had become mayor, his mother a teacher, then a principal, and every single day they lived a golden example of marriage that Gabe had always admired but considered a near impossible act to follow.

Brianna and Seth—another marriage uniting the Harpers and the Mannions—appeared to be following in their footsteps. As were Aiden and Jolene Wells, and who would've ever seen that coming? Honeymoon Harbor's former bad boy was now the chief of police, and the bullied girl from the wrong side of the tracks, whose father had died while serving time in prison, had not only been nominated for an Emmy for makeup artistry but, with his angel investor financial assistance, was growing her cosmetics business into a regional West Coast chain, even while continuing to work on the occasional film. They were seemingly another perfect couple.

So, it wasn't impossible. But in his world of the rich and often infamous, Gabe had had a front-row seat at enough failed marriages to know that the odds of a happily-ever-after storybook ending is a crapshoot.

But so was any relationship. Look at Chelsea and him. She was not the woman he'd been looking for. But he'd found her. That first day in the shop, when he'd known she'd be trouble, he hadn't wanted her. But she had turned out to be the woman he not only wanted, with every fiber of his being, but needed.

Having watched the wreckage Carter had delivered to his four children, Gabe was determined that if he'd ever meet a like-minded woman he might marry, children would be off the bargaining table. But then two orphaned girls had come into his life. And his heart.

He'd always thought himself a risk taker. Going off to New York, where he knew no one, with plans to become *someone*. He'd taken a risk when he'd gone to work for Harborstone, which Dr. Doogie had accurately portrayed as a Little Pond, Big Fish scenario. Unlike a larger firm, where it was possible to blend into the woodwork, make some deals, have a life outside the office and not have to get up every morning geared for war, he'd chosen war. And the risk had paid off. Until now.

Gabe had no doubt he could wrest his power back and take Carter's senior place on the board before the brown slushy New York City snow melted next spring.

But why would he want to?

He'd gone to Wall Street firmly believing that there'd be some crystal clear moment when an imaginary bell would ring, like in that Christmas movie his mom made them watch every Christmas Eve, announcing not that he'd earned angel wings, but that he had achieved absolute success. Such as getting a senior seat on the board. He'd also believed that once he'd reached that lofty place and had all the money he'd ever need, he'd be happy.

However, his conversations with Chelsea had him realizing that would never happen because the goal line would keep moving. And as hard as it was to admit, like all the other guys who hung out at those finance bars, he'd been chasing the high like an addict. Since returning home to Honeymoon Harbor, he'd had so many reminders, including from his own family, and even love-struck Jarle, that family, friends and love were what brought true and lasting happiness.

His mind wandered to the French Alps, where Dr. Doogie's brother was taking the summer off to spend with his family, forgoing the money he could make from teaching wealthy skiers with enough time and money to move around the world with the snow to build a better, richer life.

Quinn had thrown his high-paying, prestigious attorney gig away and risked starting his brewery and reestablishing the preprohibition family pub. And now he was obviously as happy as a Puget Sound clam.

When was the last time he'd been happy? Gabe asked himself. Oh, yeah. Earlier when he'd watched his sister and brother dancing back up the aisle after exchanging those lifetime vows with their spouses. He had not a single doubt that their risk on love would turn out as richly rewarding as his parents' had.

He'd been born into a family of risk takers, Yet, unlike the Mannions before him, he was afraid of taking the ultimate risk of putting his heart on the line. And in reality, it wouldn't even be a risk. Because there was a warm, beautiful woman and two great kids in Honeymoon Harbor who'd already given him their hearts.

They loved him. And he felt shame for how he'd treated their gift.

They'd reached the ferry terminal just as the cars had begun to load. In another minute he'd be on board, headed to that Learjet waiting on a Sea-Tac tarmac to fly him back to the battlefield.

"I need you to turn around," he told the driver, who looked up at him in the rearview mirror.

"Why? Did you forget something, sir?"

"Yes." He'd forgotten what was important, what life was, or at least *should* be all about. He'd forgotten that love was both the greatest risk, and the greatest reward of all. "I need you to take me back to Honeymoon Harbor."

"Yessir."

She wasn't going to let him off easy. But like Seth did to win Brianna back when he'd almost lost her, Gabe was willing to grovel. Whatever Chelsea wanted, he'd do it. If she didn't want to live in the lake cabin that had begun to feel like home, he'd build her a new one. Any kind, anywhere.

If she wanted him to crawl naked down Water Street over broken oyster shells, he'd do that. If she wanted him to give away all his money, he'd even do that. But hopefully she'd agree that he could do more good using it to help others then throwing it to the winds, then living with his wife and two, hopefully more, kids and a dog. Because after what he'd done to the kids today, Hailey was definitely getting her dog.

Whatever Chelsea wanted. He'd do anything for love.

THEY WERE STALLING. None of them had that much to pack, but Chelsea understood that this had been a special place for them. The first, probably, in a very long time that despite its excesses felt like home. Where, despite Gabe's insistence that he'd be gone with the geese come summer's end, they'd felt like a family. She knew that deep in their young hearts, the girls had believed that he'd change his mind. That he'd stay. Because they'd all been so perfect together. How could he not see that? She knew what they'd been thinking, because she'd been thinking the exact same thing.

He'd miss them. Terribly. He might not realize it now, but all the bright and busy days filled with all the expensive, shiny things were worth nothing in the end. There was one thing that all the money in the world could never buy. One thing that endured. The one thing only she and the girls could give him. Love. And he hadn't accepted that gift.

Having changed from her bridesmaid's dress into a pair of khaki capris and a T-shirt with the Einstein quote *The only thing that you absolutely have to know is the location of the library*, she was sitting in the library while Hannah took Hailey down to the beach to collect a final bag of shells and rocks, and maybe even a piece of sea glass, like the heart-shaped one Aiden had given Jolene so many years ago.

Chelsea wondered if years from now, when the girls were grown with their own families, they'd remember this day, and Gabe, and have sympathy for the man who'd chosen to live atop his gilded New York world alone.

"Chelsea!" Hailey came running into the library, dropping shells and rocks and spreading gray sand everywhere. "He's here!"

"Quinn? I know. He's taking us to the farm."

"Not Quinn," Hannah, who was following slowly behind so as not to drop her collected treasures, said. "Gabriel."

It was true. Hearts really did stop. Fortunately, Chelsea's began to beat again, albeit at a rhythm that couldn't possibly be healthy for anyone. She put a hand on her chest, as if to calm it. Momentarily closed her eyes and drew in a breath. Held it. Then blew it slowly out. Again. A third time.

"What are you doing?" Hailey demanded, with more than her usual impatience.

"She's meditating," Hannah said.

"Why?"

"Maybe to calm down so she won't stroke out. Or so she won't shove him into the water. Which is what I'd do."

Chelsea opened her eyes. "Don't tempt me. I'm supposed to be the adult here… Okay." Her heart was no longer in danger, her head was clear. "Clear eyes, full hearts, can't lose."

"What does that mean?" Hailey said.

"It's from a TV show," Hannah said. "And I think a movie. And maybe a book. It means Chelsea's planning to win."

"And Gabriel will live with us, and we'll be a family? Forever and ever?" Hailey asked.

"We don't know why he's come back," Chelsea said. The hope in that young voice was breaking her heart all over again. Especially since, dammit, she was sharing that same hope. Maybe she would take Hannah's suggestion and shove him into the water. "He could have forgotten something."

Like her. And the girls.

"Or maybe he's come here to apologize," Hannah said. "You should probably give him a chance to try to fix this. And FYI, I wouldn't go easy on him."

Chelsea blew out a breath which finished clearing her mind. "I'll be back," she promised.

"Don't come alone," Hannah said.

Despite what had proven to be a horrible end to what had started out as a lovely day, Chelsea managed a ragged laugh. "You realize that I am, literally, going to be the boss of you. For many years to come."

"It's not my fault I haven't had any loving parental discipline for a very long time. You'll have to work on that, I suppose."

"*We'll* work on that," Chelsea amended. "Together."

With that, she walked out of the library, down the hall into the foyer and to the front door where Quinn was standing.

"If you need any help, just yell," he said. "I can take

him, easy. That manly jaw so many women have swooned over is pure glass. Just so you know."

"I'll keep that in mind," Chelsea said. Not that she intended to hit him. Although there'd admittedly been a moment at the reception when she'd been tempted to.

GABE STUDIED HER as she walked out the door. For a woman whose every thought was always written on her face, and in those bright as sunshine eyes, she wasn't giving him a clue this time. *And what did you expect? Her to run into your waiting arms like a woman in a perfume commercial?*

"I forgot something," he said.

"Oh?" He didn't realize she could arch a brow like that. It was definitely a librarian brow. He remembered Mrs. Henderson using it like a light saber. "What would that be?"

"You."

"I see."

"I had my priorities all screwed up. I have for a long time, which is how I ended up in the hospital with what the EMTs thought maybe was a heart attack."

Her eyes widened, revealing a flash of emotion. "You had a heart attack?"

"No. It turned out to be an anxiety attack, but it got my attention enough that I came home to regroup. And get my mojo back. But even after I got here, I was too blind, or stupid, to realize how screwed up my life had become until I got to the ferry and knew that I didn't want to spend my life anywhere else with anyone but you."

The crickets were back. Bunches and bunches of them. Or, as he remembered his mother teaching them one summer evening, an *orchestra* of crickets. All playing a someone-done-someone-wrong song.

"I'm sorry," she said finally. "Was that a proposal?"

He rubbed his jaw, saw Quinn standing in the doorway behind her, and hoped that he could get out of this mess he'd created without landing back in the ER.

"Yes. It was."

"And you came up with the idea to propose when?"

"At the ferry."

"Which you didn't board."

"No, because, well, there wasn't any reason to. Because you were here."

"That would be true. As are the girls."

"I'm hoping that they're a package deal."

"That's a big decision. Taking on a wife and two children. A proposal so important doesn't seem something that a person should make impulsively. It should be given a proper amount of thought."

He glanced over and saw the two faces pressed against the window. *His girls.* Just the thought of turning this real estate showplace into a proper home with the three of them gave him more happiness than any Wall Street deal had ever provided. He was going to have to write Dr. Doogie a thank-you note. Or better yet, invite him to the wedding. Then maybe, next year, they could all go summer skiing to meet the brother. Who wouldn't be working. But then again, neither would he. Because it would be a vacation from the philanthropic equity fund he intended to run out of the housekeeper's cottage.

The kids would definitely need a dog. One big enough not to slip through the spaces in the wrought iron fence surrounding the main part of the property.

He thought about taking them sailing in the bay. Not in the faering, which he was still sticking to his promise of auctioning off, but in a boat large enough for them to spend the night anchored in Serenity Cove. He thought about grilling fresh-caught salmon on the back deck, of family barbecues on the velvety green expanse of lawn. Of Christmas at his family's farm, of the girls riding in the sleigh his father brought out every year for the festival.

He thought of growing old with Chelsea Prescott Mannion. Of sitting in rocking chairs on the deck, watching the lowering summer sun gild the lake to shades of gold and copper. He thought of watching the stars come out, glistening like diamonds in a dark blue velvet sky. Then later, finding yet new places and ways to add to the list.

"I think I'm going to be a dirty old man."

"That's a point in your favor. So long as you plan on keeping it home."

"Anywhere you are."

Chelsea's slow smile gave him hope that she might not require the crawling on oyster shells penance. "That's exactly the right answer."

"I've thought about it."

"And?"

"It *is* a proposal."

"It took you long enough. I was getting a little worried that Hailey was going to come running out and do it for you. And how would we explain that to our grandchildren?"

"If you're talking about her kids, they'll totally understand."

She laughed. Then closed the distance between them, went up on her toes and touched her lips to his.

"Welcome home."

* * * * *

ACKNOWLEDGMENTS

During the writing of *Summer on Mirror Lake*, I've had reason to be grateful for a number of special people: Dianne Moggy, who reached out and invited me home to HQN; Susan Swinwood, for her keen eye, thoughtful editorial advice, and who's a joy to work with; Denise Marcil and Anne Marie O'Farrell who are not only the wisest, most supportive agents in the business, but also managed to score amazing theater seats to *Dear Evan Hansen* during a super memorable NYC visit.

Again, thanks to Sean Kapitain and his fabulous art team, who not only patiently put up with all my photos and suggestions, but created another stunningly beautiful portrait of my beloved Pacific Northwest for this book cover.

Also huge appreciation to the always cheerful HQN publicist Lisa Wray for all her wonderful advance work; the terrific sales team who even laughed at my jokes; and all the others working so hard behind the scenes who kept *Summer on Mirror Lake* on track during its publishing journey. And I can't leave out super-efficient Mandy Lawler, who frees up valuable time for me to write. I promise I'll master Excel one of these days!

A shout-out to all the wonderful booksellers and librarians for getting my books into the hands of readers, and last, but certainly not least, smooches to all those special readers who've allowed me to live my dream for so many years. Because it's truly all about you.

Once Upon a Wedding

CHAPTER ONE

ONCE UPON A TIME, in the early 1900s, a newly married royal couple of a small European principality decided to take a tour of America on their honeymoon. When the King and Queen of Montacroix had learned of the lush green majesty of the Olympic National Monument from their friend former President Theodore Roosevelt, they'd added it to their itinerary. As soon as that news reached Washington State's Olympic Peninsula, the residents of the once prosperous but dying Victorian seaport town nestled up against the mountains had immediately voted to rename the town Honeymoon Harbor in hopes of using the royal visit to garner publicity.

It worked. As the years passed, the town became a popular wedding and honeymoon destination. Honeymoon Harborites had long grown accustomed to seeing brides decked out in white princess dresses and grooms in tuxedos exchanging vows in the town center's lacy white Victorian gazebo, on the sand beside impossibly blue water, and barefoot in mountain meadows carpeted with wildflowers dancing on the breeze.

But they really perked up when the couples were locals. And any wedding became an event when it involved the Mannions or the Harpers, whose feud, mostly long past—but still occasionally simmering—had begun when Nathaniel Harper was the sole person to vote against the name change. Or, as some old-timers claimed, when, generations ago, Nathaniel and Gabriel Mannion were both courting the same woman, who'd ended up choosing Gabriel.

Today's wedding between Kylee Campbell and Mai Munemori involved both families. Seth Harper had remodeled the Folk Victorian house for Kylee and Mai to live in, and they had chosen the back garden as the perfect location to exchange their vows. Meanwhile Seth's fiancée, Brianna Mannion, had stepped in as wedding planner when the couple found attempting to coordinate events while learning the ropes of mothering their newborn adopted daughter more time-consuming and exhausting than they'd expected. Although the last wedding Brianna had organized had involved two King Charles spaniels, as a former executive concierge to the top rollers at the Las Vegas Midas Resort and Casino, she had no doubt that the small, intimate garden wedding would go off without a hitch. Little did she realize that she was about to learn the unfortunate lesson of best-laid plans.

DESIREE MARCHAND HAD loved baking ever since she'd been old enough to stand on a stool in her grand-mère Dupree's kitchen, learning the many variations of French pastry dough, beginning with the basic distinction between *viennoiserie* and *patisserie*. "The Viennese may have given us pastry," her grand-mère would say, "but we French are the ones who put the magic into the dough." According to family lore, an old-line Creole ancestor, who could trace his roots directly back to France, had started the family's first *boulangerie* in 1736, making bread for the patients at New Orleans's Charity Hospital, which had continued to operate until Hurricane Katrina.

Today Desiree was in Kylee and Mai's kitchen, singing to herself as she put together the happiest of pastries, a wedding cake. She was spreading French buttercream frosting on the three layers of cake, when an all-too-familiar baritone voice from her past began singing along. Spinning around, she found herself looking straight into a pair of dark chocolate-brown eyes.

"What are you doing here?"

Bastien Broussard lifted his hands. "Apparently I'm here to get stabbed with whatever that weapon is that you're holding."

She glanced down at the stainless-steel bench scraper she'd been using to smooth the buttercream. And lowered her hand. "I meant here." She inadvertently swung it again as she waved her hand around the kitchen. "In this town. In this house."

Before he could answer, Brianna came rushing into the kitchen, appearing nearly as flustered as Desiree felt. "Don't tell Kylee and Mai, but we have a problem."

She was not alone. What was the man Desiree had loved with all her heart, then walked away from, doing here, in the far northwest corner of the country?

"What is it?" she asked, trying for a reasonably calm voice. But from the way a corner of Bastien's mouth quirked, he knew that he'd rattled her. As he'd always been able to do. In so many ways.

"We've lost our musician."

"Lost, lost? As in you can't find her? Or lost as in she's not showing up?"

"The second. She's in the hospital getting stitches for a cut she got opening a can of dog food," Brianna answered on something close to a wail. She closed her eyes, took a deep breath, seemed to be counting to ten, then opened her eyes again. "I don't know what's wrong with me. I've dealt with being stuck in an elevator with snarling little dogs trying to rip each other's tulle bridesmaid's dresses off. I don't know why I'm panicking over a musician."

"Because this wedding is personal. Kylee's been your friend all your life. You want everything to be perfect."

"I always expect everything to be perfect," Brianna returned sharply, then pressed her fingers against the bridge of her nose. "I'm sorry. I've been working on that." She took another breath. Let it out. "It's not the end of the world." Desiree couldn't quite decide whom she was trying to convince. Her? Or herself? "If I can't find a wedding singer in the next ninety minutes, I'll simply have Seth figure out how to hook up my phone to a sound system. He's a genius at that tech stuff. It won't be the same as an actual performer, but it's better than nothing."

Do. Not. Say. A. Word. Desiree was afraid to even look at the man standing behind her for fear that he'd know that she knew what he was thinking, and she didn't want to encourage him.

"What type of wedding singer was she?" he asked.

Damn.

"Marian Oberchain's very versatile. She can sing pop, the oldies, ballads, even country. She could also play a classical harp, an acoustic guitar and the ukulele, which I really wanted because Mai's from Hawaii, and Marian was going to play the 'Hawaiian Wedding Song'… I'm sorry. I don't believe we've met."

"I'm an old friend of Desiree's," he said. "Bastien Broussard."

"You're French?"

"Cajun." He gifted her with one of his knee-melting smiles. Not the full-out sexy kind he used to turn on Desiree, but it was enough to bring a bit of color to the usually cool and composed Brianna's cheeks. "A few centuries removed from France. But I lived in Paris for a while."

As if that smile had emptied her head, a feeling which

Desiree had experienced too many times in the past, Brianna appeared to have forgotten her immediate problem.

"Perhaps you'd better go find Seth so he can hook up that system," Desiree suggested.

"I suppose I should. Oh, I'm sorry, I just realized that I was so distracted that I didn't introduce myself. I'm Brianna Mannion."

"And *your* family would have come here from the auld sod," he said, somehow pulling off what sounded to Desiree like an actual Irish accent.

"Like yours, from a few generations back," she confirmed. "It's good to meet you, Mr. Broussard. Enjoy your visit. In fact, I just had a wonderful idea."

No! Desiree begged inwardly. *Don't go there.*

"Why don't you stay for the wedding? I know Kylee and Mai would welcome having you here and that way you and Desiree can catch up."

Damn. She'd gone there.

"I'd enjoy that," Bastien said. "Although I'm afraid I'm not dressed formally enough for the occasion."

Both women skimmed a look over him in his dark, slim-cut indigo jeans, a white button-down linen shirt worn open over a black body-hugging T-shirt, and cobalt-blue loafers that looked so soft they had to be pricey Italian leather to allow him to go without socks. He still looked like a Cajun bad boy blues rocker, but he had taken on a definite Parisian flair since she'd last seen him. His hair, as black as her own, was no longer down at his shoulders, but had been cut to a shaggy style that just reached his collar and begged a woman's hands to run through it.

"You look great," Brianna said. "We're very casual here in Honeymoon Harbor. The only reason I'll be dressing up is that I'm the maid of honor."

"*Bien*, then," he said. "I'd be honored to accept your

invitation. But I do have another suggestion that might solve your problem."

"Oh?" Brianna lifted a perfectly arched blond brow.

"As it happens, I'm a singer. And a musician."

"Really. What instrument do you play?"

"A tenor sax typically. Which is in my rental car. But I can also play the alto sax, keyboard and guitar. And once, while I was in Hawaii, I had a lesson in the ukulele. Coincidentally, it was the 'Hawaiian Wedding Song.'"

In full official wedding coordinator mode, Brianna folded her arms. "I don't want to risk insulting you, Mr. Broussard, but are you any good? Because this wedding is the most personal event I've ever planned."

"*Je comprends*. I'd feel the same way myself." He reached into the pocket of his dark jeans, pulled out a cell phone and opened YouTube. "This was at a live concert in Australia."

He hit Play and there he was standing alone in the spotlight onstage, wearing much the same outfit as he was wearing now, but with a black leather jacket and black rocker boots, his beautiful voice crooning a blues ballad about love and loss Desiree knew that he'd written about them. Bastien had played it for her in Paris, on the balcony of their room in the Hôtel Plaza Athénée with its perfect view of the Eiffel Tower their last night together.

"Oh. Now I feel really foolish." Brianna looked up at him. "You're famous."

He shrugged in that casual Gallic way he had. "A bit," he allowed. "In my own circle. There's no reason you should know of me."

"He won a music award," Desiree heard herself saying before she could stop herself.

"Three," he corrected her with a self-deprecating grin that was sexier than any male swagger. "But who's counting?" He turned back to Brianna. "If you'd like to give me the bride's playlist…"

"It's right here." Brianna pulled it out of a white binder and handed it to him. "I'll have to talk to Kylee and Mai, but I'm sure they'll agree that you should feel free to play whatever you'd like. And what feels appropriate. I don't know what you usually charge, but—"

"Consider it my gift to the happy couple," he said. Then tilted his head and looked at Desiree, who knew very well what was coming. "Desiree sings, too. In fact, we were in a band together. She was the front singer, of course."

"You were in a band?" Brianna looked at Desiree as if she'd been keeping some big secret from everyone in Honeymoon Harbor.

"It was a very long time ago. I was nineteen, working in my father's bakery as an apprentice with plans to attend culinary school in France. Then I got sidetracked for a few years."

Plans which she'd put off after Bastien had approached her in New Orleans's Jackson Square, where she'd been singing Christmas carols with a choral group. And hadn't her father exploded when she'd told him that she'd agreed to join the band of a stranger whom she'd met that very same night? That had caused a split between them for two weeks, until Augustin Dupree had thrown in the towel. Only after threatening to slice Bastien into pieces with a filet knife and feed him to the gators if he ever hurt his baby girl.

"I was three years older," Bastien said. "Mood Indigo, that was our band. It was blues rock, but to be honest, we'd play whatever someone would pay us to play. Including our share of weddings, until Desiree decided that baking would provide her a steadier income. Which, at the time, she was correct about." He touched her with his melting dark gaze. "What do you say, *cher*? Want to relive our young and foolish past for a couple hours?"

"Oh, that would be so romantic!" Brianna actually clapped her hands. The outward display of excitement from the warm but usually composed woman was like a brass Mardi Gras band marching through the kitchen. "Would you, Desiree? I know it would mean so much to Kylee and Mai."

"Your cake appears nearly finished," Bastien noted.

"It just needs the topper," she said. "Which I'm going to wait to add until right before rolling it outside."

"Wonder Women." He nodded his approval, not that she needed it. "I like that."

"You like all women," Desiree retorted.

Brianna's brow furrowed again. "Mr. Broussard—"

"Bastien," he said easily.

"Bastien it is," Brianna said in an outwardly casual tone that didn't fool anyone for a moment. "Perhaps you could get your saxophone from your car while Desiree and I go over a few last-minute details about the cake cutting?"

"Fine." He met Desiree's gaze. "I'm parked down the street. I'll be back soon.'

They both watched him walk away. "I've always been mad crazy in love with Seth," Brianna murmured. "But looking never hurt, did it?"

"Every other woman always has," Desiree said, sounding a bit too sharp to her own ears. "I'm sorry. That sounded snarky and I certainly didn't mean it that way."

"I'm the one who should apologize, inviting him to stay without talking with you alone first. Is there a problem?"

"No." She wouldn't allow it. "Don't worry, nothing's going to screw up Kylee and Mai's special day."

"You loved him," Brianna guessed.

"Yes." Desiree sighed. "I was young and naive."

"I've been there. It's hard. Are you sure…"

"It'll be fine." She forced a smile. "I haven't sung in public for years. It could be fun." Right up there with a root canal.

"Being a wedding, there are going to be a lot of love songs."

"As long as I can avoid singing 'Unchained Melody.' Because that always makes me cry when I think of Patrick Swayze getting murdered."

"You're not alone. That one's not on the list because Kylee cries like a baby whenever we watch *Ghost*. Jolene would be really upset if we ruin the makeup she spent so much time applying."

"Then it'll be fine," Desiree said.

"Perhaps this could turn out to be a romantic reunion for the two of you."

"Nope," Desiree said as Bastien walked back into the kitchen, looking good enough to scoop up with a spoon. "Not happening."

CHAPTER TWO

ONCE SHE'D CALMED DOWN, Brianna, who was no longer in the kitchen, had reminded Bastien of one of those old Hitchcock movie blondes. Like Grace Kelly. Cool and calm in a crisis.

Desiree, on the other hand, sticking with the '50s/'60s movie theme, was more Natalie Wood. He'd always found her more stunning than the girl-next-door, with an undercurrent of recklessness and sensuality humming beneath the surface that her strict and proper New Orleans Catholic French upbringing usually kept hidden. Until she was onstage. Or, he thought, as bittersweet memories caused both his body and his heart to ache, in bed.

"What are you doing here?" she asked as she finally put the possible weapon down on the counter.

"I came to see you."

What else could have brought him to this small, quaint town that was nothing like Paris? Nor New Orleans. He found it interesting that she'd kept her singing career a secret from a woman who appeared to be a friend. Bastien had always known that of the two of them, she could have been the true star. But she'd given up her chance for fame to bake croissants and, apparently, wedding cakes. He'd stopped by her bakery on the way here, where a young woman had sent him to this house. The *boulangerie* had matched her personality. Tidy and organized, as baking required, yet the desserts in the window and glass display case were lovely, even sensual, and enticing. Just like her.

"How did you find me?" She made it sound as if he'd

discovered her in the witness protection program. Nor did she seem at all happy to see him. Bastien could have taken that as a sign he stood no chance of winning her back, but he had always been an optimist. He decided that there'd be no reason for her to put up that protective wall if she weren't susceptible to being won over.

"Well, I could have Googled you, but decided that could be considered a bit stalkerish, so I simply asked your father."

"You asked Papa? I don't understand. Did you call him all the way from Paris to ask, 'Hey, Augustin, where can I find your daughter? I know you've always believed she's much too good for me, but I want to see her.'"

He found it interesting that she knew he'd been living in Paris. True, he did appear in music magazines like *Rolling Stone* and on various entertainment shows, from time to time, and had even written a song for a Disney movie, but perhaps she'd occasionally checked up on him. As he admittedly had her.

"No, I asked him where to find you while having coffee and beignets at the Café du Monde, which is admittedly touristy, but nevertheless, they do make great beignets. And it's conveniently near the French Market where we both happened to be shopping for greens, boudin and shrimp."

Her eyes—a vivid clear blue of the Caribbean Sea that contrasted so sharply with tawny skin that was a beautiful blend of her Creole father and islander mother—widened. They'd always had a way of focusing in on you as if you were the only person in the room. He wasn't the only man to get lost in those thickly lashed eyes. He'd witnessed audience members react the same way when, after looking for an individual to sing directly to, she'd single one out.

"What were you doing at the market?"

"Like I said, shopping… I've been living in New Orleans for the past two years."

"But I was visiting Papa just a few months ago and he never said a thing."

"I doubt he wanted to encourage a reunion. Also, I asked him not to."

"Why? Were you still angry about me leaving? Not just about having broken up the band, but after that night in Paris, two years later?"

After playing a gig in Madrid, he'd taken a train to Paris, where he knew she should be finishing up her two years of culinary training. Bastien called the number he'd never gotten out of his head, suggesting they meet for coffee at a café not far from the school. They hadn't bothered with the coffee, but had instead gone straight to his balcony room at the Hôtel Plaza Athénée, which by then he could almost afford.

They'd been drinking champagne on the balcony when he'd sung her the song he'd written just that morning, about the love of a man for a woman, and the loss Bastien knew was going to break his heart.

Afterward, they'd made love in the deep soaker tub that had a perfectly framed view of the Eiffel Tower, and then went on to spend the night making up for all the time lost since she'd left the band. The next morning, they'd shared a continental breakfast in bed. As if it were yesterday, he could picture her plucking an elegant, golden crusty croissant from the basket, biting into it, intently studying it as if preparing for the Superior Pastry Certificate she'd only just achieved at Paris's Le Cordon Bleu school.

"I could make a better one," she'd decided. "But the hint of almond admittedly marries well with the buttery flavor." She'd held it out to him, inviting him to take a bite.

"I'd rather take a bite of you," he'd said, nevertheless tasting the croissant because he'd never been able to deny Desiree anything. "Good," he'd decided. "But not as tasty as my angel." Putting their mimosa glasses on the table beside the bed, he'd pulled her down on top of him.

Bastien suspected, from the way Desiree's gaze moved from his to out the French doors of the cottage toward the garden, that she too was remembering those golden twenty-four hours. After breakfast, they'd wandered the streets of Paris, had lunch at a little bistro next to the Seine before going up into the Eiffel Tower to look out over the city, which was in full, glorious spring bloom. At the end of the sun-brightened day, the flowers he'd bought her from a small stand outside the Jardin de Tuileries still in hand, she'd boarded a night flight to New York City. She was going to work for the man who'd go on to be named the best pastry chef in the world. Bastien had stayed behind in Paris, having decided to use the city for his home base.

"I wasn't angry about you leaving the band," he said, bringing both his mind and the conversation back to the present. "Truthfully, I was surprised you stayed as long as you did. Every morning of those five years we toured, I'd wake up thinking, 'This will be the day Desiree leaves.' I understood that you did what you had to do. For yourself and your career. And I've done okay for myself going solo."

"You've done more than okay. You truly are a star."

He shrugged. "It's a living. I'm not going to lie and say it didn't hurt, watching your plane fly away, off to New York, but the same way we were destined to first meet, I consoled myself with the knowledge that eventually we'd meet again when the time was right, and stay together forever."

A dark brow lifted over those expressive eyes, which had begun to spark with a bit of temper he'd always enjoyed uncovering. "You were that sure of yourself?"

"No. I was that sure of us," Bastien said mildly. "Unfortunately, due to contractual concert agreements, I couldn't follow you to New York. Also, if you want me to be perfectly honest—"

"Of course I do."

"All right. The truth was that I didn't know how many more chances we'd get, and I didn't want to risk screwing up what could have been our last time together."

"You were always superstitious."

Bastien grinned as he shrugged. "What can I say? It's the Cajun in me." He was also the more romantic of the two of them, but decided this wasn't the time to bring that up. "But like I said, my situation, when you were visiting your father, was complicated."

"Because of your concert schedule?"

"No. I'd stopped playing live concerts by then."

"But I bought… Never mind."

Ah. Desiree was talking about the new album he'd had engineered at a studio in New Orleans. Bastien liked that she still listened to him sing and wondered if she'd ever realized that all the love songs he wrote were always for her.

"I stopped because of my grand-mère."

"I've always liked Abella."

"As she liked you. I always wondered how she and your father could be so close, while at the same time he disapproved so strongly of me."

"My mother died when I was born," she reminded him. "And although my grand-mère lived with us and took care of me as if I were her own daughter, we lost her to cancer when I was twelve. Along with the understandable grief at his mother's death, I suspect Papa was at a total loss on how to handle a hormonal adolescent girl who was growing up faster than he would have wished. He was merely being protective."

Looking back on the young man he'd been when they'd first met, Bastien decided that if he ever had a daughter, he'd feel the same way.

"Also," she continued, "they undoubtedly grew close because they were both in the business of making people happy with their food. And your grand-mère Abella always bought the bread for her restaurant from my family."

"That's why he called me."

"My father called you? In Paris? When?"

"A little over two years ago. He found me through my manager. He wanted to let me know how ill Abella was becoming. I knew she was growing older, but she'd always had such strength, you know? And she'd raised me, much as yours did you, after my parents took off."

Bastien's father had been a blues musician who, like many musicians, had unfortunately become too fond of drugs and alcohol. Because LeRoy Broussard had left the family when Bastien was a toddler, he had no memory of him. He did remember his mother, who was also too fond of her "hot and dirty" Cajun martinis, taking off with an oil man who'd had no use for children. The memory of watching her drive off in that big fancy car when he was seven years old had been burned into Bastien's mind as if by a red-hot branding iron. Over the years, it had lost its power to wound. But it had made him vow that when he settled down, he'd only wed a woman he'd want to live with forever. Like the woman who was standing so near. And yet so far.

"Of course I knew she was growing older. But she'd always been so strong," Bastien said. "I'd call her every Sunday, from wherever I was, timing the call between when she got home from early mass and before she opened the restaurant for the after-church crowd. Not once had she so much as hinted that she had a heart condition. I learned about that from your father, who, like I said, tracked me down in Paris, where I was living in the Oberkampf—"

"Where, despite making a good enough living to live in one of the pricier arrondissements, you preferred to hang out with musicians."

"That would only be natural since I *am* a musician," he said. Although he only played in public occasionally these days. "The only time I ever was comfortable with pricey things was when I wanted to show off for you. Rather than take you to my very plain room with a cranky old landlady who watched with an eagle eye for me to bring home a woman, or a man, if I were so inclined, both of which were against my rental agreement, I splurged and booked that hotel room."

The color in her cheeks and the way her eyes turned a little dreamy told him that he wasn't the only one who had bittersweet memories of that twenty-four hours they'd spent together.

"At any rate, Augustin told me that the restaurant was wearing her heart out, but she refused to sell. She insisted that she'd keep working until they put her in a box. Which was exactly what she did until last month, two years after I came home to help her run it. In truth, at the end, she spent her last six months sitting in a chair, bossing me around her kitchen as if I were a mere line cook, but despite her failing health, we passed a good time together, her and me."

"I'm so sorry." She reached out and touched the bare skin beneath his rolled-up sleeve, warming Bastien all the way to the bone. "But at least you had that special time together."

"True. It's a debt I owe to your father. Have you ever thought what a coincidence it was that we both grew up so many years with our grandmothers taking on our mothers' roles? I've often wondered if that was another reason why we connected."

"But I never knew my mother, so I suspect that was easier for me. And my father was always there." Unlike either of his parents.

"Grand-mère's passing put a lot of things in motion. I'd already hired my cousin Octave as a sous chef. She left the restaurant to me, so, after staying a few months to make sure he could handle it, I sold it to Octave, whose wife is having their second child this fall. And voilà." He lifted his hands. "Here I am."

"Why?" Desiree asked again.

"To see you, *cher.*"

"And do you have plans beyond that?"

"*Bien sur.* I'm opening a restaurant. I checked this town out online and it's definitely lacking in dining choices. So I decided it would be a perfect location to open a Cajun café."

She tilted her head, and put her hands on her hips. "You're opening a restaurant here? In Honeymoon Harbor?"

"I am. I find the name prophetic. I saw a couple getting married in that pretty little gazebo as I drove by. What would you think of us exchanging our vows there? Or would you prefer being married in New Orleans, where your father can walk you down the aisle in the same ca-thedral where you received your First Communion and confirmation?"

"I'm certainly not going to marry you."

"Of course you are," he said easily. "Because we're soul mates. But don't worry, I'll give you all the time you need to get used to the idea."

"You gave me that soul mate line that day you asked me to join your band. After you'd heard me sing."

"It wasn't a line then. And it isn't now. It's the God's own truth. And while I'm being truthful, here's another fact for you. I wouldn't have cared if you could sing or not. I just wanted an excuse to be with you every day. That, by the way, has not changed."

"You're out of your crazy Cajun mind."

"Over you," he agreed. "And here's the best part."

She folded her arms over her white apron with *Ovenly* written in pretty script on the bib part. "I can't wait to hear it."

"I'm opening up that café in the space next to your *boulangerie*. Which will make us neighbors."

"You are not." Her remarkable eyes were now shoot-ing flaming daggers. "That space only became open last week and I'm expanding Ovenly into it."

"Have you signed a lease?"

"No, but—"

He flashed her his most sincere smile. The one that had usually charmed Sister Mary Constance out of as-signing him to detention.

"I'm sure a compromise can be worked out. But why don't we discuss that later, *cher*?" He glanced down at his watch. "We're running out of rehearsal time and you wouldn't want to disappoint the brides."

CHAPTER THREE

WHILE DESIREE AND BASTIEN were going through the song choice list Brianna had given them, editing it to take out a few that they felt had been overdone and adding others, two of the bedrooms were a hive of activity. Gloria Wells, owner of Thairapy Salon, was styling the bridal parties' hair, as well as that of many of Mai's family members who'd flown in from Hawaii for the occasion. In the other bedroom, Gloria's daughter, Jolene, who'd arrived the previous day from Los Angeles, was using her pots, pencils and powders to create her own kind of magic.

"I love it that you kept me looking like myself," Kylee Campbell said, closing her eyes as instructed while Jolene spritzed the rose water setting spray on her face. "But so much better! We need to add credits at the end of the wedding video. Just like in the movies!" She held up her hands as if framing it on a screen. "Makeup by award-winning Jolene Wells!"

"Being nominated is a long way from winning. It's a long time until the awards ceremony in September."

"But there were so many TV movies and series made last year," Kylee said. "And you ended up making the top tier! I'd vote for you to win in a heartbeat."

"Me, too," Mai, her fiancée and about-to-be wife, said. "Besides, how many more Tudor-period TV series does the world need? There is no competition."

And wasn't that exactly what Jolene had thought when she'd seen the list? "I love you," she told Mai. "You, too," she assured Kylee.

"Love is all around!" Kylee, who seemed to be talking in exclamation marks today, said.

"We probably *should* have credits," Mai seconded Kylee's suggestion. "How many people have not only a famous makeup artist, but also a three-time award-winning singer at their wedding? I can't imagine how you pulled that off," she told Brianna, who'd arrived to get her makeup done for her role as maid of honor.

"Bastien Broussard fell into my lap," Brianna said. "Actually into your kitchen. It turns out he's an old friend of Desiree's who's in town to visit her. From New Orleans, by way of Paris."

"I love Paris," Kylee said with a sigh. "I once dreamed of living there, in some little attic apartment on the Left Bank."

"You'd definitely fit in with all the other artists and bohemians," Brianna agreed.

"I would have back then. But I don't regret a thing. Because if I *had* settled in Paris, I might not have met Mai, and we wouldn't have Clara." She laughed. "Of all the ways I imagined my life turning out while I was growing up, I never, in a million years, would've guessed I'd be happy as a typical suburban mom."

"In the first place, this cottage is not in the burbs. Honeymoon Harbor doesn't even *have* suburbs. And you'll never, ever, be typical. You still do beautifully creative photography, so it isn't as if you've been completely domesticated."

"That would certainly be true," Mai said as she left the room with Kylee to get their hair styled, then be helped into their gowns.

"You're my next victim," Jolene said, turning to Brianna. "Not that you need much work. Fortunately, not everyone has your perfect skin, or I'd never get my makeup line launched."

"I've been using the night cream I bought from your mom at the salon. And the day cream with the sunscreen," Brianna said. "They're so light, I can't even feel them on my skin. When you do launch it, it's going to be a smashing success."

"From your mouth to God's ear," Jolene said as she spritzed a lavender rosemary toner on Brianna's face. "This will keep your skin hydrated when you're spending so much time in the sun," she said. "The lavender is mostly to relax you. You've been running around like the Energizer Bunny all day."

"I want Kylee and Mai's day to be perfect. As maid of honor, it's my responsibility to make it happen."

"It'll be wonderful. Beautiful. And as perfect as everything you always do."

If Brianna hadn't been so nice to her during those high school bullying days, Jolene could have been jealous of her ability to multitask seemingly a gazillion things at once without so much as having a honey-blond hair slip out of place. She began smoothing a moisturizer on her face. "And even if you messed everything up, Kylee's so high up in the gilded happy clouds, I don't think she'd even notice."

"She's definitely dialed her usual enthusiasm level up to eleven," Brianna agreed.

Jolene dabbed on a bit of foundation. "I don't want to gossip, but is Amanda Barrow always so quiet?"

"She's not the chattiest person in the world, but then again, I'm usually not, either, so I've never noticed. But now that you mention it, she might be a bit more subdued today. Why?"

"She had what looked like the last stage of a bruise

on her right cheek. And it was a little swollen, like a bruise tends to be. So, not wanting to bring it up, since we don't know each other at all, I massaged her face, to help break up the blood, with Arnica gel. It's a homeopathic herb that I've found works very well with bruises after face lasering."

"Ouch." Brianna's hands lifted to her own cheeks. "I can't imagine doing that."

"You're not in a business that requires women to remain forever young," Jolene said.

"Thank God. My problem used to be just the opposite. I was young enough that sometimes it was hard to be taken seriously. Especially by older wealthy men who were used to more staid, gray-haired butler types."

"You were young, blonde and pretty. Like nearly every other woman, you've undoubtedly encountered your share of unwanted male attention."

"And isn't that a polite way to put it," Brianna said, confirming Jolene's statement. "Getting back to Amanda—who, by the way, created a fairyland out in that garden—she's a landscaper. Although she has a crew, while she was doing the work on Herons Landing, I watched her carrying big rocks around and planting trees and shrubs. I suppose bruises could be part of that."

"Makes sense," Jolene agreed. "So, I noticed your brother arrived a while ago," Jolene casually commented.

"Seth came because his mom's officiating. I sort of coerced Aiden to come to catch up with him. He's been staying at the coast house for a few weeks."

"Really?" Jolene was proud of how her voice showed none of the nerves that had been tangling ever since she caught sight of the one man she'd rather never see again, talking with Seth and Caroline Harper in the back garden. "Is he on vacation?"

"More like decompressing. He recently came back from Los Angeles—"

"Aiden's been in LA?" What would she have done if she'd known? And the second question: Had he known *she* was living there?

True, she didn't have her face on a billboard on Sunset Boulevard, but the announcement of the award nomination was listed in the *Los Angeles Times*, *LA Weekly*, *Los Angeles Magazine* and *Variety*. And other papers she hadn't even known about until she'd discovered her mother had gone online, downloading and printing out every mention of the nomination she could find. Jolene made a note never to go to a movie she'd worked on with her mother. Gloria would probably take a photo of the screen when her name appeared. Way, way down toward the end, after nearly everyone had left the theater.

"Aiden joined the LAPD right out of the Marines. He started in SWAT, then moved to different departments. Funny, I was so caught in my own career at the time, I didn't make the connection about both of you being there. I guess you never ran across one another?"

Jolene shrugged. "It's a big city. The odds would have been against it."

"I imagine that's so," Brianna said. "Las Vegas wasn't nearly as large, but I know how we all run in our own worlds and spaces. But now you'll have an opportunity to catch up."

Fortunately, Brianna went on to talk about how wonderful Mai's family was, most of whom were staying at Herons Landing, which saved Jolene from responding.

CHAPTER FOUR

"You can't deny that we still blend together perfectly," Bastien said after he and Desiree had sung for thirty minutes.

"Our voices," she qualified. "Though you never sang all that often when we were a four-person band."

"We put you in the front because you were the prettiest," he said. He glanced out the doors again at the gathering guests. "I'm going to run out and see if any one of those guys in the Hawaiian shirts happened to have brought a uke. That'd be cool if we could sing the 'Hawaiian Wedding Song' to that."

"I doubt they'd have it here at the house, even if they'd brought it on the plane."

"True. But this is a small town, so wherever they're staying can't be that far away."

"They're all either at Brianna's bed-and-breakfast or the Lighthouse View Hotel. Neither of which are very far away."

"I thought Brianna Mannion was a wedding planner."

"She's helping out today. The brides recently adopted a baby, so their lives got too busy to take care of details, which was when Brianna stepped in. She used to be a concierge for the mega-rich at some of the best hotels in the country, then decided to slow her life down and come back home from Las Vegas. To make a long and somewhat winding story short, she and the contractor helping to restore the Victorian house she was renovating are now engaged."

"Long and winding stories that end up happily are my favorite," he said.

She refused to fall into that conversation snare. Their own road might have been long and winding, but she wasn't going to allow her heart to tumble again. She'd done the right thing breaking up with Bastien. She'd have to remember all the reasons why leaving had been for the best. And why their lives were still not compatible.

"I mostly know the melody to the 'Hawaiian Wedding Song,'" she said. "Enough to keep up if I knew the words. Which I don't. And I really can't wait for you to try to track down a ukulele. I have to go change into the dress I'm wearing to the wedding. Jolene, a Hollywood makeup artist, insists on doing my makeup along with all the other women's. She's the daughter of Gloria, who runs the salon and is in charge of hair today."

"It's going to take me some time to catch up on all the small-town connections," he said, as if he was actually going to be staying here in Honeymoon Harbor. He wouldn't last a month. "You're gorgeous just the way you are," he said, unaware of her thoughts, "but you should have time to go online and check it out while she fancies you up. You always were the quickest of us to memorize lyrics." He flashed her another of those damn cocky grins, then went off in search of a ukulele.

Shaking her head, she went off to get "fancied" up. Since baking in a hot kitchen could melt off makeup, it had been years since she'd worn anything but a bit of moisturizer. When Gloria Wells had started selling her daughter's organic products at Thairapy, she'd fallen in love with the light and smooth lotion.

"Well," Jolene said, as Desiree sat down in the chair in front of the dressing table. "I've been gilding a lot of gorgeous lilies today. But it's still fun."

"Other than a bit of lipstick and sometimes a touch of powder for New Orleans humidity, I haven't worn makeup since I used to sing, which was years ago," Desiree said.

"Brianna told me you were in a rock band." Jolene swept a moisturizer over her face, then followed up with a light-as-air primer. "That must have been fun."

"It was blues rock. And it had its moments." Desiree smiled for the first time since Bastien had appeared in the kitchen. "Who am I kidding? It was fun. For a few years. Then I decided it was probably time to grow up and get a job where I could earn a living down the road. The music business, like Hollywood, was and still is extremely sexist. Not every woman can have a career for as long as Cher or Carly Simon."

"I suppose you can probably do makeup as well as I do."

"Stage makeup is different," she said. "As you probably know from working in Hollywood. The bright lights take more. I layered it on with a trowel."

"You're striking enough to get away with going over the top." Jolene stood back and studied her. "Your eyes hold such a wonderful element of surprise when contrasted with your skin. What would you say to a smoky cat eye with some glitter?"

"That it might be a bit much for an afternoon garden wedding."

"True." Jolene sighed. "But it'd be fabulous. If I weren't leaving after the wedding to Ireland for a shoot, I'd want to really get creative with you so Kylee could take your portrait. But for today, we'll skip the cat eyes and glitter and just go with a bit of smoke."

As she got busy with her artistry gathering up her brushes and colors, Desiree went online and looked up the lyrics for the song. Which, fortunately, were short and simple. And perfect.

"I'd imagine your work allows for a lot of travel," she said, after she'd committed them to memory over two readings.

"At times," Jolene said. "But even with films set in fabulous places, many of the interior shots are done in studios in LA, so there's not as much as you'd think. Though sometimes the constant traveling for work makes it difficult to have a relationship. I'm going to be in Ireland for three months, while my boyfriend, I guess that's what you'd call him, although it sounds so high school, will be shooting in Australia and Hawaii."

"I didn't want to say anything, because you probably get tired of answering the question, but since you brought him up, I've seen the photos of the two of you on magazine covers at the checkout in the market—is it difficult dating an actor?"

"I'd never dated one before Mark," Jolene said, sweeping color across Desiree's lids. "I always stuck with guys in the trade. Electricians, carpenters, the occasional camera operator. But yes, I'll admit that it can get bothersome having paparazzi cameras in your face whenever you go out to the grocery store."

"I can imagine. When Bastien and I were together, women would send notes and even nude photos to him. Sometimes they'd even have them delivered to the dressing room we shared, or they would wait outside the club door and hand him envelopes with their phone numbers. It was hard on our relationship because, being young, I'd get jealous… I can't believe I just told you something I've never admitted to anyone."

"Hairdressers and makeup artists are like bartenders," Jolene said cheerfully. "Clients always tell us everything.

We're also like priests in a confessional. We're sworn to keep all secrets. And if I had to put up with that behavior, it would really upset me. But to be honest, my relationships never last long enough for me to get jealous." She drew a line with a black pencil and smudged it with her fingertip. "My mother said I was born leaving. She's probably right."

"I envy you," Desiree admitted. "Being able to move on so easily."

"It has its pluses." She looked into the mirror. "So, what do you think?"

"I have never, in my entire life, looked this good. No wonder you were nominated for an award."

"*Nominated* is the operative word," Jolene said. "The awards aren't until September."

"It doesn't matter. I'd vote for you in a heartbeat."

"Too bad your vote doesn't count. Close your eyes." She spritzed Desiree's face with setting water. "And if I weren't leaving right after the wedding, I think we could become besties. Now that my BFF back in LA is engaged, I suspect I'll come back from Ireland to discover I've lost her to her fiancé." She took a mascara brush and swept it across Desiree's lashes. "I don't know a woman in Hollywood who has lashes as thick and long as yours," she said. "And I'm including those who paid big bucks for extensions. This mascara is waterproof, just in case you end up crying at the wedding."

"I don't cry," Desiree said.

"Never?"

"Not since my grandmother passed when I was twelve. My mother died when I was born. There were complications with the birth. So I ended up having only my father through my teens. It didn't take me long to realize that tears really upset him, since he had no idea what to do with a girl. I just learned, the night of my grandmother's funeral, to cry into a pillow. By the time I graduated, I'd lost the tears, I suppose," she said, meeting Jolene's eyes in the mirror. "A bit like your ability to move on."

That wasn't entirely true. She had cried in the restroom on the flight to New York from Paris, but that was more information than she cared to share.

She was, Desiree told herself as she left the room to change into her dress, going to have to gather up all her strength to resist Bastien Broussard. Or she'd be right back where she'd been when the most delicious man she'd ever seen had sauntered up to her after she'd finished singing "Joyeux Noël" and, without so much as an introduction, asked, "Hey, *cher*, want to be in my band?"

It was the first time in her life she'd understood that "near occasion of sin" the nuns were always warning girls against. It was also the first time she'd wanted to experience it. In that frozen moment in time, if Bastien Broussard had asked her to fly to the moon with him on gossamer wings, she'd have accepted on the spot.

She had assured the rest of the choral group that she'd be fine, and although she'd known it would be considered foolish, she had gone with him down Pirate's Alley, where the famed Privateer Jean Lafitte and Andrew Jackson had formed an unlikely alliance to plan the successful defeat of the British at the Battle of New Orleans. Unlike the noisy holiday mood throughout the Quarter, the bar had been reasonably quiet. He'd ordered a beer for himself, a Coke for her, and he'd explained about how he had a three-piece band that needed a front girl and since she was not only the most beautiful girl in the Crescent City, but also sang like an angel, she'd be perfect.

She'd been vaguely aware of him saying something about not making much money, but she needn't worry, he'd be sure she'd be taken care of, and he'd protect her against any drunk guys who might want to harass her, and how he'd promised her they'd pass a good time together.

By then she'd already been swept away by his smooth, deep voice and dark brown eyes, and, with their fingers linked together, she'd walked with him to a little hole-in-the-wall bar on Royal, where he introduced her as his new front girl, and within five minutes they'd left with a gig that had been only two nights away.

"I don't know any of your songs," she'd complained at the time.

He'd stopped, framed her worried face in his beautiful hands and said, "Don't worry, *cher.* We have two whole days. I'll teach you." And hadn't he? About a great deal more than singing the blues.

CHAPTER FIVE

DESIREE HAD ALWAYS been a beauty, but whatever magic Jolene, daughter of Gloria, had done had turned her into a goddess. "No one will notice the brides."

"I strongly doubt that," she said dryly. "I saw them getting dressed. They're stunning."

"There must be something in the water, here," Bastien said. "Because all the women are beautiful."

"You've always had an eye for women." She didn't say it in the angry, sulky way she once had. Bastien hoped that was because she'd grown older and belatedly realized that he'd had no reason to look at anyone but her.

"For the record, all the years we were together, I never, *ever*, looked, touched or had any kind of sex with any of those groupies. Or any other woman."

"I knew that," she said. "Well, most of the time." She shrugged shoulders bared by a dress with a floaty, longish skirt that looked as if it had washed off a painting of Monet's garden at Giverny, but sadly didn't show off her long legs he could still, during long dark nights, remember wrapped around him.

"But you were always waiting for me to cheat." She hadn't trusted him then. He wondered if she'd trust him now. If not, it may take longer than expected to win her over. But fortunately, she wasn't going anywhere. And now that he'd come up with a plan, neither was he.

"Perhaps," she admitted. She shrugged those bare shoulders that gleamed as if they'd been polished. "I was young and insecure. So, did you find your ukulele?"

"I did. But I also found something, or someone, better. One of the bride's cousins has a job playing at one of those big resort luaus. He's agreed to play the 'Hawaiian Wedding Song' during the ceremony."

"That's good news."

"It would be. But he insists he can't carry a tune, and from his demonstration, he's right, so we'll have to sing it."

"That's okay. I have it memorized."

"I knew you would. Now here's the cool thing. I was talking to Caroline Harper, she's the mother of Seth, who's the fiancé of Brianna, the wedding-planner-slash-B-and-B owner."

"I know that."

"Of course you do. I was just trying to connect all the dots. Apparently, Kylee's mom died. And her dad rejected her when she came out to him."

"That I didn't know. But since Mai's dad is going to walk both brides down the aisle, I suspected something like that might have happened."

"You suspected right. So, since Mai's entire family is essentially going to become Kylee's family, Mrs. Harper, who's officiating, planned a Hawaiian ceremony. A surprise for the both of them, which she hid from them during yesterday's rehearsal. Mai's family brought leis that have been stashed in Amanda Barrow's cooler. She's apparently the landscaper who created this garden and is also one of the attendants."

"Oh." Desiree's right hand went over her heart. "That is so lovely. And thoughtful."

"She seems like a lovely woman," he agreed. "If we get married here, perhaps we ought to consider her. Unless you'd like to get married in the church I drove by on the way to Herons Landing. Or, like I said, back home in New Orleans."

"This is my home now. But that doesn't matter because you won't be staying because we're not getting married and I'm going to be the one to move into that space next to my bakery. So, since you're wasting time, what aren't you telling me?"

"There's a song Honi, the cousin, sang for me, that would be perfect for the brides' first dance. But they're not doing that, so we thought it'd make a nice song for the exchange of leis."

"I thought you said her cousin couldn't sing."

"He can't. And, just so you won't think I planned this, he swears the entire family is tone deaf. Since it's a song for a guy, we thought he could play it on the ukulele while I sang it."

"I'm still not getting the problem."

"It's a love song called 'I'll Weave a Lei of Stars for You.'"

"Oh, that sounds beautifully romantic." Then she caught on to the possible problem. "You want to sing it to me."

"Well, if there weren't two of us, I suppose I could sing it by myself. But it would look a little odd and take away from the romanticism of the day if you suddenly either walked away, or just stood there not looking at me, while I sang it by myself."

He watched as she ran both those scenarios through her mind. "You're right. So obviously you'll sing it to me."

"It won't bother you?"

"Not at all. Believe me, I'm impervious to your Cajun charms."

"Ouch." It was his turn to cover his heart. "Direct hit."

"I'm sorry if that wounds your male ego. But you don't have to worry about my delicate sensibilities. It won't be any different than if we were two singers who'd never had a relationship."

"But we did. For five years." When he'd watched her become more and more unhappy touring with the band. "And that one night three years ago."

Score one for him. He watched her eyes soften and knew that she was sharing the same memories of that twenty-four hours that had so often haunted both his waking moments and his dreams.

"Well," she said finally, "I guess we should both just think of it this way... We'll always have Paris."

THEY DECIDED THAT Bastien would play from the list that Kylee and Mai had compiled as the guests gathered, while Desiree brought out the pastry trays and attached the Wonder Women to the base she'd already secured to the top tier of the cake with straw dowels before covering it with more buttercream frosting. She'd also volunteered to help the bridal party with any last-minute needs. Not that they seemed to need her help, since Brianna had everything running perfectly.

Caroline Harper, who would by this time next year be Brianna's mother-in-law, reminded Desiree of a wood nymph in her flowing deep green dress with a moonstone on a black cord around her neck. Her streaked blond hair, cut in a smooth, jaw-length bob, was evidence she hadn't gone *completely* New Agey during this lifestyle transformation that had had all of Honeymoon Harbor buzzing. Though she was wearing a crown of flowers around her head.

Her smile was warm as she greeted old friends and Mai's family before the ceremony started. She and her husband had been traveling the country, but had returned to Honeymoon Harbor for this wedding.

One of Mai's many cousins, who was wearing a beautiful white silk Aloha shirt with red flowers that was definitely superior to the cheaper ones sold in tourism shops, led everyone to their seats. Because of Kylee lacking an immediate family, there were no sides. There were only family and friends gathered together in this magical fairy garden Amanda Barrow had created for them.

After everyone was seated, Seth Harper rolled out the white runner that led from the second patio outside the master bedroom's French doors to the arch covered with summer wisteria, under which the brides would exchange their vows.

Her work completed until it was time to cut her cake, Desiree went to stand beside Bastien. Although it had been years since they'd sung together, as he paused to smile down at her, it was as if time had spun backward and she was precisely in the place she was meant to be. Dangerous thinking, that, she reminded herself as an older man came forward to stand at the end of the runner.

Brianna's attention to detail was demonstrated by Mai's three brothers, who were accompanying Brianna; Chelsea Prescott, Honeymoon Harbor's librarian; and Amanda Barrow down the aisle wearing Hawaiian shirts in the same colors as the dresses worn by the women they walked beside.

Brianna, maid of honor, had chosen a sapphire blue that brought out her blue eyes. Amanda had gone with a sunny yellow that worked with skin tanned from years of working outdoors, while Chelsea's bright purple was a perfect choice for her burnished brunette hair. They looked like beautiful flowers in this lush summer garden Amanda had created.

They walked up the aisle, carrying small bouquets of

tulips in the colors of their gowns mixed with white, to "All You Need Is Love."

It was such a positive song, one that was often requested at weddings, and one Desiree wished could be true. But she'd learned that love, while sometimes wonderful, could also be painful. And it wasn't always enough. Still, when she got to the part about it being easy to be where you're supposed to be, her voice faltered just a little. The guests didn't notice, but she felt Bastien's knowing glance, as if reinforcing the song's message.

As they split when they reached Caroline, the men to the right, women to the left, there was a momentary pause, allowing for suspense as everyone waited for the brides.

Then an older man, who'd been introduced to Desiree last night at the rehearsal dinner as one of Mai's uncles, stood at the end of the runner and lifted a conch shell, and blew a deeply rounded tone that spiraled over the garden and could probably be heard all over the harbor, announcing the arrival of the brides. Watching the bridal couple carefully, Desiree saw Mai's gasp of surprise as she touched her cheek, as if wiping away a tear.

While they might have gone a bit old-school with Elvis's "Can't Help Falling in Love with You" for the processional, there was nothing ordinary or expected about their gowns.

While getting dressed earlier, Desiree had been awed by Kylee's beautiful black fitted strapless midi dress embroidered with oversize red, yellow and purple beaded flowers. Dottie and Doris, who'd come to help the women into their gowns, had told her they'd ordered the dress from a designer Kylee had met on a photography trip through Italy. The more flamboyant of the two, she was wearing a pair of red sequined low-top Converse tennis shoes.

According to Dottie, the more talkative of the elderly

twin sisters, it was traditional for Japanese brides to wear white for the ceremony, then change to red for the reception. Wanting to be modern, while paying homage to all the women in her family who'd married in the traditional style, Mai had embraced both looks in a Western-style white strapless sheath gown, with a red sash embroidered with gold butterflies that fell down her back instead of a train. She'd chosen to wear simple white ballet-style flats. They were accompanied by Mai's Japanese-Hawaiian father, who walked down the aisle with a bride on each arm. He kissed both their cheeks, then sat down next to his wife in the front row.

"Greetings. And *aloha*," Caroline said. "We're gathered here today to celebrate the love of Kylee and Mai as they exchange vows in this very special union of marriage. Before we begin, I'd like to ask all the family and friends here today to take the hand of the person next to you and unite with us with one heart as we close our eyes and picture those who could not be here with us today. The Hawaiians have gifted us with the lovely knowledge that when the breeze stirs in a wedding, as it's doing lightly at this very moment in this garden, it's the presence of their *ohana*, or family, who are physically absent but are surrounding the brides at this moment with their love, support and blessing."

As she felt her eyes moisten at the thought of her mother and grandmother, Desiree was glad Jolene had brought along that big waterproof mascara tube, especially when Bastien's fingers lightly brushed the back of her hand. The touch was as quick and light as a butterfly's wings, but it struck like a gilded arrow straight to the center of her carefully guarded heart.

"The traditional Hawaiian lei signifies love and respect," Caroline said as she continued the ceremony. "Like a wedding ring, it's an unbroken circle that represents your eternal commitment and devotion to one another. Just as the beauty of each individual flower isn't lost when it becomes part of the lei, but enhanced by the strength of its bond, so will you, Kylee and Mai, remain unique individuals, enhanced by the strength of *your* bond."

"May the lei of life you weave together as wife and wife be as beautiful and fragrant as these two you give to each other here today," Caroline said as Mai and Kylee exchanged leis. Singing the song he'd learned from Mai's cousin, Bastien looked deep into Desiree's eyes and when he got to the part about always greeting her with a kiss each time she wore her lei of stars, she knew that she wasn't alone in remembering all those kisses they'd shared.

The blessing of the rings involved dipping them in a Koa wood bowl filled with water from the Pacific Ocean, meant to represent the cleansing of past relationships to a new beginning. As Caroline explained *Ho'oponopono* signified a reconciliation, a letting-go, Desiree felt Bastien glance down at her, but she steadfastly kept her eyes on the couple.

While Kylee poured water from the harbor and Mai poured the water her family had brought from the ocean outside their home into a wooden bowl, Mai's cousin came forward with his ukulele to play the "Hawaiian Wedding Song." As Bastien and Desiree sang the lyrics, she couldn't help noticing they were, as they'd once been both onstage and off, in perfect harmony.

Kylee spoke her vows first. "My darling Mai, when I went to France to take photos for my book of World War Two American soldiers' cemeteries, I never expected to find my best friend and the love of my life. As a family, with our daughter, Clara, we will create a home filled with laughter and compassion. I promise to respect you and cherish you as an individual, a partner and an equal, knowing that we do not complete but complement each other. May we have many adventures and grow old together." She took Mai's hand in hers, and said, "I give you this ring as I give you myself, with love and affection. Wear it in peace always."

A collective sigh rippled through the guests as she slipped the ring on Mai's extended finger. The open love shining in her gaze as she looked into Mai's eyes reminded Desiree of the way she'd once looked at Bastien.

And then it was Mai's turn. "Dearest Kylee, when I took my grandmother to visit my grandfather's grave in France, I never expected to find *my* best friend and the love of *my* life. I promise to laugh with you, cry with you and grow with you. I promise to share my whole heart with you and Clara and love you loyally as long as I shall live." She slipped the ring onto Kylee's extended finger. "I give you this ring as I give you myself, with love and affection. Wear it in peace always."

At that moment the breeze blowing in from the water picked up, stirring the air as it sighed in the tops of the tall fir trees and set the garden's flowers to swaying.

Caroline returned the wooden bowl to a small table draped in white linen. "Dearest Kylee and Mai, as you embark upon this wonderful shared life, I ask that you remember this special day in your beautiful garden with joy and thanksgiving. May your love and understanding grow throughout the years. May yours always be a shared adventure, rich with moments of serenity as well as excitement. May your home be like a peaceful island where the pressures of the world can be sorted out, brought into focus and healed. And may you love to live, and live to love.

"To all present, I invite you to remain after the ceremony, for the christening of the couple's beautiful daughter, Clara, who has brought such joy into all the lives of those who've met her.

"And now, with the blessings of everyone who is present here today, and by the power vested in me by the State of Washington, it is my pleasure to pronounce you legally married. You may kiss your bride."

As the conch shell sounded and the brides shared their wedding kiss, the guests stood and applauded. All stayed standing as Mai's mother, Tamami, walked down the runner in a pink kimono embroidered with white lotus flowers, carrying a baby girl whose white christening dress, Desiree had learned as the women dressed, was the same one Mai had worn.

The christening was brief but meaningful, and it was impossible not to see the love and wonder in both Kylee's and Mai's eyes as they gazed at their adopted baby girl. This time, when Bastien looked down at Desiree and smiled, she smiled back. It was impossible to keep a closed and guarded heart when she was surrounded by so much joy and love.

Then the brides, followed by the grandmother and daughter, walked down the aisle to "From This Moment On" as the guests showered them with white rose petals.

Her heart feeling so much lighter, Desiree began flirting with the harmony, which had Bastien winking at her, the way he would those times onstage, when their eyes would meet, and it would feel as if they were the only two people in the world. Once again, time spun backward, to that first Christmas they'd met, when this Cajun sax player had stolen her heart.

Oh, yes, Desiree admitted, she could feel herself falling all over again. And even as her wary head warned her she could be in trouble, her newly emboldened heart didn't care.

CHAPTER SIX

THE RECEPTION WAS BUFFET-STYLE, catered by Luca's Kitchen, and with Desiree's bakery providing not just the cake but various pastries and cookies. Bastien played his sax and Desiree sang for the gathered guests while they ate.

Brianna was finally breathing a sigh of relief at how well everything had gone when Kylee, who'd changed into more casual attire, came up to her.

"That was amazing," she said, throwing her arms around Brianna. "Thank you for providing memories for a lifetime."

"It was truly my pleasure," she said. "Although I'll admit Mai's family made it easy. Once Caroline came up with the idea to make her feel more at home, they'd arranged for so much of the ceremony. Including bringing the leis, bowl and conch shell."

"It made Mai cry a bit. In a good way... I was glad to see Aiden here," Kylee said. "I haven't seen him since he returned to Washington."

"I wasn't certain he'd show up," Brianna admitted. "He's hidden away like a hermit at the coast house. But I played the Catholic guilt card and pointed out how important it was for him to get out with people again. Also, quite honestly, Seth has been worried about him."

It had been painful for Brianna to watch Aiden suffering and Seth worrying about not being able to get through to his best friend.

"It had to have been hard on him, having his partner

killed. Not to mention being shot himself." Kylee glanced over to where Aiden was standing across the lawn, talking with his older brother Quinn. His expression was nowhere near as happy as the rest of the guests.

"It was also good to see Jolene again, and thank goodness she used that waterproof mascara, because I got so emotional during the wedding, I was on the verge of weeping like the willow Amanda planted in our front yard. And speaking of Jolene, would you have ever guessed someone from Honeymoon Harbor would end up on the cover of *People* for dating a movie star?"

"I'm happy for her," Brianna confided. Jolene had been the subject of bullying through middle school and up until she'd suddenly dropped out of high school at sixteen.

"Me, too. So, what's going on between her and your brother?"

"Which brother?"

"Aiden."

"I had no idea anything was going on." Brianna's gaze turned toward Jolene, who was currently amusing Clara with funny faces. "What do you mean?"

"I've been watching them. They've stayed on the outskirts of the crowd the entire reception, seeming to make sure they're on opposite ends of the yard. If she moves, he moves. And vice versa. It doesn't seem accidental and I'm definitely picking up vibes."

"I haven't a clue. Although Jolene would come over for the occasional sleepover during middle school, before she suddenly dropped out of high school, I never noticed Aiden paying any attention to her."

"Well, he sure is now."

"They both live in Los Angeles. She told me they hadn't run into each other, but maybe their paths have crossed in the past few years and she didn't want to talk about it for some reason."

Before Kylee could comment, one of the young women hired to keep the tables cleared and the buffet table looking tidy came over to ask Brianna a question and the subject was forgotten.

BASTIEN WENT INTO the kitchen, in search of Luca Salvadori, who was taking a fresh antipasto platter from the refrigerator.

"Hey, man," Luca said, "that was some wicked-cool music you two pulled off at the last minute. I was surprised Desiree sang. She's never mentioned a word about singing to anyone in town that I know of. And believe me, if she had, it would've been in bold print on the town's Facebook page."

"We were in a band together for five years. That was some time back."

"You didn't record anything?"

"I scraped up enough dough to pay for studio time to have an album engineered. But it's a catch-22. You need a name to be signed. And you can't be signed if you haven't gotten enough attention to get a label interested. So it never went anywhere."

"I'll bet it would now," Luca said, putting the tray on the counter. "I'm a fan, by the way. I've got all your blues rock albums. I was wondering about that gap of time. Between albums."

"Thanks. As for the time…" Bastien shrugged. "Life happens."

"I know about that," Luca said. "The question of the moment is how you let her get away."

Another shrug. "Stupid also happens. But life on the road wasn't ever for Desiree. She's been baking all her life and decided it was a more dependable way to earn a living."

"She could work in any high-end restaurant in the country, and from what I hear, she turned down a bunch before settling down here. I buy some of my pastries from her, although I make the tiramisu myself from my grandmother's recipe."

"Speaking of grandmothers, the reason for the gap is that I quit the road to go home to New Orleans and help my grand-mère run our family restaurant. But she recently passed, so I sold the restaurant to my cousin, and now that I'm free, I intend to win Desiree back."

"A man with a plan," Luca said with an approving nod. "Good for you."

"The thing is, I don't want to go back on the road. So I thought I'd open a restaurant here."

Luca's dark brows rose. "Why would you open a restaurant here in this small town when you could probably put your name on one in any city in the country and fill the place every night?"

"Because Desiree isn't in any other city. She's here."

"Wow. You *are* serious. But I don't get what that has to do with me."

"I wanted to make sure there wasn't going to be a problem with me giving you some competition."

"Hell, no, I think it's great. You may be able to tell from the town's name that we're a destination wedding town. Not like Vegas, but we get our share of tourists. A bigger variety of places for people to go out to eat can only make the town more appealing, which in turn brings in more visitors with dollars to spend. Right now, for dinner choices, there's Mannion's, which is a great pub; Taco the Town's food truck; Leaf, which, as it sounds, is vegetarian, and me. Adding you to the mix will help people get into the habit of going out more. Especially in the winter when tourism slows down and the locals start getting cabin fever. What are you going to name it?"

"Sensation Cajun."

"I like it." Luca held out his hand. "So welcome to Honeymoon Harbor, and good luck. With both the restaurant and Desiree." He picked up the tray again to take it out. "She's a helluva woman."

"Thanks. You called that one right."

ALTHOUGH THEY'D STOPPED SINGING, the wedding reception showed no signs of slowing down. And, as long as Kylee and Mai seemed to be enjoying themselves, why should it? The best thing about summer was the long days when the sun wouldn't set until after nine o'clock and the twilight glowing with shades of gold and amber would last for another thirty or forty minutes.

During that time, Honeymoon Harborites expressed surprise to learn that the town's baker had once been in a band.

"It's as if you two had been singing together all your lives," Dottie enthused.

"It was five years," Desiree repeated what she'd been saying for the past twenty minutes. "A long time ago."

"Well," Dottie's twin, Doris, said, "it may have been long ago, but it's obvious the connection between the two of you is still there. I suspect we'll be fitting you for a wedding dress before this time next year."

"I wouldn't bet the store on that," Desiree said with a laugh. A laugh that faded as she saw Bastien heading toward her, setting off those all-too-familiar butterflies in her stomach.

After greeting the elderly twins and accepting their compliments, he took Desiree by the elbow and led her to the far end of the garden. How could such an innocuous touch send heat flowing through her entire body?

"I talked with Luca Salvadori," he said. "I wanted to make sure he was okay with me opening up a restaurant. He thinks it's a great idea that will create more business for everyone."

"I'm delighted he approves," she said, folding her arms to steel herself against the charm offensive she knew would be directed her way. "Perhaps you may have thought to ask me how *I* felt before you made your plans to attempt to steal my building space."

"What would you say to taking this conversation somewhere more private, before we start garnering even more attention?"

She narrowed her gaze. "Where?"

"First to the building in question. I have an idea. I also have a question. When was the last time you ate?"

"I've been busy." She thought back. "A croissant this morning."

"Then you should be hungry. Let's take off. I'll show you my idea, then cook you dinner."

"Where are you staying?"

"At the Lighthouse View Hotel. I was lucky to get the only available room. It seems that you were right about Mai's family filling both Brianna's B and B and the hotel."

"I didn't realize they had kitchenettes at the hotel."

"They don't." There it was. That slow, devastating smile she'd been expecting. "I thought maybe I could use your kitchen."

Her initial thought was to turn him down on the spot. Then again, if he actually did intend to stick around, and Desiree sincerely doubted it, since small towns weren't his style, there were other spaces Seth could remodel for him. He didn't need hers. Which was what she was going to convince him of. Over his damn dinner.

"I could use something to eat. And I've missed New Orleans food. Also you're right about it giving us an opportunity to discuss the flaws in your impulsive plan in private."

"Believe me, *cher*," he said, his eyes turning as serious as she'd seen him since he'd put her on that plane to New York, "there was nothing impulsive about it."

And didn't that have her thinking about how he'd been spending the past two years? Family was important to Cajuns, and Bastien was no different. The fact that he'd give up a successful career to take over his grandmother's popular, but small, restaurant proved that under that hot, sex-on-a-stick exterior was a huge and caring heart.

Bastien had never been a bad man. He'd just proven to be the wrong man for her. Or perhaps they'd met too soon and she hadn't been ready for him.

"So, what do you say?"

"I don't have anything in the house to make a meal with," she said. "We'll have to stop by the market." And wouldn't that have Mildred Marshall posting about Desiree buying dinner groceries with the hot new stranger in town on the Facebook page before they'd left the parking lot?

"Sounds good to me. I'm guessing, since we're on a harbor, there's a fish shack?"

Desiree glanced down at her watch. "Kira's Sea House should still be open. For another twenty minutes."

"*Bien*. We'll start there."

HE WAS A fast shopper who knew what he wanted. Kira packed up some Dungeness crab and Gulf shrimp. He wanted the ones with shells, he told the fishmonger, to make stock.

Which admittedly impressed Desiree. And apparently Kira, who asked for the recipe.

"I'll have Desiree write it down for you as I fix it," he said. "I learned to cook in my grandmother's restaurant, and neither of us have ever been the type to use recipes."

"That must have been an adventurous experience for diners," Kira said as she wrapped the shrimp in white waxed paper and put them with the crab in a bag with ice to keep them cool.

"Food should be an adventure," he said. "Otherwise, what's the point?"

"You won't get any argument from me," Kira agreed cheerfully. Then turned to Desiree. "But please, write down what Chef Adventurous here does, okay?"

"I'll try," she agreed. "Just remember. I'm a baker, not a cook."

The farmer's market was down the street, and although the stands were beginning to close up for the day, Desiree was not surprised when both men and women stopped to sell him what he needed. Charm. Say what you want about it, Bastien was definitely born with more than his fair share. And when you tossed in that slow, sexy Cajun accent, well, he was pretty much irresistible.

One of the buskers, playing an alto sax for tips at the front of the market, recognized him immediately and looked on the verge of having a seizure from excitement. Especially when his alleged musical hero signed an autograph, then invited him to perform with him at the preopening trial run dinner at Sensation Cajun. By the time they escaped, Desiree was worried about the kid driving home safely.

The rice, unfortunately, had to be bought at Marshall's

Market, where Bastien had the usually stone-faced Mildred Marshall giggling like a schoolgirl as he laid on a Cajun accent as heavily seductive as Dennis Quaid's in *The Big Easy*. But a great deal more authentic.

"You're like the Pied Piper," she said as they walked out of the market to their cars. Having driven to the wedding alone, they had to take two cars to each of the stops. Which kept her from being in a confined space with him before she worked out her feelings about him appearing so unexpectedly.

"Just being friendly," he said. "Bein' as I'm going to be part of the community."

"You are not."

"Of course I am. And for old time's sake, your first dinner at Sensation Cajun will be on the house."

OVENLY WAS PAINTED a soft green the color of pine needles with white trim and double doors that looked as if they'd been taken from some old building in France. A green awning extended over the sidewalk, allowing for three bistro tables and chairs. Since she didn't serve dinner, the bakery had closed for the day.

"There's a brick patio in back," she said. "Normally I'd only be able to use it about two or three months a year, but I extend the season into fall with portable post heaters."

"That's a good idea. And something I'll have to consider for my place."

"I still can't believe you'll actually build a restaurant here in Honeymoon Harbor."

"Want to bet?"

"I'm not a betting person."

"You took a bet on me," he reminded her.

"And look how that turned out," she snapped, then pressed her fingers to her forehead, where a headache was beginning to throb. "I'm sorry. I didn't mean that the way it came out."

"You're hungry," he said. "And undoubtedly tired. Besides, your leaving was partly my fault. I was young, too cocky and we clicked so well, in every way, I forgot to let you know how much I loved you."

"That's all in the past."

"The past isn't dead. It's not even past," he said, quoting William Faulkner. From his outward appearance, Desiree never would have taken him for a serious reader, but in all their years together, she'd never seen him without a book. "But here we are, *cher*. So, let's deal with who and where we are now, and the rest will fall into place."

He'd always been that way, looking for the positive in a situation. Despite having been abandoned first by the father he'd never known, then his mother, Bastien Broussard had somehow remained the most optimistic person she'd ever met. She also wasn't all that surprised that he would have given up a career, just as it was skyrocketing upward into the stratosphere, for family.

"Tell me about your idea," she said. She still didn't believe he'd stay, but she was willing to listen.

"First off, I want to paint my part pink."

"Pink?" She'd been about to point out that it wasn't yet *his* part, and wouldn't be if she had anything to say about it, when his words sunk in. "Tell me you're kidding."

"This town came of age during the Victorian Era. Pink was a popular color for houses back then. They're scattered all over New Orleans."

"But not here in the Pacific Northwest," she said.

"That's exactly my point. I don't want people thinking of being in the Northwest, as stunning as the scenery is. I want them to feel as if they've been whisked away to the Big Easy. I want Sensation Cajun to be, well, a sensational experience."

"Okay. I get that. But why pink?"

"Brennan's is pink. It's also been a destination landmark for decades. Tourists who go to New Orleans are willing to wait in line to get in for a meal. And mine wouldn't be Barbie pink. I'm thinking of a deeper rose that will stand out when people are coming in on the ferry. With big arched windows on either side of the door with an awning over it. I'd already thought of green, which works perfectly with yours. It would also be great if you extended the exterior color to yours, so they'd be more uniform."

She folded her arms. Tried to picture Ovenly painted pink. "Why would I want to do that?"

"Because along with the larger windows on both the street and harbor side to let in more light, I'd like to take out that wall between our places."

"You want to invade my bakery?"

"*Invade*'s a bit harsh. My idea was to have Brianna's fiancé build some sort of archway between the two, keeping the old brick. New Orleans and French styles aren't that different."

"That's true enough, given that New Orleans is the closest you'll come to France in the States, thanks to our ancestors."

"You're getting it. Our styles could blend well together, Desiree. And not just outside, but on the menu. Luca told me he buys pastries from you."

"He does. And Brianna buys cookies and croissants for her B and B."

"See? You'd have a new outlet. We could set up the dessert cart with items you chose for each day. After diners taste how good your pastries are they could go into your bakery after their meal and take some more home for their evening dessert, a late-night snack, or even breakfast the next morning.

"And," he pressed on, "you said you wanted to expand. There's plenty of space for you to do it. Especially since I'm putting smaller, more intimate dining rooms upstairs. I believe together we'll draw from neighboring towns along with visitors to the National Park. I'm also going with green shutters on either side of the windows across the second floor and putting wrought iron on a little extension. Not an actual balcony, but to give the impression of one."

"This is sounding more and more like Brennan's exterior."

"I doubt I'll be taking any business away from them. But for those who've been to New Orleans, dining at Sensation Cajun could feel like reliving their time there. And for others who've never been, it'll give them a Big Easy experience.

"You've thought this through."

"I have, ever since your father complained that you hadn't come home to work in the family business. Luca thinks my name will bring in some people, too, though I'm not sure that this is blues rock country."

"You'd be surprised. Don't forget, Jimmy Hendrix was from Washington State. You wouldn't, by the way, be the only famous person in town. Brianna's uncle Mike is an artist."

"Michael Mannion lives here?"

"He has a studio and a gallery. Like me, he lives above the store on the third floor of a building he bought. But he's turning the second floor into space for various local artisans. Brianna talked him into doing wine painting evenings which have proven quite popular."

"I went to a showing of his work at a gallery on Julia Street. He'd done a book of paintings from each of the fifty states. We hit it off, and though his original paintings are above my budget, I could definitely use some of his Louisiana prints. With little tags beneath stating his name, with the address of the gallery. It might even drive some business his way."

He smiled at her, obviously pleased with that idea. "Small-town interconnections," he said. "This isn't turning out to be that different from New Orleans, which is, in its way, several small, close-knit communities within one city."

She couldn't deny that. Still, as they entered her bakery, Desiree wondered if a man whose dream was once to play concerts all over the world could truly be happy running a restaurant here, in a town that didn't get the number of tourists in a year that New Orleans or Paris did in a day.

"I realized I've dropped a lot on you today," he said.

"Whatever gave you that idea?" The sarcasm didn't have the edge she'd intended. He was getting to her, the sane, sensible voice in her head warned. *Be strong.*

"Just think about it," he suggested easily. "What could that hurt?"

"Nothing." But her hopeful heart, as tended to happen whenever she was anywhere around Bastien, was disagreeing with her head. "I suppose."

"I'd never make you do anything you don't want, Desiree," he said, just as he'd told her that first night he'd made love to her. Damn. That memory had long-neglected body parts jumping into the interior conversation, siding with her heart. *Dinner,* she reminded herself. Then he'd be on his way, back to the Lighthouse Hotel, and hopefully New Orleans, or Paris, or wherever the gypsy musician might roam.

"I've mostly given up making bread," she said as they passed the pastry case, which her two employees had emptied for the night. "I prefer the art of pastry making. But I do bake bread once a week for Luca. He uses whatever he needs for that night, then vacuum freezes the rest and warms it as he needs it. I kept out a loaf to eat with some cheese along with Roma tomatoes and basil when I got home tonight. So, I can contribute that to our dinner."

"Great plan. We'll have bruschetta while the sauce simmers.

"I do have another idea that we can talk about over dinner," he said after she'd retrieved the bread from the back workroom and they were walking up the stairs that Seth had insisted on replacing.

"I'm not going to bed with you," she said, wanting to get that settled right off.

"Did I say anything about sleeping with you? That wasn't my idea. Well, not one I wanted to talk about quite yet. Though anytime you want to ravish me, I wouldn't say no."

"There will be no ravishing."

"Whatever you say, *cher*," he agreed cheerfully. Too cheerfully, Desiree warned herself.

CHAPTER SEVEN

"Wow," Bastien said now, as they entered the apartment that took up the entire floor. "I wasn't expecting this."

"What were you expecting?" she asked as she put her purse on a small curved table painted in a pastoral scene by the front door. A gilded bronze mirror in one of the Louis styles—she forgot which one—hung on the buttery-yellow wall above the table.

Desiree was well aware that her apartment didn't fit in with the typical Northwest design style. Or the heavy, and to her mind cluttered, historical Victorian homes throughout town that always showed up on the annual home tour circuit. Fortunately, Seth, who'd remodeled both what had once been Fran's Bakery and this upstairs apartment, which had only been used for storage and, it had turned out, a home for mice and spiders the size of her hand, had caught on to her vision right away.

"I don't know because I hadn't given it a lot of thought," Bastien said, taking in the buttery-yellow walls that brightened up the long, dark days of winter and the rains of spring. "But it wasn't this."

Tall blue draperies hung from the tops of fifteen-foot-high walls boasting wide white crown molding to puddle on the floor. Desiree never would've been able to afford that luxury if Sarah Mannion hadn't sewn those drapes herself. There were prints and paintings in a variety of frames and eclectic styles—scenes of Paris, of New Orleans, bright and colorful modern art and more classic art prints, like the mother bathing her child in a porcelain bowl—all of which she'd unearthed at various garage sales and flea markets Sarah had taken her to visit.

"I knew wherever you lived would be pretty, like you. And feminine. Again like you." He swept a long, slow look over her that once would've had her panties melting on the spot. But not tonight, she sternly told the rebellious, reckless body of her youth. "But I didn't expect to find myself back home. Though this is more like the Garden District than my grand-mère's double shotgun house."

There were times, whenever she'd have people over for the first time, when she'd watch their eyes open wide and she'd wonder if she'd perhaps overdone the formality. But that feeling would only last a moment as her guests would immediately settle in and she'd watch the cares of their day fall away, just as hers did whenever she came upstairs from the bakery.

"Brianna's mother, Sarah, designed it for me. She's principal of the high school, but is taking design classes at the community college so she can have a new career in retirement. She used this apartment as a class project that entailed adding residential space to a commercial building. Usually people go industrial loft style in these old places. But I don't feel at home in that type of space.

"Some of the things, like the Mardi Gras masks on the bookshelves, we ordered online, and the art on the walls were all my choices, but it was as if she somehow was inside my head, reading the thoughts I couldn't quite put into words."

She definitely wasn't going to put into words the thoughts she was having now. Like how much she wanted him to lift up her skirt and take her hard and fast against the door. *Stop that*, she told her bad, bad head, dragging it back to a safer topic.

"Both Seth and Sarah had understood that as much

as I love Honeymoon Harbor, I wanted a blend of New Orleans and Paris."

Bastien stuck his hands in his back pockets, looking up at the oversize bronze-gold chandelier dripping with crystals that created rainbows on the walls. "That looks like an authentic plaster medallion."

"It is. Seth found it down in Portland. It was badly chipped, but his father, Ben—"

"Who would be the husband of Caroline."

"That would be him." She smiled at the way he kept mapping out the connections between all the people he'd met today. "He's one of the few remaining old-time master plasterers. His family built most of the original buildings in town and, as you can see, he managed to repair it beautifully."

Sarah had covered a reproduction curved Louis XV–style sofa in a deep blue velvet. Desiree had decided against sanding and repainting the cracked and peeling paint that gave the piece character and enjoyed imagining all the families who'd owned it before her. As they passed the sofa, an unwanted image of making love to him on that soft velvet flashed through her newly sex-crazed mind.

An archway through the tall brick, much like the one Bastien had suggested to connect her bakery to his restaurant, led to her kitchen, where she'd replaced the top cabinets with open shelves, and had Seth install a deep farm sink, marble countertop and a vintage, butcher-block-topped wheeled table to use as an island.

Bastien put the groceries down on the marble countertop while she went out onto the wrought iron–railed balcony that allowed her to keep a small kitchen garden in pots and sit with her morning coffee, breathe in the aroma of fresh herbs and watch the boats on the water.

"Nice setup," he said when she'd returned with a tomato and leaves of basil. "I like the espresso machine."

"During the day, I'll run down to Cops and Coffee. But this is my sanctuary, so I like my coffee French. And before you ask, I do leave out the chicory."

"Not a bad call, in my opinion," he agreed. "It took a while, but I talked grand-mère out of putting it in the café coffee."

"Would you like some wine?" she asked.

"I wouldn't turn it down. I'd say we earned it today. Especially you, who, along with stepping in to perform, also did all that baking."

"Ah, but you're cooking dinner when we could have ordered out. Or picked up an already cooked chicken at the market."

"Bite your tongue," he said as he laid out his ingredients. "So you still don't sing at all, *cher*?"

"Only to myself." She got out a bottle of an Oregon Sauvignon Blanc that always reminded her of the Pouilly-Fumé they'd drunk with that lunch at the little bistro beside the Seine and poured them each a glass. "When I'm alone baking."

"Thanks," he said. "You still have some amazing pipes."

While she got the ingredients for the bruschetta out of the refrigerator, Bastien washed the vegetables, then began chopping carrots, green pepper and onion—the "Holy Trinity" of Cajun food. "The first time I heard you, singing that solo for 'Joyeux Noël,' I thought I'd died right there in Jackson Square, because I knew only an angel could sound so sweet."

He looked up from peeling the shrimp. "You looked like an angel come down from heaven, too."

"It's not going to work this time, Bastien." Oh, but it

was. As it had been more and more all day. She sliced the bread on the diagonal and rubbed it with a garlic clove.

"What?"

"The famous Broussard charm offensive," she answered as she brushed olive oil onto the bread, then put it beneath the broiler.

"It's the truth." Behind her, shrimp shells boiled in a pot along with leftover bits of vegetables to make stock.

He'd always been as serious about his cooking as she was about baking. The difference, she thought now, was that baking was chemistry, while cooking, at least how he did it, was more art. Each fit their personalities. Except when it came to this man, her head tended to rule her heart, while he'd always worn his heart out in the open on his sleeve.

"It's good to be back in the kitchen together," he said. "The same way it was good to sing together at the wedding."

There was no point in lying about the connection; it had felt like that first night they'd strolled through the Quarter, singing together. On Bourbon Street, as they'd stood on a corner, waiting for the light to change, a man had come up and handed Desiree a dollar. "You're a true professional now," Bastien had told her, making her laugh. But it had still felt rewarding.

"I'm sorry the musician Brianna hired cut her hand, but it was fun to sing again," Desiree admitted. The bread had browned. She put it on the butcher-block island counter, cut up the tomato, rolled up the basil leaves and cut them *en chiffionade* from either side up to the bitter stem, which she tossed away. "Especially at such a happy occasion." She spread on the goat cheese, then topped the bread and cheese with tomato, basil and capers.

"That was a nice story about how they met at that World

War Two cemetery in France," he said. "And each knew, at that moment, that they were meant for each other."

"I suspect it was more lust at first sight," she said, her tone as dry and crisp as her wine.

"I don't remember you being so cynical. I believe it was true love. I certainly fell in love when I heard you, even before I turned around and saw you. But I'm not going to deny that while you looked and sounded an angel, my thoughts had nothing to do with heaven. Perhaps lust is merely fate's way to get us to pay attention to the person we're supposed to fall in love with."

"I've never met a man who says the *L* word so easily," she said.

"Known a lot of men, have you, *cher*?" Bastien took a bite of bruschetta she held out to him.

"Most of the students in pastry classes admittedly tend to be women. But I've met my share of male bakers, and both students and restaurant chefs tend to sit around and drink late into the night talking about all sorts of different personal things. Sex included, naturally. But love is never mentioned."

"Now see, that's the difference. It's not like I throw it around like confetti or Mardi Gras beads. Had I been with other women before you? Yes. Had I ever told any other woman that I loved her? That would be a hard no. It was a word I was saving. When I went back to the guys in the band the next morning, I told them that I'd not only found our front girl, I'd found the girl I was going to marry."

It had been the same for her. Except she'd been a virgin when, the third night after she'd joined the band, they'd made slow, tender love on a lumpy double bed in his small, three-floor walk-up studio apartment on Dauphine Street.

"Sometimes I wonder if I moved too fast," he mused. "Being that I was your first lover, perhaps you thought sex always felt that special, that right, and maybe took our love, not for granted, exactly, but as something you could feel for any man you were attracted to. Any other man who you might want to be with."

"You have it backward," she said. "You're right about me always connecting sex with love. I still do. I used to think it was my Catholic upbringing, but now I believe I'm just hard-wired that way. I always knew that when I did have sex with a man, he'd have to be someone I loved. And could see myself loving forever."

"Okay." He blew out a breath. "I promised myself that this time, I'd tell you how I felt and give you time to get used to the idea. So, demonstrating that I do have a degree of self-control where you're concerned, I'm not going to make love with you tonight."

"Well, for once we're on the same page," she said, not quite truthfully, remembering that flash of fantasy about him taking her up against the door.

"We always have been, *cher*." He looked at her over his wineglass. "Sometimes we just get a bit lost in translation." He turned down the stock pot. "We've a while yet before I need to make the roux. Why don't we enjoy our wine outside on that pretty little New Orleans balcony and enjoy the sunset?"

It was a perfect evening. The sun had turned the blue water to gold and copper. Sailboats skimmed across the gilded water, while more energetic kayakers paddled closer to shore.

"I've been thinking of taking sailing lessons," she said. "It looks so freeing."

"Maybe we could take them together, and then I could sail you to some hidden cove where we could drop anchor and make love in the moonlight."

"I thought we weren't going to talk about sex."

"I said we weren't making love," he corrected her. "But I don't remember you saying we couldn't talk about it." He took another bite of the crunchy bruschetta. "This is delicious."

"It's simple," she said. "But fresh herbs make it so much better. I was thinking of putting my garden on the patio, but then I'd have to go all the way downstairs any time I wanted something, and the pots would take up room I needed for customers. The balcony was Seth's idea."

"He's very talented. I'm glad there's someone local with the talent and vision to create my space for Sensation Cajun."

"As I said, his family built most of this town. Each generation has taught the next. They and the Mannions *are* Honeymoon Harbor." She told him of the ancient feud.

"So now he and Brianna Mannion will be connecting the family in a more personal way," he said.

She smiled, then took a sip of wine. "I've been told there have been inter-family marriages over the years, but John and Sarah Mannion beat them to it. She was Sarah Harper before she married John. He's mayor, she's the principal, and together they run the Mannion family Christmas tree farm. They have a big festival from the day after Thanksgiving to until Christmas Day. It's a wonderful community tradition."

"We'll have to go and celebrate my first Northwest Christmas together."

"If you're still here."

His eyes met hers and held. Her hormones were pinging around like steel balls in a pinball machine, and he was positively radiating testosterone. "I told you," he said. "I'm not going anywhere."

"What if I leave? I had some very good offers in Seattle and Portland before deciding to settle here after a visit."

"Then I'll move to Seattle or Portland."

"Even if you've finished building your restaurant?"

He lifted his broad shoulders and took another, longer drink of wine. "I'm betting that you have no intention of leaving. It's obvious you've woven yourself into the fabric of this town's life. But, it's only a building, Desiree. To be with you, I could walk away from it, as I did the one I sold to my cousin to come here, without a backward glance."

He put his glass on the little bistro table between them, turned toward her and took her hand. "Here's the thing you need to understand," he said. "I already let you leave twice."

"You never asked me to stay. Not even after Paris." And hadn't that hurt?

"Only because I was afraid you might. I knew band life wasn't for you, even though you could have been a star."

"You don't have to say that."

"It's true. You were the whole package, Desiree. But you hated the touring. Being crowded into that old van before we could afford to lease a decent bus. Never having a moment to yourself. The crowds, the fans. They weren't for you."

"You enjoyed them."

"I did," he admitted. "More so after you left."

"Well, if you're trying to make me feel better, that certainly doesn't."

"I didn't mean it the way it sounded. It was because I didn't have to watch you fight your growing stage fright every night. And I no longer woke up every morning wondering if that was the day you'd leave."

"I never told you I had stage fright. And it was more anxiety. I'm a quiet person at heart, Bastien. That's one of the things I love about baking. I do it early in the morning, when it's dark and the town is still sleeping. It's a special, silent time when I can have my thoughts to myself."

"Not so silent, I suspect," he said. "Since you sing while you work."

"You've caught me," she admitted with a smile.

"You hid the anxiety well," he said. "But I knew. There were so many times I thought I should lie and tell you that I didn't love you because I knew how we'd eventually turn out. But I was selfish and wanted every minute I could have with you.

"The first time you left, I understood that you needed to go to school and learn your craft. Having grown up working in a kitchen, I totally got that. Which is why I didn't say a word to discourage you. The second time, you were flush with your shiny new culinary diplomas and ready to spread your wings in the big city. No way was I going to try to deny you that...

"But now you've reached the stage in your life when you need a place to settle. Nest. Make a home."

How well he knew her. As she gazed at Bastien, Desiree felt all her excuses leave her heart with the setting sun.

"And I'm going to do everything I can to convince you to allow me to be part of your home. To let me back into your heart."

"You've never left." The admission in her soft voice vibrated with emotion.

He closed his eyes, drew in a deep breath, and although she hadn't realized that he'd been stressed, she could see the tension leaving his body. "I made a promise. Back there in the kitchen."

"You did," she said. "And I had every intention of holding you to it." She laid her free hand on the one that was holding hers. "But haven't you heard? It's a woman's prerogative to change her mind."

He stood up, bringing her with him. "The shrimp stock gets better the longer it simmers," he said.

"Then it's going to be the best stock ever made," she said, lifting her lips to his.

CHAPTER EIGHT

"I HAD A FANTASY," she admitted as they walked, hand in hand, into her bedroom. She'd painted it an eggshell buff that added a golden glow. A wrought iron four-poster bed added to the antique feel, while the draped netting created a lush, dreamy vibe. The room looked like it was bathed in champagne.

"I'm a big fan of fantasy," Bastien said in a voice as silky as her duvet. "What a coincidence," he said as she confessed the sex-against-the-door scenario. "I had the same one when I walked in. Perhaps because I attacked you the moment that bellman had left our hotel room in Paris." The sex had been quick, hot, and the memory of that ravishment possessed the ability to thrill after all these years apart.

"I attacked you right back," she reminded him.

"That you did," he said as he closed the bedroom door. He pressed Desiree against it, causing every muscle in her body to quiver with memory. "Brace yourself, *cher.*"

Before she could respond, his head swooped down and his mouth was on hers, the kiss hard, deep, erotic. There was no soft, slow seduction as there'd been their first night. No playful sex as they'd had so often shared, too high on life from performing to go to sleep. This was what she wanted. She needed him to take her, to claim her, to break through the last of those emotional protective barricades she'd built during their years apart.

She couldn't tell if the room or her head was spinning as his mouth broke away from hers and nipped first one bare shoulder, then the other, just sharp enough that she knew her skin would show his marks in the morning.

Then, just as he had in her fantasy, he caught her wrists, lifted her arms above her head, pressing them against the wood of the door as his other hand dove beneath her pretty flowered tea-length dress, pushing aside the bit of lace she wore beneath it to slide his fingers into her. She was already wet, needy and ready. Desiree arched her hips to that wicked hand as his mouth reclaimed hers, swallowing a sound that was part moan, part laugh at how, yet again, their minds and bodies were in perfect sync.

"There are some men, with lesser egos, who might find being laughed at in such a moment emasculating," he said. "But I take it as a challenge." He thrust deeper, bringing her to climax with a flick of his thumb.

"That's one."

He released her arms, turned her around so she was facing the door and unzipped her dress, allowing it to fall in a flowered puddle to the floor. Her bra was next with a single snap of the hook, and then he slowed the pace, kissing a line from the nape of her neck, down her spine, and lower, as he pulled her undies down her legs.

"Step out of your shoes," he instructed. The lace underwear that was down around her ankles was next. Then he kissed his way up her body again, his mouth tasting what his fingers had readied.

"I want to watch you." He nipped at her inner thighs, the way he had her shoulders, branding her with his teeth, then soothing the skin with his tongue. "I want to see your eyes, watch your face, when I take you."

Her knees were weak as he turned her yet again, to face him. As he did, she saw herself in the tall mirror leaning against the wall. She was naked, and her skin, deepened to a dusky rose, gleamed with moisture, while

Bastien remained fully dressed. The erotic contrast had her feeling helpless as his hands moved over her, cupping her breasts. His fingertips, roughened from years of guitar strings, scraped her nipples, causing an ache between her thighs.

"Tell me you want me," he said, his hands growing more possessive, more arousing, as they moved over her, demanding more.

"I do," she managed.

"Say it." He pressed the straining zippered placket of rough denim against her bare flesh. "Say my name."

Lost in a world of slick, sinful sensation, she could deny him nothing. The ability to trust completely, to give every bit of herself, was born from knowing she was deeply, truly loved. "I want you, Bastien. I *need* you."

She gripped his shoulders and moved her hips against him, drawing forth a ragged male groan that was the sexiest thing she'd ever heard. He reached between them, freeing himself, then, taking a condom from the pocket of his jeans, tore the wrapper open. He was big, stone hard and, miraculously, hers.

"I'm going to take you," he said as he rolled the latex over himself.

"Finally." She panted the word.

It was his turn to laugh. Then as Desiree clasped his shoulders, he drove into her, filling her, ravishing her against the door of her pretty champagne-colored room, setting off an orgasm that streaked through her like flaming, brightly colored Mardi Gras fireworks.

THEY FINALLY MADE it to the bed. Lying on the one-thousand-count Egyptian cotton sheets Sarah had given her for a housewarming gift, Desiree watched Bastien pull his T-shirt off to reveal a deeply tanned chest with the same mouthwatering abs she'd loved to run her hands over. She could easily spend the rest of her life watching him undress over and over again. Like a GIF, she thought with a laugh. She could use it as a screensaver on her laptop, although she'd never get any work done.

"You're laughing again," he said, as his hands pushed down his unfastened jeans.

"Not at you." As her wandering eyes followed his happy trail down to his obliques, she wondered how anyone who cooked for a living could maintain such an amazing body. "I'm just happy."

"I'm glad." He kicked off those pricey Italian loafers, leaving his long, lean feet bare. She'd never realized how sexy bare feet could be until today. He pushed a pair of navy boxers down his legs, stepped out of them and joined her in the bed. "Now that we've taken the edge off and fulfilled that fantasy, let's see if I could make you even happier."

MUCH, MUCH LATER, after he'd proven to be a man of his word, they were sitting in her kitchen eating the best étouffée she'd ever had in her life. And having grown up in New Orleans, that was saying something.

"Your grandmother taught you well," she said. She'd claimed his linen shirt as her own and was wearing it with her undies, while he had, sadly, put that T-shirt and jeans back on for cooking. "You also chose the name of your restaurant well. This is truly sensational."

"Thanks, but the company is what really makes the meal. I've missed being with you."

"Me, too. With you. And not just for the mind-blowing sex. When I left Paris, it felt as if I'd torn off a limb. I kept waiting for you to show up in New York." She took a piece of bread and spread it over the plate to mop off the last bit of sauce. "You never did."

"You weren't ready."

"You had no way of knowing that."

"You're right. I didn't. But it was the opportunity of a lifetime for you," he said. "It'd be like me being able to study under Lester Young, John Coltrane or Charlie Parker. How many people can say they were there, in that very kitchen, creating pastries with arguably the most famous pastry chef in the world?"

She laughed. "I don't think that's the type of thing that will make it into my obituary. Fortunately, I have no desire to be famous. While you, on the other hand, are a world-renowned musician."

"For songs I wrote for you."

"I wondered about that," she admitted. She'd also sung along while baking, which had made her heart ache, at the same time the songs had her feeling as if he was still with her. Just a little. "You know how the French call an orgasm *la petite mort*?"

"The little death."

"That's it. That's how I felt. But not in the amazing orgasm way. But in a lonely way. As if you'd died to me. I grieved for a long time."

"I'm sorry."

"It's not your fault," she said. "I was the one who left."

"If it's any consolation, I felt the same way. Which is why I wrote the songs. They served as somewhat of a catharsis as I'd imagine I was singing them to you."

"Once again we're so in sync," she murmured, no longer fighting the fact that in so many ways, they fit together perfectly, like two pieces of a beautiful puzzle. "Because I'd sing along and imagine I was singing with you." She blew out a long breath. "So here we are. Where

we belong, if you're honestly set on building your restaurant here."

"I never say anything I don't mean," he said. He gathered up their plates, took them over to the dishwasher,
then made two cups of espresso with hearts in the foam.

"How long did it take you to learn that?" she said,
duly impressed.

"I've been practicing awhile," he admitted. "To show
off for you. Here's the idea I was thinking about earlier
and was going to mention to you before we got sidetracked… What would you say to us singing again?"

"Professionally? Even I if wanted to, which I don't,
what would we do with our businesses?"

"You mentioned Brianna's uncle is renting out space
to artisans."

"I did and he is."

"What if I had a studio built there? That album you
bought, my last one? I produced it at a studio in New
Orleans and had it engineered there. We could do the
same thing."

She thought about that. "Wouldn't we have to tour to
promote it?"

"It's a new world. We can put some selected singles on
a website. I already have live performances on YouTube."

"I know." She sighed. "I've watched. Along with thou-
sands of other people."

"Who bought the album while I was in New Orleans
working in grand-mère's café. The only singing I've done
in public over the past two years has been in a few local
clubs. That performance on YouTube was at the House
of Blues. We could make some extra bucks doing what
we'd enjoy anyway. Pay for some trips, put some away
for our kids' college—"

"Aren't you getting a little ahead of yourself, Bastien Broussard?"

"You talked about wanting children. Did you change your mind? Because it's okay if you have."

"No. I just believe we should wait until the restaurant is up and running and we've adjusted to living a normal life together."

"We've plenty of time," he agreed. "That's totally your call. I was at the airport, waiting for my flight, when CNN ran an article about women in their fifties having children."

She slapped his arm. "I don't want to wait *that* long. I've watched Kylee and Mai with Clara and as darling as that baby is, she defines high-maintenance. Also, while *I* realize there's nothing wrong with having a baby without a formal marriage, Papa's a little old-fashioned."

"That's like saying the Pope is Catholic," Bastien said with a touch of laughter in his eyes. "I was getting to that. I should have waited to mention the college part. The reason I came here was to propose. I had it all planned out. But then I found you bustling around with cake for the wedding, and the next thing I knew I was off looking for a uke. Then we were singing, and the reception didn't seem the right place."

"It would have taken away from the brides' day," she agreed.

"Then I wanted to show you my restaurant first, so you'd know what you were getting into, and then there was the sex—which was mind-blowing, don't get me wrong. But that got me sidetracked again with the conversation about maybe singing together again, and kids, and the plan fell apart. But the most important thing of all is that I wanted to propose, Desiree Marchand, heart of my heart."

"That was on your latest album." He'd sung it in both English and French, "*couer de mon couer.*"

"So what do you say?"

"How about just asking me straight-out?" she suggested.

He dropped to one knee, took her hand in his and placed it over his beating heart. "Desiree Marchand, will you be my wife and let me love and cherish you all the days of my life?"

"Yes," she said. "I can't think of anything that would make me happier than becoming your wife and loving and cherishing you all the days of *my* life."

"Thank God." He blew out a breath.

Bastien stood up, drawing her into his arms as they sealed their pledge with a kiss.

Then, as Desiree laughed, her now-freed heart felt so light that she could feel it floating up and out the French doors, over the moonlit harbor.

* * * * *

Get 4 FREE REWARDS!

We'll send you 2 FREE Books _plus_ 2 FREE Mystery Gifts.

FREE
Value Over
$20

Both the **Romance** and **Suspense** collections feature compelling novels written by many of today's best-selling authors.

YES! Please send me 2 FREE novels from the Essential Romance or Essential Suspense Collection and my 2 FREE gifts (gifts are worth about $10 retail). After receiving them, if I don't wish to receive any more books, I can return the shipping statement marked "cancel." If I don't cancel, I will receive 4 brand-new novels every month and be billed just $6.74 each in the U.S. or $7.24 each in Canada. That's a savings of at least 16% off the cover price. It's quite a bargain! Shipping and handling is just 50¢ per book in the U.S. and 75¢ per book in Canada.* I understand that accepting the 2 free books and gifts places me under no obligation to buy anything. I can always return a shipment and cancel at any time. The free books and gifts are mine to keep no matter what I decide.

Choose one: ☐ **Essential Romance**   ☐ **Essential Suspense**
                          (194/394 MDN GMY7)   (191/391 MDN GMY7)

Name (please print)

Address   Apt. #

City   State/Province   Zip/Postal Code

> **Mail to the Reader Service:**
> **IN U.S.A.:** P.O. Box 1341, Buffalo, NY 14240-8531
> **IN CANADA:** P.O. Box 603, Fort Erie, Ontario L2A 5X3

Want to try 2 free books from another series! Call 1-800-873-8635 or visit www.ReaderService.com.